# STRANGERS
## ON THE SHORE

**ADRIEN BROOKE**

Published by
Hybrid Global Publishing
333 E 14th Street
#3C
New York, NY 10003

Copyright © 2024 by Adrien Brooke

All rights reserved. No part of this book may be reproduced or transmitted in any form or by any means, electronic or mechanical, including photocopying, recording, or by any information storage and retrieval system, without the written permission of the Publisher, except where permitted by law.

Manufactured in the United States of America, or in the United Kingdom when distributed elsewhere.

Brooke, Adrien
    ISBN: 978-1-961757-89-9
    eBook: 978-1-961757-53-0
    LCCN: requested

Cover design by: Julia Kuris
Copyediting by: Claudia Volkman
Interior design by: Amit Dey
Author photo by: Jeff Sweet
Illustrator: Daniela Ruggeri

**adrienbrooke.com**

# EPIGRAPH

"To the west, America, he said, full of greedy fools fouling up their inheritance. To the east, China-Russia; he drew no distinction: boiler suits, prison camps, and a damn long march to nowhere. In the middle..." —John le Carré, *Tinker Tailor Soldier Spy*

活着就要斗争,
在斗争中前进,
即使死亡,
能量也要发挥干净.

To live is to struggle; we advance in the struggle so that we may use all our potential, even in death.

艾青 Aì Qīng, 鱼化石 "Fish Fossil"

## WU FAMILY

胡玉英 - Wu Yukying, the oldest of the Wu siblings. Married to Laurence Li, she sometimes introduces herself as Li Yukying

胡天圣 - Wu Tinseng, the middle child, adopted by the family at age six, physics tutor turned spy

胡卓群 - Wu Cheuk-Kwan, the youngest, a doctor in Hong Kong

## MEI FAMILY

梅涵空 - Mei Hankong, a cultural attaché for the People's Republic of China, living in Switzerland for the past fifteen years

李熙鳳 - Li Xifeng, his wife, a poet, and an accomplished translator

梅今朝 - Mei Jinzhao, youngest of their two sons

## PASSENGERS

Laurence Li, born 李英东 - Li Yingtung, Wu Yukying's husband, a Hong Kong government undersecretary

林子文 - Lim Chiboon – aka Hugh Nash, a Singaporean and New York-based gossip columnist

单璕 - Shan Dao, Wu Tinseng's friend from France

Lucas Grodescu – a blackmailer

Marissa Grodescu – his wife

Mrs. Richard Lanzette – a widow from Chicago

Mrs. Duncan – an American tourist

Miss Duncan – her daughter

Rebecca Arden – an American feminist

Mrs. Biddle – an elderly Londoner

**N.B. for English-only readers** – While phonetically both Mandarin and Cantonese names are pronounced separately, they can be written together (Yukying) or separately (Yuk Ying, Yuk-Ying). The Chinese characters remain the same regardless of Romanization. In this story, the Mei family's names are Romanized in Mandarin, while the Wu family is Romanized in Cantonese; this reflects their journeys and where they live.

**Terms of Endearment**

Jiejie/jie – older sister or older female friend

Didi – little brother or younger male friend

Gege/ge – older brother or older male friend

Da ge – eldest brother

A-Seng, A-Kwan – a common diminutive nickname style

A-die – father

# CONTENTS

PART ONE—The Night Has a Thousand Eyes . . . . . . . . . . . . 1

PART TWO—Do You Want to Know a Secret? . . . . . . . . . .49

PART THREE—He's a Rebel . . . . . . . . . . . . . . . . . . . 109

PART FOUR—Mama Said. . . . . . . . . . . . . . . . . . . . . 165

PART FIVE—A Town without Pity. . . . . . . . . . . . . . . . 209

Acknowledgments. . . . . . . . . . . . . . . . . . . . . . . . . . 285

About the Author . . . . . . . . . . . . . . . . . . . . . . . . . . 287

# PART ONE

## THE NIGHT HAS A THOUSAND EYES

# PROLOGUE

*June 25, 1963. Épernay, France.*

The room was cold, and Wu Yukying was beginning to worry. When she'd first arrived, they'd led her to a room with no windows, directing her to sit in the chair directly below the vent. Afraid to contradict them, she sat with air like cold fingers tickling the back of her neck. A shudder shook the pen in her hand. The shivering was becoming impossible to suppress. She set down the pen and, though she knew it would not make much difference, slid her hands under her legs to try to keep them warm.

When she'd asked, the man in the wrinkled suit hadn't been sure of the timeline. It was busier than normal, and many people were in line to be questioned; she was just one of many. She could knock on the door if she needed anything. His smile suggested knocking would be noted in the file. She glanced across the desk to the waiting chair and wondered how much they knew.

They'd kept her waiting for over an hour now.

It had occurred to her, of course, to move to the other side, away from the vent. She was well within her rights to seek a little comfort. But who knew what might tip the scales against her? Besides, what was a few more minutes? She had her shawl, after all, well-made Irish wool, dyed blue flecked with white and gray—a gift she almost hadn't accepted and now was glad she had. She wrapped it tighter around her shoulders and imagined it a shield. The clock ticked slowly. One minute. Another. Yukying rubbed one hand with the other, trying to encourage circulation. Her fingers felt bony and fragile; she thought about small things in cages.

The detective noticed the wringing of her hands as he walked in, and grimaced.

"Ah, yes. Sorry." A gentle French accent curled the corners of his English. "The building is old. Survived the wars, so now the city thinks it should be preserved. I'd rather get decent heating, but what can you do? Can we get you some tea? A warm cup always helps me."

"No thank you," she said, and moved her hands to her lap.

"Are you sure? We have a good selection."

"That's a kind offer, but I would rather get back to my husband."

"I understand," the detective said, in the tone of unmarried men everywhere. "So, Mrs. Li." He tapped the file in front of him. "Do you want to tell me how you got involved in all this?"

# CHAPTER ONE

*Ten Days Ago. June 15, 1963. Southampton, England.*

"Yukying-jie!"

Amid the train hisses and tinny announcements, she heard her name—but no matter where she looked, she couldn't find the source.

"Yukying-jie!"

"How is it he manages to be heard over all this?" Wu Cheuk-Kwan grumbled happily, searching the crowded platform beside her. "He's worse than an air-raid siren."

Yukying patted her brother's arm and used his shoulder to rise on tiptoes, scanning the crowd. Wu Tinseng had clearly spotted her, but everyone in Southampton was so *tall*, she couldn't...

"Jie!" She heard right next to her ear, then a blur of gray swept her into a hug. Joy blossomed through her whole body, and then she was smiling, smiling, smiling as the stone she'd carried for three years finally dissolved, leaving her weightless as Tinseng swung her around.

"Put her down," Cheuk-Kwan said behind them. "Is she your doll? Where's my greeting? And why are you—"

Yukying was set down gently as Cheuk-Kwan got pulled in a hug of his own. A smile lurked behind Cheuk-Kwan's usual scowl as Tinseng slapped his back enthusiastically. Cheuk-Kwan tried to look annoyed when they parted. It convinced exactly no one.

"Did you miss me?" Tinseng asked, looking between them with an unchanged smirk, and it was as though he'd never left.

"Of course we did," Yukying said at the same time Cheuk-Kwan said, "Miss who? *You?*"

Tinseng shoved Cheuk-Kwan, then wrapped Yukying in his arms again, drinking her in with a rapt expression.

"Hi," he said as they peered into each other's faces, cataloging all the minute shifts, the new moles and wrinkles they'd collected during their time apart. Tinseng had always looked naturally mischievous, with a constant smile of some sort dominating his face. His dark amber eyes still sparkled, though crow's feet were beginning to grow around them. His black hair was overgrown as usual, cut poorly and tied back in a mess of a low ponytail; she'd have to make him see the barber on the ship.

And what did he see in return? She thought she hadn't changed at all: Same dull brown eyes, same round nose. Peasant features, her mother had called them. In three years, her black hair had started showing gray, but she stubbornly refused to dye it. She had gained weight through great effort, and it showed in her cheeks, which might be why he was smiling so softly now; her health had always been one of his biggest worries.

"I missed you so much," he said. "You have no idea."

"*Some* idea," she teased gently.

"Yeah? You missed me too?"

"Of course I did, you silly boy." She pulled his ear as he beamed. "Now, where's this friend you brought?"

Tinseng's friend hovered a few paces away with two suitcases waiting by his side. He would be imposingly tall if Yukying wasn't so used to tall men. His expression was flat, eyebrows drawn together, mouth turned down in a frown; such a stony countenance changed his full lips and striking brown eyes from beautiful to imposing. His beauty reminded Yukying of a painting. Even the black hair tucked behind his ears lay perfectly on his shoulders; flyaways wouldn't have dared. And yet, even that rebelliously long hair seemed studious on this man, more classical than modern. Every detail—from his rigidly straight posture to the way his long hands lay perfectly still at his sides—made him unapproachable. Certainly the other people around him thought so, giving him a wide berth on an otherwise crowded platform.

"Shan Dao!" Tinseng called, waving his hand high above his head. She almost laughed; at least *one* person didn't find him unapproachable, anyway.

"*Stop it*," Cheuk-Kwan hissed, pulling Tinseng's hand down. "Are you a child?"

"Living without me has made you even *more* of a stick-in-the-mud— how is that possible?" Tinseng reclaimed his hand and bounded over to his friend. Yukying caught the other man tracking Tinseng's movement, hawkish in his intent.

"I still can't believe he invited a complete stranger," Cheuk-Kwan muttered as they watched Tinseng gesture back toward them.

"Lim Chiboon and Laurence are here too," she said, trying to placate him.

"That's different. Yingtung's your husband, and Chiboon's practically family."

"Well, I think it's nice. The more the merrier."

Cheuk-Kwan drew a breath to say something else, but by then Tinseng had returned.

"Cheuk-Kwan, Yukying, this is Shan Dao."

Shan Dao bowed, though it earned him stares from passersby.

"Shan Dao, this is my brother, Wu Cheuk-Kwan, and my sister, Wu Yukying."

"Tinseng, *please*," she said with a sigh. "It's Li Yukying."

"You . . ." Shan Dao tilted his head in confusion.

"Took my husband's last name, yes."

"*Why?*" Shan Dao looked genuinely shocked. Yukying tried not to blush; she should be used to the reaction by now.

"Excellent question," Cheuk-Kwan said approvingly. "It's because her husband, Li Yingtung, is a bootlicking dog's hips for the English—"

"Wu Cheuk-Kwan," Yukying cautioned, but Tinseng was talking too: "It's because our sister is far too accommodating and also has the absolute worst taste in men. You'll see when you meet him."

"You will," Cheuk-Kwan said, nodding, "and you'll regret agreeing to come. He's that bad."

"My husband, Laurence—"

"*Laurence!*" Tinseng emphasized. "He named himself after a—"

And Cheuk-Kwan added, "Li Yingtung had the name changed by deed poll, by the way, that's how much of a—"

Yukying put a hand on both her brothers' arms. "*Laurence* is on the ship already, with Lim Chiboon. So we should probably get going."

"Yes, let's get out of here before you attract more attention," Cheuk-Kwan muttered, picking up the luggage at Tinseng's feet. "For fuck's sake, how many suitcases did you bring, Wu Tinseng?"

"Yukying told me to! It was cheaper this way, instead of mailing my things back. Shan Dao packed them, so it's all extremely efficient. Somehow, when he folds things, they don't wrinkle. He could be a minor god of laundry. I should pray to you, Shan Dao."

Tinseng's patter accompanied them through the queue into their taxi. In the quiet of the backseat, Yukying finally felt comfortable enough to ask, "Tell us a little about yourself, Shan Dao. How did you meet Tinseng?"

"It's a funny story, actually—" Tinseng started, only to be cut off by Cheuk-Kwan.

"She didn't ask *you*."

"I tell it better!"

"A mutual acquaintance," Shan Dao explained to Yukying, having clearly picked up on the need to ignore the brotherly sniping. "She was hosting a salon on Chinese poetry and invited us both."

"You don't write poetry," Cheuk-Kwan accused Tinseng.

"But I have *plenty* of opinions about it," Tinseng chirped.

"Are you a poet, Shan Dao?" Yukying asked before Cheuk-Kwan took that bait.

"No. I translate professionally. I was asked to translate Mao's Ode to the Plum Blossom into French. Tinseng . . ." With the slightest pause, during which his gaze shifted toward Tinseng, he continued, "did not agree with my choices."

"You'd lost the intent," Tinseng said.

"The intent was there. So was the form."

"Why bother trying to keep it within the confines of a 词牌名 when it's a translation?[1] The syllabic parallelism is totally lost. And your audience was French. You had the opportunity to sway them away from pessimism and say something about endurance, the way Mao intended, but instead you had them arguing about *metre*."

"Metre is the vehicle by which the poet sways," Shan Dao rejoined haughtily. "Otherwise, it would have been a *speech*."

Yukying and Cheuk-Kwan exchanged a look; they could imagine, suddenly, exactly how this first meeting went.

"Who won the argument?" Cheuk-Kwan asked.

"Neither," Shan Dao said at the same time Tinseng crowed, "I did."

Shan Dao turned fully in his seat to glare, which delighted Tinseng. Yukying watched with interest; before he'd left, Tinseng had been muted, withdrawn in a way that had worried her. But here he was, the Tinseng from her earliest memories, the full brightness of the sun in his smile.

"It seems like Paris treated you well," she observed.

"It did," Tinseng nodded thoughtfully, "but I'm glad I'm leaving. I missed you too much. Not you though." He knocked his knee against Cheuk-Kwan's, who immediately retaliated with a smack to the head. Shan Dao watched coolly as Tinseng tried to flick Cheuk-Kwan's ear; Cheuk-Kwan blocked, hitting his brother's arm away.

"They missed each other," Yukying explained apologetically. "A-Kwan, A-Seng, you're being very rude to our guest."

"How can I be rude when he's not my guest? He's my very close friend." Tinseng's sly grin foreshadowed trouble. "He'll be invited to all my lectures."

"Wait, what? Lectures?" Cheuk-Kwan's indignation filled the car. "Since when? I thought you were coming home because you'd quit your job."

"I did quit my job, but I know how much you'd complain about me not earning my keep, so I called in a favor and got a position at that new university opening up. Turns out, they needed to fill some adjunct

---
[1] 词牌名 - a poetic verse set to a common folk tune.

positions last minute. Now you don't have to worry about me. In fact, I'll probably be able to move out of Yukying-jie's after just a few months. Aren't I amazing? You're *welcome*."

So that hadn't changed, she noticed sadly, but it had probably been too hopeful to think Tinseng would come back understanding how valued he was. He'd always struggled with his place in his adopted family, though some of the pressure had let up after their mother had been killed in '49. Wu-furen had refused to acknowledge that she couldn't fight the nation's tide, and sometimes Yukying quietly thought it had been a little too easy for her mother to die with the old China rather than adapt to the new one. Tinseng was the opposite: he was ever adaptable, a survivor no matter how he had to change. Even at twelve, Tinseng had been the one to keep them all alive and safe until their father could arrange to have them secreted out of China and established in Hong Kong. But they'd lost everything, and between the loss of his wife, his familial land, and his fortune, their father had never recovered; it had been up to the three children to learn how to survive.

Now Tinseng and Cheuk-Kwan were twenty-six, and she was an ancient thirty. She wondered if they'd learned any other lessons since those days, or if they were still just surviving.

※

The line for the check-in process stretched down the ramp at the dock. Passports had to be checked, rules explained, welcomes extended. Tinseng stood ahead with his friend, having walked briskly with his luggage from the taxi. Yukying moved a little slower, a bout of pneumonia during childhood having permanently damaged her lungs. Her younger brother lingered with her, eager for an opportunity to complain out of Tinseng's earshot.

"You know what's going to happen now. We're not going to see him the whole trip. And what about this Shan Dao? Did you hear his accent?"

"A-Kwan," she scolded sharply, and lowered her voice to only reach his ear. "It's good that A-Seng brought him along. It's good that he trusts us to introduce . . . *important* people in his life. He needs us," she reminded him, "to see things he might not see."

The glance they exchanged was a promise between them. If Tinseng was a survivor in some ways, he was his own worst enemy in others. When Yukying had heard Tinseng was moving to Paris, she'd been relieved: she'd caught him only six months before with another man, and his indiscretion had terrified her. France was the only place she knew where sodomy wasn't a criminal act. Of course, he would still be a Chinese man in a European country, but in one part of his life, at least, he could live a little freer. If she had to lose him, it would be worth the sacrifice if he gained that for himself.

Cheuk-Kwan hadn't seen it that way. When Cheuk-Kwan had found out about Tinseng's proclivities, Yukying had only just stopped him before he'd confronted Tinseng; she'd made him promise not to say anything until he could discuss it calmly. By the time he'd been ready, Tinseng had already left for a five-year appointment in Paris. Cheuk-Kwan had seen it as abandonment, an invective against their family. Cheuk-Kwan had always held Tinseng on a pedestal, from which height Tinseng had seemed to control everything. When Tinseng had left, that image shattered, and with Tinseng fallen from his pedestal, it meant he was just Cheuk-Kwan's brother—and that Cheuk-Kwan might be just as responsible for their relationship as Tinseng.

"I've been worried too," she soothed with a hand on his arm. "But let's not rush to judgment. Let's try to get to know Shan Dao, OK?"

Cheuk-Kwan looked away. Concern hovered over him like clouds rolling in.

"You don't know," Cheuk-Kwan said after a few moments of silence. "Maybe they *are* just friends."

Yukying made a noise that, uncharitably, could be considered a snort. It was so immodest and unlike her that Cheuk-Kwan whipped around, but all he caught was a knowing smile aimed his way.

"I don't think so," she said gently. "I recognize the look."

"Ugh. I thought *one* of you getting married was bad."

"Laurence has grown on you," she teased. "Don't deny it."

"I'd rather die," he said grimly, then shot her a hesitant look. "You really think . . ."

They watched for a while as the line moved. Tinseng kept glancing over at his friend, his expression the same each time. Yukying wondered at it: She'd never seen Tinseng so unreserved about his true feelings before. Unrestrained, yes; he'd always been wild and impulsive. But those had been games to him, ways to entertain himself as he'd waited for the rest of the world to catch up. The look on Tinseng's face now was far from a game.

"I think we should get to know Shan Dao. We might be seeing a lot of him, especially if Tinseng followed my advice and asked Shan Dao to stay with us." Tinseng had written that Shan Dao was looking for accommodations, as his uncle would not have room for him; Yukying had written back insisting Tinseng adhere to *some* propriety and invite Shan Dao to stay with them. But when had Tinseng ever listened to good advice?

Cheuk-Kwan stared at them unhappily. "Do you think Tinseng will actually say something this time?"

"Maybe if he saw you being brave, he could be brave himself."

"So, no, then," Cheuk-Kwan muttered. "You don't think he'll say shit. Why should he? We're just his family."

Yukying sighed and changed the subject for both their sakes.

On the other side of the check-in, Laurence waited for them. When they'd made it through, he kissed her cheek then stepped in to greet their guest with the pleasantries his English mother had taught him. Shan Dao met him with Western manners of his own, a hand outstretched. Laurence took it firmly, then led the way, Shan Dao falling in beside him. Already they were discussing alma maters, tutors, the politics of university placements, Pullyblank's coup over at Cambridge for the Chair of Chinese back in '53, Cowperthwaite's invective against free universal primary education—Hong Kong's literacy rates were abysmal compared to the rapidly improving literacy rates in China. The three siblings watched in undisguised interest.

"You've brought another one," Cheuk-Kwan muttered. "You've brought Yingtung an *ally*."

"How dare you!" Tinseng hissed. "Shan Dao's nothing like Yingtung! Tell him he's wrong, Yukying," he pleaded, but Yukying held her tongue and smiled.

They had reserved three rooms in the same hallway, and slouched in one of the doorways stood their childhood friend Lim Chiboon, waiting for their arrival. He had changed the least of all of them over the years, his cherubic face still hiding the observant eyes of a journalist and artist, the two professions that kept him occupied.

"What a beautiful piece of art Tinseng's brought us," Chiboon commented at her elbow as they followed the others into her and Laurence's room first. "I think I'll be staring all trip."

Yukying covered her giggle with her hand. She'd forgotten how mischievous Chiboon could be; he and Tinseng had been a deadly combination as teenagers, trailing laughter after them like paper lanterns. Back then, she had considered Chiboon's older brother an ally in keeping their brothers on the right path, but he'd had a career and a family dynasty to rebuild, and she'd been a young woman at home waiting for Laurence to propose to her, so it'd fallen to her to get them out of whatever trouble they'd found themselves in. It'd been a relief when the Lim family had relocated to Singapore; they'd only seen Chiboon in summers then, and when he visited in the years that followed, Yukying could be charmed by their antics instead of held responsible for them. She was more charmed than ever these days. For form's sake, though, she tutted at him and murmured a platitude about being nice to their guest.

"I'm simply appreciating beauty, jiejije. Speaking of, you look more beautiful every time I see you." Chiboon plucked at the shoulder of her jacket. "Did you make this yourself?"

"Do you like it?" It was a suited trio pattern she'd ordered from London. The boxy jacket and skirt she'd sewn with leftover yards of lightweight flecked wool; the blouse was crushed rose pink faille, with a neat bow at the collar. She straightened the bow self-consciously.

"It looks off the rack from Bergman's," Chiboon said.

"It does," Laurence agreed loyally, walking back into the room from the bathroom where he'd been putting away their toiletries. "The wives at the club complimented her dress the other day—said they couldn't believe it was a pattern."

Yukying and Chiboon exchanged a look of long-suffering fondness for her husband, who had trouble realizing his compliments could sound like insults. Unlike her brothers, Chiboon found Laurence just as endearing as her.

"Ah, jiejie, speaking of sewing..." Tinseng called, "I have a jacket—the liner was torn..."

"Bring it to my room later," she said with a smile. "I'll fix it."

"And a pair of trousers?" he asked hopefully.

"Whatever you need."

"See, Shan Dao? Didn't I say she was the best?"

---

For an hour, everyone flitted in and out of one another's rooms, excited by their reunion and all the discoveries the rooms had to offer. The staterooms looked just like the brochure: a full bed (or twin beds, in the other two rooms), a table with two chairs for writing and eating, a set of drawers with vanity atop, a porthole looking out. Laurence was already taking full advantage of the hangers in the slim closet behind the door. There were bags for different kinds of laundry service, and towels folded into swans had been left at the foot of the bed. Yukying would take the pen when she left; she had a collection at home.

After some attempt to unpack, there was the rest of the ship to explore: they wandered in twos and threes through deck upon deck of rooms, pools and libraries and bars, a large ballroom and a grand hall, a gymnasium, a movie theater. At the entrances to various lounges, paper signs announced the night's activities: horse racing on the radio at 9:30 p.m. in one, a bingo meeting in another, dancing in one of the larger lounges after dinner. In the grand hall music by the ship's band started at 9:00 p.m., with a celebration of castoff at 10:45 that promised to be resplendent.

"Shan Dao will be asleep for all of this!" Tinseng said. "He has a strict bedtime of 9:30 p.m., 10:00 if he's *really* wild." Tinseng winked at Chiboon. "I, on the other hand, plan to be up all night. What about you, jie?"

"Oh no, I shouldn't. My joints."

Chiboon grimaced in sympathy, while Tinseng said, "Last time you wrote, you didn't mention how the new powder worked?"

Yukying smiled at him. He was always so eager for her to try new things. He cut advertisements and articles out of French newspapers and translated them for her, writing about oils and machines and techniques. She didn't have the heart to tell him they never worked.

"The powder is good," she told him kindly, "but a good night's sleep is just as important."

By the time dinner started, Yukying was thankful to sit down. She ate the first course of chilled honeydew melon in silence as the rest of her group learned more about the three strangers assigned to their table: an older accountant in a rumpled jumper finally indulging his lifelong dream to photograph Europe, a young banker meeting his mother in Italy, and finally Mrs. Richard Lanzette, a widow whose husband had made her promise to live well after he'd passed.

As the only two women in their group, Yukying and Mrs. Lanzette were expected to have more in common with each other than anyone else at the table; to the men, nationality, age, and experience were secondary to the condition of womanhood. Yukying was all too familiar with being thrown together with women who wanted nothing to do with her—most often at the church Laurence's family attended, a predominantly British crowd of politicians and their families. After it was clear to Laurence's mother that she wouldn't be able to persuade Laurence out of the marriage, his mother had insisted Yukying join at least one committee. After a few stressful attempts, she'd finally found a good Bible study group on Wednesday nights, but she wouldn't forget the looks from the women on the jumble sale committee anytime soon.

Thankfully, Mrs. Lanzette didn't seem to be like that. In the course of exchanging the usual pleasantries—Yukying's husband, Laurence, worked for the British government in Hong Kong, Mrs. Lanzette's husband had been a professor of semiotics at the University of Chicago; this was Yukying's first time in Europe if you didn't count England, which of course you never should; it was Mrs. Lanzette's third time, but the first without her husband; the salad course was always overrated, didn't you think?—Yukying got the impression of comfortable loneliness. After sharing a ribald story about a nude costume ball held by the university every year, the elder woman leaned back with her whiskey and gave Yukying a shrewd look.

"So tell me, how do you plan to while away the hours on this tub?"

"I'm excited for the films, of course. I hope they show something with Cary Grant."

"They're sure to. Which one's your favorite?"

Yukying didn't even have to think about her answer. "*Bringing Up Baby*."

"With the tiger? That one's a romp. I'm partial to *Suspicion*, myself, I like seeing him play against type. You like comedies, then?"

"Yes, and romances." Yukying looked down at her *saumon poché* in hollandaise, but such rich food would surely disagree with her. She ate one of the cucumbers slices instead. "I like knowing they'll be together by the end. I get nervous otherwise."

"Why, that's nothing to be ashamed of, dear. In fact, it's very understandable. Look at everything there is to be nervous about! Who *wouldn't* want a little predictability these days, with Korea, and the riots in Alabama, and—well, I mean, I don't have to tell *you*." Yukying braced herself slightly, but Mrs. Lanzette only added, "We women are more attuned to these things."

Yukying thought of her conversation with Cheuk-Kwan earlier. "I suppose we are." Across the table, Cheuk-Kwan and Laurence were arguing about something; at least they were keeping their voices down. "Laurence's father says it's natural for women to want happy endings."

"Hmm. A big man, is he?" Mrs. Lanzette asked archly. "Talks a lot, never seems to actually say anything? My dear, I'm from Chicago, we're a city defined by men too big for their britches. They flock around the radio in the smoke room to squawk about politics—as if they have anything to do with it, hah! I saw my fair share of that at the university, believe *me*."

Yukying leaned in. "Laurence often hosts large dinner parties at our apartment. His father has big contracts with the government. That's why he wanted Laurence to go into that work."

"So you know, then. To hear them tell it, they should've been the one giving the orders to MacArthur, not the other way around. Who was your MacArthur? I'm afraid I never followed much outside of headlines."

There was no easy way to sum up the complicated web of opposing internal and external forces during the Resistance Against Japanese Aggression. Between the KMT, CCP, and interlopers like Stilwell, Yukying chose the least offensive option to an American, and the only name one was likely to recognize: "Chiang Kai-shek."

Mrs. Lanzette nodded amiably. "And I just bet when you're sitting there listening to them around the dinner table, they sound like Chiang should've been wiring them for every troop movement."

Yukying could recall a dozen instances of this exact sentiment. "Yes, the war would have ended years earlier if only they'd been in charge."

"Or never begun at all, if you'd let 'em at Hitler and Hirohito from the start, right?" Mrs. Lanzette speared a potato. "Sometimes, when you walk past, doesn't it sound *exactly* like a bunch of old biddies gossiping over their knitting?"

Yukying held her hand over her mouth to hide her laugh. Mrs. Lanzette sipped her whiskey victoriously.

"I like you, Li Yukying; you're the first clever girl I've met on this ship. Do you sew? Of course you do, I see your work on this dress—it's flawless. Why don't you join my sewing circle tomorrow? How I've already been dragooned into one, I couldn't tell you, but I'd just adore some good company."

"Well . . ." Yukying considered the effort it would take to navigate a group of unknown women. On the other hand, the boys had already discussed how much tennis they wanted to get in on this trip, an activity she couldn't participate in. She had planned to sit on the sidelines with Lim Chiboon, but she'd also brought a thorny knitting project in the hopes of making some progress. "That's very kind of you to offer. Thank you, I will."

She ate one last cucumber coin to assuage her guilt for how much she couldn't finish as the waiters swept away their plates for the fourth course.

"Are you looking forward to our first port?" she asked.

"Lisbon? Afraid I don't have even the start of a plan. I have my *Frommer's*, of course, but nothing beyond that."

"Oh, well, may I introduce you to my friend?" Yukying grabbed Chiboon's attention. "Mrs. Richard Lanzette, Denise, this is Mr. Chiboon Lim, but you might know him by his nom de plume Hughland Nash."

Mrs. Lanzette goggled. "Hugh Nash? *No.* You did that tell-all interview with Debby Walley in last month's *Photoplay!*"

"Yukying . . ." Chiboon was all false modesty behind his glass. "Stop . . ."

"He's syndicated in over two-dozen newspapers," Yukying boasted, trying not to grin at his antics. "And he's planned this whole trip for us, so we're quite in his debt."

"It was nothing much," Chiboon said with the same pleased smile she remembered from muggy afternoons staying inside together, when she would praise his sketches or his rearrangement of the shelves so the knickknacks looked less cluttered.

"We were wondering what there is to do in Lisbon, Hugh," Yukying prompted.

"Well, there's the Museu Nacional dos Coches, which has a remarkable collection of historic carriages, and an artillery museum for the fellows. But all that's a little pedestrian. The real point of interest are the casinos." He leaned forward, eyes gleaming. "They were *riddled* with spies back in the war."

"Now we're talkin'!" Mrs. Lanzette nodded enthusiastically. "I adore spy stories. I've read every Bond novel, can't get enough."

"Oh, then you must go. It's all rumor, of course, but they say the Palácio and Casino Estoril were the refuges for the Allies, and the Atlântico was for the Reich. They even say Ian Fleming frequented Casino Estoril while he was a spy."

"*Really.*"

"I'm just repeating what I've heard, of course," Chiboon winked at Mrs. Lanzette. "But the source was *very* good."

"Mr. Nash, you should write a guide," Mrs. Lanzette gushed. "I'll certainly take your advice. Have you read that new man on the scene, le Carré? He writes better than Fleming, though I can't say I enjoyed his realism; the ending was so bleak. If I wanted that, I'd read the headlines. Who do you prefer, Mr. Nash, as a writer?"

"I think I prefer writing the stories to reading them."

Mrs. Lanzette agreed, praising his coverage of the Mei Affair especially, a scandal that had intrigued and shocked the world a year ago when the story had first broke. Mei Hankong had been a cultural attaché to the Chinese Embassy in Switzerland, a longtime post. He had been cleared as far as anyone knew, as had his wife, Li Xifeng, a translator of poetry and a private tutor. In December 1961, it had been quietly reported that both had died in a tragic accident. Speculation had flown behind closed doors, but hardly anything was written; the press, Chiboon explained, had a strict embargo on writing about spies—at least, he added, in every civilized country.

Which was why it had come as a shock when a Swiss rag had broken an unbelievable story: they claimed Li Xifeng had been spying for Russia for years, right under the embassy's nose. That would have been more than enough for scandal. But the rag went on to claim that her husband had known; instead of loyalty to his country, he'd hidden her secret instead.

"How could I resist? Everyone else was writing about it." It was the spy story of the century, even better than the Rosenbergs. Where most columnists had used the scandal to moralize, Chiboon had instead analyzed Li Xifeng's poetry translations. "It was a hard sell to my editor, but I promised him I wouldn't linger on the stuffy parts."

Cheuk-Kwan's harsh chuckle made them all look his way. "You've spent too much time in America. You're able to swallow the official reports without choking."

Chiboon didn't acknowledge Cheuk-Kwan. He smiled at Mrs. Lanzette instead. "You see, that's why Yukying and I are such fast friends: I loathe talking politics, unlike most of my companions here. There's nothing Yukying's husband and brothers love more than boring us to tears with their debates. Me, I wonder what the point of all that is. I'm far more interested in art."

"Scandal isn't *art*." Cheuk-Kwan's voice rose, then fell as he caught Yukying's glare. "And there's no such thing as art for art's sake, you *know* that."

"But what is scandal but the gutter version of a tragic play?" Chiboon asked. "When Joan Bennett's husband shot her agent out of jealousy just for talking to her, what was that but Othello jealous over a handkerchief? And when Mei Hankong covered up his wife's espionage, choosing her over his beloved People's Republic, that's just Faust choosing the earthly over the spiritual. Whether we call it gossip or tragedy, it's all the same muck."

"And you the muckraker?" Mrs. Lanzette asked playfully.

"Where else do you find the best stories but the mud?" Chiboon smirked. Cheuk-Kwan made a noise of disgust and gave up. The waiters were circling again. Yukying looked down at her plate. Someone had pushed extra broccoli onto it, but when she looked around no one would meet her eye.

~~~

Yukying hoped the conversation would move on, but the other woman finished her whiskey and asked, "Do you think Hankong Mei killed her, Mr. Nash? Or was it assassination, like the bolder papers say?"

"Is it really so obvious they were killed?" Yukying asked before she could help herself. She had, secretly, been holding on to the hope that it had been just a robbery gone wrong. She hated to think that Mei Hankong had killed his wife and himself in shame and, though she tried not to be naïve, she also hated the idea that governments went around killing their citizens. She never wanted to assume the worst.

"Ah, jie," Lim Chiboon said, "Robbery, heart attack, or suicide—that's always the excuse. There's a reason all the retired spies write those into their novels. No, I don't think he killed her."

Chiboon's reasoning, he told them while the waiter brought them fresh drinks, was that Mei Hankong had already hidden his wife's activities for so long. Why suddenly change his mind to such a degree? And if he *had* decided he'd had enough, why not turn her in instead? He would have been a national hero, albeit a secret one, for catching such an important Russian spy. Given a medal, or probably two since it was his wife.

"Horrible," Yukying murmured.

Mrs. Lanzette shook her head. "Their poor sons."

"Tinseng-ge knew one of them, you know," Chiboon said.

"Really?"

"Oh, yes, his brush with infamy. Wu Tinseng!" Chiboon elbowed the man next to him. "Tinseng, we're talking about the Mei Affair. Tell Mrs. Lanzette about how you knew Mei Jinzhao back in the day."

Until now Tinseng had been oddly quiet, paying attention to his friend or else staring at the other passengers around the room. Now he turned fully and settled his drink in his hand.

"I didn't really," he said. "It was for eight weeks when I was sixteen. A lifetime ago."

"Tinseng doesn't know how to tell a story," Chiboon said, and proceeded to tell it himself. They had met at New Asia College in Hong Kong, where Mei Jinzhao's uncle taught philosophy. Mei Jinzhao had been sent by his parents, an emissary of sorts for China, and at sixteen taking the responsibility seriously—too seriously, Chiboon said, but who wasn't a radical for their beliefs at sixteen? Wu Tinseng had already been taking university classes for a year and a half; at sixteen, he excelled in all the sciences, but his tutors were urging him to round out his studies. "They could see he needed philosophy and the arts or risk becoming an absolute bore like his brother over here." So he had agreed to take the intensive on Chinese literature; taught by a staunch Neo-Confucianist, the course had been just as much history as language. Wu Tinseng and Mei Jinzhao had argued all term over politics.

Yukying remembered the arguing. Tinseng had come home every night, unable to afford the dormitory fees, full of stories about the other boy. Looking back, Yukying understood much better why Tinseng hadn't been able to stop talking about him: she'd nursed a few secret crushes herself. She had wondered, when the headlines first broke last year, if Tinseng had felt for the boy he'd once known.

"Mei Jinzhao was his father's son," Chiboon said, nodding meaningfully at Mrs. Lanzette. "Isn't that right, Tinseng?"

"He *was* his father's son back then," Tinseng said. "Absolutely principled. And stubborn: we could have died arguing and he would have found me in the afterlife just to continue on. But it was stubborn in a good way, a righteous way." His smile spoke of faraway sunlit memories. "And when he decided on his loyalties, he never wavered."

"How fascinating that he didn't stand by either of them, then," Cheuk-Kwan said. "Or his country. You'd think such a loyal person would have stuck around, instead of disappearing into thin air like he did."

"Who knows why he disappeared." Tinseng pointed his fork at his brother. "Maybe that *was* loyal, and we just don't know why."

"How could letting your parents be flogged by every reporter alive be loy—"

"I'm telling you," Tinseng interrupted, "if Mei Jinzhao did something, it was for the right reasons."

Next to him, Shan Dao huffed. Strangely, his ears were bright red. "You flatter him too much."

"Oh, that's nothing," Cheuk-Kwan said, then confided gleefully, "Back then, he wouldn't shut up about him."

Shan Dao raised his eyebrows. "I recall a comrade describing Mei Jinzhao as sour. Uninteresting. Stuffy. Not the type Wu Tinseng could ever befriend." It sounded like he was reciting something. Now Tinseng's ears were red too.

"Well, you're wrong about that," Cheuk-Kwan said, "Tinseng would have kidnapped him back home if he could."

"I know more about Mei Jinzhao than some of my own cousins," Chiboon agreed. "Mei Jinzhao likes boiled tofu over fried, Mei Jinzhao's read *Les Misérables* in the original French . . ."

"Mei Jinzhao can recite dozens of Mao's best speeches by heart," Cheuk-Kwan threw in.

"Mei Jinzhao hung all the stars individually."

"You make it sound like he was all I talked about!" Tinseng moaned.

"You *were* very detailed," Yukying said. "I think I can still remember some of the pranks you said you were planning for him. The poor boy, he didn't deserve any of that."

"Yeah, *he* didn't know you torture your friends," Cheuk-Kwan said.

"I didn't want to be his friend," Tinseng snapped, then his head whipped up and he said quickly to Shan Dao, "I mean, I—I *did*, but I didn't know . . . Oh my *god*," he concluded, and drained his drink.

"So he thought Mei Jinzhao was his rival?" Shan Dao asked, ignoring whatever was going on with Tinseng, which Yukying thought was very sensible of him.

"It seemed so," Yukying nodded. "I think he liked that he'd found his match. I remember him saying he couldn't believe someone so smart could think the way he did, so staunchly Maoist. Tinseng wanted to prove Mei Jinzhao wrong. You know how Tinseng gets. They were always fighting over politics." She looked between them and smiled. "That doesn't seem to have changed."

Shan Dao nodded solemnly. "Tinseng has very steady preferences. In friends."

Tinseng groaned again and buried his head in his hands. "I've died. I must have died. This is hell."

"This is the best day of my life," Cheuk-Kwan declared with a huge grin.

"*Anyway!*" Tinseng said. "Shan Dao doesn't know him! It's not important right now! Chiboon, save me, change the topic. Tell us more about Lisbon, huh?"

With a pitying smirk, Chiboon obliged him.

Laurence waited to comment until they were back in the room, finishing the last of their unpacking.

"Tinseng's friend seems . . . nice." Laurence shook out his sweaters and casual slacks from his valise, then refolded them one by one into the dresser. "I won't mind having him stay with us."

"I'm not sure he is," Yukying fretted.

"Oh. Tinseng hasn't said anything?" Laurence shook his head. "Well, Shan Dao would be welcome. One never knows about these foreign types, if they only know how to eat 面包 and not 面条.[2] His accent, did you hear it?"

Yukying attempted to do the same with her own clothes, folding and refolding the same capris with no improvement. "If he's friends with Tinseng, I'm sure he's nice. He was very polite earlier." She didn't know how to address the other things. She wished she knew what to say, but the enormity of her disagreement overwhelmed her; she didn't know where to start. So, she ignored it all and changed the subject. "I wonder how long they've known each other."

"He didn't mention Shan Dao in any of his letters?"

"Just the one introducing him, telling me about his move and wondering if he could come along. But that isn't very surprising, is it?"

"I wouldn't be surprised if he showed up with an arm missing and forgot to mention it."

"Laurence."

"Well, I wouldn't."

He crossed their stateroom and plucked the capris out of her arms.

"Why do you fold clothes so poorly?" He asked, folding it for her and placing it in her drawer. Others (her brothers, mostly) would only hear reproach in his tone. But they were hypocrites, her brothers. They grew up in the same home she did; they should know words could hide all manner of intention.

---

[2] One never knows if they only know how to eat bread (mian bao) and not noodles (mian tiao); a.k.a., they've forgotten their roots.

She watched as Laurence shooed her aside to unpack the rest of her suitcase for her and understood that each emotion was its own language. Laurence spoke Mandarin, Cantonese, English, and a little French. But unease and insecurity were his most native tongues, and he'd never learned to speak tenderness. Tinseng spoke his giving and ambition fluently but struggled to speak a word of vulnerability. Cheuk-Kwan spoke every dialect of anger and panic, and his protectiveness always muddled his tongue.

She wondered what languages Tinseng's friend spoke.

"Did he mention any prospects when he gets to Hong Kong?" she asked.

"He didn't say much of anything. Tinseng did all the talking for him. An odd choice for him, don't you think? Strong and silent? Wouldn't he want someone who could keep up?"

"Tinseng has a funny heart. He likes people who have the things he admires." *The things he thinks he lacks*, she thought but didn't add; that seemed like too much of a secret to share.

"Do you think they're—" Laurence started, then stopped.

"Hmm?" she said, distracted by holding up two dresses in the mirror and trying to decide which to wear tomorrow.

"Do you, uh . . ." He cleared his throat. "Do you think they'll want to sit together at dinner?"

"Oh, yes. You know A-Seng. Once he's got his mind on something, he never lets go." She decided on the blue dress, and sighed. "I hope A-Kwan will be able to adjust."

They turned and grimaced at each other—no further words needed.

"He'll adjust," Yukying said again, firmer this time. She'd make it happen if she had to commandeer one of the ship's kitchens and force a reconciliatory meal down both their throats.

"They should send you to Saigon," Laurence said, kissing the crown of her head. "The Buddhists and Catholics would have come to an agreement weeks ago with you to set them right."

"Laurence, please." She hated when he spoke of politics so cavalierly. He'd inherited the trait from his father, and it scraped against her own upbringing. "Don't make light. The situation is so bad there."

"It will calm down," Laurence said with unearned confidence. "They'll announce an agreement any day now, Diệm will give concessions and let the Buddhists have their flag, and that will be that. He doesn't want to lose American support."

With piercing clarity, she saw herself around her childhood dinner table listening to her mother's commentary on the war and all its players. Her mother had always prided herself on being honest in front of her children; she was equipping them to survive the real world, she'd say when their father tried to rein her in. Yukying heard her mother's voice echoing in hers when she said, "We should be more worried. The Americans can hide their ambition behind Diệm for now, but someday they'll grow tired of it. Look what happened in Cuba last year. Some people eat more than their share and still covet their neighbor's bowl."

"Yukying." Laurence sighed, pursing his lips.

"No politics on the trip. Yes, I remember." It had been her idea in the first place. "I haven't told A-Kwan that rule yet," she admitted.

"I hadn't noticed," Laurence deadpanned. She met his eyes in the mirror. The impulse to laugh was there, but they didn't indulge it. They'd never been that sort. Instead, their shared amusement lingered like perfume as they continued unpacking in the quiet content of two people finally at ease.

※

Sleep stole her away the moment she laid her head down. One moment she had been reading by lamplight, the next she woke in the dark. Laurence lay asleep by her side. A sound in the hallway startled her. People walking back from dancing—that must have been what had awakened her. She blearily checked her watch to find it was just past midnight. She rolled over and watched Laurence in the dark for a moment; his face always looked so young in sleep. She sighed and shifted for a few minutes, then gave up and slid out of bed.

As she came back from the bathroom, she noticed the bag of laundry by the door. Laurence had forgotten to put it out, and she'd wanted tonight's dress pressed for the Lisbon casinos. Setting her water down, she grabbed the bag and opened the door slowly so she didn't wake Laurence.

As she set out the bag, movement three doors down caught her eye. She looked up to see Shan Dao walking back to his suite. He wore different clothes than at dinner: dark slacks and a tapered white button-down shirt. The clothes flattered his height, quite unlike the bland gray suit he had worn to dinner. He didn't look her way as he slipped into his room, closing the door with a gentle click.

*Strange*, she thought, *didn't Tinseng say he went to sleep at 9:30?* But she could think of a dozen reasons why someone would stay up: the excitement of vacation, the discomfort of an unfamiliar mattress, the rocking of the ship. Besides, maybe Tinseng had been exaggerating about his habits, and he only went to sleep earlier than Tinseng—not a difficult thing to do.

Yukying left the bag outside and went back to bed. It was best to forget about it. If she needed to worry, someone would tell her eventually.

# CHAPTER TWO

*Nine Days Ago. June 16, 1963. At Sea.*

Yukying considered herself an expert in the tricks the ocean could play—she'd lived near water her whole life—but as she stared out from the bow that first morning, she found herself humbled. No matter where she stood on the deck, the ocean stretched out all the way to the horizon, daring her to consider how small she was. The ocean knew all, and she knew nothing.

When she had walked upstairs earlier, she'd noticed Shan Dao a few chairs over, looking out at the view. In the morning light, some of his severity lessened; he wore light gray slacks and a white polo, and his upper body was wrapped in a beautiful knit shawl, tucked into the crooks of both his arms. It looked incongruous on a man, more the soft kind of layer one expected on a woman. Then Yukying scolded herself for thinking that way; Shan Dao could wear anything he wanted, of course.

She did not speak with him, but they acknowledged each other silently, and when she sat, it was one recliner chair over from his—enough space to imply that she would not bother him, but close enough for him to know she would not reject his company. It was pleasant. It was rare to feel so at ease with a stranger. Eventually, the rest of the ship woke up around them, and by mutual silent agreement, they got up and walked down to breakfast together.

Tennis was first on the agenda that morning, according to her brothers. Yukying followed them to the courts, planning to put in a short appearance before searching for Mrs. Lanzette's sewing circle. Once again she was left with Shan Dao, who seemed to be there against his will; he appeared unaware that Tinseng was showing off for him.

"You don't play?" she asked. He did not. He could play football if pressed, but (here he smiled self-deprecatingly) chess and go were his sports. In return, he didn't insult her by asking what sports she played but instead asked about her hobbies. Cooking, she had to admit, was as much a hobby to her as a household chore. It was different for her than for the British housewives of her acquaintance, she told him. Those women showed their love other ways, if they showed it at all, and talked of cooking mostly as labor; she knew her experience of kitchens was vastly different than that of Europeans.

"Not all of them," Shan Dao said. "There are farmers and workers there too. The rich who live in Hong Kong don't represent them all."

"Oh, I didn't mean to—of course, it's all . . . I'm sure the struggle is the same everywhere," she said, her voice trailing off.

"I meant to say you would find your people there," Shan Dao said with a faraway look; he had been transported by memory. "You would recognize their kitchens. Be at home in them, perhaps."

She imagined being in a kitchen with Shan Dao; it was a much more peaceful image than navigating a kitchen with her brothers.

"Tinseng said you're a vegetarian," she said. "Do you eat fish at all? Or shellfish?"

"I . . . have. I prefer not to." Yukying heard concessions in the pause. Between their births and now, there had been far too many reasons why a boy might starve, and why he might tear into whatever scraps he could find without asking what it was or where it had come from. There had been times Yukying had starved too. Almost everyone in their generation had. It wasn't an experience she wanted them to share.

"If you don't mind me asking . . . the diet can't be for religious reasons?"

Shan Dao shook his head. "Religion is not needed for a man to feel moral responsibility or to advocate living without exploitation."

Yukying smiled out at the court where her brothers were swinging rackets to test them. "An answer even Cheuk-Kwan wouldn't find fault with."

"Would that stop him from trying?"

"Probably not," she said, and laughed, delighted that Shan Dao already knew both her brothers so well. She put a hand on his arm. "Tell me, what are some of your favorite foods? Have you craved anything since you left home?"

He paused for so long that she wondered if she'd insulted him in some way, and she was about to change the topic entirely when he finally admitted, "*Röstis bernois und spinat* . . . a Swiss food." His hesitance made sense now: He had assumed she would reject his Western answer. After all, hadn't Laurence said it last night? *One never knows about these foreign types, if they only know how to eat* 面包 *and not* 面条. She wondered if he felt he could be open about missing Paris. Tinseng had said he'd spent the majority of his life there. It would be a shame if he had to pretend that wasn't a part of him, and yet they both knew that would be the expectation when he settled in Hong Kong: to assimilate, to learn the language and forget all his others, to eat rice and not bread.

Shan Dao expected her to say something dismissive now, perhaps about how they didn't eat that kind of thing in Hong Kong. She'd have to disappoint him.

"Ro… rowstees?" She smiled and shook her head. "Once more?"

"*Röstis bernois und spinat.*"

"Spinach," she guessed, "and . . ."

"Do you know—" he had to reach for English, "hash browns?"

She shook her head.

"Mm. Then… it is a little like 葱油饼 . . . no." he shook his head ruefully. "That's wrong."

"Whatever it is, I'm sure it's delicious. Do you think you can get me a recipe?"

"Why?"

"So I can make it?" She would have thought that obvious, but Shan Dao looked up at her quizzically.

"Why?" he asked again.

"Well . . . for when you're homesick."

He began to protest, but she hushed him with another pat on the arm. "It will be easy to add your ingredients to my list." She didn't cook *every* meal—she shared the responsibility with Laurence's mother and sisters—but she did buy most of the food because she loved going to the markets first thing in the morning when the ocean air still smelled like crisp possibility. "Though, please use the kitchen whenever you'd like. You're probably used to cooking for yourself, and I want you to think of the house as your own."

"As . . . my own?" Shan Dao's frown deepened.

"Yes. Has that been worked out?" Yukying tilted her head at Shan Dao's confusion. "Tinseng explained your situation, and we asked him to let you know we insist that you stay with us. . . He *did* tell you, didn't he?"

"I . . . no." Shan Dao frowned. "No, he didn't."

"Oh . . ." Her stupid, *stupid* brother. "I'm sorry; I probably misunderstood something."

They both looked over at Tinseng, currently pointing and laughing at Cheuk-Kwan—until his younger brother threw a tennis ball into the air then aimed the serve directly at his face.

"The fault is *not* with you," Shan Dao muttered.

Yukying suppressed a sigh and decided to search out Mrs. Lanzette. Even a sewing circle full of wary strangers would be easier to navigate than these boys.

※

She found the group in one of the smaller lounges, which was decorated like a cozy library. Unlike a regular library, there were delicate metal grates over all the shelves—it wouldn't do to have books dropping on guests all the time, she supposed. She meandered between occupied tables and individuals reading on couches, shy about approaching the group of women directly; the sewing circle was the largest group in the room. She pretended to read the book titles on a nearby shelf as she listened to one of the women say, "Betty Friedan says the younger generation hasn't suffered a crisis of identity yet. We think we don't have to look into the future or plan what we want, really *want*, for our lives." The voice was nasally American and imperious. "Here, let me find it... 'They had only to wait to be chosen, marking time passively until the husband, the babies, the new house decided what the rest of their lives would be.'"

"You carry that thing around like the Bible, Rebecca," a woman with an English accent said.

"We might be better off if it replaced it."

The group tittered at the casual blasphemy. As Rebecca started speaking again, someone else called out, "Mrs. Li! I thought that was you." Mrs. Lanzette waved her over. "Thought you'd escape me, eh? No such luck. Come join our little band of firebrands. I see you've brought your basket."

The women had fallen silent at the sight of her, but Mrs. Lanzette was a battle-axe of a woman, accepting no awkwardness at *her* table. Introductions were made, and Yukying was thankful the table hid more diversity than their whiteness implied. She shook hands or nodded to them all: Mrs. Biddle, a stately London woman with seven grandchildren (there were pictures) and with whom Mrs. Lanzette had kept correspondence over many years; Rebecca Arden, the American typist who had "gotten the hell out of Ohio" and now lived alone in New York City; Mrs. Duncan from a place called Maine, who seemed no firebrand but did, to her credit, seem absolutely uninterested in anything but cards and drinking; her daughter, Miss Duncan, the only daughter of Mrs. Duncan's five, openly mooning over Rebecca and her defiant freedom; and a young woman from the Eastern Bloc, Marissa Grodescu, who lived in France with her husband. Yukying pounced on the topic of France eagerly.

"I wanted to visit Paris while my brother lived there," she said, as they all went back to their sewing and conversation. "He was there three years and I never visited once. The time slipped by so quickly."

"Paris can be beautiful in spring, but not now. The heat makes the city sweat."

"Oh, if you think it's hot there, never visit Hong Kong in summer..."

While they worked on their projects, the table exchanged horror stories of the various heat waves they'd survived. From there the topic turned briefly to the wars past, then to the wars present, but no one wanted to speak on either for very long; the table split into smaller conversations, and soon Yukying found she'd passed forty-five minutes talking mostly to the Polish woman who lived in France. The other still stumbled over her English, but all her words were spoken with steel. She was a woman with hard eyes and a quick tongue, and Yukying liked her very much.

"Remind me of your name again?"

"Marissa Grodescu." She set aside her needles to light a cigarette.

"Yukying Li."

"Is Li *your* name? I have heard that Asian women do not take their husband's name when they marry." She offered a cigarette to Yukying, who politely declined.

"Oh, well, yes, that's usually the case. But my husband was born and raised in Hong Kong; his mother is English, and his whole family is..." *More bread than rice*, Yukying thought wryly. "And he works for the British, so it was easier. And a little bit expected," she added, uncertain to whom she was being apologetic.

Marissa scoffed. "Is that not always the way? Always *expected*." She stared at the bookshelves over Yukying's shoulder. "And what is expected of *them*?"

"Them? The English?"

"Men," Marissa said with enough venom that Yukying thought she might spit on the floor to complete the curse.

"Ah, have you read this book from America, Marissa?" The woman from earlier, Rebecca, inserted herself into the conversation, pulling *The Feminine Mystique* from her bag and sliding it over. "It's the book of the century. You should borrow it. Either of you," she said, smiling at Yukying. Yukying had heard of the book, of course. It'd just been released, but already it was infamous. The feminism it discussed was distinctly Western, and through lenses that didn't all apply to Yukying's understanding. In 1950 the People's Republic of China's first official act as a new power had been to pass the New Marriage Law, giving women equal rights of ownership and property management when women in America couldn't even have bank accounts. It also let women initiate divorce—an act still impossible in most of the world over a decade later. Of course, Yukying couldn't exercise those rights herself, living under British rule, but they shaped the way she thought, and she thought of the Americans as backward, and the book itself as a little behind the times. Still, the Kowloon Kaifong Women's Association had set up a series of dates in the fall to discuss the book, and she'd been disappointed her copy hadn't arrived in time to read on this trip.

"May I?" She looked over at Marissa, who gestured at Yukying to take it.

"What good would it do me?" Marissa asked. "I already know the words, and words cannot help. Action is what is required."

"Hear, hear," Miss Duncan muttered, then smirked when Yukying had to smother her laugh.

"Then why not divorce him, dear?" Mrs. Lanzette asked. "You live in Paris; it's de rigueur for the French."

"That's right—doesn't everyone over there?"

Yukying and Marissa exchanged a look; it always seemed so simple from the outside.

Marissa Grodescu smiled grimly. "Not everyone in France is of one mind on the issue. My husband believes a wife is an investment."

The table murmured their sympathy, but really, what was there to say? Every woman there had heard this story before. Old Mrs. Biddle probably believed a husband was right in this belief. Yukying silently thanked whichever ancestor had sent her Laurence; she really had gotten extraordinarily lucky with him.

Thinking of Laurence reminded her to check the time—she was supposed to meet him for lunch in fifteen minutes. She clucked her tongue and began packing her things, making sure to tuck the book in her bag as she promised to return it to Rebecca before the end of the trip.

"Have tea with us this afternoon," she invited Marissa, but the other woman shook her head.

"Don't invite trouble to your table, Mrs. Li."

Yukying pursed her lips. That wouldn't do at all.

"Then borrow this." Yukying dropped a pattern into Marissa's basket. "You'll have to return it tomorrow."

Marissa looked down at it. Her frown made it very clear what she thought of Yukying: a foolish, silly person who didn't understand what was really going on. Yukying had been on the receiving end of that look her entire life. She just smiled and left Marissa with a single thread of connection to someone who cared.

<hr>

After lunch, Yukying claimed a deck chair and started in on Rebecca's book of the century. The shade of the deck and the white noise of the guests in the pool lulled her eyes closed. Time drifted in a gentle haze until Tinseng and Chiboon's voices coaxed her awake. They both dripped with pool water, puddles accumulating at their feet.

"Oh, jie, did we wake you?" Tinseng hit Chiboon on the arm. "I *told* you to be quiet."

"No, I shouldn't have fallen asleep in the first place." She scrubbed at her eyes and patted down her hair. Her hat sat crooked on her head. "In public, too—how embarrassing."

"No, no, half the people out here are asleep," Tinseng said, pointing to a few. "Her, and him, oh, and definitely him."

"But how can you tell? She's wearing sunglasses. And maybe he's just reading."

"Oh no, he's asleep. The grip on his book, for one. The way he's propped it against something so it won't slide down, but you can see his hand is loose. He planned to nap."

"When did you get so observant, Tinseng?" Chiboon asked.

"When I realized I could learn secrets that way," her brother said with a sharp smile. "Now I always know when a student is trying to cheat."

"Imagine if *your* teachers had been able to tell when you'd cheated," Yukying teased.

"Ahh, unfair," Tinseng whined, "We were geniuses in our time. My students are just lazy."

"That's right, we were wasted on our teachers. They never tapped our potential." Chiboon looked at his watch and hissed. "I promised Cheuk-Kwan I'd meet him for the movie, he's going to flay me!"

"Run fast!" Tinseng called merrily as Chiboon pulled on a shirt and dashed off. Yukying laughed and settled back against her chair; Tinseng sprawled out next to her. When he broke the silence, he was uncharacteristically hesitant.

"Jiejie? Can I ask you something, and you won't ask why?"

"Of course," she promised without hesitation.

"How do you know if you . . . how did you know you loved Li Yingtung?"

Her heart constricted even as she tried not to smile at her silly little brother who thought he needed to be shy about his feelings. There were many answers to this question: answers that were true, answers that were helpful, answers Tinseng maybe wanted to hear. A few years ago, she would have told him something very different. Now, though, she mostly told the truth.

"I knew when we spent that weekend with everyone in Macau."

"But he was so awkward then!"

"I know." Yukying smiled down at her hands, remembering. "I'd wanted him to make a good impression so badly, to show you all the man he'd become. But he sort of failed, didn't he?"

"Well . . . he wasn't *that* bad," Tinseng said generously, since they both knew it really had been that bad.

"I thought I would be embarrassed," she said. "I was afraid I would . . . want to scold him . . . or hide him." *Like Mother had been with Father,* she thought; she'd been so afraid of finding that inside herself. "I had an image of the Laurence I wanted him to be for you. I wanted to show you the Laurence I saw when it was just us. But . . . it was okay that he wasn't. I ended up liking the sarcasm you drew out of him and the way he followed along when you and Cheuk-Kwan talked. No matter which part of him I saw, I still wanted to stand next to him, to help him, support him, be proud of him. When I realized that, I realized I'd found someone I could always be with, no matter the circumstance. He could trust me with every part of himself, and I would never reject him."

Tinseng nodded, focused, like he was trying to memorize every word. "How do you show someone that? That they can trust you with every part of themselves?"

Would Tinseng listen if she told him the best way to build trust was to show the vulnerable parts of yourself first? Would he stop avoiding difficult conversations for once? It was unlikely; sincerity wasn't a currency Tinseng used. His pockets had always been empty of trust.

"You can also show them with your patience, and your attention. With your honesty. And by listening." She leaned over and tapped his nose with a finger. "By not interrupting."

"What if they like being interrupted?" he wheedled.

"Then it must be fine," she teased back. "What else do *they* like?"

"*They* like being challenged. They like getting the rug pulled out from under them, even if it irritates them at first. Excellence—they love anything that excels. Games, as long as no one gets hurt and everyone wins. Unless he's being competitive—then he loves crushing his competition into a fine powder. It's the best; it really is. He's so effortless about it! Oh, and he loves showing off. He'd never admit it, but he does. He likes seeing people be good." His voice quieted as he added, mostly to himself, "He likes when he catches me paying attention. He likes knowing I'm . . ."

"Knowing you're what?" she prompted gently. Tinseng shook his head, still lost. "A-Seng, if you feel this way, why haven't you asked him to stay with us?"

"Who says I haven't?"

"Shan Dao himself, this morning."

"Ah. Ha-ha." An embarrassed flush spread across his cheeks. "It's complicated."

"Is it? Or are you making it more complicated than it has to be?"

He paused long enough that Yukying almost believed he'd lost his thought entirely. Finally, he planted a theatrical kiss on her cheek. "You're so wise, jie. Let's get back in the water, eh?"

In the end, she let him get away with it; she *had* promised not to ask why. *Besides*, she thought as she followed him down the steps into the shallow end of the water, *what are older sisters for, if not to hide behind their skirts?* They had the rest of the trip to work things out. With how deeply Tinseng felt about Shan Dao, she was certain he wouldn't be able to hide himself forever.

———

After dinner, their group claimed a corner of one of the smoking rooms. Without the burden of their tablemates, they were free to speak in Cantonese, and conversation flowed to more personal topics. They had three years of news to catch Tinseng up on, nearly three for Chiboon. Cheuk-Kwan related to Tinseng and Shan Dao the refugee crisis that had only worsened, the typhoon that hit last year, the water crisis being mismanaged by every level of government. It was a hard time for Hong Kong, but then, it was a hard time everywhere.

"Tell me about you, Yukying." Chiboon looked over at the brothers, who existed in their own little world. "Since I don't think we'll get them back for a while."

"Oh, there's not much to tell . . ." she started to say. "Just a little volunteering."

"Don't listen to her," Laurence broke in, then heard how that sounded and stammered, "Ah, sorry—what I meant was: She's being modest."

"Well then, I'll go to a more trustworthy source," Chiboon said. "Tell all, Laurence-ge."

Ignoring Yukying's protests, Laurence told Chiboon that her work wasn't just volunteering. The refugees from China had caused a real crisis for the city. There was new public housing, but obviously it wasn't enough. The refugees were fleeing the famine more than anything, and they were all poor, hardly a skilled worker among them. "It's not like we need more farmers," Laurence said. "So Yukying started a literacy program." It mobilized student groups and church committees, and was training volunteers to go to homes rather than making the already overtaxed refugees travel to a center. "It should be supported better," he admitted, "but right now it gets by on donations."

"I never thought I'd hear you openly critical of the governor, Li Ying-tung." They turned to Tinseng, who watched Laurence with a neutral sort of attention Yukying knew could be dangerous. "I remember you being very vocal in your support before I left."

"That was before," Laurence said.

"Before my sister, you mean."

"Yes. Before Yukying, I was an ass."

"I always knew, but it's nice to see you finally admit it."

Laurence rolled his eyes. "Anyway. Just as the refugees slowed down, we had the typhoon."

"It was fucking bad," Cheuk-Kwan agreed. "Entire sections leveled."

Tinseng shook his head. "They published that only a few thousand were left homeless, but I knew better than to trust it."

"A few thousand." Cheuk-Kwan snorted. "Try more like seventy thousand."

"Or more," Yukying agreed. She'd seen it. Tinseng blinked, a little pale.

"Seventy thousand. That's . . ."

"And Yukying's organization is one of the biggest groups helping," Laurence said, chin in the air. "She's doing more for them than anyone else in the city."

"Oh, that's not—"

"I'd expect nothing less," Tinseng spoke over Yukying's denial. "How much have they rebuilt?"

"The parts you'd expect," Cheuk-Kwan said. "Tourist areas, the British neighborhoods, you know. And that's not even the biggest problem anymore. The water shortage is getting worse by the day."

Tinseng grimaced. "Sounds like we've got our work cut out for us when we get home," he said, with the same unbreakable spirit he'd always shown, no matter the problem. He sounded ready to roll up his sleeves and wade into the rubble right then. His mood hit those who had stayed behind like a sunbeam breaking free of the clouds. Yukying, Cheuk-Kwan, and Laurence all exchanged looks, and Yukying knew they were all thinking the same thing: No matter how Tinseng might get under their skin, he'd been deeply, terribly missed.

Chiboon was talking about Gibraltar when she drifted back. "You'll all come with me, right? My editor gave me a checklist for each stop, as though I couldn't write about that boring rock in my sleep."

"Aww, but Yukying and I are excited for Gibraltar, aren't we, jiejie?" Tinseng said. "I want to see those monkeys steal someone's glasses off their face."

"You and monkeys, that's the *real* family reunion," Cheuk-Kwan quipped, and earned himself a punch in the arm.

"Would you take notes for me, then?" Chiboon asked Tinseng.

"Only if you finally tell me that secret about Dean Martin."

"No deal. I'll . . . buy your drinks for an entire night."

"With how much he drinks?"

"A whole night," Chiboon insisted.

"Done," Tinseng agreed. They shook on it, to the amusement of the rest of the table.

"You're the best, both of you," Chiboon gushed.

"That's half-true," Cheuk-Kwan told Laurence, who pressed his lips together in an effort not to laugh.

"And what are *you* contributing to Chiboon's research?" Tinseng crossed his arms and looked his brother up and down. "Ten tips for single men on cruises? How to not look desperate while sitting alone at the bar?"

"*You're* single," Cheuk-Kwan said pointedly. Tinseng stammered, caught out. Laurence sent a baleful look to Yukying, pleading with her to intervene.

"Which port is everyone looking forward to the most?" she asked the room.

"Barcelona," Laurence answered.

"Naples for me," Cheuk-Kwan said.

"Why's that?"

"Because it means we only have a single plane ride until we're home."

Everyone groaned and shouted abuse in Cheuk-Kwan's direction. As he defended himself loudly, Yukying asked quietly across the table, "What about you, Shan Dao? Which port are you most excited for?"

"Villefranche. But I, too, look forward to reaching Hong Kong."

"How long are you planning to visit Hong Kong?" Chiboon asked.

Shan Dao looked over at Tinseng, then back to Chiboon. "The timeline is currently ... flexible."

Yukying and Cheuk-Kwan exchanged raised eyebrows, and Yukying quickly jumped on the opportunity to ask, "Where are you planning to stay? We live in King's Park and have plenty of room. We've already asked Tinseng, though he hasn't given us an answer yet ..."

"Tinseng mentioned he was still deciding," Shan Dao's voice sounded strangled. "I have a room at a hotel. It is sufficie—"

"A room at a hotel?" Cheuk-Kwan turned to Tinseng. "You're going to let him stay at a *hotel*?"

"Nonsense," Yukying agreed. "You have to stay with us. We have more rooms than we know what to do with."

Tinseng shook his head. "J–Shan Dao is his own man—"

"The hotel is temporary," Shan Dao insisted. "It will likely only be for a few days until I find a room to rent."

"See? He's made up his mind," Tinseng said. "Besides, he might not even stay in Hong Kong that long. He wants to go back to China and teach there. Soak in his presence now; we might never see him again if Shan Dao gets his way, ha-ha."

Tinseng's forced laughter fell into the stunned silence with a thud. Shan Dao looked down at his hands. Cheuk-Kwan stared at his sister in disbelief, but Yukying didn't know where to start.

"Tell us about your new position, Tinseng," Chiboon said for want of anything polite to say about the trainwreck in front of them.

"Adjunct for now, but it could lead to tenure." Tinseng preened a little. "One physics lecture, but they mostly have me teaching French to first years."

"Weren't you tutoring Chinese and English in Paris?" Cheuk-Kwan narrowed his eyes. "How does someone go from a language tutor to physics professor?"

"I don't know, Cheuk-Kwan. I *did* get a degree in it. Or don't you remember those years? All the science books I used to carry around? Besides, how does a doctor grow such a large private practice yet still have such shit bedside manners?"

"*Some* patients need to be put under," Cheuk-Kwan hissed.

"Scary. When we get back, I'm ripping up the floorboards of your office—I bet you have jars of eyes and fingernails under there."

"Ahh, I've missed this," Chiboon said, leaning back. "Haven't you missed this, Laurence?"

"Like a toothache," Laurence muttered, and Chiboon chuckled. But Yukying *had* missed this, the sniping and talking over each other and the laughter and the yelling—all the familiar noise of love.

---

All the love in the world, however, couldn't keep these men from arguing. The mood had shifted after the exchange about where Shan Dao would stay, and it seemed inevitable that the conversation would turn to politics. Cheuk-Kwan and Chiboon picked up their conversation about the Mei Affair from the night before and, without their American tablemates to keep them in check, voices quickly rose.

"'Every Party member, every branch of work, every statement and every action must proceed from the interests of the whole Party.'" Shan Dao's tone was quiet and even, with steel cable underneath. "'It is absolutely impermissible to violate this principle.'"

"Exactly." Cheuk-Kwan pointed at Shan Dao. "*Exactly*. Where was Li Xifeng's loyalty? The only thing she ever did to protect the Party was to die before there could be a trial."

"If only there had been a trial," Chiboon mourned. "Killed in cold blood is sensational, but I might have gotten invited to sit in on the trial. That's a career-maker."

"We're lucky there wasn't a trial," Cheuk-Kwan said.

"And why's that?" Tinseng asked with a smile that informed everyone there was about to be a fight.

Cheuk-Kwan obliged him by saying, "You were in France. You saw what they wrote in the papers. The wife of a Chinese diplomat recruited by the USSR? There's nothing the West loves more than our own infighting. Not to mention Li Xifeng set back relations between China and Russia how many years? A trial would've made it that much worse."

"So we're supposed to throw out the potential for the truth, for *progress*, which you apparently care about, just because you're stupid enough to believe the shock and outrage from the CCP? Of course they know there are spies, Cheuk-Kwan—it's the bloody Cold War! It's all to save face, nothing more. No one's asking questions now about why she might've been interested in leaving the CCP in the first place. Real, legitimate complaints with the way things are being run—instead, all that's been silenced. Behind the scenes, I guarantee they're ecstatic. They succeeded in burying it all, every stinking corpse."

"And you think exhuming all those corpses in a trial would be better? The fact of it's bad enough. It's made the situation in Hong Kong a complete clusterfuck, Tinseng. If you hadn't fucked off to France, you'd know that."

"Oh, so now it's my fault?"

"*And* it's weakened our international support," Cheuk-Kwan talked over him. "What the Party needs is unity, across all countries, just like the capitalists have. If Li Xifeng had problems with her Party, she should have tried to address it internally. What she did just divides us further."

"Better these things end quickly, without fanfare," Laurence agreed. "Bad enough it was leaked to the press."

"Without answers?" Tinseng asked, voice rising. "Without justice?"

"Did the Rosenbergs get justice?" Cheuk-Kwan asked. "Did the truth come out in *their* trial? Given the death sentence by their country without a second glance at all that sham evidence, even with so many of their own citizens protesting in the streets. How do you think a trial in China would end? Death by assassin or by jury—how's it any different?"

"We could have heard her arguments! *Why* she did what she did. People need to know." Tinseng's gaze moved to Shan Dao, then swept over the rest of them. "Isn't public debate in the interest of the Party?

It's important that people hear the reasons she lost faith in the CCP. It's silence of the truth."

"She didn't believe in truth," Cheuk-Kwan spat, "or she wouldn't have thought it so easily conquered."

Shan Dao stood abruptly.

"I . . . dinner is not sitting well. Excuse me," he said and left the room. Tinseng hissed at his brother and hurried after him. Silence reigned for a few beats before Laurence and Cheuk-Kwan turned back to each other as if nothing had happened.

"The least she could have done was sell those secrets to the Western Bloc," Laurence said, shaking his head. "Our government would have given her sanctuary in a heartbeat."

"You really think it's the same?" Chiboon asked. "I read all her published letters and notes for my articles. Nuclear policy was her largest concern—what future would be left for her sons, and their children. Khrushchev believes in disarmament. She thought he would pursue peace."

"Khrushchev ends every day pissing on Lenin's grave," Cheuk-Kwan snarled. "How could she—"

"Cheuk-Kwan!" Yukying scolded sharply.

"All I'm saying is," Laurence doubled down, "if she'd wanted to undermine the CCP, she could have defected and taken her knowledge anywhere. But selling to the Soviets? 损人不利己."[3]

"Anywhere?" Chiboon asked. "Maybe I'm misremembering, but weren't some French spies killed just last month?"

"Exactly." Cheuk-Kwan nodded. "Why the f— ahem. Why would she run to imperialists when they can't even keep their own safe? Besides, she could have wanted out from the CCP but still believed in the Party, Laurence, it's not as mutually exclusive as you seem to think."

---

[3] To harm someone without any self-benefit. A play on 损人利己—to harm others to benefit self. English equivalent: "like cutting off your nose to spite your face."

Yukying sighed as her husband and brother started another round of their endless argument. It was probably too late to ban political topics, she thought; even if she tried now, no one would listen.

※

That night, pain in her joints kept her awake. No matter how much she tried to distract herself, no matter the lotion Laurence carefully rubbed into her skin, she still found herself cataloging how every shift of her body strained a different part of her. If she lay on her stomach, it put pressure on her knees. On her back, her neck complained. She didn't want to get up, but she knew the only thing to do was walk around, stretch, and try to breathe through it. Eventually, she had to hope, exhaustion would win over pain.

She rose with a sigh. Her key went into her dress pocket as she slipped out the door to wander the halls, zigzagging in a large circle that took her upstairs, down her own hallway, downstairs, through the lower hallways of the staterooms, then back up to her own floor. She heard noise behind different doors as she walked, saw laundry and dirty dishes left out. She tried to imagine the people who fit these little clues, but that was more Tinseng's kind of game.

As she walked down the stairs to complete another loop of the lower staterooms, a cabin door at the opposite end of the hall opened. On instinct, she paused on the stair to see whoever emerged before they saw her.

It was Shan Dao. She blinked, not understanding. He walked out of the stateroom as he rolled down his shirtsleeves. The door shut behind him. He looked unbothered, but when the door was fully closed, he turned back and stared at it—as if he debated knocking again, or maybe like he'd left something inside. He stared with such focus that he startled when the ship creaked. Then he remembered himself and started walking toward his room—toward the staircase where Yukying stood watching him.

Panicking, Yukying half-ran up the stairs to their floor, then ducked into the recess with the cigarette machine. She turned away from the hallway to listen. The footsteps grew louder. When Shan Dao reached her, she ducked her head low pretending to fiddle for change in her pocket. Shan Dao passed, not looking her way. He stopped outside his and Tinseng's door, unlocked it, then disappeared inside.

She stared down at the cigarettes in their neat rows. *What was that?*

She'd never be able to sleep now. She started up her circuit again, mulling things over. In the lower hallway, she stood a safe distance away and stared at the door of the room she saw Shan Dao leaving. Number 208. There was nothing about this door to distinguish it from the others. What was in room 208? No, that wasn't the question. She thought about the rolled shirtsleeves and the intense look on Shan Dao's face. *Who* was in room 208?

Someone walked down the hallway from behind. Yukying turned, startled, and placed a hand on her chest when she saw who it was.

"Mrs. Grodescu," she cried, relieved to see a friendly face.

"Mrs. Li. It's late."

"It is. I couldn't sleep. Were you at the dance?"

"Yes. I came to check on my husband. He was supposed to be upstairs at the dance some while ago. Usually he would not like me there unchaperoned."

"I see. I hope he's well?"

"Most likely distracted by work," Mrs. Grodescu said, thin-lipped. "It was the first thing he unpacked."

"Well, please don't let me keep you, then. Will I see you at the circle tomorrow?"

"Likely not. We plan to be all day at Tamariz Beach."

"Carcavelos for us. Have a marvelous time."

"You as well. Goodnight." Marissa Grodescu nodded to her and walked past. Yukying turned and watched as Mrs. Grodescu took her key from her pocket and entered room 208.

# PART TWO

## DO YOU WANT TO KNOW A SECRET?

# CHAPTER THREE

*Two Years Ago. December 1961. Paris, France.*

The knock came at five past midnight.

It was an erratic thing, its rhythm too strong, then tailing off as if the hand had fallen from sudden lack of strength. Wu Tinseng sat up and stared at the door. He could read a knock like tea leaves, and this one meant fucking trouble. Getting up from his chair, he grabbed his gun from the drawer and hid it behind his back as he opened the door a sliver.

"Mei Jinzhao!" He tucked his gun into the back of his waistband and threw the door open. "You're supposed to be in Switzerland! What do I owe . . ."

His words stalled as his eyes caught up with his mouth. His professional instincts took over, sweeping over the man standing in the hallway and cataloging him from head to toe: unwashed hair, bloodshot eyes, wrinkled suit, scuffed shoes. His usual beauty dimmed from exhaustion. Constantly shifting weight, a restlessness he'd never seen from Jinzhao before. A foot barely touching the floor—favoring his left side. An injury, and a bad one.

"What happened?" Tinseng demanded, all pretense dropped.

"They're dead," Jinzhao said, and Tinseng went numb.

"Who?"

"My parents. They've . . ." Jinzhao's eyes were unfocused. "It was not an accident."

*Oh, fuck.*

"Come inside." He had to get a door between Jinzhao and the outside world. When Jinzhao remained unmoving, Tinseng tugged at his sleeve, not thinking much of a gesture he'd made a hundred times. He was horrified when Jinzhao swayed and lost his balance. Darting forward, Tinseng snaked his arm around Jinzhao's back, taking the majority of his weight. It felt strange to be so close again. After Jinzhao had learned about his proclivities two months ago, Tinseng had been keeping his distance; the last thing Tinseng wanted to do was make his friend uncomfortable. But just now the situation demanded it, and Tinseng knew how to keep his touch impersonal.

"Don't fight," he scolded when Jinzhao tried to pull away from the help. "I know you hate to be close, but you're lucky I'm not carrying you." They limped to the couch. Jinzhao slumped down on it, strings cut. Tinseng pulled over the chair from his lone table and sat closer than he should, knees nearly touching.

"Now," he said, "I'm sorry we have to do this, but I think you need to tell me everything. It might be important later, and you might forget."

Jinzhao nodded. He understood and licked dry lips, trying to start.

"My mother sent me a telegram. I have it . . ." he began, patting his pockets.

"It doesn't matter," Tinseng told him. "Find it later."

He settled again. "It was unlike her usual tone. You know my parents have been fractious in the past. I thought perhaps she was finally leaving him. I took the soonest train I could. I did not telegram back, in case she wanted to keep anything from my father. When I arrived, it was night."

"Do you know the precise time?" Tinseng interrupted as gently as he could.

"I—no. The train ticket, I could . . ."

"That's okay. Keep going."

"She was in their bedroom. He was in his study. There was a note. His hand."

"Do you have that?"

"The police took it. I wrote down what I could remember. But that wasn't . . . Tinseng. It wasn't. It doesn't make sense."

"Okay. Okay." Who wouldn't say that? It was the thing you always thought, after something like this. "Jinzhao. I'm sorry. How?"

"A gun. Both of them. Tinseng, I heard someone leaving."

The hair on Tinseng's neck prickled.

None of the windows were open, Jinzhao told him. It hadn't been a sound outside. Jinzhao sounded defensive; the argument had played in his head already. "It was the back door. I ran downstairs. It was unlocked." They weren't people to ever leave the door unlocked, Jinzhao insisted.

*Who knows what people do the night they destroy themselves*, someone might say. But Tinseng's instincts tingled up and down his skin.

"What next?" he asked.

"I called the police." The odd thing was that someone from the embassy arrived even before the ambulance. How, exactly, had they known something had happened? Jinzhao had been grateful for their arrival, though; when the police did arrive, they begun insisting it was a murder-suicide, with the note and the gun underneath the body. But Jinzhao had heard someone leaving. He'd been *sure* of it. Could the embassy man help him plead his case? Assurances and platitudes had been given.

Then the Swiss police took Jinzhao in for questioning. "I stayed for three hours until—"

"Wait. And the embassy *let* them? Did they send someone to go along with you?"

"No. I expected it from the Swiss but—"

Tinseng and Jinzhao exchanged a look. Though Jinzhao himself was no one special, his father held a position at the embassy. Usually no one in the West was willing to act against anyone like Mei Jinzhao, so closely associated with the Chinese embassy, for fear of retribution. Expel one Chinese spy, and the next day five of yours would be kicked out of the PRC. Mistreating an attaché would find your foreign diplomats denied visas. One of the CCP's favorite ways to express displeasure was to refuse to let foreign companies negotiate contracts; nothing made the Americans sit up and notice like loss of profit. China was harsh whenever relationships were strained, protective of their people in a way Tinseng sometimes envied. So why had their embassy man left Jinzhao out in the cold?

"He knew me," Jinzhao said, dazed, thinking along the same lines as Tinseng. "He worked across the hall from my father. We went to the opera together." His brow furrowed, as though this betrayal was a confusing puzzle he couldn't work out. Eventually the police let him go and told him not to leave town. The embassy man was waiting in the lobby for him and offered an invitation to stay at his house. Jinzhao politely refused. The embassy man walked him to his hotel, and that was when Jinzhao knew he was being watched.

———⁂———

They had to take a break. Beads of sweat dotted Jinzhao's upper lip. He needed a drink but wouldn't touch the cheap whiskey Tinseng kept. Tinseng insisted he lie down while he made tea.

"No, not the couch—through here. It's fine, don't be like that. You think I was going to use the bed tonight? How often do you find me asleep on the couch? Look at the sheets: undisturbed. You're not inconveniencing anyone. Now, let me take your coat. There are pajamas in the top drawer. If I don't find you changed when I get back, I'll withhold tea. Don't think I won't! I'm known to be very cruel."

Tinseng closed the bedroom door behind him and took Jinzhao's coat and bag into the kitchen. He put the kettle on, then turned the bag and coat inside-out looking for any clue about what could have caused this. Unmistakable flecks on the lower hem: bloodstains. In the pockets: his datebook, wallet with both French and Swiss francs, ID cards, and a ticket stub from Switzerland. Switzerland, and his parents, a cultural attaché and his wife, dead, and *not an accident*. On paper, Mei Hankong's job had mostly been to organize lectures for universities and various societies, booking them speakers from the PRC and generally touting all the cultural and intellectual advancements of the People's Republic to the Swiss. Obviously, it had been more than that.

The papers had a gag rule about reporting on intelligence affairs, but if these had been assassinations, surely Tinseng in his line of work would have heard something.

He thought about calling the office, but if he hadn't heard anything by now, they were purposefully keeping him out of the loop. Instinct told him he needed to keep as low under the radar as possible. Instead, he shamelessly flipped through Jinzhao's datebook. It was mid-December and most people would still be using their 1961 datebooks, dragging their feet until a day or two after New Year's when they absolutely had to switch. But of course, Jinzhao had already started using his brand-new 1962 datebook with November and December '61 pages conveniently included for overachievers. On the very first page, Jinzhao had inscribed a poem, presumably to set the tone for the year:

> *Des humains suffrages, Des communs élans Là tu te dégages Et voles selon.*
> *Puisque de vous seules, Braises de satin, Le Devoir s'exhale Sans qu'on dise : enfin.*
> *Là pas d'espérance, Nul orietur. Science avec patience, Le supplice est sûr.*
> *Elle est retrouvée. Quoi ? - L'Éternité. C'est la mer allée Avec le soleil.*

> From human prayers, / From common spirits / You free yourself / And thus you fly.
> Since from you alone, / Satin embers, / Duty breathes / No one says: at last.
> No hope here, / No emergence. / Knowledge with patience, / Torment is certain.
> It has been rediscovered. / What? Eternity. / It is the sea fled / with the sun.

Tinseng's smile hurt. The poem was so deeply Mei Jinzhao: thoughtful and quiet, a little melancholy, but so *good*. The smile fell from his face. How much would this tragedy change his friend? How much of his goodness would Tinseng need to mourn? How much of his kindness now lay dead with—

Not wanting to think about that, Tinseng flipped to the current month's page; there, Jinzhao had written a hasty note—*Mother*—on Tuesday last. Tinseng checked the train ticket: a 2:35 p.m. train on the same date. There were a few other inconsequential reminders for lunches and appointments, but only one other note that interested him: his own name, "胡天圣, 19:00," written on December 25. Tinseng ran his finger over his name in Jinzhao's beautiful handwriting. That's right—they had plans for Christmas, didn't they? They probably didn't anymore.

Thinking there might be something useful in the back, Tinseng thumbed to the contacts list, then breathed in: His name was the very first entry. *Not even alphabetical, Jinzhao, how unlike you*, he would tease under other circumstances, but there was something that stole his humor about seeing his name here. He'd ranked above Jinzhao's parents, even; Mei Hankong and Li Xifeng were entries two and three respectively. Before his parents, his brother, his uncle in Hong Kong, his more-established acquaintances and friends he'd known far longer than Tinseng... before anyone else, Jinzhao apparently wanted to remember Tinseng first.

Tinseng hadn't known they were *this* close of friends. He'd hoped, of course, when they'd reconnected, but they'd only been reacquainted since April; he hadn't wanted to assume. Seeing proof of his importance in Jinzhao's world made his brain swirl off into distant galaxies of fantasy, visions of what it might be like if...

The egg timer dinged. He shook himself back to his senses and brought the tea into the other room.

❧

In the bedroom, Jinzhao lay asleep on the bed, only his shoes and shirt removed. How long had he been pushing himself? Tinseng took a moment to stare. Even exhausted, Jinzhao still looked beautiful. *What luck some people have,* he thought, the teacup scalding his hand, *to be born so striking* and *smart* and *kind*. And what luck he had, that such a person would ever consider being friends with someone like him. With slow movements, he started removing one of Jinzhao's socks, careful around the swollen ankle. Jinzhao's skin was clammy, as if it had absorbed a chill. A warm bath was definitely needed, but first Tinseng examined the leg, feeling for anything like a break. All around the ankle were horrible bruises, deeply mottled things that spoke of violence.

He pulled the pant leg down and walked to the bathroom, counting his breath, one-two-three, through his nose. He turned on the tap and stood for a moment clenching and unclenching his fists. When the water ran warm, he plugged the drain and returned to the bed, where he called softly to Jinzhao. No response. Gently smoothing the sweaty hair from Jinzhao's brow, he murmured, "Jinzhao, wake up for me."

Jinzhao frowned deeply, his eyes still closed. On an exhale, he made a noise, the sound of a wounded animal.

"Tinseng?"

"Yes, I'm here. What do you need?"

"Don't leave," Jinzhao whispered. Grief flared through Tinseng. He had always wondered about his capacity for violence, but in this moment he knew he was capable of anything if it promised Jinzhao even a moment's relief. Jinzhao wouldn't want that, though. He didn't know what Jinzhao wanted; he could barely admit what he himself wanted. Something dangerous and irreversible, most likely.

"Do you see me going anywhere?" Tinseng joked, because he could not say any of the first ten things that had come to mind. Jinzhao opened his eyes to glare half-heartedly, but the expression fell off and he turned his head away trying to hide emotions not meant to be witnessed.

Tinseng watched, helpless. Half-formed impulses warred in him. He allowed himself no grace. "How about a bath, Jinzhao—does that sound nice? No? Well, I'm sorry you thought you had a choice. Come on."

By the time they stood in front of the tub, Jinzhao was shaking with exertion and shock. Tinseng turned off the water and tested the temperature.

"Do you need help with your clothes?" Jinzhao shook his head. "Okay. I'll go get fresh towels, then I'm checking your injuries. Don't give me that look; I know there are more. Your modesty will be preserved; I promise I won't make any jokes. Just pretend I'm the family doctor." They both winced. "Sorry. I—sorry. But if we're not going to a hospital? Then I have to."

He almost said please; the turmoil in his chest had him halfway to begging. Some of it must have shown, because Jinzhao stopped putting up a fight. With slumped shoulders, he started unbuttoning his shirt. Tinseng took the cue and left. Just outside the closed door, he gripped the bedside table and tried to breathe through the spots of rage. His heart spluttered like a dying engine, pounding with emotion he couldn't afford to have. Jinzhao needed him calm. He'd come here trusting Tinseng with this. Tinseng would rather die than let him down.

---

After examining his injuries and confirming no bones were broken, Tinseng pulled a chair into the bathroom and sat facing away from the bath. Jinzhao picked up the story again: The next morning, he went back to the house, only to be told he wasn't allowed in. He went to the embassy, and they told him he couldn't go beyond the lobby. He even went back to the police station; they told him they would call him at the hotel when they had news.

That went on for three days. The embassy questioned him on the second day, and the police again on the third. By this time, the story had changed. What had first been termed a murder-suicide by the police on the ground was now being called a robbery by detectives, with the coroner backing up this assertion.

"Tell me more about the house," Tinseng said. "Had there been drawers left open? Papers rustled through?"

"There were no obvious signs of robbery," Jinzhao said, though he admitted he hadn't been looking hard at the time. When the police had questioned him, he remembered that his mother's bedside had looked more chaotic than usual. But that had been where she was killed, or at least moved; perhaps that was to be expected.

"And your leg?" Tinseng asked.

Six days after he'd arrived in Bern, they had blocked him from every avenue of questioning. He was beginning to feel pressed in. And all the time he was being trailed by men who were not trying very hard to hide. When he'd asked the embassy man, Jinzhao was told he was jumping at shadows. He got desperate. He stood outside his parents' house until he saw someone he recognized, a secretary from the embassy; when she left, he followed her and begged her to help him.

She nearly fled at the sight of him, telling him to stay away, saying she couldn't be seen with him. That scared him more than anything else. Until then, he had been trying to convince himself his parents were killed by others—the Swiss, the English. The Russians, even. But the way his own comrades were acting, the distance they wanted from him, made him realize he needed to leave.

A block away from the train station, they jumped him. They spoke Swiss German, but they were both Chinese. They tried to drag him into a car. Jinzhao only escaped because of the self-defense lessons his mother had insisted on when he was a boy. The son of diplomats could never be too safe, she'd said.

"And then you came here?"

"Then I came here. After ensuring I wasn't followed, to the best of my ability."

"You used all of Raymond Chandler's tricks?" Tinseng made a joke of it, but he needed to know. Jinzhao nodded, wry; he had switched trains and tried to memorize all the faces of the other passengers. But he had been distracted hiding his injuries, too, and wasn't sure of his results.

"I've put you in danger," he said, looking out the bedroom window. They had moved from the bathroom to the bed during the retelling.

"Don't worry about that," Tinseng said, getting up to close the curtain. "I'm just glad you're here. Though what you thought a mere translator could do . . ."

For the first time that night, Jinzhao looked a little like himself as he stared Tinseng down.

"Wu Tinseng."

Tinseng laughed awkwardly. "What?"

"Why do you never take any papers from work home? Why does the department you work for have no presence? Why does a translator need a gun?"

"Okay, okay, okay." Tinseng held up his hands in surrender. "When did you get so inquisitive?"

"I'm hardly able to ignore it."

Tinseng scratched his nose. He'd always been able to hide from everyone else; he only found it impossible with Mei Jinzhao. The problem, he thought, was that he didn't *want* to hide. He was always begging the world to call him on his stories, and there was no one he wanted to see past his bullshit more than Mei Jinzhao. It'd been true back when they were sixteen. By now, it was possibly the only truth Tinseng had left.

"Okay, Jinzhao. Tomorrow. Ask me tomorrow."

*Tomorrow, Jinzhao. I'll tell you who I am and what I do, and if you don't reject me completely, I'll be whatever you need me to be.*

---

*Two Years Ago. February 1962. Paris, France.*

They'd first recruited him from the physics classrooms of New Asia College in Hong Kong to translate scientific documents. Tinseng hadn't been persuaded by British politics, not really; their definition of justice didn't align with his own. But Yukying was always telling him to do good with his life, and he'd once truly believed he would be able to wrench the world away from its corrupt trajectory. Certainly, signing up to work on the nuclear problem would help more than blowing up lab equipment and getting drunk on weekends, so he'd agreed.

His first handler had quickly recognized his potential and flagged him for the higher-ups; increasingly, he'd been pulled into rooms with sources and assets, asked to translate in real time. After only a year and a half, the chief of Hong Kong Station, a man named Weir, had promised him he was on track to become a field agent. They wanted to send him overseas for proper training, then place him somewhere he could begin recruiting a stable of assets; as their handling officer he would be in charge of their safety and see they were well taken care of. His other option was to stay in Hong Kong and keep his desk job, moving up the ranks in scientific intelligence work, perhaps pursuing a teaching position at New Asia College to become a recruiter himself.

In the end, the choice had been made for him: Yukying had cornered him one day about his other secret, and he'd realized just how much social danger he'd put his family in; his secret would break Yukying's engagement, would send his brother's patients running. He'd taken the promotion and left for training not long after. He had been trained to pair his paranoia with pattern recognition in order to draw out secrets, from texts as well as flesh.

"Tinseng." From across the room, Jinzhao called his name. Tinseng ignored him, burying his nose deeper in Li Xifeng's journal.

"Wu Tinseng."

"*Shh*, I'm focusing."

The package had been in Jinzhao's mailbox when he'd returned from Bern, full of his mother's papers and journals. A note on the front read, *Keep these safe for me.* The package was postmarked December 11. By the 15th, she was dead.

"Let it go, Tinseng."

"This," Tinseng said as he tapped Li Xifeng's journal with a bitten nail, "this means something, I know it."

Every professional instinct told him this journal held a key. A secret lurked behind Li Xifeng's beautiful penmanship, something to explain why Li Xifeng had been killed. It wasn't just hope that made him think so: He was fluent in Cantonese, Mandarin, English, and French, and passable in Russian and Korean—he *knew* language, and there was something about the way Li Xifeng translated some of these poems . . .

Besides, his contacts were getting nowhere, his digging around at work fruitless. They were no closer to knowing who killed Jinzhao's parents or why. It felt like failure. It *was* failure: As long as those questions remained unanswered, it wouldn't be safe for Jinzhao to return to China.

"Tinseng."

Tinseng looked up. Jinzhao sat across the table now, looking at him with concern.

"She sent it to you for a reason," Tinseng insisted weakly, but Jinzhao wasn't letting that persuade him this time.

"We will continue trying," Jinzhao promised, "but not tonight." He gently pulled the journal from underneath Tinseng's hand; Tinseng let it go.

"I'll work harder," he began, but Jinzhao was there, leaning over him, surrounding him, pulling him up into an embrace. Ever since that night two months ago, Jinzhao had stopped keeping his distance. Now, and with increasing frequency, there would be fingers wrapped around Tinseng's wrist, a hand on his back when Jinzhao read something over his shoulder, and even, when Jinzhao was feeling particularly distressed, hugs like this one that enveloped them both. Tinseng knew it had nothing to do with him, not really, but that didn't stop him from enjoying it. Tinseng closed his eyes and rested his cheek against Jinzhao's shoulder. He felt his chest move against Jinzhao's as they both breathed. When he inhaled, the scent of Jinzhao's familiar cologne traveled through his veins. On his exhale, his shoulders dropped—how long had he been so tense? His neck twinged. He took another deep breath and returned the embrace, properly relaxing for the first time in hours.

"You're right," he murmured, though Jinzhao hadn't said anything. "Come on, let's go for a walk."

On the street, Tinseng's head cleared of its fog. "I'm sorry, Jinzhao. It's just that, as long as we don't have answers, you can't go back to China, and that's the goal."

Jinzhao looked down at his shoes. "It is what I should do," he agreed.

"I know, I know." Tinseng could hardly think of anything else. "When we're done with this, I promise I'll get you on the plane to Beijing myself. Everything will be cleared up, and you'll be able to go whatever you want."

Jinzhao's mouth thinned. "The same applies to you. You could pursue any profession you want."

"Hah." Tinseng had to disagree. "I don't know if I have the right temperament for most jobs. I can stick it out two more years here, then go back to Weir."

"Tinseng."

"What?" Tinseng couldn't help but feel a little insulted. "I liked it there. Even if it's changed a bit, I can adapt anywhere."

Jinzhao looked a little incredulous. "Tinseng."

"What, you don't believe me?"

"You hate them."

"I hate it *here*. Hong Kong was better. Weir had his priorities straight."

Back when he worked in Hong Kong Station, his chief Terrance Weir was a crusty old sinologist turned spy, a legend to anyone who'd worked more than a month in Asia. Weir was loyal to his assets, then to his friends, then to MI6—in that order. He knew what was important. If Tinseng had still worked for Weir when Jinzhao had come to him back in '61, he would have taken him in, no hesitation.

"You should quit," Jinzhao insisted.

"I can't just quit," Tinseng said, as he always said. This was not the first time they'd had this discussion, or the tenth. "I still have to pay rent, you know!"

"Tutor instead."

Tinseng sighed and dropped the act. "We need their resources. And if it ends up that you need protection, or a totally new identity, they're still our best bet. Let me get in contact with Weir. Maybe there's something he can do there. Maybe we could even send you there. At the very least, you'd be closer to home."

"Home," Jinzhao repeated.

"Beijing? Where your brother is?" Tinseng was confused now.

"Oh. Yes." Jinzhao looked back down at his shoes. "Don't trouble yourself."

"Jinzhao. Trouble myself? It's not trouble! It's the right thing to do. Besides, isn't this why you came to me? So I could help?"

"Not at the expense of yourself."

"Oh, please. Let me tell you what I think, Mei Jinzhao," he said, just to say something, with no real intent to continue. He liked to hear the cadence of words out loud. But Jinzhao searched his face, taking him seriously.

"What do you think, Tinseng?" A thrill ran through Tinseng. There was a time when Jinzhao never would have asked, would have thought his opinion irrelevant or simply wrong. Now he asked for Tinseng's advice as though he truly valued it. Tinseng had to honor that by giving a true answer.

"I think you're worth all the effort in the world. Every person is. Isn't that the point of it all? I know that can tilt too individualistic for you, but lately I've been reading Louise Michel's speeches," he began to warm to the topic, "and there's this common ground between the Confucians and the anarchists: They both stress self-cultivation as the starting point for change. A path that leads to mass enlightenment. That second one's a little loftier, hah. But we can start the change here, you and me. Me, choosing to help you."

"路见不平," Jinzhao said quietly. "拔刀相助."

*The road is rough and full of injustice; draw your sword to help.* It was the kind of thing you said about a hero. Tinseng felt the blush on his cheeks.

"Jinzhao, that's way too much. I'm not like that."

"You intervene when others would not."

"Well." He couldn't exactly deny that. "I try." It was Tinseng looking down at his shoes now.

"And you *should* quit," Jinzhao said, making Tinseng laugh. Stubborn as always, that Mei Jinzhao. Tinseng wished he didn't find it so endearing.

"I'll think about it," Tinseng promised. "Once this is done, I'll think about it."

<hr />

Nothing was as simple as Jinzhao made it sound. Mei Jinzhao still saw the world in black and white. He wanted a grand sweeping code of morality that would somehow be applied to the entire world and create harmony, if only everyone would adopt it. Back when they were sixteen, Tinseng had told him that outlook was naïve at best and dangerous to the world in the wrong hands.

Yes, but so was every outlook, Jinzhao had said, and the right hands were the hands of the workers.

"And how was that working out in China?" Tinseng had asked, because from where he stood it looked like the same old hierarchy—one that Mei Jinzhao and his parents were complicit in.

The summer had ended with an explosive argument after Tinseng had nearly gotten kicked out for hosting unofficial debates in the dormitories after visiting hours and inviting women into the men's dorms. Tinseng considered the dorm rules arbitrary, sexist, and—if you really got him going—indicative of the kind of authoritarian tendencies the college should really curb before it became fully fascist. Jinzhao had been unrepentant in his smug assessment of Tinseng's rule-breaking and subsequent punishment, accusing Tinseng of hyper-individuality. If everyone acted like Tinseng acted, following whims and acting outside the bounds of accepted values, they would have no society at all. Not only that, but Tinseng's actions were a danger to himself and others. Tinseng accused Jinzhao of only caring about the theoretical—he didn't care about real people at all; he had no heart.

He didn't think that way about Jinzhao anymore.

Two days ago, drunk, Tinseng had said, "You know, you could sell me to the CCP. *That* would convince them you're loyal." Jinzhao had walked out of the room. If he had still owned his own apartment, he would have left entirely, but since he now lived with Tinseng out of an abundance of caution, he had holed up in the bedroom and refused to speak to Tinseng for the rest of the night.

Jinzhao wasn't willing to do whatever it took to help; Tinseng was. That was what it meant to draw a sword when you saw injustice: if you drew a sword, you had to follow through. You had to commit to death before the steel left its sheath, or the gesture was an empty one.

He'd always known he would die for the people he loved; he just hadn't known he'd kill for them too. Looking back, he must have always felt this way, but he hadn't known it about himself until Weir had seen it and drawn it out of him. It was as though they'd told him all the mirrors in the world had been fake, what he'd seen in them a lie. He had never wanted to know. He could have gone his whole life without the realization that Jinzhao had been right about him back then: He *was* a danger to himself and others.

But he was who he was now; he was who they made him. Could he really regret it if it meant helping Jinzhao? If they'd forged him into a person Jinzhao could rely on, it was easy to believe it was all worth it.

———

Despite treating the mystery of Jinzhao's parents as his new full-time job, Tinseng still had to go to work, which he was resenting more and more. Once he'd been transferred to Paris, they'd pushed him into interrogations and other, less pleasant work. They saw him as inferior, and he saw them as brutish. He really did need to quit. Jinzhao was right about that too, unfortunately, though Tinseng had no plans to tell *him* that.

That morning, Tinseng called in sick. He planned to spend all day at the library looking up references he didn't know from Li Xifeng's journal. Jinzhao listened from the kitchen and set down a mug of tea in front of him after he'd hung up.

"Do you think they believed me?" Tinseng picked up the tea and walked over to the dresser to pull out clothes for the day.

"No."

"Oh, come on. I can be very convincing." Jinzhao had no reaction, so Tinseng pushed. "You, for example, always believe my lies."

Jinzhao slowly looked around. Anticipation crackled between them. "When did you lie?"

"When I said I liked that Proust you bought me."

Jinzhao's eyes flashed. "You loved the Proust."

"Did I?" Tinseng asked neutrally.

"You did." Around Jinzhao was a low buzz of irritation. Anyone else would have taken a step back. Tinseng stepped forward.

"How do you know? I'm a spy, you know. I'm a very good liar."

Jinzhao snorted. "You are *not*."

"What!?"

"You have a tell."

"What! No I don't! What is it? Tell me."

"No."

"Jinzhao!"

But Jinzhao walked away. Tinseng stood staring at him, mouth agape in shocked delight. "You're going to regret that!" he called—and couldn't stop grinning all morning.

The next day, though, that moment of joy felt as far away as his sister in Hong Kong. He'd had another row at work: Under pressure for results, the head of Paris Station had finally looped him in on Mei Hankong and his wife, and had rounded up some usual suspects for Tinseng to question. Tinseng had little interest in their machinations. Lately he'd begun refusing to do interrogations, asking for more translation work. They'd been reluctant to meet his requests.

"I hate them, Jinzhao, I really do. They're shortsighted and reactive, yet somehow it takes a million years to do anything."

"The others aren't the same?" Jinzhao asked.

Tinseng opened his mouth to argue. Hong Kong had been better. Weir had been good, right? Or had Tinseng just thought that because he'd been twenty and eager to prove himself in the world? He thought of MI6, the CID, the CIA, the KGB. Lay out files from each, strip the names and locations, translate them into the same language—Tinseng bet not even the heads of service would be able to tell their work from the others. The same tactics, the same justifications. He sighed. He needed a drink.

"You know," he said as he poured whiskey from his one cheap bottle and looked anywhere but Jinzhao, "I once saw a man named Cyril slice a man's eyeball open. We had to tape his eyelids open first, and Cyril made me do that part. Told me I had to learn this kind of thing if I wanted to move up. The tape left this residue on my fingers, and I kept pressing my thumb and forefinger together, pulling them apart. That's what I remember. That tape. The stickiness on the pads of my fingers." He sat on the couch next to Jinzhao. "I can't really remember anything else."

"Tinseng." Jinzhao's face was blank, but they were sitting close enough that Tinseng felt the sharp rise and fall of his chest.

"That's what Paris Station sees in me: a scalp hunter. They'd love to pay me to do that to their enemies. They all would."

"Even Weir?"

"Well, no. Not him. But he told me when we talked that they're pushing him out. He's the only good one I know. If he's gone, I don't know what I'll do."

Jinzhao watched him, waiting for more. Tinseng found himself saying, "I never wanted to be a spy, you know. But I thought I was doing something to help the people I loved. It was easier to think that in Hong Kong. But whose country is that, really? Which one is mine? You know," he said, rubbing his nose, "I know I was on the recruitment list for the other side too. I never told you that? I think that's why they were so pushy—trying to recruit me before the enemy could get me first. Originally, I wasn't supposed to be a translator. Weir gave me that when he saw they were losing me. They wanted me to sign up for communist party activities and report back. A mole. A rat, that's what they wanted me to be. But I wouldn't."

"Why not?"

"Because I—" Tinseng hit a brick wall. He usually didn't allow himself to think about any of this. How they'd wanted him to report back the names of innocent, curious people whose only crime was interest in the possibility of a better world. They'd wanted him to ingratiate himself in a community only to betray it—a community to which his brother belonged, and so had he once. But to which community did he belong now? Which of them came first? He was born in China, still thought of himself as Chinese, wanted to go back so badly sometimes his whole body ached from it. The only thing that stopped him was the knowledge that he'd get himself thrown in jail or killed almost as quickly as his adoptive mother had. He ran his mouth too much, broke too many rules. But sometimes it seemed correct to die fighting to make *that* place better: his birthplace, his first home. Then he would think of Hong Kong, his ten years there. Didn't all the people there deserve his efforts too? To whom did he owe his obligation? Which debts were most important to pay?

He laughed, amused at himself. Who was he to think himself so important? As if *he* could change the world. He shook his head and did what he always did when he encountered a wall: he climbed over it.

"Because I'm lazy and selfish," he said. "Didn't you know?"

Jinzhao frowned very prettily at that. "Tinseng."

"Fine, you're right," he said with a gusty sigh, all the fight going out of him. "They're exactly the same. Not in words but deeds. It's not about philosophy in the end."

"It *is* about philosophy. But not to them."

"No, not to them."

"To us. To us," Jinzhao repeated, "it matters. It matters what you do on this earth; it is the life and death of our souls. Your talents, your mind, your heart, should not belong to *them*." Jinzhao raised his eyes to stare at Tinseng. "It belongs to the people."

Tinseng inhaled. "Which people?" he asked, not breathing, staring across the very short distance at Jinzhao.

Jinzhao did not look away. "The people in front of you," he said, and then Tinseng was kissing him.

---

*One Year Ago. June 1962. Bern, Switzerland.*

On the sixth-month anniversary of the murder, Wu Tinseng and Mei Jinzhao traveled to Bern to pay their respects. Tinseng left work early, and they took the Friday afternoon train. When they arrived, they wasted no time, only stopping to buy some flowers before joining the rush-hour traffic in a taxi to the house.

The street was quiet. Its perfectly spaced trees swayed gently, beckoning them closer to the neat little brownstone. It was a sign of the CCP's favor—a sign that Mei Hankong was on his way up and that Li Xifeng's translation work was seen favorably by the Ministry of Culture. At some point, they had lost that favor. Tinseng still didn't know why, though he hadn't given up the search.

Today wasn't the day to think about that. Today was for Mei Jinzhao, who stood next to him still as a jade statue. Tinseng knew better than to speak. He couldn't hold Jinzhao's hand in this country, couldn't lean against him for comfort, wouldn't even risk a hand on his back. He settled for passing over the flowers. Jinzhao took them, and they stood in front of the house in silence.

---

Later, in the hotel room, Tinseng watched Jinzhao's spiraling mood until he couldn't anymore.

"Hey, Jinzhao? My lips are cold." He pouted to show how needy they were. The shadow behind Jinzhao's eyes darkened as he stared. He wanted to be distracted, just as much as Tinseng wanted to distract him. A few seconds later, Tinseng was on his back.

"We'll have to be quieter here," Tinseng warned. "The walls are thin."

"They're thin in Paris too."

"That was Paris. This is—ah! This is . . . Jinzhao." He let his head fall back; if he watched, he wouldn't be able to stop talking. It hadn't been surprising to discover Jinzhao was incessant and unyielding in bed and never seemed to tire of torturing Tinseng. Long after Tinseng would have wandered to other things, Jinzhao was still teasing him, sometimes gently, sometimes so cruelly it felt like a heel against his throat.

"Please," he let himself whimper. "Jinzhao, please."

He knew how to stay quiet these days, which was possibly the most drastic change from when Jinzhao had known him before. Tinseng was silent the way doors could be opened and shut without the rest of the house hearing. It wasn't natural for him, but he'd been told he wore it well. It'd become so second-nature, this unnatural stillness, that he'd forgotten, a little, what he'd been like before. No one knew him in Paris, so no one knew to wonder until Mei Jinzhao had shown up and cracked him open—like he was doing now, his attention agitating Tinseng in the best-worst way.

"Jinzhao, god, will you ... just ... like that, keep going like that ..."

In the silent room, his voice was the giveaway creak of a floorboard. It knocked them both askew. His ears might have been ringing. He said the words again, just to hear his own voice the way it used to sound.

"Jinzhao. Please. *Please.*"

He didn't know what he was begging for—perhaps nothing. Perhaps simply for the joy of saying the word, asking the way a spoiled child asked. Over the past few months with Jinzhao, he'd learned to ask without reserve, arms outstretched, expecting everything, denied nothing.

"Please," he said to Jinzhao, and Jinzhao gave him everything.

After, he could only lie still a few minutes before the need to ruin the moment overtook his better sense.

"I see why they call it *le petit mort*. Someday, you're going to actually kill me."

Torn between smugness and exasperation, Jinzhao chose to ignore Tinseng's obnoxious smile and lavished Tinseng's collarbone with long, lingering kisses. Quietly, deep in the back of his mind, Tinseng congratulated himself on the successful distraction and tried not to feel too guilty. Was it manipulation if he was distracting himself too?

---

Walking from the hotel to the train the next morning, they passed a newsstand with the first edition papers. Jinzhao's eyes were downcast as he walked past, but Tinseng kept an eye on license plates and corners, and his eyes swept over the headlines. One read:

**SCOOP: CHINESISCHE DIPLOMATEN WAREN USSR SPIONE**

Tinseng couldn't read Swiss German, but he didn't need to. Ominous dread built in his stomach.

"Jinzhao." He pointed to the paper. "I think there's trouble."

# CHAPTER FOUR

*Ten Months Ago. August 1962. Paris, France.*

What happened next was mayhem.

Desperate for scandal, the world descended on Mei Hankong's sons. The eldest in Beijing gave an official statement condemning his parents' actions but had otherwise been unreachable by Western reporters. The youngest, a translator living in Paris since January of '61, should have been easier to harass. But Mei Jinzhao was like a ghost and had been since he'd graduated from university. The most recent official picture anyone could find was from his passport, taken when he was eighteen. At twenty-five, Jinzhao looked much different. People looking to make a few francs sold other photos to the papers, but Jinzhao was always a pale figure in the background, usually blurry; unlike Tinseng, he never attended the kind of parties where rolls of film were wasted.

Jinzhao's lack of presence had been a deliberate tactic encouraged by his mother; previously, Jinzhao had believed she'd merely been concerned over his privacy. Now, like the rest of her advice, the lesson had been warped. Tinseng, for one, felt grateful for her foresight. His solitude made it easy for Tinseng to move Jinzhao across the city to a predominantly Senegalese neighborhood where none of their old acquaintances would come looking for either of them. From there, he set up a new identity for Jinzhao. And then they started their hunt again.

Well... he said they, but really Jinzhao was there only in body. In spirit he was far away, absorbing the double betrayal. His mother's activities as a spy for Russia were a shock, but it was his father's collaboration that hurt Jinzhao most. His father, who was supposed to have embodied all the Chinese Communist Party stood for, all Mao stood for. To betray the Party like this was unthinkable, a nightmare for Jinzhao who simply could not understand why his father hadn't immediately turned his mother in, or at least refused to participate in her illegal activity. Why hadn't he tried harder to turn her from the wrong path?

The press, the nightly news, the headlines—the Mei Affair became unavoidable as reporters combed through the leaked files someone had stolen from the house in Bern. Suddenly the disheveled dresser next to Li Xifeng made sense. Tinseng's money was on one of the assassins, but the embassy man they'd sent to clean up was high on the list too, and there had been a lot of people in and out of that house that night.

Tinseng tried to shield him from the worst of it. He preferred avoidance anyway, so he simply stopped taking newspapers home and only listened to the evening news at cafés. It didn't help. Jinzhao sat in their new flat, a book in his lap, staring at the wall with a blank expression Tinseng would do anything to fix.

In the meantime, Tinseng kept his head down. Now, suddenly, Paris Station was too interested in Tinseng's known acquaintance Mei Jinzhao. Tinseng bought them time by promising to keep Jinzhao from going to ground and to relate back any information he could wring from him. That was a lie, but they hadn't known Tinseng had already been working on Li Xifeng's journal for months; it was easy to mislead them with scraps he knew led nowhere, as he scrambled to stay ahead. For once, he held all the cards. He just had to figure out what to do with them.

"Do you still want to go back to Beijing?" he'd asked Jinzhao, but Jinzhao had no answers for him.

In some ways, the scandal was helpful. It had given Tinseng what he'd been lacking: information. This time, he wasn't looking for the murderers—it was fairly clear now why the CCP had killed them. It even made sense why they'd left Jinzhao out in the cold: they couldn't trust that Jinzhao wasn't in on it too. What Tinseng needed, now, was to clear Jinzhao's name as much as he could so that when Jinzhao's head cleared, he could return to Beijing. His real home, Tinseng kept reminding himself. His real family.

So, what work had Li Xifeng been doing for the Russians? And was Jinzhao implicated in any way? That night, sitting at the foldaway desk they'd attached to the wall next to the front door, Tinseng pulled out Li Xifeng's journal and flipped to the poem that matched with the translation of "Solitude" by Chou Meng-tieh the paper had printed. He looked down at the journal's version again, reading:

缺月孤懸天中
又返照於苻藻交橫的溪底
溪面如鏡晶澈
紙偶爾有幾瓣白雲冉冉
幾點飛鳥輕噪著渡影掠水過

An incomplete moon hangs lonely in the sky
Reflected in the reed-tangled bed of the stream
The surface of the stream as clear as the glass in a mirror
With now and then a floating wisp of white cloud
And the shadows of birds crying softly as they skim the water

The lines from "Solitude" were the same . . . almost. Except . . . he leaned in, holding up the paper to the lamp to read the cramped handwriting better . . . yes, there, a subtle change hardly anyone would notice unless they were looking. In the newspaper, and therefore on the paper stolen from her home, she had copied down the original character for character. But in the journal, she'd written something else: On the third line, instead of 澈, she'd written a very smudgy 湛. He stared at it, disbelieving. He hadn't noticed before; his eyes had skimmed right over it.

It was only a first name. Likely, the other half of the name would be somewhere else. Still, it was extremely clever. He wondered if anyone else had figured it out. If they had, any of the names she'd listed would be in danger. Terrible danger, if they were operatives. More likely, though, this was a list of potential recruits. She'd been communicating with other agents in Bern, sending leads their way. Tinseng was impressed, actually. It was like the old crossword trick. He thought back to all the poems in her journals—he'd known something was wrong about them! There had been so many; now he would have to go back and check each one. There had been that one about lovesickness by Emperor Yuan, and quite a few from Xu Zhimo, and Nalan Xingde, and . . . Mao Zedong's "Snow."

"Snow," the poem from which Li Xifeng and Mei Hankong had taken the characters to make Jinzhao's name. It was an ambitious poem. One befitting Jinzhao, Tinseng had always thought. It spoke of past heroes, but at the end, it drew attention to the present hero, the author himself and all his generation—look what I'm going to do, the poem said. Li Xifeng had written out the stanza in her journal, and Tinseng had skimmed it once, then never returned to it. It had seemed like a maternal reminiscence, sweet but meaningless. Nothing had stood out. Surely she hadn't . . .

But it seemed she had. Or at least, she'd thought about it. There it was, clear on the page: She had written down her own son's name as a potential collaborator. A possible traitor.

With grim determination, Tinseng tore out the page and took out his lighter, ready to destroy it before Jinzhao could ever see it.

Before he could, the man himself walked in.

"What are you doing?" Jinzhao asked.

Tinseng looked down at the page. He had one chance to lie and spare Jinzhao this knowledge, a betrayal that would change him forever. For a split second, the choice stood before him: Carry this secret for Jinzhao or let him know the truth. If Jinzhao had walked in just a few minutes later, there would have been no choice at all. Tinseng would have taken it to the grave. Unfortunately, Jinzhao stood in front of him now, and he was right: Tinseng was a terrible liar. It had to be the truth.

"You know how I thought I figured out what your mother might be doing for Russia? How maybe she was identifying potential Chinese recruits, those who might be interested in switching sides?"

"Those weak in their conviction, like her. Yes."

Tinseng didn't wince somehow. "Well. I was right. And I figured out how she was doing it. It was poetry. She changed characters, subtly. It could have been seen as a sloppy translation, bad handwriting, even an artistic choice. It was really clever, actually. I never would've figured it out if we didn't have the journal."

Jinzhao walked around the desk to see the page he had ripped out. Tinseng held it to his chest. His heart pounded as though it were his own secret. He didn't want to be any part of inflicting pain on Jinzhao.

"Tinseng?" Jinzhao didn't understand why Tinseng wasn't already showing him the discovery.

"This has another name. One she—she hadn't sent it yet, Jinzhao. The newspaper printed another one of the poems, and it didn't have the name like the version in the journal had. So these were her personal notes; that's why she sent them to you. With the date written on top, she'd been sitting on it for months. Maybe she never sent it."

"Whose name is it?" Jinzhao asked, eyes flickering down to the page in Tinseng's hand. A part of him must have known already because he asked unsteadily, "Someone we know?"

"Jinzhao..." Tinseng watched Jinzhao's hand reach for the paper. He didn't stop Jinzhao from taking it. It didn't take long to read. It was only four lines. Tinseng watched and didn't know what he was waiting for— only that he was terrified in a way he'd only been once before, in a kitchen with his sister, waiting for her judgment. He was startled when Jinzhao held out his hand.

"Your lighter."

Jinzhao sounded calm, but Tinseng still hesitated before handing over the lighter. Jinzhao lit the page and threw it in the bin. They stood in silence watching the paper burn.

When there was nothing but ash in the trash can, Tinseng turned and started, "Jinzhao, we—" *We have to find out if there were copies*, he'd planned to say, but Jinzhao cut him off.

"No." It was as harsh as Jinzhao had ever spoken. "I am going for a walk."

*Do you think that's a good idea?* Tinseng thought but didn't say, because he wasn't a fool. Instead, he took his cigarettes out and slid them into Jinzhao's inner jacket pocket. Jinzhao avoided his eyes, saying nothing, taking nothing, shutting the door quietly behind him, and leaving

Tinseng in the middle of the room. As he turned to collapse into the chair, he caught a glimpse of himself in the hallway mirror.

"Well," he told his reflection, "fuck."

✧

*Nine Months Ago. September 1962. Paris, France.*

"It will prove my innocence if I return now."

"You don't know that! They could shoot you on sight."

"I cannot have them think me a traitor."

"We don't know if they do! We don't know if she—we just don't know. And I'm trying to find out, I am; I know how much you want to fucking leave, but you have to give me *time*. I," Tinseng said, swallowing hard, "I wouldn't even be able to write to you, if you left now."

"That cannot be a consideration. I have to think about—"

"About what? The greater fucking good? What good are you to the Party if you—"

"Do not belittle my values just because you—"

"Some values are more important than others!"

They glared at each other from across the room. Very deliberately, Tinseng walked over to the desk and opened the file. Jinzhao's nostrils flared. He walked past Tinseng into the kitchen. These days, whenever Jinzhao saw Tinseng pull out Li Xifeng's journal, he left the room entirely. It was a cowardly way to win an argument, but Tinseng didn't know what else to do. As he watched Jinzhao withdraw yet again, Tinseng had to admit that maybe his strategy of never talking about it wasn't working—but how was he supposed to start? Whenever they tried to discuss even the simple facts of the case, it ended in arguments like this one. They disagreed so fundamentally about what his parents did that any conversation ended in a fight. It was like they were sixteen again, and Tinseng hadn't known what to do then either.

Maybe it was impossible for Tinseng to help. Mei Jinzhao had the kind of personality that wanted to be unwaveringly loyal. He wasn't equipped to deal with such complete betrayal. His father had loved his country, but he had been loyal to his wife first, betraying all the state-first ideals he had raised his sons to hold above all else. His mother had loved her sons, but she been loyal to her ideals over family and state. From what Tinseng understood, she had been the only person to ever show Jinzhao unconditional love, and the boy in turn had loved his mother with his entire heart. But love, to Jinzhao, was completely synonymous with trust. With his trust in his mother shattered, he spent his days wondering if her love—the love that had shaped and defined him—had been a lie.

Tired down to his atoms, Tinseng wondered if life had been easier back in the age of Mencius or some other ancient time. If the moral battles had been simpler, if conclusions on right and wrong had felt easier to reach. The times they lived in now felt too complex. Anything he thought to say to Jinzhao felt insultingly insufficient.

He looked through the doorway to where Jinzhao had retreated into the kitchen. He stood over the stove, head down, shoulders slumped.

What could he say that Jinzhao would believe? *Nothing*, he thought. But he could do other things. He could find who leaked the secrets and track down whether they had taken any papers with the poem "Snow" on them. He could untangle this mess and make sure no one thought Mei Jinzhao capable of betrayal. He could punish anyone who threatened Jinzhao's happiness.

While Jinzhao floated around the flat like a ghost, Tinseng would track down whatever he could about this source. That was the goal he gripped between his teeth, and he wouldn't let go for anything.

༺❦༻

*Eight Months Ago. October 1962. Geneva, Switzerland.*

The paper that had confirmed the story and branded it the "Mei Affair" was a reputable pillar of Swiss journalism. But the paper that first broke the story, *Die Morgenzeitung*, was little more than a gossip rag—its owner the type to sell his mother for a scoop, its editor a vindictive cretin, and its writers willing to fill gaps in their stories with lies. *Die Morgenzeitung* was the kind of paper that felt no integrity, only the motivation to sell more papers, and had held on to their advantage over their competitors as long as they could. Now that every paper reported on the Meis with breathless coverage, *Die Morgenzeitung's* staff were bitter about sharing the limelight.

Tinseng used this against them. First he'd cleared the job so he could travel for more than a weekend at a time, and surprisingly, his boss had liked the idea. They'd even helped smooth the way for him with the other British agents working in Geneva. Then, over the course of multiple weeks, he'd hung around the bars near the *Die Morgenzeitung* offices, introduced himself as a translator to the beat writers, dropped hints he'd do anything for a check, did a few odd jobs for the paper and brought them one major story, then suggested he might be able to get more out of their primary documents. Maybe they were sitting on another scoop, but it was hidden in the Mandarin. If they let him have a look . . .

*The desperate and greedy are always easiest to trick,* Tinseng thought triumphantly a month later as he stood in the *Die Morgenzeitung* office ready to look at their other caches of Li Xifeng's papers. The editor hadn't wanted any documents to leave the office, and Tinseng acted disappointed he couldn't take the work home. He proceeded to work four eighteen-hour days in a row. He worked late hours, presumably to show his dedication, and each night a bored junior reporter had to monitor him. After the first week, he was able to give them far more accurate translations than they'd had before. With his sincerity and usefulness proven, they began to trust him. The next Thursday, when he announced another long night, the young man assigned to watch him had groaned: He had finally scored a date with the blonde down in accounting. (That too had been Tinseng's doing.) Casually, Tinseng mentioned that if the young man wanted to slip out to meet his date, Tinseng would cover for him as long as he was back by one or two to lock up. And so, wishing the young man luck on his date, Tinseng was left alone on the floor. 笑裏藏刀.[4]

---

[4] Literally "hide a knife behind a smile." To charm and ingratiate oneself with the enemy; one of the thirty-six stratagems.

He made copies of all the papers first to take back to Paris Station. There, in the back of one of the files, was a page with the poem "Snow." And—yes. There was the little imperfection that implied Jinzhao's name. Fuck. Well, at least they hadn't printed it yet. Tinseng took the page, folded it, and put it in his pocket. The filing system at *Die Morgenzeitung* was haphazard; they only kept one copy of primary documents. Even if someone realized this page was missing later, they'd have no way to prove it.

After tucking all the copies in his bag, Tinseng picked the lock on the squat two-drawer file cabinet of the reporter who first broke the story. What he needed was the name of the source. Who had the originals? Tinseng had to know, so that he could track them down and burn every last copy of this page from the face of the earth.

He didn't find anything else useful in the reporter's desk—reporters didn't write down their sources for this very reason, and he had to admit he was a little relieved for the reporter's other sources—so he moved on to a department he *knew* would have useful information: accounting. In this new age, when wars were fought with secrets, financial records were a reliable goldmine, and they didn't let Tinseng down now: He found a bank account number. That was plenty. He wrote down the number and slid it into his pocket next to the poem.

To keep up the pretense, he sat back at his loaned desk and continued to work on translating. His babysitter came back at 1:30 a.m., flushed and grateful. Tinseng would translate for the next week or two so he didn't arouse suspicion, then make a fuss about not being paid enough and get himself fired. More than reasonable for what he was walking away with.

As he walked back to his hostel, dark satisfaction curled like shadows around him. He kept touching his pocket, hardly willing to believe his luck and eager to wield his new lead to cut through to the truth.

*Three Months Ago. March 1963. Paris, France.*

Paper was the currency of the Cold War. A napkin with a scribbled chemical equation could mean a tectonic shift in world politics. A photograph of two men in a café could mean a bullet in the head. The only problem was the quantity of the stuff: that napkin might be buried under hundreds of pages of trash, and one photo could easily be lost. No one had the time or resources to sort through it all.

Lucas Grodescu had made it his business to provide that service. Files on Grodescu listed him as a blackmailer, thief, and information source; Grodescu called himself a courier. He was never the one who discovered the secrets. He was the middleman the secrets passed through, the one who got secrets where they needed to go.

Any two-bit thief could bring Lucas Grodescu information and expect a predictable payday based on quantity; later, they might get a second payout based on quality. It made Grodescu one of the most popular middlemen to work with, and that, in turn, protected Grodescu: He made very few enemies and always had some helpful tidbit to toss any authority coming after him. Every government had used him, in fact; his access was unprecedented, his results undeniable—a fat spider in the middle of an intercontinental web.

The bank account number Tinseng had found led him on a merry chase through multiple countries, banks, shell businesses, and more paperwork than Tinseng could stand, but finally it had given him Lucas Grodescu's name. That in itself was a bad omen: Grodescu worked from France, and Tinseng had heard of him before. He wasn't a man to do anyone favors, and MI6 would never be interested in buying these secrets at the price Grodescu was likely asking. It was a game between the CCP and USSR, and possibly the Americans who were rich and impulsive enough to be tempted by any bidding war. Tinseng had no hope of getting near it.

While Tinseng considered what to do about Lucas Grodescu, he'd been working the problem from the other side. He'd finally been able to convince Jinzhao to make a deal with the British. He would talk and let them ask their questions in exchange for a new life in Hong Kong. The deal let Tinseng go too; he'd become more trouble than he was worth to them, a liability and a nuisance, and he offered them an easy out: get him a job at the new university being established in Hong Kong and he'd recruit for the Circus. They agreed with insulting alacrity.

Tinseng didn't mention that if, at any time, Jinzhao felt it was safe to return to Beijing, Tinseng would help him get back and damn the consequences. He didn't mention that achieving this goal would be far easier in Hong Kong than in France. And he especially didn't mention that he had absolutely no intention of holding up his side of the bargain. He would never recruit a single soul to be fed to this grinder. He would rather them put a bullet in his head than trick any student as he'd been tricked.

That had been settled two weeks ago. When he'd written Yukying the day after, he'd started and scrapped four different letters. His handwriting looked worse than ever.

He was terrified of returning to Hong Kong.

Once, Cai Hesen had written to his friend Mao Zedong that he had traveled to Europe to "understand the ultimate goals of human beings, to break apart the numerous constraints of the world, and to realize the nature, status, and responsibilities of freedom." Tinseng hadn't been that ambitious. He'd *left*, rather than *traveled to*. Fled, coward that he was. He thought he'd have more time and that somehow time would make him braver. It hadn't.

---

"What did your sister write?" Jinzhao asked two weeks later. He sat on the bed, book in hand, legs extended out in front of him, pillow stuffed against the small of his back. It was so domestic Tinseng wanted to cry, or take a picture, or throw something heavy out the window. His record player, maybe.

Instead of any of those things, he joined Jinzhao on the bed.

"She wrote about my brother," he said.

"What about your brother?"

Tinseng ignored the question, bunching his own pillow underneath his neck to stare up at Jinzhao. "Have I ever told you you're beautiful?"

"Yes." Jinzhao's countenance didn't flicker. "Your brother?"

"Significantly less beautiful. What about brilliant? Have I used brilliant?"

"Many times." A beat. "Maybe you're running out of words."

"Me? Never! Effusive. Exemplary. Cataclysmic." Nothing. He framed Jinzhao's face with both hands and smiled up at him with all the tenderness he had. "Crackerjack."

That got a flicker. Tinseng counted it as a win, but just when he thought he was in the clear:

"What did your sister write?"

You really couldn't distract Mei Jinzhao for long. He sighed.

"She said my brother is happy I'm coming home."

"And that's . . . bad?"

"It means he never forgave me for leaving in the first place. And he offered for me to stay with him."

"This is also bad," Jinzhao hazarded.

"It's just complicated. I'd love to live with Yukying, but her husband . . . and where she lives is annoying too—too many British. And if I lived with Cheuk-Kwan, I could help look after our father, but . . . well, let's just say we're a bit much together."

"But they both want you to stay with them?" Tinseng nodded. "Whom will you choose?"

"I don't know. Maybe neither. I'm not going to think about it right now. There are more important things going on, you know?"

"You can't ignore your family."

He snorted. "The past three years say different."

"Tinseng."

"Can we not talk about this?"

"Why?"

*Because you can't let things go. Because once you argued with me for three days about the test ban treaty, and you didn't even care about that very much.*

*Because I don't know how long I get to hold on to you, and I don't want to fight with the time we have left.*

"Because I'm tired."

Jinzhao's gaze softened. Tinseng looked away. "Do they know?"

No, you really couldn't distract Mei Jinzhao, could you? After so many years, Tinseng still hadn't learned.

"Yukying does. Her husband, Li Yingtung, thinks I'm eccentric. He looks the other way deliberately, I think. It's easier. If we lived together, you and I, I mean, he'd go to his grave thinking we're good friends who want to save money on rent. The same goes for my father. He's kind enough to pretend."

"And your brother?"

"Cheuk-Kwan . . ." He grimaced. "He has his suspicions. I don't know what he'd do if he had to live with it under his nose every day. His Party friends think homosexuality is a White man's disease. Mainland China didn't have this problem until they showed up, that kind of thing. I've never heard him say anything that extreme, but it's just one more way I'm a problem, right?"

"You are *not* a problem."

"You say that now."

"I say that always."

Tinseng's heart clenched. "Always?" he asked, because he was weak and wanted to hear it again.

Jinzhao wrapped a hand around the back of his neck and stared him down as he repeated, "Always."

Tinseng hid his uncontainable grin in Jinzhao's shirt. *Always, always, always.*

"How do you feel about running away?" Tinseng muttered into the rumpled cotton. "Possibly disappearing forever? The countryside is nice; we could have a field of sunflowers and grow grapes."

"Do you know how to grow grapes?"

"I'd learn." He turned his head to the side so he could breathe in Jinzhao's scent. "Ugh. You're lucky you don't have to deal with any of this. With the British giving you that stipend to help for your first three months, you could rent anywhere. Well, anywhere cheap. You'll finally be a free man—no more dealing with my dirty mugs."

"Mm."

"And you'll have your own space again. I won't be hanging like a limpet. You won't have to fight for the sheets."

The hand on his neck tightened, then let go.

"Time for sleep."

"But—"

"You said you were tired." Jinzhao turned off the light. "And tomorrow, write back to your sister."

※

*One Month Ago. May 20, 1963. Paris, France.*

"Change the record, would you?" Tinseng called from across the room. "I'm trying to forge this, and Buscaglione is distracting. I have to think in English."

Jinzhao turned off the record, and Tinseng got back to his letter. It had to be good enough to trick the most cunning blackmailer in Europe.

"Shan Dao," he called out, a test.

"Yes?" As predicted, there was no hesitation on Jinzhao's part; after only a week of practice with his brand-new cover name, he was already flawless.

"'When I look at Shan Dao, it's like climbing a mountain and looking down far; far from the world,'" he quoted just to watch Jinzhao frown against his blush. He sniggered. "Come here and look at this. You're getting very good with the name, by the way. You don't mind if I start calling you that in bed, do you?" Jinzhao materialized by his side and pinched the top of his ear. "Okay, okay! It was just a question! Anyway, what do you think?"

Jinzhao looked at the letter meant for Lucas Grodescu: it arranged to meet him in Villefranche in order to exchange an extraordinary amount of money for some papers that had once belonged to Li Xifeng.

It was the third communication they'd had with the man, and the most important.

"Good." Jinzhao handed it back.

"I think so too." Tinseng folded it and slipped it into an envelope. "Well, what's left?"

"Packing."

"Nooo . . . there must be something else."

"Nothing else." Jinzhao pointed at a pile of Tinseng's clothes. "We are moving across the world. Pack."

"But not for a whole *month*. It can wait! There are so many better things to do. Like . . . Come on, Jinzhao, don't hide. Or is it that you've grown bored of me already, after a few months of having me whichever way you want? What can I do to keep your interest? I'm but a mere mortal, I can onl—*mmph!*"

Jinzhao showed him, thoroughly, how to hold his interest, and made sure that Tinseng paid very close attention. Tinseng was nothing if not an attentive student; he even added his own ideas to the curriculum.

Afterward, Tinseng reached for his cigarettes and kept talking. "Let's go through the plan again."

"Mm."

"Assuming he's hooked on our bait about a buyer in Villefranche, he'll have the papers by the time we rendezvous. You're going to pose as a petty—or is it pretty?—thief with some old British codes to sell. It will be hard to check your story since we're mostly at sea. You'll ask to meet him in his room for a first sweep, then ask to meet again at port in Lisbon. While he's ashore, I'll search the room more thoroughly."

"And if he's carrying it on his person?"

"They say these ports are full of pickpockets and thieves." Tinseng smiled. "Anyone could be a victim."

"Risky."

"I could also slip something into his drink one night. We have options; I'm not worried about that."

"If he has them couriered to Villefranche?"

"Then we steal them at the meetup."

"Duplicates?"

"Unlikely. With regular blackmail, maybe, but these are state secrets. They're worth a lot more if there's only one copy ... if you know the other side doesn't have them too. The more people know a secret, the less worth it has. If word got around he was keeping copies, his stock would plummet. Besides, he likes to think of himself as better than other blackmailers who try to dip from the same well. He's the one-and-done type."

"But if he does," Jinzhao said, and Tinseng heard the worry.

"Then they'd probably be in his house in Paris or his estate about two hours outside it. They *could* be in a safety deposit box at the bank, or some hidden bolt hole in the city, but I don't think so. A controlling spider like him would want to keep them close." He kissed Jinzhao's shoulder. "We'll find out when we steal the ones he does have. If he calls off the meeting with the buyer in Villefranche, we'll know there was only one copy. If he doesn't, we'll have to intercept."

Tinseng couldn't lie around any longer and went to shower. When he went back to the room to change, he found Jinzhao folding clothes into a trunk.

"What will we tell your family when we leave Villefranche?"

"Oh," Tinseng said with a laugh as he pulled on trousers, "*That* doesn't matter. They expect these kinds of things from me. If nothing else, I'll pick a fight with Cheuk-Kwan, then leave in a huff. My shameless reputation has its perks." He winked at Jinzhao but the other man wasn't amused. "Anyway, I can apologize back home once this is all over."

"And my name?" They would be introduced to Jinzhao as Shan Dao, but once they returned to Hong Kong, he wouldn't go by his cover name forever.

"That you were worried about the CID—rightfully so, I might add—and a person is most vulnerable to 'accidents' when they're traveling. We wanted to make sure you arrived in Hong Kong safely, and so not even they could know your real identity while we were on the move."

It was even true, mostly, which he knew would appeal to Jinzhao. Still, Jinzhao looked upset. It was the way he sat, feet tucked under him, staring down at the clothes instead of where Tinseng always wanted him to be looking, which was, of course, himself. He plucked the sweater from Jinzhao's hands and crowded into his lap, making himself too much of a nuisance to ignore. Jinzhao looked up with a warm expression, but there were still shadows behind his eyes.

"Nothing is assured. You're right. And I know you're worried, but if you wanted me to worry with you, you shouldn't have fucked me so well." The expression unfurled into amusement, which meant Tinseng was on the right track. "Besides, what is there to worry about? We caught a break with his wife booking that cruise. Cheuk-Kwan took my bait about arranging the trip, and he even invited Chiboon too. It's the perfect cover. Traveling in groups is always better. Grodescu thinks he's meeting his buyer in Villefranche, so the papers will either be on board, in which case we'll steal and destroy them, or they'll be in Villefranche when we arrive, and we'll steal them then. You'll be safe, we'll fly back to Hong Kong, and get fat on marinated crab until you finally get sick of me. It's the perfect plan."

# CHAPTER FIVE

*Ten Days Ago. June 15, 1963. At Sea.*

It was the perfect plan—right up until dinner the first night.

They met Yukying and Cheuk-Kwan at the train station, and both were too polite to ask too many questions of the stranger Tinseng had brought on their family trip. Jinzhao's fake passport sailed through all its checks, and soon enough they were safely ensconced in their new home for the next ten days, door locked and gray Southampton light shining through the porthole of their stateroom.

Tinseng felt so good he'd been indulging almost every impulse to tease Jinzhao as it entered his mind. As he finished his haphazard unpacking, he looked over his shoulder to find Jinzhao was neatly hanging all his shirts, even the undershirts. *Of course he is*, Tinseng thought fondly. He was so good.

"What should we do now?" Tinseng asked nonchalantly, making a show of looking at his watch. "We're on vacation, remember? We have some time before we're expected for cocktails." He unhooked his watch and set it on the dresser. The cufflinks were next, then the tie. "And we have the run of the entire boat."

"Ship."

"Whatever. It's better for our cover if we're seen taking part in activities." He took off his suit jacket and let it crumple on the floor. "What about a drink at the bar? A Shirley Temple for you, extra cherries. Or we could join a round of cards. Maybe sit in the smoke room and discuss Korea?"

As he listed things Jinzhao would never do, he unbuttoned his pale purple-heather shirt. Jinzhao walked slowly over to him, eyes dark as they lingered on Tinseng's exposed chest.

Tinseng managed to keep a straight face as he continued, "There's a movie starting in a few minutes. But I don't know if I should sit in a dark room with you, Jinzhao. I've heard you can't be trusted. I've heard about the kind of things you get up to in the dar—"

He laughed into the kiss and wasted no time pulling Jinzhao down on top of him. Each long kiss left Tinseng dizzy.

"This can't be your answer every time I ask what you want to do," he said.

"Why not?" Jinzhao asked as he unzipped Tinseng's trousers.

Tinseng couldn't think of a good answer to that, not with Jinzhao lowering himself between Tinseng's legs. It only took a few more moments for him to stop thinking completely.

They ended up being late for cocktails. Tinseng found he couldn't bring himself to care.

※

So it was all going very well, and Tinseng was beginning to think it might be *too* easy, that he'd have to find fun elsewhere, until he walked into the dining room and actually saw the man.

He'd known he would have to share a room with their target, of course—their whole plan hinged on it. To Lucas Grodescu, Tinseng would be just another foreigner, no one of interest or import. Tinseng would be able to observe him that way, pick his moment more carefully, and steal what they needed. Grodescu would end up empty-handed and none the wiser who had robbed him. That had been the plan.

But a plan never survived its execution.

Lucas Grodescu was more handsome in person than in pictures. His curly salt-and-pepper hair had been tamed back with product. His nose proclaimed his French heritage, and his teeth gleamed through thin lips. His high forehead wrinkled pleasantly whenever he smiled or frowned, but his eyes never lost their sharpness even when his soft cheeks were pushed up by his mirth.

Tinseng sat down to dinner, seething.

For most of the meal he couldn't stop sneaking looks at the man across the room. He heard himself entertain Mrs. Lanzette and laugh at Chiboon's jokes, but he'd set himself on autopilot: the conversation mechanical, the laughter hollow. Only a familiar name snapped him back to his surroundings. Restless anger moved under Tinseng's skin. He smiled around a piece of fish, took a few drinks of wine, and turned in his seat, presumably to speak with Chiboon. Grodescu looked good in his dark-blue three-piece suit; his wife looked better in her yellow satin dinner dress. No one would know the man holding court at his table was one of the most successful blackmailers alive. It would be impossible to tell, looking at his handsome face, that he had ruined dozens of lives, all for power or perhaps just the sheer fun of it. And now he wanted to ruin Jinzhao. And would, unless Tinseng stopped him. The injustice of it gathered in him, simmering.

※

Evenings on a cruise like this were busier than the days, with revelry and music winding through every deck. Between dinner and the sendoff celebration, Jinzhao excused himself from their company, and Tinseng made an excuse to follow him. As he stood in front of their room searching for his key, Cheuk-Kwan called out from behind them.

"Go ahead," he told Jinzhao, and walked over to his brother. "Yeah, what is it, didi?" he started to ask; even as he did, his brother pulled Tinseng into his room.

The moment the door closed, he whirled around. "Why are you being such an asshole?"

"What can I say? I missed you so much, it's hard not to—"

"Jiejie said you haven't answered about staying with her. You hate Yingtung. You hate his house. What's the problem? You're not even going to *ask* to stay with me? Not going to help look after your own father? What, is your—" He lowered his voice to a harsh whisper, "your *friend* too good for us?"

Tinseng's eyes widened, then narrowed.

"Careful."

"That'd make one of us," his brother scoffed.

"He *is* my friend."

"Then he should have no issue staying with us."

"He's his own man. It's not like we . . . he has his own agenda when we get home."

"What do you mean, agenda?"

"I mean he might not even stay in Hong Kong permanently."

Cheuk-Kwan threw up his hands. "You brought him halfway across the world, introduced him to your family, and he's not even staying? He knows how that looks, right? He knows how rude that is?"

"Oh, he knows," Tinseng muttered at the ground, then looked up at Cheuk-Kwan's growl of frustration. "Look, it's complicated! It's not his fault! I'm helping him."

"Of course you are. Let me guess: He started following you around in Paris. Saw the way you lived and wanted a taste of it. Agreed to follow you and then, what? Having second thoughts? Realized it's not all laughs-a-minute with you?"

"It's not like that," Tinseng said weakly, but he could hear the doubt in his own voice.

"Right." Cheuk-Kwan reached around Tinseng to open the door. "I'm going to talk with him."

"No! No, you're not." Tinseng plastered himself against the wood. "Fuck no. Listen to me." He pressed a hand flat against Cheuk-Kwan's chest. "Hey. Listen. You've got the wrong idea. Really. He was—his parents just died. And he had me all to himself before. I think seeing me with you and Yukying makes the grief real. He won't have what we have ever again." Tinseng's smile asked something of Cheuk-Kwan. "It's not second thoughts. It's..."

"Mourning," Cheuk-Kwan supplied. Tinseng's fingers gripped slightly on his shirt.

"Yeah. That's it." They stared at each other, neither saying the thing each wanted to say.

"I said I'd help him start fresh," Tinseng said eventually. "But I wanted him to know he wasn't beholden. No debts owed, you know?"

"Then what exactly are you getting out of it?"

"It's just the right thing to do, didi."

Cheuk-Kwan glowered at Tinseng. "You're an idiot," he said but let him go.

The moment he was behind his own cabin door Tinseng flopped face-first on the nearest of the two twin beds. Tinseng didn't think Cheuk-Kwan was wrong, but he was an idiot for reasons his brother couldn't even imagine. After a moment the mattress dipped. A warm palm spread across the center of his back.

"What did he say?"

"Nothing important. Really, Jinzhao, I'm fine." He pushed off the bed and stood with a burst of pent-up energy. "Well, I'm fine about my brother anyway. Grodescu's ugly face nearly put me off dessert, that's all. Imagine having to stare at that every morning. We should feel sorry for him, living with such a burden. Anyway, I should be asking you: Are you okay?"

"Fine," Jinzhao echoed dryly.

Tinseng walked over to look out the porthole at the unending blue of the ocean. "How was it, hearing their names tonight at dinner?" Jinzhao's silence spoke for itself. "Everyone talks too much for knowing so little," Tinseng said.

"We don't know either."

Tinseng wrinkled his nose, disapproving. "Yes, we do. I've read your mother's journal; I know she did what she did because she didn't want the world to end. She believed in the workers, and she didn't believe the CCP lifted them up anymore."

"Your brother was correct."

"My brother's an ignorant, blind, stubborn, narrow-minded . . ."

"Tinseng."

"Your mother wanted *justice*, Jinzhao. And she saw the best in you."

"Then why did she see betrayal?" Jinzhao's anger shuddered through the room. "Why did she mark me to be turned?"

"It wasn't betrayal she saw, it was—" Tinseng reached for the right words. "'There is no such thing as the State, and no one exists alone.' She saw your heart, your obligation to the whole, and thought she could find a better fit for your ideals, that's all. Maybe the CCP is where you fit, maybe it isn't. You could create a lot of change there if you go back. And maybe it wasn't her place to assume that she knew better than you, or that you would be miserable working for the CCP just because she was. But you can't fault her for loving you so much that she cared about where you spent the rest of your life." He took a deep breath, then added, "'We must love one another or die.'"

Jinzhao's eyes widened. The words hung in the air too much like a confession, and Jinzhao's silence was far too close to rejection. Tinseng laughed it off, waving his hand through the moment.

"Ah, it's almost time to meet the others for drinks. You know what you're doing tonight?"

Jinzhao nodded over at the note they'd written out together, establishing them as petty thieves looking to connect with a big fish, asking to meet with Grodescu tomorrow in his cabin. Jinzhao would slip the note under his door while Tinseng kept an eye on the couple upstairs.

"Make sure to wear different clothes, some of the nice ones we bought, in case anyone sees you. They'll be so distracted by your beauty they'll forget about anything else."

"Ridiculous."

Tinseng tried to smile.

"You're upset," Jinzhao said. There was no point hiding it, so Tinseng didn't try. He looked down at his hands. These hands had held the confession papers of his countrymen. He'd bloodied the knuckles on their faces in interrogation rooms on the orders of men who'd refused to learn his real name. He'd spent countless hours cutting and burning tape, editing agent debriefs to leave out all the things that couldn't be on official record. They'd asked him to cover up actions so dirty he'd felt unclean for days after, as though the tape had left its oily black film under his skin. He'd covered his hands in blood and ink and mud, but they'd never shaken until tonight.

"You know, I never respected those men whose job it was to get close to the targets. All they had to do was talk—how hard could that be? I'm the most accomplished talker they've ever hired." He grinned wide at the meaningless boast. "But could those ambassadors and politicians do *my* job? They'd quit after a day, even if they could speak the languages. I guess I owe them an apology," he said. "They wouldn't have been able to do my job, but I don't think I could do theirs either. Seeing him tonight..."

He knew the problem, of course; it wasn't difficult to diagnose. The problem was the fantasy he kept imagining, the one where he calmly excused himself from the table, walked across the room, and shot Grodescu two times in the head. The job was too personal, and rage had clouded his mind like mustard gas and mist.

Knowing the problem didn't stop the tremble in his fingers.

"Tinseng," Jinzhao started, but Tinseng couldn't bear that softness right now, or Jinzhao's sorrowful eyes, or anything that would get sliced to ribbons against the whirring blades of his anger.

"Don't wait up for me," he said flippantly, moving before he said something worse. But when he kissed Jinzhao's cheek, he couldn't help but murmur, "Be careful."

Jinzhao's hand squeezed his waist, a promise Tinseng carried with him the rest of the night.

---

The next day was a full day at sea. Overnight, they'd received an answer to their note in the form of another note, slipped under their door sometime in the night. Tonight, Jinzhao would meet with Grodescu for the first time. Jinzhao actively fretted throughout breakfast, but Tinseng tried not to think about it; worrying wouldn't change anything, and in the meantime, he was on vacation. Tinseng planned to throw himself into every activity today: tennis with Cheuk-Kwan, swimming with Chiboon, dinner and records in Yukying's room, late night dancing with anyone he could convince to join him.

During breakfast, he watched Yukying for any sign she thought it strange seeing Jinzhao last night. She acted normal, though, so Tinseng dismissed it. If she'd really wondered, she could have asked when she and Jinzhao met early this morning. Jinzhao's cover of being an early-to-bed, early-to-rise sort was already paying dividends; it even had the added benefit of not being a lie.

When Jinzhao asked Tinseng if Yukying was going to be a problem, he shook his head.

"It's fine," he said to Jinzhao as they stood outside their room, locking the door. "If she hasn't said anything by this point, she's probably forgotten about it."

"Forgotten about what?" Cheuk-Kwan asked behind him.

"Do you *really* want to know?" Tinseng pasted on a leer and waggled his eyebrows for good measure.

"On second thought, no."

Tinseng shot Jinzhao a triumphant grin before skipping ahead to walk alongside Cheuk-Kwan. "After all these years you're finally learning, didi! Now, what's this I hear about me beating you in tennis?"

As they waited for a court to be available, he and Cheuk-Kwan went to the other side of the deck and tried out rackets. Tinseng found his right away, but Cheuk-Kwan took forever, insisting that Tinseng weigh in on each one. He disagreed with all of Cheuk-Kwan's assessments just for fun, and while his brother fumed, he watched Jinzhao talking with Yukying across the deck. Seeking out conversation with the same person twice in one day was a major mark of approval from Jinzhao, and Tinseng let himself bask for a moment. It was easy to slip into fantasy: Both of them moving into that sprawling Western-style apartment Yingtung's mother had insisted on buying, the one Yukying had subtly complained about in her letters. The empty space made her feel lonely, and Tinseng understood completely; he wouldn't want to be rattling around like a lone marble in that huge place either. But what if he did accept Yukying's offer, and what if Jinzhao stayed? Tinseng already had their room picked out: the eastern-facing one, so Jinzhao could spend his mornings in the sun. And Tinseng could wake up next to Jinzhao every day—well, more likely he'd wake up to an empty bed with the sunlight streaming in and wander out to find Jinzhao and Yukying in the kitchen. He even added Yingtung to the fantasy for jiejie's sake; he could read quietly in a corner, gazing adoringly at Yukying while staying absolutely silent.

In this fantasy, Jinzhao wouldn't even notice Tinseng enter the room, and Tinseng would get to watch as long as he liked: Jinzhao's careful cutting, his economical movements, the way he tilted his head to listen. He imagined Yukying would like this kind of audience, so different from her brothers and husband. Jinzhao's attention was intoxicating and addictive; once you'd earned it, nothing else really compared. He would listen so well to Yukying, too, whose quiet voice often got drowned out. Tinseng always felt guilty about it even as he couldn't help his nature. But Jinzhao would be the perfect match. Yukying would be able to read his silences, and they could listen to each other in their attentive, quiet ways.

*It would be perfect*, Tinseng thought, imagining it so clearly it might be happening in front of him right now. They'd convince Cheuk-Kwan to move in, too, and keep a pallet for Chiboon when he visited, and then everyone would be together again—all the people Tinseng loved under one roof. He'd always loved living in apartment buildings, hearing the large families together. He wanted that for them, wanted noise and clatter and constant comings and goings.

And in the mornings, when he rose later than everyone else, he could love them all from a distance. Maybe he'd even join Yingtung in his quiet corner, stealing whichever section of the newspaper his brother-in-law was reaching for, just to torture him. Then he could pretend to read while watching everyone over the top of the paper, noticing all the little things he'd step all over if he was closer.

Everyone assumed Tinseng loved disturbing any calm he came across, throwing himself like a stone into still water. But the secret truth was that he wished he was the still water; he yearned for it, coveted it, watched it with itching envy whenever he saw it. If he wanted to get closer, to try to figure out how to snatch a little of that peace for himself, what could he do but disturb it?

On the other side of the deck, Yukying smiled and laid a hand on Jinzhao's arm. Tinseng twitched sympathetically as he saw Jinzhao tense—Yukying couldn't know that Jinzhao didn't like to be touched—then watched, amazed, as Jinzhao's shoulders fell. There was the slightest sway of his torso, as if Jinzhao was considering tilting forward. Moving *closer?*

A string of unintelligible shrieks raced through his head. It was happening. His two favorite people—

"Didi, Cheuk-Kwan, you won't *believe* it." He clutched his brother's shoulder and shook it aggressively. "Shan Dao let Yukying touch his arm. She touched his arm and he didn't pull away! He even looked like he *liked* it. Do you know what this means???"

"No, I fucking don't, and I absolutely don't want to know."

"It means my plan is *working*," Tinseng said, knowing he sounded unhinged but not caring in the slightest. "You're next, didi. You're next!"

"No I'm not, you lunatic. Leave me out of it." Tinseng cackled and let Cheuk-Kwan throw off his hand. "Come on," Cheuk-Kwan continued, and Tinseng caught him hiding a smile with a shake of his head. "Are we playing tennis or not?"

On the tennis court, Tinseng and Cheuk-Kwan play-fought just the way they used to, putting on a show for the ladies who'd come to watch handsome young men in tennis whites. It was so easy to fall into their old routine that Tinseng easily tricked himself into believing nothing had changed. He showed off for Jinzhao, too, who did an admirable job of pretending to ignore him except for all the times Tinseng caught him staring. Eventually, the match devolved: Cheuk-Kwan laughed at Tinseng for smacking himself with his own racket, which prompted Tinseng to jump over the net to chase Cheuk-Kwan around the court until he got a few hits in. Jinzhao and Yukying were long gone by then, so they ate lunch together, and Tinseng thought of his daydream again and how incomplete it was without Cheuk-Kwan there, the only person who humbled him so completely, and the only one who fully called Tinseng out on his bullshit. He didn't want to live without his brother, he realized. How could he have forgotten that?

He was still daydreaming in the late afternoon when something possessed him to ask Yukying when she fell in love with Yingtung. She pulled his head out of the clouds with her answer. It was too dangerous to think this way; after all, it wasn't as though he planned to confess to Jinzhao or ask him to stay in Hong Kong. It was all just idle fantasy, something to pass the time. He'd told Cheuk-Kwan he had a plan, but of course that was a lie. He had a hope, nothing more, and he knew better than to put any faith in that.

***

He'd promised Jinzhao that if the topic of the Mei Affair came up, he'd stay out of it. The first night he'd been able to hold his tongue, mostly. Tonight, he simply couldn't keep that promise. Neither could Jinzhao, apparently.

"'Every Party member, every branch of work, every statement and every action must proceed from the interests of the whole Party.'" Jinzhao spoke softly, but they all quieted down to listen. "'It is absolutely impermissible to violate this principle.'"

Cheuk-Kwan thought Jinzhao was speaking of Li Xifeng. Tinseng knew better. Jinzhao spoke of his father; it was his father who had really betrayed the Party, his father who had chosen a single individual over the dozens Li Xifeng could have ruined with her list. Jinzhao hated his mother for seeing a traitor in him, but it was worse that his father was a hypocrite.

"We're lucky there wasn't a trial," Cheuk-Kwan said.

Tinseng turned on him. "And why's that?" he asked, because as long as he was breaking promises, he was going to speak his full mind. For months he'd been holding back his opinions from Jinzhao, but there was nothing holding him back from a few vicious rounds with Cheuk-Kwan.

"No one's asking questions now about why she might've been interested in leaving the CCP in the first place," he said, feeling Jinzhao's attention like a brand. "Real, legitimate complaints with the way things are being run—instead, all that's been silenced. Behind the scenes, I guarantee they're ecstatic. They succeeded in burying it all, every stinking corpse."

Old blood smelled of rotting iron. You could never mop it all away. He knew Jinzhao would have wanted a trial, instead of the coverup that had left him questioning everything. It would have been painful, but Jinzhao pursued the truth unsparingly no matter the pain it caused him. It made him a truly good man: he upheld his values, even when it didn't benefit him. It was why Li Xifeng had put his name on her list in the first place.

"Better these things end quickly, without fanfare," Yingtung said, the absolute slug. "Bad enough it was leaked to the press."

"Without answers?" Tinseng asked, voice rising. He was forgetting himself. "Without justice?"

"Did the Rosenbergs get justice?" Cheuk-Kwan pushed back. "Did the truth come out in their trial? Given the death sentence by their country without a second glance at all that sham evidence, even with so many of their own citizens protesting in the streets. How do you think a trial in China would end? Dead by assassin or by jury—how's it any different?"

*It would have been different for their sons*, he couldn't say, but instead heard himself saying as he pressed his palm flat on the table, "We could have heard her arguments! *Why* she did what she did. People need to know." Tinseng couldn't help looking at Jinzhao then. Jinzhao's face held a faraway look, the one that meant Jinzhao was trying his hardest not to have any emotion at all. Tinseng's eyes snapped away. "Isn't public debate in the interest of the Party? It's important that people hear the reasons she lost faith in the CCP. To do anything else is silencing the truth."

"She didn't believe in truth," Cheuk-Kwan spat, "or she wouldn't have thought it so easily conquered."

Jinzhao stood, and Tinseng knew he'd fucked up. As soon as he could, Tinseng followed.

"I'm sorry," he said the moment he caught up with him in the hallway. "Hey, I'm sorry, J—Shan Dao, I'm—"

"Don't." It was an instruction.

Tinseng pressed his lips together. Through the hallway to the staircase, he maintained silence, but as they passed the grand hall, he pulled Jinzhao by the elbow. "Come on, in here. It's better to be seen, and I need to wait for the Grodescus here anyway."

Jinzhao reluctantly followed Tinseng into the ballroom where the band was playing a standard Tinseng recognized from the radio. They walked to the shorter edge of the bar, Jinzhao facing inward, Tinseng pressing his back against the wood to look out at the room. The noise of the music and crowd gave him an excuse to stand close.

"Do you want to dance?" he asked. A joke, of course, and a poor one. Two men couldn't dance together. They never had before, and only now Tinseng realized they never would. He rubbed his forehead. "Have I said sorry yet?"

Jinzhao looked down at the bar's polished top as Tinseng ordered a whiskey neat and took out his cigarettes. There were words lodged in Jinzhao's chest, Tinseng could tell. Tinseng felt them in his own throat; he could barely swallow around them. It could have been any number of secrets. They kept a lot from each other still, out of necessity. Out of fear.

"You really think she believed in truth?" Jinzhao asked eventually.

"I do."

"Is that why he did what he did? Because he could see that?"

"I don't know. You knew him better than me." He regretted the words as soon as they left his mouth, but Jinzhao only smiled wryly.

"You once said you wanted to be a spy because you wanted to do something to help the people you loved." Jinzhao took the cigarette from his fingers and took a drag. It was rare that he smoked at all. Tinseng shook out another, letting Jinzhao have his. "I thought the same about my path."

"Your father's plans for you?"

"A good path. The right path." Jinzhao shook his head. "That's all gone."

"What do you mean?"

"'Truly great men look to this age alone,'" Jinzhao said, quoting the poem he'd been named after, the poem his mother had used to mark him weak in his own conviction, or maybe the other way around. Mao had written the line to urge his country to look toward the future; the heroes of old had little poetry in their souls, he'd said. In 1936, the year Jinzhao was born, Mao had written in verse the longing in Mei Hankong and Li Xifeng's hearts; the dreams for their country had been the same as the dreams for their son.

But no two people dreamed the same.

The bartender came and went with Tinseng's whiskey. The first sip cleared some of the lump in his throat.

"You know why I picked Shan Dao for you?"

"Because you delight in the absurd."

"Well, yes. But no. Because of one of the stories in the chapter about praise. 'Shan Dao could not be described or named. Pure, deep, mysterious and silent—no one saw his limits, yet all agreed that he had, indeed, entered upon the Way. Therefore no one who saw him could say what he was but bowed nevertheless before his greatness.' Anyway, I can see why your mother wanted to recruit you." His voice was a little watery. "You could convince anyone of anything."

Jinzhao's face gained a shadow, the way it always did when Tinseng mentioned his mother's list. But Tinseng had lived with these shadows for a year now, and he thought this one was different. More thoughtful, maybe.

"Are you still okay to meet him tonight?" Grodescu would be waiting for Jinzhao in his room while Tinseng made sure everyone was distracted here.

Jinzhao nodded. "Yes. Thank you."

Tinseng didn't know what he was being thanked for, but he smiled anyway. "Any time, Shan Dao," and it felt good to say, because it was true.

In the end, Tinseng was stupid to think he'd be able to feign calm while Jinzhao prepared to meet Grodescu. He checked his watch compulsively until Chiboon asked archly whether he was waiting for something, then he slipped his hand into his pocket, keeping it in a fist. Finally, around the time he knew Jinzhao would be in Grodescu's room, he headed back to the room to wait.

In the silence of the room, for the first time in days, Tinseng couldn't outrun his thoughts.

He kept imagining the moment when he finally had the papers. For dramatic effect, his mind pictured it dissolving like self-immolating paper, and with it, all the fear and pain Jinzhao had lived with since showing up at Tinseng's door. If he had the papers, he could ensure Jinzhao would never look like that again. No one would question Jinzhao's loyalty; no one would mark him as a traitor; there would be no reason to consider him a threat better silenced. The information would simply disappear. The question, and the threat, would die a quiet death on that piece of paper. Tinseng was going to make sure of it.

When Jinzhao finally returned, Tinseng immediately knew something had gone wrong.

"What happened?"

"Your sister saw me."

"Are you sure?" Jinzhao just looked at him. "Okay. Well, that's . . . not great, but not the end of the world. Maybe she'll just forget about it. Yukying's never been a gossip; she stays out of people's business. I'm proof of it."

"What do I say if she asks?"

"That you were borrowing something. He's as tall as you, almost. I don't know, we'll think of something. It's not important, Yukying's not our problem. What did Grodescu say?"

"He will meet me tomorrow. Tamariz."

"Okay, remind me to leave notes under Yukying's and Cheuk-Kwan's doors. Did he seem interested in the bait?"

"Yes. Are you sure we can give it to him?"

"Oh yeah. Those codes are long blown, but he won't know that. He accepted your location? Arrogant of him. Okay. Then I'll start in on their room once I see them leave the ship and meet you at the beach afterward."

"Tinseng..."

"It's fine. If I don't find them in his room tomorrow, there's always Villefranche. Now let's get some sleep. It's past your bedtime."

They changed in silence and lay in silence, and during it all Tinseng tried not to worry too loudly. Yukying was a complication, but the plan was still strong. He'd have all the time he needed to search the room, and they'd be one step closer to all of this being over.

---

Now. June 25, 1963. Épernay, France.

"And did any of the passengers stand out to you?" The detective in the wrinkled suit asked, pen poised over his notebook.

"Hmm, let me think." Tinseng made a three-act play of it: reaching back in his memory, considering, ultimately shaking his head. "No, I don't think so. Why, was there someone important?"

"And when did you meet Lucas Grodescu?"

*Aha,* Tinseng thought, *you won't get me that easy.* "Who?"

"A passenger named Lucas Grodescu."

"Never heard of him. Are you holding him here too?"

"Mr. Woo," the detective said, mispronouncing the name. "It is critical that you take this seriously."

"I'm taking it as seriously as you."

"What do you mean by that?"

"You kept my sister for questioning for over an hour. I didn't know questioning an innocent woman took so long. What was the reason?"

"We had to keep Mrs. Li longer than anticipated. She was very understanding."

"She is, isn't she? Whereas I,"—Tinseng tapped his fingers on the table—"I'm impatient. Disruptive, unable to focus, a nuisance to others.

It's all documented in my file. Do you have it there?" He reached for the folder on the table and laughed when the other man set his meaty hand on it. Tinseng grinned as if to say, *can't blame me for trying.* "What do you have in your file? There are so many things to know about me. For example, I love leftover zha liang, I have no feeling in two of my fingertips, I'm afraid of bees..."

"Mr. Woo." A thin vein of exasperation cracked through the detective's veneer. Tinseng leaned back in the chair and crossed his arms. Just a thin crack for now, but he was just warming up.

This was going to be fun.

# PART THREE

## HE'S A REBEL

# CHAPTER SIX

*Seven days ago. June 18, 1963. Lisbon, Portugal.*

On the morning of the third day, they awoke anchored in Lisbon. Only Yukying and Laurence had planned to go ashore with the first group, rising early to join the other eager guests queuing for the boats. The moment they emerged outside, Yukying was struck by what they'd done: traveled thousands of miles to a completely foreign place—strangers in a strange land. The air smelled different, felt different against her skin. London had been foreign, too, but she'd been to London before, and besides, she lived in Hong Kong; the English had transplanted their way of life there, and she'd had long exposure to it. Lisbon, though, was truly unknown: she'd never met a Portuguese person before, never heard their language spoken, knew nothing except a sheet of information the cruise staff had slipped under their door during the night. The paper, which they received for every port, listed recommendations for bars, museums, cafés, cabarets, shopping centers, and casinos, as well as little tips about the region such as food specialties, wares for which the area was famous, and even the price of taxis so the tourists didn't get too fleeced. But those were just lists, words flat on a page. They captured nothing of the spirit of the place where they'd landed. They had two days and one night to absorb as much as they could. It was a daunting, thrilling challenge, a once-in-a-lifetime experience she knew she was privileged to have.

So it rankled how little attention she was paying as she took Laurence's hand and stepped off the boat into Portugal for the first time.

Yukying wished she wasn't so distracted. But how could she think of anything but what she'd seen last night? It'd kept her awake until close to dawn as she'd stared at the ceiling trying to think of explanations. Shan Dao and Mr. Grodescu had been in the room together, alone. Shan Dao had left the room rolling down his shirtsleeves. Mrs. Grodescu had come back to check on her husband; he had left her alone, uncharacteristically.

There were perfectly innocent reasons for all of that. She shouldn't jump to conclusions.

She trailed a little behind Laurence as they walked, half-listening to his recitation of *Frommer's*.

But there had been the first night, too, when Tinseng had been at the dance and she'd seen Shan Dao in those nice clothes sneaking back into his room. Where had he been then?

Had he been meeting with this other man?

Perhaps she'd misunderstood the relationship between Shan Dao and Tinseng. True, Tinseng had asked her how she'd known she'd been in love, which was very unlike him. He'd spoken like he'd been sure of his feelings. But it was presumptuous to think Tinseng had expressed those feelings to Shan Dao. It might even be presumptuous to assume Tinseng had admitted his feelings to himself; he could remain very ignorant if he decided he'd rather not know.

But even if he and Tinseng weren't together, even if Shan Dao couldn't see how Tinseng felt about him, how could Shan Dao be so reckless? Even talking about these acts could be enough to land Shan Dao in jail and bring scrutiny to everyone around him, which would mean disaster for Tinseng, surely. She couldn't understand what Shan Dao was thinking. He seemed so conscientious and thoughtful. She must be wrong.

But if she wasn't . . . if Shan Dao was putting Tinseng in that position . . .

"May I carry that for you?" Laurence asked, startling her.

"Hmm?" How long had her thoughts been wandering? She looked around and realized they'd already walked blocks away from the pier.

"You keep adjusting your bag. Is it too heavy? Here, let me—"

"Oh, thank you." She handed the bag over and sighed. "I'm sorry. I slept poorly last night."

"Your back again?"

"A tension headache. I woke up and walked around the ship."

"Wake me next time, I'll walk with you. Also," he looked around, "Do we get a taxi or take the train? Which beach did you and Tinseng agree to last night? Carcavelos?"

That had been what they'd decided; veterans of the cruise had recommended it. But this morning there'd been a note under the door in Tinseng's distinctive scrawl, informing her the plan had changed to Tamariz Beach. Perhaps it was coincidence. But Yukying thought about Mrs. Grodescu's comment last night and didn't think so.

"Actually we thought Tamariz would be less crowded."

Laurence shrugged. "As long as they have cabanas to rent, I don't care."

She kissed his cheek, thankful her husband wasn't one of those overbearing types, and guilty that she was taking advantage of it. She told herself again she was overreacting.

***

If praia do Tamariz lacked in size, it insisted on impressing in views. To the east, Portugal's white stone forts jutted into the water on their precipices and peninsulas. From her chair at the front of the cabana, Yukying watched the sun sparkling on the water and the huge variety of people vacationing from all over the world. Laurence couldn't be happier reading his book and sipping colorful drinks brought to him from the hotel that rented the cabanas.

Cheuk-Kwan, Chiboon, and Shan Dao joined them at eleven. Shan Dao made Tinseng's excuses while he settled into the cabana chair next to Laurence, then looked over curiously at Laurence's book. Laurence held out the spine for Shan Dao to read aloud: "*The Second World War, Volume Three—The Grand Alliance.*" His mouth thinned as he saw the author. "Winston Churchill."

"The third in his six-volume set," Laurence explained. "Published in 1951. I finished the first two years ago, but never seem to have the time to read the rest. I brought the other four and mean to finish them all by the end of the trip."

"Churchill was—" Shan Dao started, but Laurence held up a hand to stop him.

"You're shaking the wrong mulberry tree," Laurence informed him. "I'm not the political one. That one and his brother are," he pointed out to the water where Cheuk-Kwan had already submerged himself in the Mediterranean.

"You aren't political," Shan Dao repeated slowly, "But you work for the British government."

Laurence turned a page. "That's right."

"You have little interest in the way imperialists rule your country?" Shan Dao asked archly. "You follow without thought?"

"I'm told it's one of my strengths," Laurence drawled, catching Yukying's eye and smirking just for her. The first time Laurence had truly stopped following his parents without thought, it had been to defend his love of her. She blushed even though they'd been married for four years.

"There are better perspectives, even from the west," Shan Dao insisted, as if he could not believe Laurence's attitude and thought perhaps it was simply that no one had brought it up with him before. "Klaus Epstein's essays, for instance."

"That depends on the perspective Yingtung's looking for, doesn't it?" Chiboon said from his spot on the sand; he had brought a beautiful blanket—from a state called New Mexico, he'd said—and had settled next to Yukying's chair with a huge spread of magazines from New York he'd promised to share. He looked up from one with Liz and Richard on the cover and said, "For perspective on the English he takes those orders from, there's little better than the man they revere like Jesus."

Shan Dao blinked at this reframing. "Insight rather than perspective?" Laurence inclined his head. "Then, let me know what insight you gain."

"What?"

"Let me know. I'll be living under them soon," Shan Dao said, and turned to his own book. Yukying, Chiboon, and Laurence all exchanged raised eyebrows—was that confirmation he planned to stay in Hong Kong?—but no one was quite brave enough to comment.

With everyone settled in, Yukying walked to the north end of the beach and gathered a small feast from the vendors lined up along the outskirts. Thankfully, most of the handwritten signs had English as well as Portuguese. She bought pão com chouriço, espetadas, and rissóis de camarão, and a few other items she didn't know the names for, pointing at what looked good and hoping for the best. She also bought croquettes, which were Chiboon's favorites in Hong Kong, and this variation looked so delicious she couldn't help buying three servings.

By the time she returned, Tinseng had finally joined them, and Cheuk-Kwan was back, too, drinking water. They fell on the food the moment they saw it. A few moments later, food in their mouths, they whirled away, chasing each other into the water. The cabana's cloth sides flapped in their wake, and a stunned silence was only broken by Chiboon's groan.

"They ate all the croquettes." Chiboon sounded truly pitiful as he pouted at the grease-stained paper plate. "Rude, so rude."

Smiling, Yukying reached under her chair and brought out a hidden plate.

"These only have potato," she said. "For Shan Dao, too, because he's vegetarian."

Chiboon nearly wept his thanks, while Shan Dao had almost no reaction at all, except to search her face. What was he looking for? Did he know she had seen him last night? Did he think she might be cold to him because of it, or did he think this was some kind of trick? She reminded herself not to make assumptions and pushed some food into his hands.

---

The hours slipped by easily on their slice of beach. Chiboon lured impressively large seagulls closer and closer with crumbs from their lunch, then, once he grew bored of that, sprawled out with Yukying and provided her with a running commentary of fashion faux paus as they people-watched. Laurence kept to his book.

"Technically, you could do this at home," Tinseng pointed out during one of his breaks eating cold food and applying more sunscreen.

"Then I wouldn't have the pleasure of your company," Laurence replied dryly, not even looking up from the page. They heard a snort from the other corner of the cabana, but by the time they were looking at him, Shan Dao had schooled his features back to neutral.

"Betrayal!" Tinseng cried. "This tent is full of traitors! I'm leaving!" He looked around for someone to plead with him to stay.

"Bye," Chiboon said, still bitter about the croquettes.

"Tell Cheuk-Kwan to come reapply his Glacier Cream soon," Yukying told him sweetly, battling a grin at Tinseng's growing pout.

"I see how it is," he said, sticking out his tongue at them, then immediately dropping the performance for a genuine grin. He swooped in to kiss Yukying on the cheek. "See you in an hour or two!" With a wave, he was gone again.

A few minutes later, Shan Dao rose and announced he was going for a walk. No one paid him much mind, and Yukying kept her eyes on her magazine until Shan Dao was a few steps away. She watched him walk down the beach toward the east where an old fort was open to tourists. She flipped through the rest of her magazine for show, the words swimming in front of her eyes. When she reached the end, she conspicuously put it down and sighed.

"What is it?" Laurence asked, immediately attentive to that particular sound of dissatisfaction.

"That was my last magazine."

"I'll ask the boy if the hotel has any."

"Oh, no, that's too much. I'll walk into town. I need to stretch my legs anyway."

"How far away is that?"

"Not very far, just across the tracks, but I might walk for a while. It'll be nice to see more of the area."

"Do you want me to come with you?" Laurence asked. She looked at him: book in hand, drink by his side, his usual pinched expression completely smoothed over by a look of relaxation she hadn't seen since their honeymoon. Even if she didn't have ulterior motives, she'd be loath to interrupt such comfort.

"No, you stay here, keep everyone out of trouble."

"Good luck with *that*," Chiboon muttered, picking up Yukying's magazine. "Jiejie, can I—?"

"Of course. I'll be back in an hour or so," she said, kissing Laurence briefly. "Would you like anything from the pharmacy?"

Neither needed anything, so she slung her bag over her shoulder and walked away from the cabana toward town. After looking over her shoulder to make sure no one in her group could see her, she changed direction and headed east.

※

She'd noticed the fort when they'd arrived, of course. It sat on a hill, sternly disapproving of the revelry on the beach beneath it. The fort was miniscule compared to the ones they'd toured in England, but that didn't stop tourists from cramming themselves through the narrow stone hallways. At least she didn't have to worry about losing Shan Dao. As she followed him through the main entrance, she read *Forte da Cruz*, and wondered if Cruz was a who or a where.

She followed behind a large family as Shan Dao took a sharp turn to walk up a narrow spiral staircase. There wasn't much room in this cramped fort built for safety, not comfort. She'd toured some walls and forts as part of school trips and remembered those places now as she climbed. Strange, the things that were universal: the coolness of stone safe from sunlight, the reverential quiet of a place seeped in history, the echoing presence of soldiers hurrying up and down. She stepped where hundreds of men had stepped before and wondered if they ever hurried for something happy— a nice meal, perhaps, or a mail call expecting a letter from home. She hoped so; she hoped it wasn't all terror hastening their steps.

The ghosts of the past dissolved as she stepped through them into the blinding afternoon sunlight. She'd only been in the staircase a few moments, but her eyes had already adjusted; she blinked hurriedly and scanned the crowd quickly for Shan Dao.

He stood by the wall looking out at the ocean. Trying to find a spot where no one could see her, she ducked into a shallow room with an open doorway. According to the plaque, the room had been used as storage. She moved to the narrow open window to the side of the doorway where there was another plaque and pretended to read it as she watched Shan Dao through the window.

She felt a bump against her and turned on instinct to bow an apology before remembering she was in Europe. It was a little girl, looking at her with wide eyes. When she registered Yukying's attention, she turned to her mother and said something in a language Yukying couldn't begin to recognize. It sounded soft like the French Tinseng spoke, but with unexpected flourishes, a roll of the tongue that reminded her of the downward sweep of a brush. In the midst of unknown words, she suddenly heard a burst of English:

"*Ji rengiasi kaip* Audrey Hepburn."

"Audrey Hepburn?" Yukying repeated. The girl nodded and pointed at Yukying's dress. It was a white dress, softly bloused above the waist with a pale-purple silk ribbon. Cross-stitched bands of turquoise bordered the bateau neckline and hemline. She'd knitted it herself from *Vogue Knitting*'s summer pattern, and now all that effort had paid off from the girl's adoring gaze.

"Ahh." Yukying smiled and nodded, then swooshed the skirt with her hands so it fanned out. The girl's eyes lit up, and she clapped.

"*Vėl! Vėl!*" the girl demanded, but before Yukying understood what she was asking for, her mother clucked her tongue to chastise her.

"Sorry," the woman said in hesitant English.

"No, no," Yukying said, waving the apology away. Out of the corner of her eye, she checked on Shan Dao; he still hadn't moved. She turned back to the girl. "Audrey Hepburn? Good, yes?"

"Yes," the girl nodded furiously. "*Funny Face*. That's for me,'" the little girl sang. Yukying joined in, and they sang together, "*Bonjour Paris!*"

They grinned at each other—two strangers who'd found a single thread of connection strong enough to transcend language. A cloud drifted and the shifting sunlight caught the little girl's gap-toothed smile. As Yukying smiled in kind, she saw movement over the girl's head. Shan Dao had started moving toward the exit.

"Goodbye!" She said, the only word mother and daughter were likely to understand, though she would have liked to say so much more. The little girl waved as Yukying hurried away.

Shan Dao moved more quickly now. *It must be because Mr. Grodescu hasn't shown up*, Yukying thought. An external set of stairs down one of the fort's walls led to the street; she descended only after Shan Dao was far down the sidewalk, trying to keep lots of people between them. Shan Dao crossed the street turning north and walked past Casino Estoril into the city. Where was he going? *Maybe he's just sightseeing*, she thought; it would be nice to be wrong about all this, a misunderstanding she'd blush to remember later. She would take embarrassment if it meant Tinseng was safe. The pedestrian traffic turned more local, making her presence more obvious than ever, but she wasn't about to start ducking behind newspaper stands. She had just as much right to be here as anyone.

Finally, Shan Dao stopped at a café and sat at one of the outside tables. He spoke with a server then pulled out a newspaper. Yukying felt another flicker of doubt; this was all normal behavior. She scouted the opposite side of the street and found an angled alley where she could keep herself mostly concealed. Unseen, she watched the back of Shan Dao's head and tried not to feel immensely foolish.

Just as she'd convinced herself to give up and go, Shan Dao looked up from his paper. Yukying saw him then: the man who must be Mr. Grodescu. She had seen him at dinner, but she'd never had reason to look closely before now. He was, to Yukying's eye, the perfect specimen of a French gentleman. Willowy height, gold-framed glasses perched on a patrician nose, a healthy tan that spoke leisure. Some men tried to deny their age by dressing too fashionably or putting too much product in their hair, but Mr. Grodescu wore his middle age comfortably; he gave the air of a quietly assured man—or perhaps arrogant, she corrected as he sat down with a bored countenance.

She watched a pantomime play out. Shan Dao set down his paper. Grodescu gestured. Shan Dao leaned forward to talk, and Grodescu stared at him, lips unmoving, nodding occasionally. The server came again, and both men leaned back in their chairs, calling a draw. Grodescu looked up at the young woman and smiled as he ordered. Yukying didn't like the smile. She didn't like any of this.

As she watched, her surroundings slipped away from her. The noise of pedestrians passing by, the rumbling of engines, all faded to the background as she stared, intent on absorbing every detail. She was so focused that she didn't hear the footsteps until it was too late.

Three things happened at once: A presence stepped up behind her, a hand covered her mouth, and a sinister voice said in her ear, "Don't move. Don't scream."

She couldn't move, *couldn't* scream. Her mind blanked completely, shock a barren white void. The danger pulled her backward into the alley, the hand on her mouth tensing its fingers into her soft cheek as they walked away from safety. When he'd dragged her all the way to the back wall, he spun her around roughly.

"Tell me what you're doi—Yukying??"

The man scrambled back. Yukying stared.

"Tinseng? What . . ." Her hand went to her cheek. The pressure of his silencing hand had sunk into her skin like dough. "What's going on?"

"Fuck, there's no time for this. Just stay here, okay?" He moved forward to the lip of the alley. She watched him for a moment, still stunned. She didn't know who he had been just a moment ago. Ignoring Tinseng's command, she snuck forward until she was just behind him.

"I'm not kidding, Yukying, go back," Tinseng said without taking his gaze away from the café.

"Do you know that man Shan Dao is with?" she asked. "Tinseng, why did you—"

"It's fine, jiejie. Stand behind me, at least. Jesus. How long have you been here?"

She bit her lip. "I've been following him since the beach."

"Since the . . ." he chuckled under his breath. "Oh, I can't wait to hear his side of this."

"Tinseng." The voice in her ear was not the one laughing now. The hand around her mouth had not been her gentle brother's. She'd been helpless. The fear had curdled and sat, churning, in her stomach.

"Tinseng," she said again. Tinseng finally turned back. He took the time to really look at her—her arms hugging her torso, her wobbling lip, whatever he found in her eyes—and crumbled, taking a step toward her.

"Yukying, I didn't mean to be so rough, I really didn't. I thought you were . . . did I hurt you?"

She sighed. "No, but . . ."

"But I scared you," he surmised. Horrifyingly, she felt tears prickling the corners of her eyes. "Yukying, I'm sorry. What can I do? What do you need?" he asked, even as he looked over his shoulder to check on Shan Dao and Mr. Grodescu.

"I need to know how Shan Dao knows that man."

"He's just an old friend. Nothing to worry about."

Tinseng expected her not to call his bluff; he expected the Yukying of three years ago, who would have let him get away with it. But if he could change, so could she.

Instead of capitulating, she swallowed and asked, "Is that why Shan Dao was in that man's room last night?"

"What . . ." Tinseng turned back to her with a narrowed gaze. "Whatever you think is happening, it's not." At her pinched frown, he added, "I know I haven't always made the best decisions. But I promise I know what I'm doing. And I trust Shan Dao with my life." He looked over his shoulder again, clearly desperate to give his attention back to the café. "Now, will you go back to the beach, please?"

She almost said yes. She considered walking back to the beach, pretending to pay attention to the conversation around her, checking her watch every few minutes and wondering when Tinseng would be back, what news he'd have. She thought about waiting patiently. She was so good at that; she'd been doing it her whole life. As expected from someone like her: A woman fragile from childhood illness shouldn't be in this alley.

But neither should her little brother. He should be back at the beach, too, laughing in the sun, not here doing—whatever this was.

She raised her chin. "I'm fine where I am, thank you."

A noise came from the square. They both turned in unison. Tinseng fidgeted.

"Fine, fine, fine, but if your mother rises from the dead to kill me, it's your fault. They should be almost done anyway." She heard him muttering an apology to their mother under his breath as they situated themselves so they could both see the table.

"This is a good spot, by the way," he said. "You have a good eye. Ugh, I hate his face. Why couldn't you choose a place where I could stare at Shan Dao instead? He looks interested, though, that's good."

They watched for long minutes until Grodescu waved at the server. "Hah, paying the bill. Generous of him," Tinseng said dryly. "Oh, he's leaving. Okay. Okay. Okay," he said again, reassuring himself. "That looked okay."

"Should we go over to him?" she asked.

"No. We should go back to the beach; Yingtung will worry where you've been."

"I told him I was shopping in town. Oh, I don't have . . ." She looked down at her empty hands.

"There's a shop on the way back," Tinseng said. "I saw it earlier. Come on."

An awkward silence pulled between them as they walked to the pharmacy and bought a basket of trinkets and snacks. Tinseng had always hated silence in the past. Now, instead of filling it with chatter, he stayed an aisle away. In the years he'd been gone, it seemed he'd decided distance was a better weapon than distraction.

When they'd made their purchases and were once again side-by-side on the sidewalk, she tried again.

"I hope you know you can tell me anything, didi," she said in her softest, saddest voice. She wasn't above a little manipulation right now.

Tinseng wrung his hands, keeping them clasped as if not allowing himself to reach out. "I would. Believe me, I would. But this is bigger than just me. Please, you can't tell Yingtung or anyone else. Not even Cheuk-Kwan."

"Are you or Shan Dao in trouble?"

Tinseng shook his head. "No, no trouble." He put a hand on his heart. "I promise I'd tell you if I was."

"Then why was Shan Dao in his room last night?"

"Ahh, ha-ha, hmm. Well, you see . . . a purchase for . . . Shan Dao's uncle in Hong Kong. This man, Grodescu, is an antiquities dealer. He has a lead on a piece Shan Dao's uncle wants. Grodescu doesn't exactly keep his nose clean, and he's paranoid, so he's careful about meetings."

Tinseng's smile was shameless, and his lie was unconvincing at best. She knew he was lying, and he certainly knew he hadn't gotten away with anything. But he had an air of desperation that felt like he needed her not to call him out. It made her wonder. She'd rarely ever seen Tinseng lose his airy, uncaring demeanor. He let very little matter, so that very little could hurt him. Usually his lies were smooth and easy to believe; whatever he was protecting must be precious.

Yukying decided to let it be for now. She'd never seen anything work on Tinseng except a large dose of guilt, and she didn't want to use her only card just yet. She let him peel away at the park and walked back through the train station to the cabana alone.

It had been an hour since she left, maybe a little less. Laurence and Chiboon hadn't moved an inch. She showed Laurence the postcards she'd bought, and they spent a pleasant time writing to their friends. When they finally left, they stopped to mail the correspondence so it bore a stamp from Lisbon. The post office was full of travelers with a similar agenda, the lobby full of wide-brimmed hats and beach bags, the smell of tanning oil and sun-warmed flesh. Laurence's hand sweated in her own as they waited, and she squeezed it every so often, just to see him smile. At least one thing was still uncomplicated.

After the intense day, Yukying took a well-deserved nap. She woke up feeling like the world had reset itself while her eyes had been closed. As she showered and reapplied her makeup, she reasoned with herself. This was still a vacation. Her brother's drama, whatever it was, didn't have to interfere with that. He clearly didn't want her involved; perhaps she should listen.

With that in mind, she wandered in search of Mrs. Lanzette's sewing circle. It moved around the ship like a weather pattern, and this time she found them in one of the bars, having entrenched themselves at a table until dinner.

The ladies were quicker to accept her into the fold today; she only had to endure a few beats of awkwardness before conversation started again. They all knew by now that she spoke English fluently, so at least the rude comments in front of her had stopped. Mrs. Lanzette drew her into the conversation but Yukying politely kept herself apart, focusing on her dress until the teenager from America, Miss Duncan, leaned over.

"Pardon, but what pattern is that? It's exceptionally pretty."

"Thank you," Yukying said. "It's from the fall '61 *Vogue Knitting* . . ."

By the time Chiboon found her, she and Miss Duncan had become fast friends. The group watched warily at the man interrupting what was clearly a woman's space, but Yukying assured them, "You can trust Mr. Lim; he's darned his share of stockings. He was placed with cousins in the war," she continued. "Six girls."

The ladies chorused low murmurs of understanding and relief. The excuse didn't have to be believable; it just had to be repeatable. Some of them might know, or suspect, the truth. Some might even accept him for it, were all else equal. But the truth was illegal, and so the charade was necessary. *It is what it is*, Yukying thought as Chiboon pulled up a chair next to her.

"I wish I'd had stockings to darn," mourned Mrs. Biddle, who worked a story of surviving the Blitz into every conversation, "We ran out in '40. My sister tried dyeing her legs with tea bags, but it never looked right. I never bothered; who had the time with the war on?"

"Tea bags, horrible," Chiboon sympathized. "Did she ever try gravy?"

"No, but her friend did. A horrid disaster." She didn't sound very mournful. Chiboon got a gleam in his eye Yukying knew well. She left her friend to pry gossip from an eager Mrs. Biddle and turned back to her work. After realizing what a good audience Chiboon was, the other ladies eagerly shared their wartime workarounds and follies. When he bored of that, Chiboon mentioned he wrote for a magazine and made his audience work for his pseudonym, demurring until finally revealing his name with modesty so false Yukying's silent laughter fouled up three stitches.

She let the conversation flow around her as she thought about the morning's surprises. It was unfortunate Mrs. Grodescu wasn't here now. Before she could convince herself out of it, she heard herself ask Miss Duncan, "I believe the Grodescus sit at your table, is that right?"

"Grodescu? I'm not sure. Mother?" Miss Duncan tapped her mother on the shoulder. "Which ones are the Grodescus?"

"Grodescus? The Polish woman with the French husband. Honestly, Eloise." Mrs. Duncan shook her head and returned to the other conversation.

"Oh, *that* woman." Miss Duncan rolled her eyes, but only once her mother couldn't see. "Sorry, I feel like I've met every stinking person on this ship—how am I supposed to keep them all straight? I ask you. Anyway, yes, I remember now. What about her?"

"I heard she excels at shuffleboard, and I was hoping to convince her to play with me. Did they happen to mention their plans for today?"

"Hmm. The beach, for sure. One of the ones in Estoril. And then tonight a club. The famous casino, I think. Everyone wants to go there, that's all the boys are talking about. Can I tell you something?" Yukying didn't have the time to answer either way before Miss Duncan barreled on. "Some of them are going to try to sneak in with fake IDs."

"How daring," Yukying said neutrally, not sure what reaction Miss Duncan wanted.

"How stupid, you mean. You know the worst part? They'll probably get away with it, and then they'll be *really* insufferable. How come boys can get away with everything, and I'm stuck here knitting a jacket?" Miss Duncan asked with disgust.

"I don't know," Yukying said, looking down at her own knitting. It was a very good question.

※

"Laurence," Yukying said a few hours later, "what do you want to do tonight?"

"I don't know, darling," he said distractedly as he sat at the vanity putting on cufflinks for dinner. "A club or something, wasn't it?"

"Do you care which one?"

"Why? Have one in mind?"

"What about Casino Estoril? Chiboon mentioned it at dinner the first night."

"The one your brother mentioned he and Shan Dao are going to?"

"Yes, but we'll hardly see them."

"It's fine if we do. It has to be," he insisted when she started to protest. "He's coming home. He's living with us. He's important to you. Besides, he has the right to be protective. I, I know I have a lot to answer for."

She crossed the room and wrapped her arms around his shoulders.

"He doesn't get to make that judgment." She met his eyes in the mirror. "I do."

"What judgment will you make, then, Empress Wu Yukying?"

"That you are going to look very good on my arm tonight." She kissed his temple, then his cheek. He turned his head so she could kiss him properly, with a hand sneaking to the back of his head to steady him. He pulled her into his lap and they kissed there for long minutes, languid and unrushed. When they finally pulled apart, Laurence trailed a finger down her neck, tracing the collar of her dress.

"In that case," he said, "should I bring out the tuxedo?"

※

At night, the park in front of Casino Estoril served the purpose of red carpet and grand staircase, a long dark stretch that muted all surrounding distraction as taxis used the circular drive to drop off their fares: locals, high rollers, and tourists alike stepped out in their splendor before the dazzling neon building with its imposing modern blocks, wanting to see and be seen. Through the front doors, a cacophony of excess awaited, ready to swallow everyone whole.

Yukying's deep violet evening gown floated just above the ground. The rich color stood out against her pale skin, the material lush after the grit of the beach. While the gown itself came from a shop, she'd hand-embroidered a gold sash pinned around the middle, pulling in her frame and accentuating her waist, narrow even by Hong Kong's standards and absolutely diminutive compared to the Americans on board, who'd been far better fed during the war. Laurence wore a classic tuxedo, the lines impeccably pressed. He was no one's idea of beauty except for Yukying's—the only reason he gained attention back home was because of his family name—but even he glowed a little tonight, offering his arm as they stepped out of the taxi and up the steps.

Inside, Yukying took her time scanning each area for the Grodescus, finally finding them in the large ballroom where a live band played standards. The couple twirled expertly on the dance floor between slower couples. In the same room, she wasn't surprised to find Tinseng and Shan Dao sitting in a corner booth. She quickly pulled Laurence aside so they weren't seen by her brother and directed them to a high-top table. A waitress materialized instantly, then hurried off to bring them their champagne. Laurence lit their cigarettes and prepared to settle in, because she hadn't informed him otherwise. Usually, if they attended a party, Laurence avoided all the social aspects he could get away with, wanting only to enjoy a quiet conversation with his wife or, if the situation was truly dire, one of his work acquaintances. Tonight she would have to disappoint him.

When the Grodescus finally sat down, she turned to Laurence and said, "Darling, you see that couple over there? The woman in red and the man in gray? I met her yesterday. Can we go say hello? We can be friendly faces."

"Another one of your charity cases?"

"She's nice, and very lonely," Yukying said, which just proved Laurence's point. But for her sake, he visibly gathered himself and nodded. She silently apologized and promised herself she'd make it up to him tomorrow by not forcing him to do any activities with her brothers.

A strange look passed over Marissa Grodescu's face when she saw them approach. Yukying hoped it was simple awkwardness as the other couple stood up for them. She kept her focus on Mrs. Grodescu as she smiled widely.

"Hello, Mrs. Grodescu. Mrs. Yukying Li," she said, reintroducing herself to save Marissa embarrassment in case she couldn't remember. "We're on the cruise together. This is my husband, Mr. Laurence Li."

Introductions and handshakes were exchanged, and the strict politeness of society granted them chairs at the table. The men started in on the usual topics: Mr. Li was born and raised in Hong Kong, undergraduate at Yale, graduate studies at Oxford, and now in government work; Mr. Grodescu was born and educated in France, but spent both wars out of country with relatives, which was how he met his wife, and was in the trade of antiquities. That part of the story matched the one Tinseng gave her; she didn't know what to think. But instead of asking more questions, Yukying had something else in mind, a plan that had blossomed the moment she saw the couple on the floor.

"Mrs. Grodescu, your husband dances marvelously," she said quietly under the talk of the men. "My husband was born with two left feet. No amount of lessons have helped." She sighed wistfully and looked out at the dance floor. "Sometimes I miss having a more varied dance card. Not that my husband isn't a wonderful partner, of course!"

Mrs. Grodescu looked amused. "I understand. Doctors say eating the same foods every day is not nourishing."

"Yes, exactly. I do think I'm lacking iron in my diet sometimes." They exchanged a look every woman knew: a secret, knowing smile. Then, before her nerves failed her, Yukying asked, "Could I bother him for a dance?"

Another flash of something passed over Mrs. Grodescu's face. This time, Yukying could see the grimace, almost like fear.

"Lucas is . . . particular," Mrs. Grodescu hedged, her gaze nervously flittering to her husband.

"I'm sure if I just asked." Yukying internally apologized a dozen times for her rudeness and turned to interrupt the men's conversation about the various ways to move antiques out of China. "Mr. Grodescu, I was just telling your wife you dance wonderfully. Would you mind if I imposed on you for a song?"

"If that is what you wish . . ." Mr. Grodescu addressed her husband while he asked. Laurence for his part looked immediately over at Yukying, who told him it was all right with a smile.

Confused but glad it wasn't him being asked to dance, Laurence said, "You would be doing me a favor. She loves dancing. I can't keep up."

And so Mr. Grodescu offered his hand.

Until now, Yukying had refrained from looking over at Tinseng or Shan Dao in their back booth. They'd existed in her mind like hot spots on a heat map, but she hadn't let herself think about it. Now she saw them in snapshots as Mr. Grodescu led her around the floor. Tinseng looked horrified in the first instance, furious for the rest. She caught Shan Dao's hand on his arm, Shan Dao's mouth by Tinseng's ear. The final time, Tinseng stared directly at her, as if waiting for her eyes to meet his; the look on his face made a fist clench in her belly. Shan Dao wasn't looking at her; his face was turned toward Tinseng, his expression in shadow.

Part of her flinched away from the mere idea of their disapproval. Another part of her knew she was the type to ask forgiveness rather than permission. They all were, the three Wu children, and she couldn't even blame it on her younger brothers: she'd been this way her entire life. She'd learned how to sneak in order to get what she wanted.

*Really*, she thought as she spun gracefully around the room, *Tinseng shouldn't be surprised by this development at all.*

She stopped looking their way after that. She didn't want to be a neglectful partner.

"Are you enjoying the cruise?" she asked Mr. Grodescu.

"My wife is enjoying it."

Yukying thought of the way the other woman spoke of him, how miserable Mrs. Grodescu looked in the lounge yesterday, the strange looks on her face tonight.

"She's lucky to have such an thoughtful husband."

"You could remind her of that." They spun around the stage as the strings crescendoed. "And what of yourself? Are you enjoying the trip? No seasickness?"

"No, no, I'm lucky. I grew up around water, spent plenty of time on boats. I'm very used to it."

"Then you must like taking late night walks? It was you I heard talking to Marissa last night, wasn't it?"

Yukying stared at Mr. Grodescu, whose eyes sank needles under her skin.

"Yes, it was. I," she swallowed, "I have back pain; it wakes me. The doctors said walking would help."

"I'm sorry to hear it. Pain is a hard thing to bear." Her feet barely touched the floor as he moved them. "You should be more careful walking around that late, Mrs. Li. Even on a ship like this, there are advantageous sorts."

"I will. Thank you. It helps to know there are good married men like you who keep late hours."

"I keep all hours," he said, and his attention crawled all over her. She knew, down to her marrow, that no matter where she walked on the ship now, she'd imagine coal-dark eyes watching from places she could not see. She wanted to shiver to shake out the fear so it couldn't spread. But his hand was splayed across her back, and he would surely feel it.

*Men love fear,* her mother used to say; *they love it more than they will ever love you.* Once, not long before she died, her mother had repeated this advice while she'd fixed Yukying's hair, staring at her daughter in the mirror. *You're weak,* she'd told her as she pulled Yukying's hair ruthlessly into place. Yukying had winced, then offered a smile, more reflex than anything calculated. To her surprise, her mother's frown had relaxed just a little. *But there, you see?* she'd said. *Not as weak as you think, if you can smile through pain.* Yukying had not understood but had kept smiling. Anything to earn her mother's approval.

Those words drifted up around her now, echoes as soft as the drummer's brush on the snare. *Never show them how weak you are or they'll eat you alive,* her mother had said, intense in her insistence. *Hide behind that smile. Cultivate whatever weapon you can.*

Mr. Grodescu watched her, hungry. She twisted up her emotion and pulled it tight.

"I hope we run into each other again, then," she said, and her knot of a smile held fast.

⚜

It took all her focus to walk calmly back to the table. Once she settled back in her chair, she counted excruciating minutes until she could politely lead Laurence away, wishing the other couple a pleasant evening. She felt Lucas Grodescu's attention on her, though when she looked over, he wasn't ever looking her way.

Tinseng was never far from her mind. After another drink, she excused herself to the ladies' room. She walked slowly so Tinseng would notice her movement. In the privacy of the stall, she sat for a few minutes just breathing. Then she got up, washed her hands, fixed her lipstick, and ran her hands down her dress. She stared at the reflection in the mirror. There was a flush high in her cheeks. Was this a woman a mother could be proud of?

She picked up her clutch and walked out. Tinseng was waiting, leaning against the wall examining his fingernails, the very picture of a bored man about town. The effect was ruined as his head snapped up at the sound of heels on tile. He hurried over to her.

"Yukying," he hissed, "What the *hell?*"

She did have some shame and looked down at the floor. "I'm just worried. I want to help."

"I can see that! You might as well have lit an incendiary! Who taught you to be so unsubtle??"

They stared at each other. A moment later, they collapsed in their own ways, Tinseng throwing his head back, Yukying muffling laughter into her fist.

"But really, jie, what were you thinking?" Tinseng asked as they found a bench to sit on; in the casino there was no lack of alcoves and corners. "Don't you want to have a nice vacation? You need to forget this."

She wondered how to articulate what she was thinking—or more importantly, how to make her brother believe her. She would run into far more dangerous situations than this to ensure her brothers' safety. Flashes of what they'd done to survive getting to Hong Kong weren't as close to the surface of her thoughts these days, yet they were never too far away. But even before that. When Tinseng had first started living with them, no one had quite known what to do with him. One day he'd tried to climb the rigging of a sailboat on the river, and had frozen halfway up. After half the town had tried to get him down, it'd been Yukying who'd coaxed him to jump into the water, promising he would be okay; she would catch him. He jumped, trusting her. Ever since, a part of her heart had been his.

"No," she said. "I won't forget it, Tinseng. Not if it hurts you. I need to stay, so I know you're okay."

He stared, then laughed again, rueful and wrung out.

"God." He shook his head. "You and J—you and Shan Dao can never be on the same side. I would die." He took a huge, gulping breath. "This is kind of dangerous, jie."

"Then you shouldn't be alone. At least tell me what the danger is. *Please*," she interrupted before he could start, "please don't lie."

Tinseng's teeth rattled shut. He chewed on his answer.

"There's trouble," he finally said. "A little . . . a lot. But I'm taking care of it."

"I'm sure you are. You're very responsible. And Grodescu?"

Tinseng fidgeted. "I shouldn't talk about it here."

"Would you like to go outside?"

Her insistence made him uncomfortable. It made her uncomfortable, too, like wearing a skin that wasn't hers. They'd never been so fractious with each other before. They'd laughed earlier at the invocation of her mother, but her presence was between them now, a ghost they'd never been able to put to rest.

He wrinkled his nose, then sighed.

"Okay. Tomorrow morning. Come to our room, but not too early, for my sake. Not Shan Dao's—he gets up around six."

"Six isn't so early," she admonished out of habit.

"You're both as bad as each other. Well, if you want company, you should ask him. Anyway, I'm not cracked like you two, so if you insist on bothering us, will you bring me something from the breakfast spread, jiejie? I missed it this morning; what kind of continental breakfast closes at nine?"

His whine, and his arm looped in hers, were his way of asking if they were okay. It settled the fractured pieces of her heart. These well-worn roles were as necessary to her as she knew they were to him.

"Of course," she said, "Anything for my A-Seng." And she meant it.

# CHAPTER SEVEN

*Six Days Ago. June 19, 1963. At Sea.*

After seeing Yukying dance with Grodescu that night, fear followed Tinseng into his dreams.

He found himself in front of Jinzhao's parents' house in Bern. The street was quiet in the way he remembered, its perfectly spaced trees swaying gently, beckoning him inside the neat little brownstone. When Jinzhao had stood across the street after racing from Paris to Bern, he'd sensed something wrong and hurried inside. Was Tinseng to relive that night with its bloody bodies? But no, there were no bright explosions, no muffled gunshots, no screams. Whatever was in store for him, it wasn't to walk in Jinzhao's footsteps.

The house stood abandoned and whispered its emptiness to Tinseng. He knew what it wanted him to do. He didn't want to do it. He made the house wait, walking down the street instead. But in the dream it was midnight, and midnight was patient. It wrapped itself around Tinseng until he was shivering, so cold he began to freeze. If he didn't get inside he'd stick to the sidewalk, rooted here forever. The dream was forcing his hand.

He didn't want to go. He had to go.

Across the street, the gate opened.

The moment he crossed the threshold, he heard a loud creak. At the path's end, the front door waited like an open mouth. He took a deep breath and stepped inside—but nothing happened. Typical, he thought with a roll of his eyes.

His feet remembered the layout from blueprints and moved him from the foyer into the parlor. Inside, he found Lim Chiboon. His torso sat on the couch, his intestines spilling over the side where his legs should have been. A canvas sat on an easel next to him, on which Chiboon painted calmly. When his brush ran dry, he dipped it into his gaping stomach, wetting the bristles with blood. This all seemed normal enough, except:

"What are you doing here?" Tinseng asked. "You're supposed to be in New York."

"You couldn't protect me," Chiboon said, "so I ended up here."

"Oh." Tinseng took a step forward, but Chiboon hissed at him.

"Hey, hey, hey, it's not done yet!" He gestured to his painting. "You can't see it until it's done, or you'll ruin the surprise."

"Sorry, sorry!" Tinseng backed up, hands raised. "Hey, do you know—"

Something crashed upstairs, just above their heads. A familiar shatter. They looked up, then back down at each other with twin smirks.

"Your mother's vase?"

"That or the time we let the cat into Auntie Guo's dining room."

"Ahh, those were good times," Tinseng said.

"Too bad they're over," Chiboon said. Before Tinseng could answer, the house creaked around them. Tinseng felt himself pulled back through the doors. He waved at Chiboon, who waved back with his paintbrush, sending splatters of blood paint on the couch. *Jinzhao isn't going to be very happy about those stains*, Tinseng thought as he was sucked back into the hallway. As if on a track, the dream took him down the hall to an oak door and pushed it open.

In the study, Mei Hankong sat behind his desk. Jinzhao rarely spoke about him, even now. But Tinseng had read a few letters, and his wife's journal, of course. And there was everything that came out during the scandal. How unhappy she'd been, how she'd considered many different ways out, from divorce to suicide, but only as thoughts passing like mayflies. Then, when she thought she'd finally escaped through her betrayal, her husband had surprised her. Instead of turning her in, he'd remained faithful. Held her in his arms. He had never seen his wife's unhappiness with him, only her discontent with the state. That in itself had been a trap.

Mei Hankong looked up from his writing. He had no face, only a smudged blankness of skin. Tinseng had never heard his voice. Some of the skin bunched into a facsimile of a mouth and rasped, "So you're him."

"What an interesting philosophical quandary," Tinseng said cheerfully, unwilling to yield any ground. "Am I him? I am certainly me."

The featureless face somehow managed to portray annoyance. Even Tinseng's dream found him insufferable. He grinned.

"What do you seek here?" Mei Hankong asked.

"Not the truth," Tinseng said. "I have enough of that already."

"Not even my truth?"

"Is that important? You don't have anything I need. I'm sorry to disturb you. I'll leave you to your writing."

"Wait—"

Tinseng ignored him and walked to the door.

"Wait, I—I have things to tell you—don't leave yet . . ."

Tinseng had become too complacent in the dream. He opened the door to find Mei Hankong standing on the other side. Tinseng's head whipped back around, but Mei Hankong stood behind him too.

"Don't leave me alone."

Something tickled Tinseng's ankle.

The man in front of him said, "Come back inside."

The man behind him said, "I want to help."

And they said together, "You'll be safe here."

There were . . . *things* . . . growing up from the floor around his legs. They were thin and curious, deceptively light. He knew he could not look at them. If he looked, they would jump up and devour him. The only thing keeping him alive was his devotion to the pretense that he did not know what was about to happen.

"You have to stay," the two men said, now four. "If you are to be part of this family. We'll listen." A dozen circled him entirely. "We'll make you comfortable here." They stayed at a respectful distance; they didn't need to touch. The things growing out of the floor did that for them.

"Stay, Wu Tinseng." The house pulled him down against its coffin-wood floor, and he heard all around: *Stay, stay, stay, staystaystayst—*

If he waited any longer, he'd die. He pulled a knife from a sheaf on his belt (had that always been there?) to slash his way out. Some of what he slashed felt like vines; some cut more like flesh. He didn't look. He pushed and cut until he could flee.

The hallways expanded and contracted like a heaving chest. The staircase turned, then turned again. When he thought he'd reached the top, he stepped through a stair and started over. Frustrated, he tried to outsmart the dream with fairy-tale tricks: drawing a line on the wall, leaving breadcrumbs he found in his pocket, tying a string to the banister at the start. Nothing worked but time. When the house finally tired of the game, it spat him out on the second floor.

The moment he opened the door to the bedroom, Cheuk-Kwan fell into him. He clung to Tinseng as they sank to the ground. Cheuk-Kwan's mouth was full of blood.

"Why did you come back?" his brother asked. "If you'd just stayed away, none of this would have happened."

"I know, I'm sorry," Tinseng said. He didn't know what he'd done, but knew it was his fault. He patted down Cheuk-Kwan's body to find a wound to heal. "What happened? Where are you hurt?" If he didn't know what was wrong, he couldn't help. "Hey, Cheuk-Kwan, what happened? Tell me," he insisted, getting frantic. "I don't see anything!"

"If you wanted to help, you should have . . ." Blood dribbled over Cheuk-Kwan's lips as he spoke.

"And leave you to die? Who do you think I am?"

"Go away," Cheuk-Kwan said, then repeated louder, "Go away!"

"No, no, not until I—"

The scream rattled the entire house: "*GO AWAY!*" It flung Tinseng back. The sound cut ribbons into him as he slumped against the wall, and the slicing didn't stop. His flesh kept peeling from invisible blades. If he stayed, he'd die.

He slammed the door shut on his brother and ran down the hallway, panting, sobbing. He heard his own voice even though he didn't speak: *Some values are more important than others.*

He went blank for a while, the dream losing focus as he sunk into unconscious terror. When he emerged, the house had become darker, more menacing. He knew what came next, but all he could do was walk toward it.

"S-stay back," she said, "My brother is here, he'll be coming back any minute."

"Yukying, it's me." He spread his arms in a surrendering movement; as he did, he realized he was holding a knife. Had he always been holding that knife? Yes, perhaps he had. Her eyes tracked it, darting between its gleam and his face.

"Who are you?"

"It's me—it's Tinseng."

"I don't know you," she repeated. "Stay away from me. Do you want money?" She held out her hands. Fistfuls of coins clattered to the floor. "Please take it, whatever you want."

"I don't want anything, Yukying, it's *me*."

She shook her head, tears streaming down at whatever horrors she saw in his face. He moved forward, but she scuttled back, so terrified of him she couldn't speak.

"Yukying, I know what's doing this. It's the house! It's not me, it must be the house. If we leave, you'll remember. Come on!"

He reached out to take her hand. All the lights flickered. "Come on, this will work. Trust me. Please?"

She shook her head. *No, no no no.* The scream trapped in her throat made the lightbulbs rattle in their fixtures. Impatience welled within him: he knew how to fix it, and she wouldn't listen. He stepped forward to pull her outside. He knew the answer, and if she wouldn't listen he'd make the choice for both of them—

He knew what came next. There was a knife in his hand, and the dream wanted to use it. It would be an accident. He wouldn't mean to do it. But it was coming, and he couldn't stop it. Did he even want to stop?

After this, there would only be one person left. He would be waiting for Tinseng in his mother's library, reading the poem. He was waiting, and Tinseng would go to him.

*There's no stopping any of this*, he thought as the knife slipped between Yukying's ribs. There never was.

※

A hand shook his shoulder.

For all his desperation to escape the nightmare, Tinseng didn't wake immediately. His mind folded the sensation into the dream, a piece of the house trying to capture him. He shuddered trying to shake it off. The hand shook him again, a little harder. This time the dream finally shattered as he heard, "Tinseng." It was his favorite person's voice.

"We brought you breakfast," his other favorite person added. He opened his eyes to find them both smiling down at him. He searched Yukying's face for any of the fear from his dream.

"You look tired, A-Seng. Did you rest well?"

"Bad dreams," he admitted, then felt guilty when they both looked worried. "But I'm fine now. Did I hear something about breakfast?"

At the little table, he and Yukying took the chairs. Jinzhao sat perched on the very end of the bed. Once he finished eating, Tinseng fumbled to shake a cigarette from his crumpled package. Jinzhao held the lighter, cupping his hand to keep the flame steady.

With no further distractions, Tinseng sighed. "So, Yukying. What do you think you saw?"

"Our first night," she said, "I saw Shan Dao returning to his room around midnight. I thought it was odd, since you said he always went to sleep early. The second night, I saw him leaving Mr. Grodescu's room, with Mr. Grodescu inside. Mrs. Grodescu mentioned they planned to visit Tamariz Beach, and then I got a note from you saying our plans had changed from Carcavelos to Tamariz. I didn't want to assume anything, and I'm sorry I thought that about you, Shan Dao. I just wanted to make sure Tinseng was safe."

"No apology necessary," Jinzhao said, as Tinseng insisted, "I can take care of myself, you know."

"Of course," Yukying patted his hand.

"So, I suppose you're curious what really happened?" he asked.

She indulged him with an equally nonchalant, "A little."

"Well," Tinseng settled back in his chair. He loved telling a good story. "The first thing you need to know is that Lucas Grodescu is a dangerous man. Maybe the most dangerous you've ever met. He calls himself a courier, or a middle-man. He started as a blackmailer, but he's much more than that now. He sells secrets to governments. They all buy from him, and they'd be sorry to see him go, because they need intel and he's one of their best sources. I'm only telling you this so you understand. We've had to be careful."

"I understand."

"Grodescu is motivated only by money. That's why he can't give up the personal blackmailing. He'll sell anything and ruin anyone. If you can't pay, he'll toss your secret to the press, or the police, or your spouse—whatever will do the most damage. He's like a tic, getting fat off his host. He's merciless underneath all that charm."

"Charm?" She repeated skeptically.

"You're right. Sleaze is better. You weren't taken in by him, were you?"

"I entertain politicians every night, A-Seng," she admonished softly. "And I've talked with his wife. She's scared of him."

"I wouldn't be surprised if he's holding something over her," Tinseng said. "But I bet you're wondering why we know about Grodescu in the first place. Why are we involved with him?"

Here was the part he'd been dreading. Tinseng didn't mind lying in general; he saw it as a means to an end, and the lies he told were mostly harmless. But lying to Yukying had always been difficult.

"Because . . ." Tinseng inhaled his cigarette and looked at Jinzhao. "I've run into some trouble."

"Grodescu knows about Tinseng," Jinzhao added.

They'd decided Jinzhao would talk rarely and would tell Yukying the biggest lie. Considering how Jinzhao felt about outright lies, it had been a startling offer. Tinseng knew it came from guilt. That hadn't stopped him from accepting; it was a smart plan. Yukying would be watching for lies from Tinseng but wouldn't know Jinzhao's tells.

"Knows wh—" They watched Yukying's eyes grow wide. "Oh."

"He is blackmailing him," Jinzhao continued. "He has photographs."

"*Oh.*" Yukying blinked a few times. "Oh, I'm so sorry, Tinseng." Worry lines deepened around her eyes. "So yesterday, you were . . ?"

"Understanding his terms."

"We'll pay whatever he wants," Yukying said in her most serious voice, covering Tinseng's hand and staring so intently that he blinked. "Whatever it is."

"Ah," Tinseng cleared his throat of the sudden emotion stuck there. He'd imagined Yukying's reaction to this lie to be . . . well, not this. "Jiejie, you're too good. But it's not so simple. We'll never be rid of him, as long as he has those photos." That much was true, at least.

Yukying stared down at the floor.

When the quiet stretched too long, Tinseng said softly, "It'll be fine. Like I said yesterday, I'm taking care of it. The main thing is, we don't want you to worry."

Yukying sat a moment longer, thinking. Tinseng tried not to rush her. Eventually, she folded her hands in her lap and said, "I think you should tell Cheuk-Kwan."

Tinseng actually laughed. "You think that would go well?"

"He could help."

"Could he? *Would* he? I think I remember his friends saying homosexuality was simply the product of trauma under capitalism. Or was it fascism? They could never agree," he explained to Jinzhao.

Yukying pursed her lips. "That was a long time ago. He doesn't have those friends anymore, and he doesn't think that way, A-Seng."

"How do you know that?"

"You should tell him about this," she insisted instead of answering his question. "He might surprise you."

Tinseng's laugh was harsh and dry, tinder eager to light. He was losing his grip on the mask of the brother Yukying knew; he saw the confusion and worry in her face. He shook his head.

"You see the best in everyone, jiejie."

"He loves you. He wants what's best for you. We both do. We just want to see you happy." She lowered her voice. "He would understand, and he *would* help. And if Grodescu sends what he has to someone, Cheuk-Kwan should know before that happens."

Tinseng sucked his teeth and wished his sister weren't so nice. "I'll think about it. But for now, please keep this to yourself?"

Yukying nodded. "Of course."

For a moment the only noise was the ship's engines. Then Yukying picked up her head and asked, "What do you plan to do next?"

"Next? Uh." Tinseng thought through what he'd do if this lie was the truth and found it very similar to his actual situation. "We need to find out where he's hiding the photos. It could be in the briefcase he carries sometimes. I searched his room yesterday before I came to the beach but didn't find anything."

Yukying blinked, shocked. "That was dangerous, Tinseng."

"It had to be done," he said with a shrug. "And now we have to find a way to figure out if it's on him."

"His wife might have some idea where he keeps things," Yukying said. "I've talked to her a few times now. I could say it's because of . . . well, I'd think of something."

"No, no, no," he said, shaking his head against the idea.

"But I think she trusts me," she said. "What harm is there in asking? We're on the ship all day and most of tomorrow besides the stop in Gibraltar. Why don't we use the time wisely?"

Tinseng felt himself unraveling a little. Jinzhao must have sensed it, because he returned his gaze from where it had been far away, and said, "Your brother worries for you. The worst thing he could experience is being responsible for you getting hurt."

It was just like Mei Jinzhao to gather everything in Tinseng's heart and express it as concisely as possible. When Jinzhao said it, it sounded true and immutable, which was exactly how it felt to Tinseng. He couldn't imagine what he would do if anything happened to Yukying, but he knew he wouldn't want to survive it.

"Shan Dao speaks so eloquently," Tinseng said, staring at his lifeline. Jinzhao met the stare, a little misty around the eyes.

"Shan Dao," Yukying's gentle voice pulled them back, "it sounds like you might be part of this family someday."

"I hope so," Jinzhao said.

Tinseng's head whipped around—that was news to him. But Yukying just nodded as if she'd expected that answer.

"Well, then. You should know we have always taken care of each other, no matter what." Yukying took Tinseng's hand. "Family helps each other and stands by each other's side. There is nothing I wouldn't do for Tinseng. Knowing that in my heart means I can do anything."

That old catchphrase of their parents—the sentiment that had gotten his adoptive mother killed—should be something he hated. He'd read the text so many times as punishment that he still knew it by heart. He should hate to hear it, but the words never failed to make him shiver, as though feeling their power for the very first time. The idea had been written on his sinew and muscle, growing as he'd grown; not what he was born with but what he was made from.

"You're right," he said quietly. He didn't look at Jinzhao, who would be upset; he could deal with that later. Instead, he said more loudly, "Of course you're right!" He pulled her into an embrace and declared, "You've never been wrong, ever, not a single time."

"That's not true, you silly boy." She hugged him back tightly. "Thank you, A-Seng," she murmured in his ear, words just for him. "Thank you for letting me help."

Tinseng closed his eyes and rested his forehead on her shoulder, and tried not to think of everything that could happen to this woman in his arms, all because of him.

∞

Once they'd agreed to a plan and Yukying left, Tinseng collapsed back into his chair, exhausted. Yukying had never been the impulsive one or the one with the temper. But she'd seen just as much destruction, he realized.

Not as much death, maybe, but perhaps more devastation: Over the last few days, as she'd shared stories about families she'd helped, she'd been careful to only share happy endings. But sometimes the silences spoke for her. In all the time he'd known her, he couldn't think of a time when her kindness had really wavered. For the first time, he wondered how exhausting that must be. He was angry, so angry, that she'd taken this risk. But wasn't she doing exactly what he would have done? Wouldn't that be too hypocritical, even for him, to deny her the right to action?

He sighed as he sat back with his cigarette and wished that just *one* time his plans would turn out the way he wanted.

Jinzhao had been quiet since Tinseng agreed to let Yukying help, withdrawing in on himself. Tinseng had ignored it, but now his time had run out. His head dropped back against the chair's back.

"What happened to doing it my way?" he asked the ceiling. "You wanted me to tell her no? After how determined she was to help yesterday? Trailing you, dancing with Grodescu. She was already thinking of befriending Mrs. Grodescu; she would have done it with or without our permission." He rolled his head to peer at Jinzhao. "Better to have it in our control, trust me."

"She believes this is for you."

"You think she wouldn't do the same for you? Didn't you hear her before? You're practically family. You're going to love the dinners," he snickered. "Besides, it's okay to help those you love."

"Even if it violates her principles?"

"Some principles are more important than others," he said slowly, knowing they weren't talking about Yukying anymore. "Her first priority is to her family. She loves me, and to her, that's more important than lying to a stranger."

"What about lying to her husband?" Jinzhao pushed.

"It won't come to that."

"What about lying to the authorities?"

"I won't let it get that far."

"What about—"

"Jinzhao."

They both breathed heavily.

"It is *wrong*," Jinzhao asserted.

"What's wrong?"

"To selfishly insist on one's individual gain at the expense of others. To have others suffer for my secrets. They're my responsibility; to make others bear them is immoral."

"*Tsk*. Who knew Mei Jinzhao would be such a martyr? Have you always been this bad at sharing your things?"

Tinseng closed his eyes and waited for the rebuttal, then drifted a little until he sensed something wrong about Jinzhao's silence; he couldn't articulate why, only that he'd learned the sound of his silences, a dialect all its own. Tinseng peered over to find pain twisting Jinzhao's face like silk clenched in a fist. Tinseng immediately dropped into a state of panic, agitated into an explosion of movement that propelled him in front of Jinzhao.

"Hey, hey, no, no, no being sad." He shook Jinzhao's shoulders a little, as if he could rattle the sadness out of him. "No, you hear me? I can't handle it. Don't do this to me. I really will go kill him, Jinzhao; don't think I won't."

Peeking out from his pretense, he tentatively asked, "Is it just Yukying being in danger?"

Jinzhao slowly shook his head.

"Is it what I said about being a martyr?"

A slight shrug, so he was getting closer.

"I didn't mean it, and it's not like you to listen to me anyway—who told you to start now? You should listen to Yukying, she's much—"

Jinzhao's shoulders tensed under his hands.

"It's what Yukying said?"

A nod.

"About us? About . . . I know she assumed too much, but it didn't seem worth it to correct her, but I'll go now, to correct her, obviously—"

He cut himself off as Jinzhao raised his head. His eyes were bloodshot as if he'd been crying, though no tears had fallen. Jinzhao's voice was so quiet Tinseng had to lean in to hear.

"I," the words came slowly, "am going to ruin another family."

*Fuck,* Tinseng swore in his head. *Fuck you, Mei Hankong, Li Xifeng; you never deserved him.* He didn't know if that was actually true—Jinzhao seemed to have really loved his mother—but from where Tinseng was standing, all that house seemed to produce was pain. He thought of his dream and struggled not to wince.

"Ridiculous, Jinzhao. *I* haven't ruined the family, so how could you?"

That was the wrong tactic to take, from Jinzhao's expression.

Tinseng immediately tried another: "And arrogant, too, to think it was you alone who ruined things. It seems like your parents were doing most of that work themselves."

Jinzhao shook his head again, though it seemed more reflex than rejection. They were getting closer; just a little more work, and maybe Tinseng could coax out a smile.

"Hey, aren't we supposed to be on vacation? Like Yukying said, we have all day today, all day tomorrow, Málaga, then Barcelona. Villefranche isn't for four whole days. What are we doing, worrying so much?"

"We're worrying the correct amount," Jinzhao said, but it was petulant, clinging to sadness already half-dissipated.

"Well, you can worry in the pool, can't you?" Tinseng took his hand and pulled him up. "Come on, I need to be out of this room."

# CHAPTER EIGHT

*Four Years Ago. December, 1959. Hong Kong.*

It was all because she'd forgotten her datebook. Nobody was supposed to be home that afternoon, and the laughter when she opened the front door surprised her. Curious, she walked toward the sound.

Tinseng's bedroom door was cracked open, and she peered through. Tinseng was on the bed with another man. Both their shirts were off. Tinseng was the one laughing, his head thrown back, as the other man . . .

She slipped away quickly, unobserved.

The rest of the day passed in a fog. As she floated through her errands, she could smell hay; around corners, when she tilted her head, a phantom smell lodged in her nostrils. They'd hidden in the back of a cart to get to the border. She had been sixteen. The hay had tickled her nose, and she'd been so afraid of sneezing. She thought about Tinseng getting caught and dragged out into the street, being beaten or worse—she thought she might throw up.

What was she supposed to do? Should she confront Tinseng? Pretend she hadn't seen anything? That would be easier, but she was the oldest; she had to be responsible.

A small, young part of her missed her mother so much she wanted to cry.

The other volunteer at church sent her home early, and Yukying didn't fight the decision. She left in a daze and started down the street. She still had to buy ingredients for the ching po leung tonight. With a head full of noise, Yukying went to the market and tried to think of what to say.

The pot was at a rolling boil when Tinseng walked in, threw his bag on the floor, and yelled a welcome.

"Tinseng, come here," she called to him.

"Of course, jiejie! Ooh, is that soup?"

"It's not ready yet. Here, eat this if you're hungry." She took a deep breath, swallowed down her fear, and looked him in the eyes. "Tinseng, I forgot my datebook today. I had to come back to get it."

"You did? But I didn't see you."

"No," she said, "You didn't. You were busy with other things."

"I don't—" Tinseng's mouth fell open a little, then closed tightly. She watched him take a step back from her: her little brother putting distance between them, pulling taut the threads they'd sewn between their two hearts—any further, and they'd all snap.

"It isn't what you think," he said in his most convincing tone, and with horrible clarity, she realized she had to find a way to keep him here in this kitchen. If she said the wrong thing, he'd bolt. The next time she saw him, he'd be a stranger; she already saw the mask falling into place. She had to think quickly if she didn't want to lose him.

"I think I need help chopping these green onions," she said.

"I . . . what?" He blinked, confused.

"Come here and help me cut these. If you're going to eat, you should help," she insisted, and after a moment's hesitation, he picked up the knife and started chopping. She watched a moment, then laughed quietly and crowded his space.

"I remember teaching you better than this. Look, you still don't put your thumb where you should." She covered his hand with hers, but he startled, the knife clattering to the board. They avoided each other's eyes. "Some things never change, do they, A-Seng?"

"You don't change," Tinseng said earnestly. "You're always the best."

"And you'll always be my little brother," she said.

"Your little brother who can't hold a knife properly."

"My little brother who forgets to take care of himself." Quietly, still not looking at him, she said, "You know you have to be careful now."

"I know." His voice was barely audible. There was no one else in the house, but it still felt dangerous to speak of it out loud. "I'll never let anyone drag you into this. It will never come back to your family, Yukying, I promise. I'll go bow before your mother and promise her too."

Yukying sighed and took the knife from his hand. "All you need to promise me is that you'll look after yourself and stay out of trouble."

"I will."

---

*Six Days Ago. June 19, 1963. At Sea.*

Four years later, she stood over her brother as he had a nightmare. She touched his shoulder gently to wake him and then listened to his story about a man who blackmailed for a living, an immoral man motivated only by profit. Tinseng painted the picture of a greedy mouth slavering to devour, and Yukying wondered what this had to do with any of them, except she knew. How could she not know? She had carried the fear in her heart since that day in December.

So, four years later, when Tinseng sat nonchalantly smoking a cigarette in his pajamas and said, "Because I've run into some trouble," Yukying knew what this was about. What it was always, inevitably, going to be about.

Over the years, some part of her had wondered whether it would be a relief, almost, if something did happen—at least then there would be a resolution. Now with the fear realized, Yukying saw what a fool she'd been to think that. How could she ever have thought certainty would be a comfort in the face of losing her brother's safety?

Head spinning with secrets, Yukying left Tinseng and Shan Dao in a daze. She walked down the hall to her own room and lay down, hugging a pillow for comfort as she tried to think.

She'd had four years to come to terms with her brother being homosexual, or at least having those tendencies. She hadn't gone out of her way to seek out books on the subject, as that would have drawn attention; where would she get them, anyway? Instead, she listened where she wouldn't have before. From a Party friend, she heard homosexuality was the cause of fascism. "Like Gorky says," the friend proclaimed at dinner, "exterminate all the homosexuals, and fascism will vanish." From one of her brother's coworkers, she heard instead that homosexuality was simply trauma suffered under capitalism. When she visited refugees from Shekou, she heard it called the White man's disease from Chinese families who don't know their own history. No one seemed to know what kind of immorality homosexuality fell under, or what was to blame for its existence.

Her conservative church friends often discussed the newest psychoanalytic theories in drawing rooms after dinner: how to stop the masculinization of women that was producing a breed of increasingly feminine men, and whether Freud was correct when he wrote that a man's love for other men masked his forbidden love for his mother. Her liberal church friends insisted that legalization of buggery was coming to England in the next ten years, possibly five—it was inevitable, they said, as the tide of public opinion turned. And once it was legal in England, surely it was only a matter of time for its colonies. But Yukying couldn't imagine that for Hong Kong, not when the vitriol was so vast and so varied. Perhaps if the rejection was coming only from the British, or only the Chinese. But with enough agreement from both sides on the issue, they would never see change.

She hugged her pillow tighter at the thought. It was so bloody hypocritical, she thought, for Hong Kongers to call her brother a deviant. After all, what would Westerners call the majority of marriages in Hong Kong? Most of the marriages she knew weren't Western registry marriages; they were customary marriages following the six rites. And yes, those marriages were legal under British code, recognized as a fundamental part of their way of life, but what would Mrs. Lanzette say, or Mrs. Duncan? Or, worse, if she explained to them that concubinage was still quite a common practice in Hong Kong, that a concubine in Hong Kong had more legal protections than wives in most Western countries, and that she herself found it perfectly acceptable? Would they listen? How would they react if she tried to explain that she knew of no single marital tradition and held no importance to the union between one man and one woman?

She knew exactly what would happen. They would look at her with pity and dismiss her culture whole cloth with the wave of a hand.

How was she supposed to accept the same dismissal from her own people? How was Tinseng? How was he supposed to live in this place they so desperately wanted to call home, and how could they call it home when it wanted to kill him?

By the time Laurence returned from his morning tennis, there was something strange buzzing under her skin like summer heat. She had always been cold—iron deficiency, a recent doctor diagnosed—but this felt like it could keep her warm for a long time if she let it catch. She couldn't do that. She had watched her mother live in her anger; she saw A-Kwan doing the same. She couldn't let her anger at the injustices of the world turn her into an inferno. Yukying would burn quickly, and the rage would leave nothing behind. That was how it went in her family. She had to let it all go; she didn't want to be the type of person who carried this around inside. But how did one get rid of anger, except to let it burn?

"Are you resting?" Laurence asked as he set down his racket. He began to say something else but she interrupted,

"Laurence." She meant to say more, but her voice cracked.

"Oh—what, um, are you—"

"Come here, please?"

He obeyed, lying down next to her. Before he could ask, she pressed her face into his shirt and started to cry. Her tears were silent, but her shoulders shook; his hands rubbed soothing circles on her back. The motions of simple comfort made her cry harder, but her tears dried quickly; soon she leaned her cheek on his chest and breathed slowly, gathering her calm back to her center.

"How can you be crying?" he asked as he smoothed her hair down. "We're on vacation."

Her laugh came out a hiccup. She didn't always appreciate his distance from emotions, the way he rarely understood how a person could be overcome by them, but now she let him ground her. She wasn't Tinseng; she didn't have to experience life as though being tossed around by a hurricane.

"You're right. We are on vacation." She accepted his handkerchief and dabbed her eyes dry. "I'm sorry."

"No reason to apologize," he said, flustered as he always was during these displays. "Did your brothers say something?"

"No, no. It's all right. I'm fine now."

"If you're sure," he said in a tone that implied he didn't believe her but wouldn't push. She hugged him again, warmly this time, and he pulled her close.

"Do you have plans the rest of the day?" she asked into his shoulder.

"None," he said. "What do you want to do?"

"Spend time with you. Let's watch this morning's movie together. What else?"

"The band is playing jazz from America tonight," Laurence said.

"Let's do that, then, just us. I'll tell Tinseng to keep everyone away for a few hours."

"Have I ever told you you're brilliant?" Laurence asked, and she laughed, easier this time. When they finally rose from bed, her anger wasn't gone, but it no longer felt like a consumption. That was all she could hope for.

The rest of the day, Yukying kept her promise. They listened to American jazz and shared an extravagant dessert ordered to their room. They ate it in robes in the middle of their bed, despite Laurence's protestations that they would drip chocolate sauce on the sheets. It was nothing they couldn't do at home, and yet they'd never done it. The day felt decadent, all the more because they planned to do nothing tomorrow. The ship would anchor at Gibraltar for a half-day for those interested, then they'd set off again that night, sailing the short distance to Málaga and docking there for the night. Yukying went to sleep knowing she'd have to find Marissa the next day, but after the despair of earlier, she found herself eager for action. Tinseng needed help and she was determined to do something. Whatever she could, to keep him safe.

※

*Five Days Ago. June 20, 1963. Gibraltar.*

On the fifth day of her vacation, Yukying woke naturally and lay in bed, pleasantly lazy, waiting for sunlight to leak in around the edges of the curtains. When it did, she rose and pulled on a simple cheongsam, slid on flats, and pinned up her hair in a quick bun, hiding the imperfections under a hat. With a kiss to Laurence's forehead, she slipped out of the room and walked up to the first-class deck.

No staff guarded the boundary at this hour, to the benefit of some enterprising children playing in pools usually off-limits to them. A few roller-skated around the empty deck. On their next pass, she waved to them, but they ignored her, uninterested in an adult; she smiled at the rejection, remembering Chiboon and Tinseng's absolute disdain for authority, and scanned the deck for a seat with the best view. Gibraltar would reveal itself soon, proclaiming its majesty out of the horizon. In one of the chairs, she recognized a familiar profile. He stared out at the sea from his chair, his gaze unwavering. It flickered when she reached his periphery, then returned to the unending stretch of blue.

"Isn't the sky beautiful here?" she asked Shan Dao. "I think I could look at it forever. It's so different than Hong Kong."

"How so?"

"That's right," she said with a laugh, "I keep forgetting you've never been. You seem such a part of everything already." That seemed to embarrass him, though she thought she caught a smile as he ducked his head. "In Hong Kong, the sky is rarely so uninterrupted. Even when I stand on the edge of the shore, the ocean doesn't feel endless. I suppose because I can still hear the city right behind me. But right now . . ."

A quiet awareness rushed into the space she left between them. In the distance, seagulls greeted the morning. The hum of the ship's massive engines rumbled beneath them. Around the corner, roller skates thumped on the wood planks. The children laughed as they skated past. Shan Dao exchanged a bemused look with her, then smiled fully as she laughed.

"Still," she said, "this is still much quieter than it ever is back home. Was it quiet where you lived?"

"Yes. Then I had to move suddenly. Tinseng was gracious and offered his home. His neighborhood was loud, but I'd visited before and knew to expect it."

They hadn't told her they had been living together. She was careful not to react in case Shan Dao thought she had already known.

"Tinseng has never lived somewhere quiet, so I imagine that brought him comfort. But I hope it didn't bother you too much."

"I adjusted."

"What was his apartment like? I never got the chance to see it." She would never know that part of his life now. Tinseng had already moved on, in that way of his that left no room for questions. "I hope he kept it clean when you lived with him."

"It was . . . reflective of his personality. Not polished, but well-loved." With fondness, Shan Dao added, "I did have to buy him bookshelves."

Yukying shook her head. "He was always tripping over something he'd left out."

"He split his lip once on *Les Contemplations*. It was untenable."

"He's lucky you were there to look after him." She turned to better face him. "Did you like living in Paris?"

"Tolerably." He seemed to recognize that one-word answers bordered on rude, so expanded, "It wasn't my plan to stay as long as I did. I was visiting to conduct a lecture series. Then I met Tinseng."

"Where did you want to go?"

"Back to China, to join my brother. It was my father's wish for a long time, and we had finally made it happen. Then . . . my priorities shifted."

"And now you're going to Hong Kong?"

"*Mm*. I will go wherever Tinseng goes."

Shan Dao's sentences sat disconnected, missing all their sinew. Yukying tried to hear everything he wasn't saying. Did he mean they had talked about their plans? Would they both be moving in with her after all? They'd lived together in Paris—but Shan Dao made it sound like a temporary situation, and Tinseng was always the type to help a friend in need. Was Shan Dao helping Tinseng through this blackmail crisis to repay his debt, or was he really as lovelorn as he seemed? And did any of that matter while Tinseng was in danger? Perhaps it mattered even more than in regular times.

"I feel so confused," she admitted with a slight laugh. "I apologize, Shan Dao, I'm being a horrible conversationalist. I just keep thinking about this man, Grodescu. Why would he want to do this? I mean," she continued, "I understand *why*. I won't ask something like, *why is there evil in the world*, that would be silly." Those had never felt like questions for her. She didn't read Proust; she read movie magazines. And yet. "But . . . ever since yesterday I've been thinking about a line from Li Xifeng's journal—I don't know if you've read it. She was writing about a dinner party of her husband's colleagues; they were discussing nuclear war and how China had nothing to fear, because even if China lost half their population in a war, there'd still be three-hundred million left to build a communist society afterward. Three-hundred million dead, but that was acceptable. And she wished she had quoted Khrushchev to them, the one when he said: 'I can't say let us make war, half would die, the other half would survive; they would put me in a straitjacket.'" Yukying ran her hands down her dress, then tucked her feet under her. "But it's really what she wrote after that. I wish I could remember exactly . . ."

"'Is everything so hopeless? Can nothing be done?'"

Yukying looked up, surprised. "You've read it."

"Closely."

"I've been thinking about that. What can be done. She wrote a question, but she already knew her answer. She didn't think everything was hopeless, or she wouldn't have tried. I was thinking about it because it seems to me that she could have gone along with the popular opinion, but she didn't. She was doing something, wasn't she? Maybe not the right thing, but . . . at least she was trying to help. If we're not trying to help, was it really the right thing to do?"

Between men who thought a sacrifice of half the population was an acceptable loss and a man who considered that idea morally insane, Yukying knew whose side she would be on, even if those men at the dinner held the more popular idea. Between the men in her life who loved differently than how the world wanted them to, and everyone who would gladly see those men destroyed, it was another easy choice.

Shan Dao had been staring at her with a strange expression for a long time, she realized.

"I'm sorry," she said, "I don't usually ramble like this."

"No, I—I was rude for staring. I was lost in thought. I . . ." Shan Dao trailed off into a murmur. "'She craves not Spring for herself alone.'"

"That's beautiful. It sounds familiar . . ."

"'Ode to the Plum Blossom.'"

"The poem you argued with A-Seng about!"

"Yes. It was a favorite of my mother's. Li Xifeng . . . when you mentioned her, I thought of my own mother." Shan Dao stopped, then continued, seemingly despite himself, "Sometimes it was difficult to understand what she wanted of me."

Tinseng had warned them not to ask about Shan Dao's parents, and Yukying could see why. His voice sounded very far away.

"I wanted to ask," she said each word carefully, "how are *you* doing?"

In the early morning shade, she could just make out his expression: confused, as if the question was out of place. Her heart ached a little.

"Of course, this has been very hard on Tinseng, but it must be difficult on you too. His exposure could harm you as well. And you're so far away from home, and your brother. If you wanted to talk about anything I would listen, not as Tinseng's sister, but as a friend."

His eyes fixed on her as she spoke. How different this gaze was than Lucas Grodescu's, she thought, the comparison immediate and helpless. She'd felt horribly pinned by the Frenchman's attention. Shan Dao's gaze was no less intense, but where Grodescu's hunger had reached outward to consume, Shan Dao's caved inward like a crumbling cliff.

"I am well. Thank you for asking." His eyes flickered away, then back. "I would also listen. As a friend. Rest assured I would not betray your confidence. Tinseng would not hear of—"

"Oh, no, I know," Yukying interrupted. "You're a very good listener."

"I've been told I keep secrets well." His tone was droll; Yukying suspected he was thinking of Tinseng.

"I believe it. How about this," she proposed with a twinkle in her eye. "When I have a secret to share, you'll be the first to know."

"A generous offer." His expression didn't change, but she felt something shift, permanently, between them. "I accept."

---

Though she had spent all of yesterday with Laurence, she had still made sure to follow through on her promise to help. The night before, she had initiated a small subterfuge in the form of bribing young Miss Duncan. She asked the girl to ask Marissa's plans at mealtime, then report back to Yukying; in exchange, Yukying had agreed to be Miss Duncan's escort to the first-class lounge, a privilege the girl desperately longed to lord over her brothers. The mutually beneficial exchange meant that soon enough Yukying knew that Marissa planned to visit Gibraltar in the morning with her husband, then cards in the afternoon with Mrs. Duncan. For an additional afternoon in the lounge of her choice, Miss Duncan agreed to ensure Yukying a seat at the card table.

And so, after the early morning conversation with Shan Dao and a pleasant half-day lounging poolside reading her book, Yukying headed down to the second-class lounge for bridge. Marissa was at the table already, paired as promised with Mrs. Duncan. Miss Duncan, who had "forgotten" to bring a fourth, waved Yukying over to the table with an unsubtle grin.

Yukying waited until the middle of the second round to ask casually, "Have you heard there were some thefts in second class?"

"Yes!" Miss Duncan leaned in. "My brother told me about it."

"Happens on every cruise," Mrs. Duncan said dismissively. "Can't be avoided."

"It was a string of real pearls!" continued Miss Duncan as though her mother hadn't spoken. "The crew is trying to keep it from getting out—it reflects poorly on them, of course—but isn't it exciting? Like 'The Adventure of the Blue Carbuncle'!"

"I don't think they'll be finding the pearls in any geese, dear," her mother said.

"Well, you never know," Miss Duncan pouted. "Who do you think it is? One of the staff? Somebody in steering? Ooh, someone in first class, stealing for the thrill of it?"

"I admit, I'm a bit concerned," Yukying said, attempting to steer the conversation back where she needed it. "With the gifts we've bought everyone, I'd hate to see them go missing. I do miss having a hotel safe."

"There isn't much to be done, is there?" Mrs. Duncan set her cigarette on the tray to play a card. "That's why I told Roger not to bring anything he wouldn't mind losing. Then what does he do? Brings his grandfather's pocket watch. For what, I asked? To tell the time, he says."

"Does he keep it on him all the time, then?" Yukying asked, trying not to sound delighted at the perfect opening.

"No. And if it gets stolen, I told him, whose fault is that?"

"What about your husband, Mrs. Grodescu? Is he worried about these thefts?"

"No," Marissa said. "He did not bring anything of value on the trip."

"Really?" Yukying persisted. "Not even something he carries on him, like Mr. Duncan's pocket watch?"

"He knew better," Marissa mumbled, more to her cards than the table.

"He knows better than *Roger*, in any case," Mrs. Duncan said, and that was the end of that. Yukying sank back into her chair and resolved to wait for another chance.

After three more rounds, Marissa rose to take a break. Yukying waited until she was away, then made her excuses and followed. She kept Marissa in sight and followed her down the spiral staircase at the back of the lounge to one of the smaller bars. She joined Marissa at the counter, but before she had the chance to make small talk, the bored bartender jumped up to take their order.

"Gin rickey," Marissa ordered as she lit a cigarette. "A double. You?"

"A sloe gin fizz, please."

As the bartender made their drinks, Yukying twisted her wedding ring and thought again about the questions Tinseng suggested she ask.

Hooks, he'd called them, but they were just lies. Yukying couldn't do that. She liked Marissa, and her instincts told her Marissa would see right through any lie she attempted. After all, Mrs. Grodescu would be used to a much higher caliber of liar. If she was to win Marissa's trust, she probably shouldn't be caught fumbling a manipulation. So, with a mental apology to Tinseng, she threw out his strategy and tried her own.

"It was lovely running into you in Lisbon," Yukying said. "Perhaps we can meet again tomorrow in Málaga, or Barcelona, if you know where you're going?"

"I am not sure."

"No plan at all? Would you like suggestions? Perhaps we could rent a cabana together in Málaga, if you like the beach."

"We spent too much time in the sun today. Tomorrow we will likely go to museums."

"Then what about tonight? Do you plan to attend the dance? Sometimes it's easier, with a crowd."

Marissa turned, eyes narrowed. "What do you mean?"

"I only mean . . ." (but the problem was no one just *said* these things, especially not to strangers) ". . . that a buffer can be welcome, on these vacations where one is trapped in such close quarters with one's husband. I would welcome your company, and I'm sure Laurence would love to talk more with Mr. Grodescu."

"You're very kind, Mrs. Li." Marissa watched her as if from a far distance. "Too kind. Sticking your nose into business that is not yours is a very sure way to break it."

"I don't mean—"

"I'm sure you don't."

The bartender returned with their drinks and Marissa walked away, leaving Yukying to trail behind in misery. She'd insulted Marissa, surely. Assumed too much, pushed too hard. What if she'd ruined her chances? Worse yet, perhaps Marissa would go back and tell her husband?

As she worried herself into a state, the table played four more rounds until the staff announced the room needed to be turned over for the next activity. Yukying was the last to leave, picking up after everyone so the waiters had an easier time. As she stacked glasses, she heard a low voice to her right.

"What are you planning to do?"

Marissa hovered just behind her. Yukying kept facing the table, sweeping up peanut shells with her hand.

"Whatever I can to help my brother," Yukying said honestly.

"Do you know what my husband does?"

"Yes." Their voices barely rose above a whisper, though none of the men filing into the room had any interest in them. "Do you?"

Marissa's laugh was jagged. "More than most."

Yukying swallowed, then straightened and looked at the other woman. "Do you help him?"

"*Never.*" In her eyes Yukying saw the same anger that had overwhelmed her in bed yesterday: that cold burning that had no name.

"Then..." Yukying brushed the peanut dust off her hands and reached out; Marissa flinched visibly, then relaxed and let Yukying grasp her arm. "Believe me, all we want is to stop him from hurting my brother, or anyone else."

Marissa shook her head. "He cannot be stopped."

"That can't be true," Yukying said gently. "Marissa, why do you think that?"

Marissa grimaced against her tears. She shook her head again, unable to speak, but that was answer enough. What had this woman seen and suffered because of this man?

"Does he..." Yukying stumbled, but her gaze raked over Marissa as if looking for visible proof, and Marissa understood.

"He does not have to. If you know his business, you know why." Marissa looked around nervously at the passengers settling in to listen to the horse races, then stepped forward. "You do not understand. He knows someone is closing in. He suspects all of you. He wanted me to get closer to you to learn more."

Yukying swallowed. "What will you tell him?"

"That you are a stupid housewife who knows nothing. He will probably believe me."

Yukying thought about the way Lucas Grodescu moved her around the dance floor. The way he'd looked at her. She wasn't sure he'd believe anyone but himself.

"Can you tell me anything?" Yukying asked. She gently steered Marissa back toward the stairs to the bar. "Anything at all that might help us? We're looking for photographs he's carrying. Do you know where that is?"

"He has many papers. No photographs."

"Are you sure? These are . . . special."

Marissa searched Yukying's face. Yukying tried to channel Tinseng, thinking of his resoluteness. He'd always taken on so much for others, and she hoped to show a sliver of that strength to Marissa.

"I have not seen any photographs," Marissa said, "but I think he plans to follow one of your group. I am not sure who, or when, just that he said a Chinese man. And he has business in Barcelona. A meeting soon after we arrive, near a post office."

"Thank you. Thank you, Marissa."

"Don't thank me. You will get yourself killed."

"If there's anything I can do—"

But Marissa was already gone. Yukying took a deep breath and pressed her palm onto the bar counter. Adrenaline drained from her body, and she started to shake.

*A drink sounds very nice*, she thought, and raised her hand to order another round.

# PART FOUR

## MAMA SAID

# CHAPTER NINE

*Four Days Ago. June 21, 1963. Málaga, Spain.*

That night they sailed to Málaga, and after dinner Tinseng led everyone down to Cheuk-Kwan and Chiboon's room to drink from the bottles Tinseng had charmed off one of the bartenders and play records on Chiboon's portable record player. Chiboon taught them to play dominos—"You *have* to know how to play in New York, it's a necessity"—and told them all about America, how it was and wasn't like the place they'd heard so much about. In turn, Tinseng shared stories of Paris—sanitized for the crowd, of course, but fun nonetheless. Then Yukying asked Shan Dao about stories from Bern, and shockingly Jinzhao obliged her, painting a picture of the Swiss Alps that had them all making a pact to rent chalets next year.

"We'll go over the holidays. Tinseng won't be teaching then!" Chiboon exclaimed, scribbling the idea into his notebook; everyone would forget this but him, and the seed would germinate in those pages until the idea became a plan, and the plan became a reality. That was the role Chiboon had always played in their group, taking their offhand dreams and turning them, alchemy-like, into experience.

By the time the party broke up and scattered back to their rooms, Tinseng was very pleasantly drunk, his tongue loose, mind fuzzy. He loved his friends, he really did. He loved his family too—he told Cheuk-Kwan this as he left, punching his brother's arm and receiving a punch in return. Jinzhao's hand hovered near the small of his back as he led him into the hall, and oh, he loved Jinzhao, loved him most of all. He wanted to tell him, but he wasn't *that* drunk: he could still remember Jinzhao's face when Yukying had mentioned being part of their family. Shock, Tinseng thought, he'd seen shock and fear. And why not—wasn't that what Tinseng felt, too, when he thought of family? Hadn't he run halfway around the world because of it? The drink made his thoughts sprint in front of him, and he fell asleep wanting to wrap his arms around Jinzhao, feeling cold without him.

The sixth day of their cruise saw them in Málaga. Málaga was a port like Lisbon with historical attractions and crowded beaches, a place to linger. Their group followed Chiboon's lead first to Alcazaba, a Moorish castle, then to a soaring Renaissance cathedral. Surely they were wonders of the world, but Tinseng couldn't focus on any of it. Yesterday Yukying had planned to talk to Marissa Grodescu, and this morning they hadn't really had the time to talk. Tinseng was waiting for a good moment to draw her aside, and until then he wouldn't be able to think of much else.

They walked out of the cathedral and wandered around the town, splitting up as moods took them. Chiboon had been expecting mail at the post office, and when he returned, he hurried up to Tinseng.

"Tinseng, you have to help me," Chiboon said, clutching him dramatically. Tinseng exchanged a bemused look with Jinzhao.

"I do? Why?"

"My Spanish friends canceled on me tonight; their message just caught up with me. I have to go, and you know I can't go alone."

"He's planning on going to Fauna in Torremolinos," Tinseng explained to Jinzhao.

"The most famous gay bar in Spain," Chiboon told Jinzhao, "about a half-hour drive from Málaga. I've been hearing about it for months. I already rented a car. I *have* to go, Tinseng, and you have to come with me, please."

Tinseng shrugged. "I really don't. We're tired."

"Tinseng, you don't understand! Brian Epstein brought John Lennon there in May! I'll eat off this story for months." Chiboon hung on Tinseng's arm. "I never ask you for anything—"

"Not true—"

"Do this *one* thing for me, gege, please?"

Tinseng wrapped an arm around Chiboon and pulled him close, only to say firmly, "No."

"You're a criminal." Chiboon stomped away in a huff.

"Not yet," Tinseng muttered to Jinzhao. Jinzhao laughed quietly and held the door of a bookstore open for him. A few minutes later, Yukying found them among the high shelves.

"What do you think of this for a-die?" He held up a book on chess.

"I don't know, Tinseng." Yukying didn't even look at the book. "Please listen."

Quickly she told them what Marissa had said yesterday.

"So," Tinseng said, "He plans to follow us and has business in Barcelona. We can work with that. Did she say which post office?"

Yukying shook her head.

"Well, that's okay. We'll split up. While we're here, let's try to find a map of Barcelona. How many post offices could there be?"

"And what about Grodescu trying to follow you?" She placed a hand on his arm. "What are you going to do?"

"He'll have to find us first. What can he do on the ship, jie? It's a locked room mystery: he knows they'll be able to figure out it was him."

"If the photos are on him, won't you have to get close?"

"We will. But we have days until Villefranche." She didn't look reassured. He took her hand off his arm and held it in both of his. "It's fine, Yukying, really! Don't worry about me. Come on, let's buy this for a-die, I think he'll really like it."

They bought a stack of books and reemerged into the Spanish sunlight. Coming out of a café across the street, Chiboon crossed over to them, gathering himself to begin an entire campaign of wheedling. Thinking of how he might avoid his friend's request, Tinseng caught a glimpse of Yukying walking down the street. It sparked a thought: Marissa had said Grodescu meant to follow them. But what if he couldn't?

He cut off Chiboon's pleading before it could start. "Hey, Chiboon, the place you're going tonight. They don't let just anyone in, right?"

"No, you have to know someone. They're very particular, with Franco and everything; they have to be. It isn't exactly France. Even England's more open than here, in some ways, which is really saying something."

"So not just anyone can walk in? They couldn't beat a password out of someone?"

"What? No, no, no, nothing like that. That's why it's so special that I'm inviting you!"

Tinseng nodded, pleased. Let Lucas Grodescu try to follow them *there*.

"Then . . . take us with you, won't you, Chiboon?"

"What, really?" He narrowed his eyes. "Just like that?"

"What can I say? I'm feeling benevolent."

"You're the best! Thank you! You won't regret it. It's going to be incredible, unforgettable, absolutely the highlight of Spain."

"What is?" They turned as one to see Cheuk-Kwan, beach bag in hand.

"Uhhh... ..." Chiboon, whose lying ability hadn't improved one iota in his years away, flailed spectacularly.

"A very scandalous cabaret," Tinseng quickly covered. "Far too risqué for a respectable doctor to be seen at."

"Is everyone else going?"

"Just the three of us."

"Shan Dao is going to a cabaret?"

"You wouldn't believe what this one's into," Tinseng said shamelessly, and was delighted to watch Jinzhao's ears turn red. "But you wouldn't like it."

"If it's the highlight of Spain, why wouldn't I?"

"Because you have no taste."

Cheuk-Kwan huffed. "If you don't want me to go, just say that," he said. He meant it as a throwaway, a stupid little thing said between brothers, but Tinseng seized the opportunity; he'd been taught to win.

"Great," he said with a brittle smile, "I don't want you to go."

"What?"

"You heard me."

Tinseng resolutely did not wince at the flicker of hurt that passed over his brother's face.

"*Fine*. Fuck you too, then." Cheuk-Kwan turned on his heel and stalked away. Chiboon hid his face in his hands, and Jinzhao merely looked at Tinseng. Tinseng threw up his hands.

"What was I supposed to do? Let him come? Some help you two were, by the way! '*Uhhh*,'" he mimicked Chiboon, then shook his head. "Useless."

"You know I'm no good at confrontation! Anyway, I'm leaving at seven-thirty. I want to get dinner first, and I have to get dressed there."

"Done. Meet you at the gangway?"

"Wait, wait, wait. This is a very important question for both of you. What will you wear?"

"Uh . . . this?" Tinseng gestured at his rumpled day suit. Chiboon wrinkled his nose.

"I'm disappointed in you, Tinseng. Give me your key; I'll pick out an outfit for you. And you, Shan Dao?" Chiboon looked him up and down. "Actually, I might have something for you. Well, not me," he said at their incredulous expressions: Chiboon stood a full head shorter than Jinzhao, "but a local friend of mine. We're getting ready together there. He always brings extras, and I can always make him run home if he hasn't. Hmm." Chiboon tapped his chin while studying Jinzhao.

Tinseng tilted his head down, watching his friend closely. "You have an idea, don't you?"

"I really couldn't say," Chiboon evaded, but he couldn't hide his growing smile.

"Ahh, I've really missed you, Chiboon," Tinseng said, tossing his room key to his old friend. "Let's get into some trouble tonight, huh?"

That night, Tinseng had hoped for a few hours alone with Jinzhao in a picturesque Spanish town. But as they settled the bill for dinner, Chiboon informed Tinseng that he was taking Jinzhao for himself.

"Eh?" Tinseng looked up from throwing some pesetas on top of the bill.

"I need company, gege. It's the west, we're Chinese; who knows what will happen."

Tinseng grimaced; Chiboon had a point. Jinzhao seemed to think so too: he straightened to his full height, which made his shoulders look just . . .

"Wow," Chiboon murmured.

"I know, right?" Tinseng agreed, deeply gratified his friend appreciated the finer things in life. Then he turned and pouted, "But what am I supposed to do?"

"I don't know—go watch the sunset? I'll take good care of Shan Dao, don't worry. You'll enjoy the results," Chiboon leered. Tinseng smothered his laugh with his hand before remembering he'd learned that from Yukying. The laugh turned into a dopey smile. Jinzhao had no idea the danger he was in, which was exactly how Tinseng wanted him. Tonight would be out of his comfort zone in the best way, and for this kind of experience, there were no better hands to trust than Chiboon's. Jinzhao deserved this; they all did.

On the sidewalk outside, Tinseng waved goodbye, calling out, "Good luck!" He turned away, cackling at Jinzhao's confused blink.

With two hours to kill, he wandered the street and sat outside drinking cheap wine—though even cheap wine was incredible in Spain—making himself visible in the hopes he'd get a glimpse of Grodescu or the men he'd sent. But Marissa Grodescu must have been mistaken, because he didn't see anyone, not even a shadow to jump at. He felt a little let down, honestly. He'd been geared up for danger, and now all he'd get was a dance.

At 10:00 p.m., he aimed himself toward the bar. He walked slowly to give Grodescu or his thugs one last chance to show themselves, but no one emerged to ruin his night. With a mental shrug, Tinseng followed the instructions Chiboon gave him for finding Fauna. When he found it, he recited the password, had his name checked by the intimidating bouncer, and slipped inside.

The moment he walked in, he understood why Chiboon insisted on choosing his clothes. It'd been lucky for all of them that every scrap of clothing Tinseng owned was currently with him; Chiboon had pawed through all his suitcases to unearth a clingy silk oxford shirt Tinseng hung on to for fancy dress parties. The scarlet of it curled around his neck, sliding down his chest where he'd been ordered to leave the top two buttons open. The suit over the shirt was a deep midnight blue that rippled black in the club's low light. Once inside, he unbuttoned the blazer because even he could admit the high waist on these slacks showed off his waist nicely. He wouldn't compare to the Spaniards who had their whole wardrobe at their disposal or the tourists who'd shown up to peacock, but Chiboon at least ensured he wouldn't be an embarrassment.

There was no chance Chiboon would appear until at least an hour after opening, so Tinseng settled at the bar and ordered more wine. He ignored the attention of interested men and casually watched the exits. He'd spent plenty of time in the gay bars of France, but here the mood was clandestine and rebellious in equal measure. In Franco's Spain, every whisper was a shout.

Tinseng remembered a similar mood in Hong Kong. The day Yukying had caught him, he had started planning his escape. It'd been very clear to him that he'd be caught eventually and bring the family down with him. He'd needed to neutralize himself. Once he'd known he'd be transferred to Paris, he'd begun imagining the freedom he thought it'd offer. Kissing a man on the street—how he longed for that one simple act. His daydreams had never extended beyond escaping a jail cell.

Then he'd actually arrived in Paris. He'd laughed at his old daydreams—how limited he'd been! There were so many ways to be hated, ones he'd almost forgotten about, but then again, he'd learned how many ways there were to love. And now here he sat with different goals, new daydreams that felt just as impossible. He was older but he felt the same as he had before.

He saw Chiboon and Jinzhao before they saw him. They entered from the door that led to the lounges and bathrooms, and murmurs spread as they made their entrance. Chiboon looked stunning, of course, drawing eyes as he—but no, Tinseng shied away from that here, in this place where things were more real, more like they should be—as *they* walked out in a floor-length green dress. Green wasn't right, but Tinseng didn't know the word, in any language; he thought of a forest in spring rain, or a flawless emerald in a gold setting. The verdant fabric against their skin made them look luminescent. The front of the dress hugged every curve, the neckline displaying Chiboon's narrow chest. Beaded detailing in a pattern like long leaves extended on either side of their hips, calling attention to their sway as they walked through the crowd. The dress had a slit running up the left side, showing off endless leg and a deadly black heel.

Men called out, lavishing Chiboon with the attention they deserved. As they turned to flutter their eyelashes at a particularly handsome man, Tinseng saw the back of the dress and laughed into his drink. No wonder they were going wild: the dress was entirely backless, exposing a scandalous amount of skin even here in Europe. The cut ended right in the small of their back, drawing the eye and calling for a hand to rest there, to feel the scratch of the embroidery and the warmth of their skin in that soft, vulnerable spot. They've chosen not to wear a wig tonight, instead tussling their hair so it fell in their eyes. It made their features sharper, their eyes darker. Framed by the soft lines of the dress, the combination was devastating. They were a siren song, and they knew it. No one else in the room was so commanding, so alluring, so untouchable yet demanding to be touched.

It was easy to see why the man by their side would be overlooked.

But Mei Jinzhao was all Tinseng could see.

Chiboon had transformed him. It wasn't garish; in fact, it was quite understated: just a black turtleneck, tight black slacks, and a black hat with his hair loose around his shoulders. A little makeup around the eyes, the hint of smoke. The impression it made was that of a single, ceaseless line down the neck, the chest, the waist, the legs . . . his entire body the stroke of a master calligrapher. Jinzhao always wore layers, buttoned up in more ways than one, and Tinseng was used to the bulk of a suit hiding Jinzhao's real figure. Tinseng had never seen him wearing modern clothes meant to impress or fit. The turtleneck actually covered more skin than usual, but it clung to his chest; the way it hugged his long neck made Tinseng want to pull down and bite.

When Jinzhao wore his usual grays and blues, it made him look flawless but light, a marble statue, a tapestry. Right now, he looked dangerous—the way a dark corridor was dangerous, the way a flickering bulb raised hairs on the back of your neck. If Chiboon was a clarion call for worthy hands to come worship, Jinzhao was a warning, a sword drawn and pointed at the throat. Tinseng wanted to swallow against the blade to feel it pressing against his Adam's apple. He wanted, a little, to bleed. It had to be the color, he thought. Tinseng had almost never seen him in black before. He thought he might go mad from it.

He didn't realize he'd walked toward Jinzhao until he stood in front of him.

"Dance with me, stranger?" he asked. Jinzhao's eyes lingered on his mouth.

"Yes," Jinzhao said, and dragged Tinseng onto the dance floor. Tinseng pressed up against him immediately, not at all coy.

"Does this offend your sensibilities?" Tinseng asked as their hips rolled against each other. "All this decadence?"

"Tinseng. I lived in Paris."

"I know, I know. But you wanted to move back."

Jinzhao's mouth thinned. He pulled Tinseng by his hip so there wasn't even the hint of space between them.

"Some values are more important than others," Jinzhao said, the bastard, but Tinseng wouldn't be bested with one blow.

"And what values are these?" He ran his hand from Jinzhao's shoulder to his arm, plucking at the turtleneck's lush material.

"Identity. Joy." Jinzhao's arm tightened around his back. "'The less you eat, drink, and buy books; the less you go to the theatre and the dance hall . . .'"

"'The less you express your own life, the more you have,'" Tinseng picked up the quote, one of his favorites, "and the greater is your alienated life.'"

"Should we count the most meager form of life as the standard?"

"No, you're right. *Well*, Marx was right, you're—"

Jinzhao kissed him; it was Tinseng's favorite way of being told to shut up.

When Jinzhao pulled away, he murmured against Tinseng's lips, "I do not want to live an alienated life."

Tinseng hid his face in Jinzhao's shoulder, afraid to find out he was dreaming.

"I want to marry you," he told Jinzhao's neck. "Barring that, I'm going to suck you off in the bathroom until you cry. Either/or, Jinzhao, your choice."

"Why are they mutually exclusive?"

"Because I say so."

"Do you."

"You say otherwise?"

"What if I did?"

"Then we'd be at an impasse, wouldn't we?"

They were grinning—well, Tinseng was grinning. Jinzhao looked like he was going to eat Tinseng raw and bloody in the street. Tinseng was just about to march Jinzhao to the bathroom when the band finally stopped fussing with their instruments and the singer leaned into the microphone.

"One, two, three, four!" The guitar struck a chord familiar to every civilized person on Earth. The entire bar erupted. In this, the first year of Beatlemania, things were about to escalate.

"Oh my god!" Tinseng cried, bouncing up and down on his toes. He looked at Jinzhao, who was already looking at him, hat crooked on his head from Tinseng's hands in his hair, his eyes hooded with want and joy and a thousand things Tinseng couldn't name yet, but he would learn, he'd *learn*. A fizzy feeling expanded in his stomach, and he grabbed both Jinzhao's hands to join the rest of the club in sheer, uncomplicated revelry.

Everyone had streamed onto the floor to participate in the elation of belonging: an entire room throwing their heads back to yell the same lyrics, moving as one body, abandoning themselves to the music and dancing themselves anew.

Later, the band played a short set of ballads. Most of the crowd took a break, clearing the floor for couples. "May I?" Jinzhao asked politely, as if the answer would ever be no. They swayed more than danced to a modest Sinatra cover. The piano lingered on its phrases as if they could all put off closing time together if only they danced slower, kissed longer. Tinseng felt safe in Jinzhao's arms—and wasn't that odd? Like the world wasn't all long shadows out to get them—like the words in love songs really were true.

"We should buy this record," Tinseng murmured in Jinzhao's ear. "I want to dance to this again."

Jinzhao didn't answer with words.

---

They didn't return to the boat until well past 2:00 a.m. Around midnight, Jinzhao had fallen asleep in a booth; they had piled their jackets on top of him, half-prank, half-nest. They'd shaken him awake when they'd left, and he'd been cute the whole way back, blinking and monosyllabic. Tinseng couldn't wait to tease him about it in the morning.

He dropped off Jinzhao in the room and went back out to get a pack of cigarettes; he'd run out tonight and he would be desperate for one tomorrow with the hangover he was likely to have. As he was feeding bills into the machine, he felt someone come up behind him. Tensing, he turned around expecting Grodescu.

"Didi," he said, laughing in relief, "don't sneak up behind someone."

"We need to talk," Cheuk-Kwan said, "come on."

"At nearly 3:00 a.m.? Can't it wait?"

"No, it can't, because you're always—you don't have a lot of time these days. Chiboon's already passed out, let's go." He turned to lead Tinseng to his room.

"Just say it here," Tinseng complained, rubbing his hand over his face.

"Your room or mine. Not here."

"No, no, we'll wake Shan Dao. Come on, there's no one around. What, are you finally going to confess you broke that vase when we were twelve?"

"Can't you listen to me? If you just *listened*, you'd save yourself a lot of trouble."

Exhaustion weighed him down. "Come on, didi, I'm tired; I was out all night."

"I know. And I know where you were."

A chill ran through him. "Yeah," he said, "A cabaret."

"No, it was Fauno. In Torremolinos. And I know what kind of bar that is."

"Whatever you think—" Tinseng planned to lie until the end, but Cheuk-Kwan didn't let him.

"You think I'm an *idiot*? You treat me like a little fool, Tinseng. But I *know*." Cheuk-Kwan's eyes flashed dangerously, and Tinseng saw the truth there. He wasn't bluffing. He was staring at Tinseng as though if he glared hard enough he could pin Tinseng down. "I've known since before you left. And I want to talk."

# CHAPTER TEN

*Three Days Ago. June 22, 1963. Barcelona, Spain.*

The next morning, they left Málaga, and once again Yukying found Shan Dao on the deck to watch the sun rise over the ocean as they sailed on to their next location. That morning he wore the most relaxed outfit she had seen yet: light gray slacks with a borrowed shirt from Tinseng, a short-sleeved linen oxford with thick pinstripes—more whimsical than Shan Dao's usual taste, too small around the shoulders and chest but clearly bringing him comfort. He wore his shawl again, wrapped higher over his shoulders this morning. He nodded to her as she sat down next to him. It was starting to feel special, though it was only the second time they'd met like this.

"How are you?" she asked, wondering how long she could hold on to her concern before it bled through. "How was last night?"

"Uneventful," he told her, understanding what she couldn't ask.

"Good." She breathed out and sat back against the chair. "Good." With the main portion of her worry addressed, she was able to add, "Was it fun?"

If she hadn't been looking, she would have missed the blush spreading from the top of Shan Dao's cheekbones over to his ears.

"Tinseng is a good dancer."

She dropped her gaze to her lap to hide her enormous, helpless smile. These stupid, foolish boys.

"I'm glad. You both deserve some happiness."

As she stared past the beautiful scenery and thought of her brother dancing, something soft was placed in her lap. She looked up to find Shan Dao had offered her his shawl, leaving him in just his short-sleeved shirt. She looked at him questioningly.

"You're shivering," he said.

She hadn't noticed. "This is too much," she protested. "*You'll* get cold." She tried to hand it back, but he retreated further into his chair so she'd have to practically throw his gift back into his arms if she wanted to reject it.

"I am sufficiently warm," he said, and now that he had pointed it out, she had to admit she was freezing. The other mornings she had remembered layers, but this morning she had hurried out later than usual, worried she would miss his company. She pulled the shawl around her shoulders gratefully and cuddled into it.

"Thank you. I'm not used to the cold anymore. We grew up in Yichang."

"Shenyang." She recognized the expression of memories crowding in, and waited patiently until he added, "I played in the snow without gloves."

"It's been ages since I've seen real snow. We've gotten frost in Hong Kong, but never snow. Will you miss having a winter?"

He thought a while, then shook his head. "It will be educational living in a new climate."

"That's a very wise way of looking at it." She examined the expert craftsmanship of the shawl and asked, "Did someone you know knit this?"

"My mother purchased it in Ireland."

"Ireland? So far."

"They traveled often for work."

"Did you travel with them?"

"Sometimes."

She stroked the soft wool as they stared out at the sunrise in companionable silence. She felt wrapped in one of the clouds lazily floating above them.

"Keep it," he said suddenly.

"What? Oh no, this was your mother's. I couldn't possibly."

"You could, easily. Keep it," he repeated.

"Surely you . . . there must be someone else who would . . ."

"No. No one else." He paused, then said, "It sits in my trunk. I haven't respected it." He smiled that ghostly smile she'd seen a few times now. "Such things were made to be used, not to gather dust. She would want it that way."

*You must miss them*, she wanted to say, but knew the awkwardness of discussing dead family. She thought instead of Ireland and the trip this shawl had taken to get here.

"They say the world is shrinking, don't they? Sometimes I don't believe it, but . . ." she found herself thinking out loud. "The person who made this probably never imagined it would be worn by a Chinese woman on the deck of a British ship sailing to Spain, talking to a Chinese-born Frenchman whose mother traveled to Ireland to buy it." A smile bloomed in her, sweet as honeycomb. "Who would have thought it possible, fifty years ago? Fifty years ago, it wasn't possible. That has to mean something, doesn't it? That things are changing for the better?"

Her words reverberated back to her, and she winced.

"It's a silly thing to think," she said. "My mother always said I was foolish like that."

"大智若愚," Shan Dao said indignantly.[5] Yukying couldn't help but be a little in awe. He was certainly a match for Tinseng, quoting Laozi like it was nothing.

"I don't know if that counts as wisdom," she said. "It's provincial, if anything."

His frown deepened. "Hope is not foolish," he said. "It's the cornerstone of progress."

"I've always thought so, but it doesn't seem true these days," she said, rubbing the soft lamb's wool between thumb and forefinger. "It feels like . . . maybe hope is too big a word. Laurence and A-Kwan always argue on such grand scales." But what about the woman who had made this

---

[5] Literally "great wisdom seems stupid." Colloquially: great wisdom can seem foolish to those who are not wise.

shawl, and the woman who had bought it? Where were they in those huge visions of war?

Shan Dao stood. "I must go check on Tinseng," he said.

"Wait."

He looked down at her. Sunlight hit the ember of his eyes, bright as the reflection of the sky.

"Did Tinseng tell you about Barcelona?"

"Yes. He has a plan."

"Okay. Good." She didn't ask any more and, once he'd left, settled back in her chair to stare out between the slats of the railing. Thin brushstrokes of cloud hovered over Spain, catching the rising light from the east. She wondered what was next. Would she be able to absorb the beauty of Barcelona today with all this in mind? She wondered, too, if she would be able to catch Marissa anywhere today, and if she would be able to help her at all. She wondered if Shan Dao would stay in their lives after this was over; but she really had no say in whether they worked out. She could only . . . well.

As she tucked the shawl under her arm on her way to breakfast, she wondered what Shan Dao's mother would think of hope.

⁂

With the largest portion of her worry evaporated, she endeavored to enjoy the morning reading on the deck with Laurence. They saw no sign of Chiboon or Tinseng, but that wasn't surprising, nor Cheuk-Kwan, which was a little odd, but Yukying was absorbed now in Betty Friedan's book, and besides, how much trouble could they get into on the ship?

*Protectiveness has often muffled the sound of doors closing against women,* she was reading, when someone's shadow darkened her page. It was Chiboon, looking a little ruffled around the edges.

"Ah, um, Yukying . . . your brothers . . ."

She sighed as she stood, handing her book to Laurence. "Where are they?" she asked and followed Chiboon's hurried steps to the other side of the deck.

They arrived too late: Tinseng and Cheuk-Kwan were already standing. She knew it was bad the way Tinseng stood up straight for once, using his height to full advantage. Shan Dao stood next to Tinseng, glaring hard at Cheuk-Kwan.

Yukying sighed again. "Boys," she said quietly, pulling their attention away from one another and onto her. "What's the problem?"

"I asked a simple question," Cheuk-Kwan said, "but I was told to mind my business."

"Because it's *not your business*," Tinseng said, uncharacteristically sharp.

"He really isn't minding his business, Yukying," Chiboon added unhelpfully.

"I'm sure Cheuk-Kwan was just curious," Yukying said, trying to soothe things.

"Curious—that's one word for it." Tinseng tilted his head. "I think it suits you, didi. You're very curious lately. Is there anything I can sate your curiosity about? Any other little questions occupying your mind?"

"You know what?" Cheuk-Kwan seethed. "Fuck you. You deserve to get caught. They have special prisons for people like you here, you know."

"I'd rather be in jail than look at that ugly face." Tinseng sniffed, unbothered and dismissive, exactly the reaction he knew would most irritate his brother. "Come on, Shan Dao." He stubbed out his cigarette and nodded at Yukying as he left; she could see the hurt in his eyes. She looked between Tinseng's retreating back and Cheuk-Kwan's hunched shoulders and wondered which one she should follow—but Tinseng had Shan Dao, after all. She turned and looked at Cheuk-Kwan expectantly for an explanation.

"Don't," was all Cheuk-Kwan said as he threw himself back into his seat. He drained his glass and held it up for another.

Yukying sat delicately and asked the waiter for a lemonade, then picked up a section of newspaper abandoned on the table. Chiboon, reading the mood, sat and unfolded the society section to hide behind, ordering a coffee. The chatter of the tables and nearby pool drifted around them as Cheuk-Kwan sulked over his juice. Whenever she took a sip of her lemonade she glanced over, but her little brother remained unmoved. Such a stubborn boy.

"Chiboon," she said, "Do you know what's going on?"

"Oh, I'm sure I don't. I was asleep for the whole thing." Chiboon ruffled his paper. "Although, I had a strange dream—you know, like how an alarm goes off in your room but becomes a rooster crowing? I think there was yelling, but in my dream it was fog horns. Or maybe it was a lot of hissing, but in my dream it was snakes. Either way, it was very close to my ear."

Cheuk-Kwan bristled. "Well where else was I supposed to talk to him about . . . *that*? The fucking hallway? Tinseng refused to talk in his room because his precious Shan Dao was asleep."

"So was I!"

"Please. You had your eyes closed, but you kept fluttering them like you were having a seizure. As if someone looks like that when they sleep."

"You—!"

"*Boys.*" Yukying set down the paper, nearing the end of her patience. Chiboon, of course, folded at the first sight of Yukying's frustration.

"He finally told him, jiejie," Chiboon admitted. "That he knows Tinseng is . . . like that."

Of all the things she had expected to hear . . . She quickly looked over at Cheuk-Kwan, who grimaced but nodded. She couldn't believe it, but there was Chiboon nodding too, with a growing smile at her incredulity.

"Really?" she asked, voice cracking. It had been too much to hope; she hadn't let herself near the thought.

"Really," her little brother said. She reached for her drink; she needed to swallow down this lump or she would start crying.

"That was very brave of you, A-Kwan," she said when she could speak again. She placed her hand over his. "I'm proud of you."

Her brother scowled, shoulders slumping. "Well, save it, because he hates me now."

"He doesn't hate you. He's probably just surprised. It's a big change." She recontextualized the fight she'd seen through the lens of this new information; she recalled the hurt in Tinseng's eyes, the hissing like a cat backed into a corner. "He might be a little scared too."

"He doesn't look scared to me."

"You might not look upset to him either," she pointed out gently.

"I'm not upset!" Cheuk-Kwan crossed his arms, then uncrossed them when he realized it contradicted his words. "I just thought—this was the big secret, right? Why he was acting the way he was. And now he knows I know, and the world didn't end like he thought. So why isn't he happier about it?"

"Did you tell him you support him? That this doesn't change how you see him? That you'll stand by his side no matter what is said about him?"

"I *won't* stand by his side no matter what's said about him. What if he killed someone or something?"

Yukying stared at him meaningfully until he huffed and went on, "I told him, I told him. More or less." Which Yukying suspected meant *no*. "He should already know, anyway! I'm his brother."

But Cheuk-Kwan didn't look certain anymore and lapsed into silence.

"You always like it when your brothers support you, right, Chiboon?"

"Oh yes, especially da-ge. I mean, who wouldn't want to impress him? It's always nice to tell others how you feel about them. That's why I always tell you how grateful I am for your mercy when we were younger, jiejie, and how sorry I am, once again, for that time with the inkpot."

Cheuk-Kwan was drinking his juice sullenly now. Yukying and Chiboon shared a glance; Chiboon raised his eyebrows to ask if everything was going to be okay, and Yukying nodded, certain they would be. They'd weathered far worse storms than this.

"It's alright, you know," Chiboon said after they'd let Cheuk-Kwan stew a while.

"It's not," Cheuk-Kwan muttered.

"But you two have always been like this. And it's always fine."

"Why'd you agree to come with us, then?" Cheuk-Kwan huffed. "Who would willingly submit themselves to this?"

"Well, see, I needed to get from London to Naples . . ."

"Oh, shut up."

"Gladly, gladly. Only . . . can I tell you a secret?"

"I won't stop you," Cheuk-Kwan said gruffly. Yukying ducked behind her lemonade glass to hide her smile.

"There was one big reason I agreed when your sister wrote."

"And that was?"

"I knew it was your idea that she ask me." Chiboon turned the page of his newspaper, shaking it out so the pages fell into the crease properly. "And I missed you too."

It was true: When she'd read Tinseng's letter describing his plan for a European cruise, she had kept the letter on the kitchen table in Cheuk-Kwan's house and wondered aloud how it would be so nice to join him. But it was just a daydream, a nice thought to pass the time pleasantly; surely Cheuk-Kwan wouldn't be able to take time off work. After a few days of this, Cheuk-Kwan had snapped at her, saying if she wanted to join Tinseng so badly, just write back and ask, but stop bothering *him* about it. And while she was at, she should write Chiboon too. As long as they were going to Europe, they might as well try to see that idiot.

"It could have been Tinseng's idea," Cheuk-Kwan protested, to which Chiboon raised his eyebrows.

"It could have been, if he was the kind of person to notice when he's left someone behind. Or the kind of person to make sure everyone gets a turn. Remember our little swimming competitions? He'd steal every prize and hardly even look anyone else's way. If he remembered to be nice, he might help one of the younger kids. But more often he was too busy showing off for you. Oh, he was happy to hear from me, ecstatic even. But asking Yukying to include everyone? Even Laurence? He isn't the type, darling, we both know that. Always swanning off on his little adventures. I'm glad he doesn't invite me. Honestly!" he insisted when Cheuk-Kwan snorted—Yukying knew her brother couldn't imagine that, *not* wanting to be invited. "It saves me the trouble of making up excuses why I don't want to go. Can you imagine? Running all over like that? Exhausting."

Chiboon looked up from his newspaper to see if his words were having the desired effect. Cheuk-Kwan was tracing lines in the condensation on his glass, his anger slowly draining away; he missed the pleased look that flashed across Chiboon's face at the sight of his turn in mood. But

Yukying was watching and saw the smug satisfaction, and she was grateful once again her brother had such good, loyal friends.

"I should go find him," Cheuk-Kwan muttered.

Chiboon clucked his tongue. "It can wait." He waved Cheuk-Kwan's concern away. "He's already forgiven you. It's what older siblings do. Right, jiejie?"

"Right," she confirmed with a firm, cheerful nod.

***

With renewed hope that her brothers might return home with their misunderstandings behind them, Yukying was in a buoyant mood all the way through lunch. Across the dining hall, she saw Marissa and Lucas Grodescu eating at their table, but even that could not deter her from thoroughly enjoying her conversation with Mrs. Lanzette about Spanish fan painting and Yan Yangchu's Mass Education Movement. After the soup, Mr. Grodescu rose and left early. Shan Dao and Tinseng left soon after. Yukying watched them go and could not help looking over at Marissa again, only to be caught: Marissa's smile held no real warmth, but at least she didn't look *too* angry. Then Marissa, still staring, rose and left the dining room.

Yukying followed into the women's bathroom down the hallway. Their eyes caught again in the mirror as they washed their hands. Yukying smiled warmly.

"Mrs. Grodescu! Good afternoon—how are you?"

"Very well," Marissa replied, not as cold as she had been the last time they spoke. "You seem in good spirits."

"I am, you know, I really am." Over the intercom, the captain announced they were pulling into Barcelona's port. "I'm very much looking forward to Barcelona. Spain is so beautiful; the pictures don't do it justice. Have you ever visited before?"

"Yes, many times. It is beautiful. You should visit Seville, if you return."

"How wonderful! I'll keep that in mind." An impulse seized her and she asked, "Do you like Spanish wine?"

"I do."

"Would you meet me for a drink later?" With a little mischief, she leaned in and added, "You could tell your husband you're spying on me."

Marissa blinked, put off by Yukying's cheer. Yukying chastised herself. Wasn't this what they were always telling Tinseng not to do?

"I'm sorry if that came on too strong. I've been spending too much time around my brothers. But I really would enjoy your company."

Marissa stared at her a moment longer. Yukying got the distinct impression she was being measured. Then Marissa turned back toward the mirror and opened her clutch.

"Are you . . . visiting the post office today?" she asked as she looked down at her bag.

"It's funny you mention that," Yukying said as Marissa pulled out lipstick. "There are more than we ever thought, and we're not quite sure which one is best. For the architecture," she added, not sure if they were still keeping up a ruse even here in the bathroom where Marissa's husband couldn't possibly be. Or maybe they were talking like this for Marissa herself; maybe it was a comfort to be distant from it all.

"You should visit the post office on Calle Comte de Salvatierra," Marissa said. She put the lipstick back in her clutch. "The ceilings are original."

Yukying's heart sunk; that wasn't either of the ones Tinseng or Jinzhao were going to.

"Well, original ceilings—that sounds lovely," she said weakly. "I'll see if we can't stop there today." She wanted to thank the other woman but understood that she wanted no acknowledgment of what she'd just done. Instead, Yukying walked around Marissa and hurried out toward the gangway. She had to find one of the boys before they left or they'd miss Grodescu entirely.

The deck was its usual swarm as they pulled into the Barcelona harbor. Yukying stayed at the railing as the staff gave the all-clear to disembark. She watched the first wave of passengers leave, but didn't see Grodescu, Tinseng, or Shan Dao in their midst. With a frown, she returned to the table; Chiboon and Cheuk-Kwan hadn't moved.

"Have Tinseng or Shan Dao been through?" When both shook their heads, she went back to the gangway. No matter how hard she looked, they were nowhere. She wondered if Tinseng had found a way to watch the gangway without being seen or if she was merely unobservant. Perhaps Grodescu had left while she was gone and Tinseng followed.

On her way down to their rooms, she found Laurence in a deck chair, smiling wryly at his book.

"I might be late to dinner," she said, "I have to go ashore and find Tinseng."

"Should I care about whatever's going on?" he asked without looking up.

"No, no." Fondness overwhelmed her as she looked at him, in his crisp shirt and the silly straw hat he'd bought from a hawker in Portugal. It was always moments like these that struck her most: the quiet, unremarkable slivers of a person no one else would ever see. Love at its most mundane was also love at its true center, she thought, when we could be the most like ourselves without fear. "It's just the usual nonsense."

"It always is with them. Good luck."

She was sure she'd need it. She hurried down to Tinseng and Shan Dao's door, fearing she'd missed them, but after a moment, Shan Dao answered; he already had his suit coat on.

"Do you know where Tinseng is?" she asked.

"Gone."

She sighed. "Well, at least you're here. I ran into Marissa, and she told me which post office is it. It's neither of the ones you chose." If Tinseng was already gone, there would be no way to contact him. Shan Dao would have to go on his own. She took in his expression: There was something there, a darkness too like fear, that made her raise her chin and say, "I'm coming with you."

# CHAPTER ELEVEN

*Three Days Ago. June 22, 1963. Barcelona, Spain.*

"I'm coming with you," she said, assuming it would be a fight the way it would with Tinseng or Cheuk-Kwan, or even Laurence. But Shan Dao simply nodded and closed the door behind him. He started walking down the hallway, then turned back when he realized she hadn't followed, his quizzical expression asking, *Are we not in a hurry?*

"You don't think I should stay behind?" she asked despite herself.

"Should you?"

The question surprised her. Shan Dao didn't know her the way her other companions did. He hadn't been there during her adolescence when she'd wheezed after a steep flight of stairs; he'd never seen her laid up for days from exhaustion or pain. She'd outgrown some of it, could manage the rest; where she hadn't grown stronger, she'd grown resilient, and she took quiet pride in that. She knew the boys were proud of her, too, but, just as she still thought of them as boys, she knew they still thought of her as fragile.

Shan Dao was free of those concerns. He thought of her no differently than he thought of anyone else. She found she liked it, seeing herself through his eyes. Adding another mark of approval to her mental tally, she fetched her wallet and passport and followed him.

They took the tram from the port into the city center and sat in tense silence as the scenery passed. Her first impression of Barcelona was the colors: deep orange sepias, pale tans, camel hair and caramel, bleached whites, washed-out stone. Almost every building was a varying shade of white or brown, none of it uniform, but somehow the palate became cohesive and deeply pleasing in a blur from the window.

Her second impression was to wonder at its size. Barcelona was the only other city in Spain she could name besides Madrid; she had expected it to be much larger.

"Did you know there were palm trees in Spain?" she asked, for want of anything else to say. Palms lined entire streets, escorting them into the city.

"No."

Silence fell between them again.

"Have you read *Don Quixote*?" she tried.

"No."

Why was conversation with Shan Dao so much easier in the early morning before everyone else was awake?

"Laurence made me read it; he loved it. It's the only novel I've read where any of it takes place in Barcelona."

Shan Dao was quiet a long moment, then offered, "*The Thief's Journal*."

"Is that a classic in the West?" She'd never heard of it.

Shan Dao almost laughed. "No."

"Would you recommend it?"

"Not to everyone." There was something he wasn't saying—a wall between them she couldn't scale.

"I'm sure if you liked it, it's worth reading," she said neutrally.

"My mother first recommended it."

"Then I would truly love to read it. Do you own a copy?"

"I used to." His mouth worked around some large truth. "We sold most of our books after Tinseng left his position."

She turned toward him then. Shan Dao stared out the window, his back perfectly straight. She knew selling possessions wasn't the worst thing Tinseng had ever done to survive, but he hadn't needed to this time; he could have asked her for help. Yet he didn't, and possibly he never would. She hated that she was finding out this way. What must Shan Dao think of them, this family Tinseng didn't trust to support him?

"Did he ever mention ... we would have—if he had written, of course, we would have ..."

She trailed off, shame flushing her cheeks. No, of course he wouldn't have mentioned his struggles. She knew more than anyone just how much Tinseng left unsaid. And what had she done about it? Written him kind, impersonal letters; waited for his occasional replies; and hoped he'd return one day, impassively letting the world happen *to* her, just as her mother had always feared.

"I'm sorry you had to do that," she told Shan Dao. "We'll be with Tinseng from now on. And you, of course," she hurried to add. "Hong Kong has plenty of booksellers, you know. You and A-Seng will be able to get your collections back in no time. It won't be like living in Paris, but you'll be able to order anything you want. And, you know, the waiting makes the books even more enjoyable," she added, a little desperately.

"Mm," Shan Dao murmured. She had no idea how to interpret the sound. Wrong-footed, Yukying remained quiet. The fact that Tinseng had run off today without telling either of them struck her again, harder this time. Tinseng assumed he was on his own, always. He hadn't changed at all; possibly he'd gotten worse during these intervening years, all alone in Paris until Shan Dao had entered his life. How was she supposed to prove she had changed when he wouldn't give her the chance? Even if he couldn't see it, surely being on this tram proved she had: She wasn't waiting for permission, and she wouldn't hold herself back. She only needed Tinseng to believe in her. She would have to prove it to him somehow.

※

As they stepped off the train, she studied the map, then pointed them north. The post office was embedded on one of the main streets of a lively neighborhood enjoying their Friday market. The crowd wove around them, uninterested in accommodating two slow tourists. The area was completely unlike Lisbon: Lisbon's beaches had been for tourists, but nothing here was for her. This neighborhood had not kept her in mind. Spices hadn't been added or subtracted, accents weren't flattened, menus didn't have a second language under the mother tongue. In Estoril, hawkers had called out to her in English; here, she heard nothing but Spanish. They had no use for her here. Homesickness jolted straight through her; she didn't fault the people of Barcelona for not caring about her, but she wanted to be somewhere familiar, where they did care. She wished she was walking through Lei Yu Mun, surrounded by *her* crowds.

Shan Dao grabbed her elbow, too hard for politeness.

"What is it?" she asked, her melancholy disrupted. "Do you see him?"

"Grodescu." He pulled her in, crowding them both behind a rotating stand of postcards. Only he could see over it; she had to peer around. Grodescu moved down the road, out of sight. Yukying and Shan Dao exchanged a grim look and followed.

They tried to stay as far back as possible without losing him in the swirling crowd. They followed Grodescu as he walked through the narrow spaces between the stalls of the produce sellers. It was the perfect place to lose someone, and Yukying didn't think it was a coincidence they quickly fell behind. Shan Dao moved even slower than she did, his politeness nearly rooting him to the spot. They must not have had these sorts of crowds where Shan Dao was from. He was stopped now behind a group of old grandmothers in simple black dresses standing in the middle of the walkway, completely unaware or perhaps not caring how they blocked traffic.

At the end of the row of stalls, Grodescu was slipping away. Yukying watched him turn right, then looked back at Shan Dao, who balefully pleaded with her over the women's heads.

She walked back and held out her hand to Shan Dao. After a moment's hesitation, he took it. With him in hand, she pushed through the flock, who shouted abuse at them, but Yukying ignored them peacefully as they hurried through the crowd.

He didn't let go of her hand and she gripped back tightly, two buoys bobbing in an unfathomably deep ocean. His grip was too strong as she pulled them through, but she didn't complain. He'd forgotten to be gentle with her. Something in her jumped at the knowledge. This wasn't endless rounds of mahjong with the church set or arranging appetizers on a plate for Laurence's bosses. This was an *adventure*.

*Maybe*, she thought, *if Mother could see me right now, she might even be proud*.

The chase ended when they peered around the corner to see Grodescu waiting in a doorway on a quiet family street. They stood out of sight, biding their time. They didn't have to wait long.

"You're late," they heard Grodescu say in English as the door opened.

"You're early," a nasally English accent whined back. "C'mon, upstairs."

The sound of hinges, then a door shutting. They exchanged a look: What now? Yukying gestured with her head: Closer? Shan Dao frowned and looked around the street. Tapping her shoulder, he pointed to a wall where rough handholds were built into the side of the building to create a makeshift ladder. He looked at her with a question in his eyes: Did she want to climb up to the roof? Yukying was already tired, and she wondered how much more she could push her body. Her knees would protest tonight. Her feet were already protesting. Her back ached, and she was bent over like a crone from a story.

But she thought about what Shan Dao had said this morning—had it been just this morning? It felt like so much longer—when he'd given her his mother's shawl. How things were made to be used, not to sit in a trunk gathering dust. She thought about that now: how this body was a gift and made to be used.

"Let's go up," she said.

"Mm." *Are you sure*, she heard, and for a moment more she did consider. But everyone else in her family was always ignoring their good sense. Why couldn't she for once? She nodded, looking up the ladder, then back at him.

Shan Dao tilted his head down with a look of understanding. "Would you like to go first?"

She beamed at him and started climbing.

On the roof, they craned their necks toward the open window below. Voices floated up to them, carried by the warm summer wind.

"Mr. Wu." Grodescu's voice held a snake charmer's melody. "Your quick work is appreciated. Tell me about the material."

"I have sorted them into personal and professional," an unknown man said, not the one who had opened the door; he spoke English, but with that accent, Yukying thought he was probably from Guangdong province somewhere. "The personal will be of no use to you; they are journal entries, nothing more. These are the ones that someone might be interested in buying."

"What's in them?" Grodescu asked.

"This one, I do not know. I cannot crack the code, but others might. These are her impressions of those in the Chinese embassy, and those who worked with her husband."

"Hmm. And what about this part here?"

"Ah, the poetry. Yes, that was strange. It was helpful to know I was looking for a name. You see this character here? It's odd. Not incorrect exactly. Dismissed as a translator's strange taste. But if you know it's hiding something, it becomes this."

"What is this?"

"A name. This is the romanization."

"You're certain?"

"Emphatically."

"Excellent," Grodescu said, and then Yukying heard what was unmistakably the sound of a man being strangled. Before this moment, she never would have thought herself capable of knowing such a thing, but the gurgling and gasping couldn't be anything else. She put a hand over her mouth and tried not to listen. After far too long, the noises trailed off, then stopped completely. Yukying shook. Next to her, Shan Dao had balled his hands into fists. She hadn't expected him to be just as scared as her, but he too was shaking slightly. She put a hand on his arm, and he stopped.

"Burn these," Grodescu's voice sounded the same as before he'd strangled a man. "No copies. Check Ming Wu's house. Burn it down if you have to."

"Sure, boss," the Englishman from before said.

"Now, what did you get on the one I asked you about?"

"Shan Dao? Nothin' much." Yukying gripped Shan Dao's arm in alarm as the man continued. "You said he wanted to sell you something?"

"That was his story, yes," Grodescu said.

"Well, he's either a great criminal or a terrible one. As far as the paper trail goes, he got into town a few months ago. Found a birth certificate and police record from Paris with small things. Drunk and disorderly, parking tickets, that kind of thing. The usual check on Chinese nationals didn't find anything except a valid passport, but that doesn't mean much. Presumably based in Paris, but then why haven't we heard of him?"

"A very sloppy cover," Grodescu said dismissively. "Focus on him. Forget the others, they're unimportant."

Yukying frowned; that didn't make any sense. Wasn't Grodescu supposed to have photographs? And weren't they supposed to be of Tinseng? Was Grodescu looking to find blackmail material about Shan Dao now?

"But you're sure it's him? All these Chinese are hard to tell apart, 'specially with their names. My guy had a fuckin' beast of a time pulling records."

"Kept forgetting their last name comes first, did he? No matter, I'm sure he did his *best*," Grodescu's disdain curled around the word. "Show me what he brought."

Yukying and Shan Dao heard the shuffling of files. Occasionally Grodescu asked questions, but for the most part he worked in silence. Finally, he said, "This is sufficient. I believe we have what we need." A rustle of something. "Follow them onshore only. The ship has too many eyes."

Oh, that was important—Yukying would be able to tell Tinseng to stay on the ship; they could keep him safe that way. It was a piece of good news among the disturbing confirmation that Grodescu was indeed a killer, not just a blackmailer.

The rest of the conversation moved on to other schemes that had nothing to do with them, but they stayed on the roof waiting until they saw Grodescu leave the house and disappear down the street. Tension crawled up her neck in a way that promised to become an unshakeable migraine tomorrow. She gritted her teeth and ignored it. She didn't have time to be distracted by pain, not when she needed to think through all they'd heard.

Shan Dao refused to engage in conversation as they took the bus to the post office where Tinseng was camped out. Instead of pleasantries, Shan Dao pulled a spluttering Tinseng by the elbow into the first café they passed. Yukying followed behind, bewildered. Shan Dao needed to be alone with her brother, so she took her time looking at the large deli counter, chatting with the man behind it in English and accepting samples of his favorite meats. When she felt enough time had passed, she ordered on his recommendation a small plate of paper-thin presunto ibérico at an eye-watering price, three ham and cheese sandwiches, and a half bottle of wine with three squat glasses stacked on its neck. She found the other two in the furthest corner of the small café, heads bent low. When she approached, they stopped speaking abruptly and busied themselves helping her with the plates and cups.

"Here," Tinseng took one of the sandwiches, picked off the ham, then placed the cheese and bread down in front of Shan Dao.

"Oh, I forgot, I'm sorry!" Yukying cried. "Where was my head? I'll go get something else, I'm so sorry."

"No need," he said, taking a bite of a sandwich.

"It's great, more for me." Tinseng placed all the ham on his sandwich. "Now," he said around a huge bite, "Shan Dao said Grodescu said to follow us onshore only?"

"That's right," Yukying confirmed.

"Well then, the plan is simple." Tinseng spread his hands. "I'll lure him out tonight, and we keep Shan Dao safe on board."

"No." Shan Dao's eyes flashed.

"You'll slow me down," Tinseng countered.

"Dangerously individualist thinking," Shan Dao retorted. "不失時機."[6]

---

[6] "I would not miss the timing."

"奮不顧身."[7] Yukying heard Shan Dao's response as concern, but Tinseng didn't take it that way, only sitting up straighter.

"舍本逐末."[8]

Both Shan Dao and Yukying bristled at Tinseng calling his safety a minor detail. Shan Dao said icily, "不以為恥, 反以為榮."[9]

Tinseng's lip curled. "Ashamed? Never. *I* draw my sword to help."

"Tinseng!" Shan Dao snapped harshly.

"J—*Shan Dao*." Tinseng made his lover's name sound like a curse. Yukying had heard enough.

"Both of you! 化干戈為玉帛."[10] She could play their game if she had to, and she knew how to win. She set down the wine she'd been pouring. "Look at you both, fighting at a time like this. Do you want to speak in anger with *him* out there? Now drink your wine," she demanded, setting down glasses in front of them.

If it had been her brothers, they would have avoided each other's gazes and focused solely on her, leaning on her to solve their problem. Tinseng did the opposite with Shan Dao, placing a hand on his arm in apology.

"You help too much," Shan Dao said, but warily now.

"I help just enough," Tinseng replied. "Besides, I plan to bring Chiboon and Cheuk-Kwan."

"More innocents in the crossfire?"

"Witnesses. Barcelona isn't Torremolinos; there will be plenty of options. And now we know there are no copies. We just have to wait one more day until Villefranche. That's where he meets his buyer, and we'll be waiting."

Tinseng must have forgotten that Yukying hadn't heard this part of the plan before. He was forgetful like that, careless in some ways. That

---

[7] To charge in without any thought to bodily risk.
[8] For someone to be nitpicky—to care about some minor detail instead of the bigger picture.
[9] "You are proud of something shameful, instead of being ashamed."
[10] "Turn your weapons of war into gifts of jade."

was how she'd first learned his secret, after all. She didn't draw attention to it now, acting as though she'd known all along.

"Then you'll buy it from him?" she asked.

"We'll get it one way or another," Tinseng promised. "Then we'll be in the clear."

They all sipped their wine.

"That poor translator," Yukying mourned. "I wonder what secrets he died for."

Tinseng huffed and took another bite of his sandwich, ripping the bread with his teeth. Shan Dao said nothing at all.

※

The ship stayed in the Barcelona dock that night; they would sail to Villefranche mid-morning. The harbor town loomed in her mind now. Somewhere on its sun-drenched streets a confrontation would happen. And tonight, her brothers and Chiboon were out in the bars as bait; would they get into an altercation? Would the steward come to inform her they'd been arrested? Would the phone ring any minute now? She sat in her room all night and kept checking the clock despite herself. She'd never been on a vacation less relaxing, even the ones with Laurence's parents.

She found sleep more elusive than ever, especially with the muscles along her spine nearly pulsing. Grodescu's voice kept circling in her head: *Follow them onshore only. The ship has too many eyes.* Laurence lay in bed reading the end of the third book in his Churchill series, unlikely to fall asleep until he'd reached the last page. She stayed up writing overdue postcards and letters until her hand cramped. She stood into an exaggerated stretch and checked her watch: 12:15 a.m. Tinseng said he would be back by one.

"I hunched over the desk too long," she told Laurence. "I think I'll take a walk. Do you think I need a sweater?"

"Definitely," he said absently. "When do you think you'll be back?"

"Before one."

"All right. Stay warm."

She left him to his book and began to walk. She didn't notice where she was going; by this point, the ship was so familiar to her she thought she could walk parts of it blind. *It's become a home of sorts*, she thought as she took the stairs from her deck up to the very top deck. Like the pretend homes they made with leaves and sticks in Yichang—the ship had that childlike sense of safety, a construct away from the real world. The sea air greeted her as she pushed the door open, beckoning her into the refreshing summer night. She stepped onto the deck and looked along its long bow. *The ship has too many eyes*, she thought, and this time the thought brought her comfort.

She saw him then: Lucas Grodescu, sitting in a chair that faced the stairway. As if he had been waiting for someone to emerge from the decks below. Their eyes met. He stood slowly, pushing himself up from the chair. Her blood ran cold—she had heard him strangle someone today. For a moment she stood completely frozen. She could not look away from his hands as he walked toward her. Then his shoe squeaked on the wood, and she jolted back into her body. She turned and barely managed not to run. Her instincts were all wrong: Instead of walking back downstairs and straight to Laurence, she walked around the middle of the ship with its huge supporting column and crossed to the back half of the deck. Even as she did, she yelled at herself: *What is your plan? What are you thinking?* She wasn't; she couldn't. She scrambled for a place to go.

Grodescu followed. She tried to keep from shaking as she walked down the deck. She'd never thought of the polished wood floor as slippery, not even with the morning dew, but now she worried she would fall if she tried to run.

On the aft end of the deck was a staircase that led to a bar, but that had closed at midnight. The pool had a staircase, though, down into the women's changing room, which in turn emptied out into a lower deck with rooms. It would have been smarter to make a loop around the deck back to the original staircase, but her hindbrain had long since panicked.

Two swinging doors separated the outside deck from the inside pool. The moment there were doors between her and Grodescu, she ran, flinging herself down the stairs to be out of sight when the doors swung open again.

She ducked down to listen but heard only silence. Had he stopped just inside? Where was he? She slipped off her shoes and took each step on tiptoe. When she reached the lower level, she hurried to the women's changing room. With her hand on the door, she heard above her,

"Hello, Mrs. Li."

Her chest rose and fell quickly, shallow sips of animal fear. She turned around. The shimmering light from the pool caught his gray eyes as he walked down the spiral staircase.

"Hello, Mr. Grodescu."

His gaze was flint as it swept her up and down in cold calculation. Yukying felt very small and unprotected in her thin cheongsam and Laurence's cardigan. She wanted to cross her arms over her chest but that would just draw attention.

"Are you enjoying your evening?" She tried to sound as insipid as possible, remembering Marissa's promise to report back that she was nothing but a housewife. "I was thinking of a swim but, silly me, I forgot my swimsuit. I'll have to go back and get it."

"Hmm." He reached the bottom of the stairs and stepped toward her. "Not a pleasant feeling, being followed, is it?"

Did he know about this afternoon? Was he guessing?

"I don't know what you mean."

"Then it wasn't you in the blue dress? And your friend Dao Shan, in the white?"

"No, it wasn't." She inched her way to the door.

"Mrs. Li, I hate to be the one to tell you this, but these men are using you. You may be in grave danger if you continue to associate with them."

"Shan Dao is just a translator."

"Is he? And your brother, Tinseng?"

"A language tutor."

"Really." He smiled as he took a step forward. She pressed back against the wall. "Just a translator and a tutor. And you believe them?"

"I, I really should go get that swimsuit. If you'll excuse me."

"Before you go, Mrs. Li, don't you want to know who I was talking about this afternoon?"

She needed to move.

"I didn't leave the ship this afternoon. You can ask my husband."

"Now, now, let's not bring your husband into this. I would like to keep you out of it too, if possible. You don't belong in this world, Mrs. Li. I've looked. You have no secrets, no skeletons as they say. You have been innocent until now. Shouldn't it stay that way?"

"I— I . . ."

She shouldn't have come down here. Surely by now someone would have walked across the deck, but no one came down here. All she had to do was take two steps to the right and walk backward through the door. *If I can do that*, she thought frantically, *if I can just get another door between us—*

"Listen very closely now," Lucas Grodescu said in a low, soothing tone, "I mean you no harm, Mrs. Li. But you know nothing about me, and I know everything about you. You have no idea what you've gotten yourself into, and now, unfortunately, you're in the middle of a very dangerous world. Your companions might have convinced you that you can be a spectator in that world. Perhaps they've made it seem like a fun distraction from your otherwise mundane existence. But there is no such thing as a bystander when it comes to secrets like these. This world can reach out and—" He lifted a hand and snapped loudly. She flinched and hated herself for it. "Do you understand?"

The wallpaper scratched at the back of her dress as she shifted her weight. "Y-you talk about the world being dangerous," she said, "the world doing harm. But it's just *you*."

"I'm a small player on this board. A pawn. If I flatter myself, a knight. But nothing more. Not like your brother and his *companion*."

"They should be left alone," she said, her voice no stronger. "They've done nothing wrong. It's the law that's wrong."

"I'm surprised, Mrs. Li. You don't seem like a seditionist."

"They love who they love. It's been legal in your country for centuries."

Grodescu blinked, frowning in confusion. Then he chuckled, low and rich.

"Oh, my. They have you *well* fooled. *Être blanc comme neige*. A shame." He clucked sympathetically. "But you have your uses, clearly." He tilted his head, studying her. There was cruelty in his eyes. "I have a message for you to deliver."

"Why would I do that?" she tried, but he ignored her.

"Tell Shan Dao I know who he is, and I know how his mother did it. I'm driving to Paris tonight. If he doesn't want your brother's name added to a poem, he will go with me. Do you understand? Repeat it back to me, please."

Her mouth betrayed her, and she did.

"Very good. Don't let them drag you down further, little lamb. Deliver my message, then stay out of this… But you won't, will you?"

She tilted her chin up. Her tongue might be numb, but she could at least look him in the eye.

"You're making a mistake," he murmured. "How can I show you that?"

Without warning, he slammed his hand next to her head. She jumped and clapped a hand over her mouth, only just catching her scream. Caught behind her teeth, it sounded like a wail of mourning. The sound echoed between them, going no further than Lucas Grodescu's sneering face.

"You see, Mrs. Li?" He stepped back, smoothing down his tie. "You're easily startled. This kind of business is not for you."

His soothing tone unsettled her, a whiplash of mood. As if the outburst of violence had been days ago, between two other people. She was terrified, she realized. She had never been this scared as an adult. As a child, yes, but that was different: fear to a child was a blurry silhouette in the shadows, terrifying because it was unknown. Now she could name all the things this man could do to her; now her fear had form, and shape, and name.

"Goodnight, Mrs. Li," Grodescu murmured and turned his back to her, retreating up the way they'd come.

She couldn't breathe as she watched him climb the stairs, didn't dare make a sound as she listened to his steps echo past the pool. The door was pushed open; she heard it swing back and forth on its frame. Then, eventually, that too fell silent.

Her first free breath was shuddering, desperate. She wanted to sink to the ground. She wanted to cry, or vomit, or both. She didn't. Instead, she pressed her palms against her eyes and breathed. Breathed.

Breathed.

Her hands began to shake as she hurried back, checking over her shoulder every few seconds—the hall was empty, always empty.

But the ship had eyes.

It only took a few minutes to reach her stateroom door. She wanted nothing more than to cry against Laurence's shoulder and be held in his arms. His steady heartbeat was the safest sound she knew, and she needed that, craved it; but she couldn't go back to Laurence like this; he'd have very valid questions, and she didn't want to lie again when it had felt so horrible this afternoon. She knew if he asked right now she would break her promise to Tinseng and tell Laurence everything. Part of her wondered if that wouldn't be for the best. She wanted her husband's perspective and his advice. He was more realistic than her and could even be cynical if pushed; she needed that sometimes and could certainly use it now.

But she couldn't break Tinseng's confidence. It would destroy whatever new foundation they were building here. So, with a lingering look at her room, she knocked on Tinseng and Shan Dao's door instead.

After a minute, Shan Dao answered in a dressing gown pulled over his pajama set, hair rumpled and eyes bleary.

"I woke you," she said in a jumble, "I'm sorry. I'll go. Please go back to sleep."

"Li Yukying," she heard as she turned, then, "Yukying. What happened?"

The prospect of having to explain overwhelmed her. As she blinked against the tears, she felt a presence next to her. It wasn't Laurence, but her heart still recognized it as someone she could trust.

"Come," Shan Dao said, and led her inside. She sat heavily in a chair and couldn't seem to meet his eyes. Part of her expected him to start hovering, visibly worrying in the same way A-Seng and A-Kwan did when they didn't know how to help. Instead, Shan Dao surprised her: he sat forward and took her hand in his, gentle as if he was cupping a dragonfly.

"What happened?" he asked again.

"Grodescu." She swallowed, but under the spotlight of Shan Dao's attention she finally felt freed from the shadows of the pool. "He saw me and followed me. I didn't tell him anything. You have to believe me, I would never; I would never betray Tinseng, or you."

"I know," he said as though her loyalty was an immovable object. It was so stubborn, so rooted in belief rather than truth, that she felt a hysterical urge to pat his head, the way she might a child. She was cracking under this pressure.

She heard herself ask shakily, "May I have some water please?"

"Of course. I apologize. I should have— yes." He cut himself off and stood.

"Thank you," she said, and drank quickly when it was placed in front of her. He watched her closely as she did. When she set down the empty glass, he reached for it and rose to fill it again. He would keep bringing her water until the sun came up, she thought. Every part of him was unwavering: his attention, his beliefs, his devotion. Perfect for someone like Tinseng, who'd never known the same home for more than a few years. Perfect for her, who'd never been anyone's first priority. Perfect even for Cheuk-Kwan, who was always watching people leave.

As she thought it, she realized what she'd been doing for the past week: imagining all the ways Shan Dao would fit into their family. She'd been imagining how they all might be less alone.

She set her third glass of water down after a few sips. "I feel much better now, thank you."

"No need."

She took a deep breath. "Grodescu said he had a message for you. Should we wait for Tinseng?"

"A message?"

"Yes, and it didn't make much sense, but—"

"It could be hours before Tinseng returns," Shan Dao said. There was a strange look in his eyes.

"But it's nearly one," she said, checking her watch, "And he said he'd be back by then."

"When is Tinseng ever on time?"

"That's true."

"I will wait up for Tinseng and inform him the moment he's returned. Please," he said, "What was the message?"

She swallowed and tried to organize her thoughts. "It didn't make any sense after what we heard today. But, oh, Shan Dao! He knew we followed him. I don't know if he knew all along, or when he might have seen us. And then what he said didn't match what we'd heard. So I'm not sure if he's trying to cover his tracks now."

Shan Dao sat listening, unmoving.

She wrung her hands and said, "He wanted me to tell you he knows who you are, and that he knows how your mother did it. And he's leaving for Paris tonight, and that if you don't want Tinseng's name added to a poem, you'll meet him there. But it doesn't make any sense—what does your mother have to do with it? And he called me a seditionist, I don't . . . oh, Shan Dao. Shan Dao?" She stood and clasped his shoulder. "Are you all right? Do you need a doctor? Should I get Cheuk-Kwan?"

His *no* was a shocking clap of thunder. Between her blinks the storm disappeared, and his face was expressionless again, but it was too late; she could still see his expression like an after-image. She took a step back. For the second time that night, she felt terror, but this had a different name than the acrid, stinking fear from earlier. This was wild fear, untamed fear: What could make a man like Shan Dao look *this* afraid?

Grodescu's mockery came back to her: *just a translator and a tutor. And you believe them?*

"What's going on?" Her heart was in her throat, but she tried to channel her father at his calmest. "Shan Dao, please tell me."

But Shan Dao had stood and looked down at her with terrifying intensity.

"Do you love Tinseng?" he asked.

"He's my brother," she replied, confused. "I—"

"Would you do anything for him?"

Her stomach dropped. "Shan Dao . . ."

"Would you?"

"Yes. Of course."

"Then you understand. It can't be him. Or you. I won't allow it."

"I *don't* understand," she protested, scared of what she saw in Shan Dao's face.

"You will." He turned away. "I'm sorry. Tell Tinseng I understand why my father helped her now."

"Why *who*—"

—and then the world went black.

# PART FIVE

## TOWN WITHOUT PITY

# CHAPTER TWELVE

*Two Days Ago. June 23, 1963. Barcelona, Spain.*

Any real operative would have noticed the body first.

But his emotions had always kept him from promotion, and his thoughts as he entered the room were solely on Jinzhao, whose company he'd been eager for, his anticipation for their reunion a low fire he'd kept stoked as he'd danced with strangers through the night. Grodescu hadn't followed or sent anyone for them, and after a bottle of champagne and seeing his brother on the dance floor, Tinseng had started to feel *good*. He'd anticipated their enemy, outfoxed him even. The game was still his to win or lose. As they'd walked back, far past 1:00 a.m., he'd placed bets with himself whether Jinzhao had waited up for him. He'd been eager to find out the answer.

The lack of Jinzhao waiting up—that was the first thing he noticed. The room was oddly empty, or so he thought until he approached the bed. A figure had been placed there, unnaturally slumped like a thrown doll. In the shadows it could have been anyone. Tinseng placed his hand on the switchblade in his pocket and approached slowly. He recognized her then—how could he not? Her hair glistened dark and wet, too thick to be water from the shower.

"Yukying!" As he propped her up, her head lolled and left a red smear against the pillow. "Yukying, wake up." He needed her to wake up. "Yukying," he tried again, shaking a little harder. Finally she stirred.

"Yingtung?" Her voice slurred as she blinked awake.

"No, jiejie, it's me. Tinseng."

"A-Seng," she breathed, smiling even now. Smiling for him, the one who deserved it least in all the world.

"Jiejie." He brushed her hair away from her face, returned her smile tenfold. "You're in the wrong room. You're bleeding. What happened?"

"What?" She looked around the room. When her eyes fell to the two chairs pulled out from the table, she gasped, "Shan Dao!" She sat upright too quickly and clutched her head with a whimper of pain.

"Hey, hey, not too fast." He wrapped an arm around her narrow shoulders, easily encompassed by his embrace. He knew she hated to be considered delicate, but right now she was nothing less than porcelain to him; he wanted to circle her in one of those thick quilts museums used to wrap priceless artifacts and then ship her back home, away from all this. He should have been here. What had he been thinking? Just how useless *was* he? The question made his hand spasm on her shoulder. She stirred in his arm, shaking her head to clear it.

"Better?" he asked, and she nodded. "Then, what were you going to say about Shan Dao?"

"Oh," she breathed. "Tinseng, you have to make sure he's safe."

Frissons of panic skittered through him. "Why wouldn't he be safe?"

"Grodescu . . . came and found me. He gave me a message for Shan Dao. Maybe I shouldn't have said anything, or waited for you, but at the time it seemed too important to wait. But after I told him, Shan Dao—" Yukying paused.

Tinseng swallowed. "Take your time," he said, though his heart pounded.

"After I told him, he was upset. He ran off. I tried to stop him, but I . . . I tripped and fell." She touched the side of her head. "I hit the table, I think." Tears welled in her eyes. "He must have put me in the bed before he left."

Upset. Ran off. Left an injured Yukying in pursuit of Grodescu, because of something the Frenchman had said.

"Why did he leave? What did Grodescu say?" Tinseng tried to keep a tight rein on his panic, but he knew his mask was slipping.

"Grodescu was leaving for Paris tonight. He wanted Shan Dao to go with him."

"What? Why?"

"He said if Shan Dao didn't, he would add your name to a poem. What does that mean? I thought he had photographs?"

Tinseng tasted iron in his mouth. The rest of his body was numb. From far away he said, "And you told this to Shan Dao?"

"Y-yes, I did, and he . . ." Yukying looked more afraid than he had ever seen her. More afraid of him now than she had been in that alley. "He told me to tell you he understands why his father helped her now."

Her words caved a bloody crater into his chest. Was he dreaming again? He must be. It had seemed so important, so *crucial*, for Jinzhao to see things his way. And now, it seemed, he did. And now Tinseng realized far too late the consequences of a Jinzhao who believed love was worth any sacrifice, just in time for Tinseng to watch Jinzhao throw his life away for him while demanding that Tinseng live with his decision. What was the point of victory when it had no winners? It was too cruel to consider. No, it had to be a nightmare; he would wake up soon, surely.

Then Yukying cupped his cheek, and the chill of her hand robbed him of the comfort of pretending. This had to be real; she never touched him in his dreams.

"I have to go." He stood. "I have to—when's the next train? Do you have any pesetas on you?"

"I-I think so. Yes, here."

She handed over the coin purse from her pocket. He had traveler's checks, of course, but they said Wu Tinseng, and that name served no purpose for what was to come. He had to consider the trail he would leave from here to Paris. A trail that could not, under any circumstances, lead back to his family.

"What's happening?" Yukying asked as she watched him pull out a drawer and paw behind his clothes. "What is this poem? Did Shan Dao really go with him?"

He didn't answer. The gun was where he had left it, six bullets inside.

"Tinseng!" she cried when she saw the gun. The holster was hidden in a different drawer. "Tinseng," she said, raising her voice, "you're going after them? Why do you need that? Why do you even have it?"

"It's fine." Had he always been such a bad liar? He didn't think so. He would have to find that cold center of himself if he wanted to save Jinzhao. "I'm taking care of it."

"Whatever it is . . . whatever Shan Dao is doing . . . surely Grodescu wouldn't—it's just blackmail . . ."

Tinseng started laughing. Once he started, he couldn't stop. It *was* funny, wasn't it, how Yukying cared so much for people who didn't deserve it—who had lied to her from the start.

She stared at him, mouth agape. He was scaring her, his rage darkening the horizon. She had weathered tsunamis in Hong Kong, but this one was in the room.

"That's not even his name," he choked out against the laughter.

"What?"

"Shan Dao. Isn't his name. He's not from Paris; his parents didn't die in a car accident. Nothing you know about him is true. For that matter, he might not even like me."

"You don't believe that," she insisted, and all his bravado disintegrated, paper in the storm.

"You're right," he conceded. "I know exactly how he feels about me." *He told me to tell you he understands why he helped her now.* He pulled out the fine leather bag Cheuk-Kwan had gifted him before he left for Paris; he shook out all the belongings then repacked with what he would need. A change of clothes; the harness and the gun; leather gloves, technically for driving; his fake passport. If they searched his bag, he would never pass the border. He would just have to hope.

"But if he's not those things, if he's not Shan Dao, who is he?"

"I can't tell you."

He kept his back to her, but it didn't help: her gentleness still gutted him as she asked,

"Who is he to *you*?"

The answer in his heart was ready to bloody his lips with its truth. Words that had sat far too long: *I'm sorry, jiejie, but I never really believed you all those times you said you loved me. It's not your fault, it's mine. But with him, I never doubt. He makes me feel things I thought I'd spend my entire life without. He makes me feel safe. And he hasn't said it yet, but, well, actually he just did, in the worst way possible, but that's okay, because I'm going to save him, then yell at him, and then fuck him until we're both crying, and then I'll say I love him too, and ask him to build a life with me. Who is he to me? He is nothing less than my zhiji. I know, I know, such an old-fashioned term, but when I first read of Yu Boya playing for Zhong Ziqi, I imagined his face, though it'd been years since that one summer.*

And then the oldest words of all, which he knew he'd never speak: *I think I was born knowing his face. Even if we'd never met, I would have died thinking of him.*

None of these words were for his jiejie. She deserved different truths. When he finally turned to face her, she had stood.

"He's someone I need to protect," he offered. "He's the one in trouble, not me. What Grodescu has will do more than just ruin him. It will get him killed. J—Shan Dao has signed his own death warrant going with him. I have to go after them. I *have* to. That's all I can say. Please don't ask me anything more," he pleaded, wiping at his eyes.

"A-Seng." She was crying too, tears spilling over like a flooded riverbank. "Someone should go with you."

"No."

"Yes," she insisted. "If you're bringing a weapon, then it's dangerous. You'll be better off with A-Kwan by your side."

"Do you see my coat?" he asked, planning to get out the door rather than listen.

"Tinseng, let me get A-Kwan. You need—"

"I *need* you to stop wasting my time!" he yelled, full volume, then paled as she flinched. His nightmare again, only too real; and really, wasn't it only a matter of time before she looked at him in fear? "Jie—"

"No," she cut him off, holding up a hand. "You're not in your right mind. You love this man—please don't argue. I think I understand. He did this for you, before you could do it for him. And you're going to waste his sacrifice by getting *both* of you killed." Then, incredibly, she took a step toward him. "If you're going to save him, you have to do your best. Your *best*, Wu Tinseng."

Her voice cut through the black mist of his anger with a power no one else on earth, not even Jinzhao, could wield. Suddenly, he was seven, looking down from the rigging of a mast as the world stretched, the infinity contained between his body and the impact, and the pain promised after the fall.

"Tinseng," she called up to him, just as she had back then when she'd held up her arms and asked him to jump, "You need to take your brother."

That, after all, was the secret of jumping: What terror could a fall hold when you knew you had someone to catch you?

He slung the bag over his shoulder and walked past her, pausing to kiss her cheek. He avoided her gaze and walked to the door. Only with his hand on the doorknob did he say, "If he isn't at the gangway in five minutes, I'm leaving without him."

<hr />

The train from Barcelona to Paris took eight hours. The drive took a little over ten hours. But Grodescu had a head start and the trains weren't known to run on time; no matter how efficient the fascists said they were, this was still Spain. If they were lucky, they'd break even. Tinseng wouldn't consider the alternative.

Cheuk-Kwan bought the tickets for the 6:00 a.m. train, while Tinseng sent telegrams to contacts in Paris, trying to prepare for a rapid response once they arrived. On the gangway, Yukying had promised to bring everyone along behind them. Tinseng couldn't think about the others right now. He had other problems. Namely—

"Here." Cheuk-Kwan smacked the ticket against Tinseng's chest. "So *now* will you—"

"No." Tinseng took the ticket and went back to writing in his notebook.

"You're such a bastard," Cheuk-Kwan muttered. He was trying to act angry, but Yukying must have said something when she'd fetched him; he couldn't stop glancing over, worry twisting his frown. Tinseng ignored his glaring as they boarded the train and, once seated, deliberately balled up his coat and rested his head against the window, pretending to go to sleep. Eventually he heard Cheuk-Kwan sigh and lean back in his chair. He gave his brother time to drift off. After fifteen minutes he opened his eyes a crack to check. Cheuk-Kwan was staring right at him.

His brother snorted softly. "What, you think I'd just fall asleep?"

"Kinda, yeah," Tinseng admitted.

"Well, you're shit outta luck. Whiskey keeps me awake."

"I told you you should've had champagne."

They stared at each other, heads both leaning on their chairs. In the dim night lighting of the car, Cheuk-Kwan looked younger. He looked like Tinseng's favorite version of Cheuk-Kwan, the one who belonged just to Tinseng. The brother in the bed next to his. In the lowest times, sharing one thin blanket on a dirt floor. The rooms had always changed, but Cheuk-Kwan's quiet huff of a laugh in the dark never had. Tinseng used to live for hearing that laugh. If they'd always suffered the next day from staying up too late, it had always been worth the pain for a glimpse of who Cheuk-Kwan was without eyes on him. Cheuk-Kwan was a different person in the dark. So, Tinseng supposed, was he.

"Hey, Cheuk-Kwan," he said quietly, "remember when we were nine, when we stayed up all night comparing girls in our class, and you said Ye Luli was the prettiest?"

"I remember your ranking being the work of a fucking lunatic. Didn't you put Kong Yun near first?"

"I had to! She would've beat me up otherwise!"

"How would she have known?"

"How do I know? She just would have. She was *scary*. She hit me once, I swear!"

Cheuk-Kwan smirked, almost the laugh Tinseng wanted to hear, but it quickly turned sour.

"So, you were lying back then."

"I wasn't, she really was mean . . ."

"No, you—about . . . when you said you liked girls."

Oh. Well, of all the truths Cheuk-Kwan would have to hear today, this would be far from the worst. Tinseng shook his head and grimaced. "No, I like girls too."

"So . . ." His brother's brow furrowed. "So, you're telling me *no one* is safe from you?"

"Hey!"

"Be quiet, people are trying to sleep. I can't believe it. I was going to write the Kowloon Kaifong Women's Association to let them know there was finally some good news for them."

"Then *I'd* have to write and inform them you're still looking for a wife."

"Fuck you," Cheuk-Kwan said, but his expression betrayed him. "You're really the worst."

"I know," Tinseng said, smile crooked with too much love. His brother's adoration was like slipping into sun-warmed water, and despite it all, Tinseng couldn't help but think, *It has to work out. We have to save Jinzhao. What can't we do, if we're together?*

⁂

Cheuk-Kwan did sleep after that, only waking up at the border when the French officials came to check passports. It occurred to Tinseng that this might cause a problem. To avoid political tension between England and France, Hong Kongers weren't automatically monitored in France the way a Chinese visitor would be, so they wouldn't have to worry about a tail the moment they stepped off the train. But Tinseng planned to do whatever was necessary to get Jinzhao back, and someone was going to ask questions in the aftermath. Grodescu used his real name on the cruise; they'd have a record of his crossing from whichever checkpoint he drove through. Cheuk-Kwan also used his real name on the cruise, and now his name would be down as crossing from Spain to France. Two dotted lines on a map, one following the other—it wouldn't take a genius detective to link them, just the moderate dedication to make calls, request records, and slog through paper files.

Thinking quickly as they watched the official stop at the seats just ahead of them, Tinseng muttered to Cheuk-Kwan, "Use a thick accent."

"What?"

"When they ask your name. Use a thick accent and don't help them."

The official moved to their seat. Their British passports sailed through inspection. Tinseng's lips twitched as he watched the official write down Cheuk-Kwan's name completely wrong next to the spelling he copied from the passport.

After the official left, Tinseng explained, "I wanted to muddy the waters. Make it harder for them to look you up. Westerners are horrible with our names. No one's adopted pinyin; they're all using a mix of other systems."

"They're not using pinyin?"

"No, it's hilarious. They just write down a bunch of different spellings and hope for the best. That's why they hired me—to try to make sense of everything. I've even had to learn the Americans' Yale system." He scrunched his nose in distaste.

"Even the British? They're in charge of fucking Hong Kong."

"Well, no, the British have a working system. Sort of. Internally. But it doesn't match anyone else's. And the French are a mess, so hopefully we'll get lucky. But the worst are the Swiss, by far. Ah, if we were in Switzerland, they wouldn't even know we were in the country! Too bad."

"Incredible," Cheuk-Kwan said and snorted derisively. "And you worked for these idiots. I'm going back to sleep."

True to his word, Cheuk-Kwan shut his eyes and fell asleep in a few minutes. Tinseng couldn't turn his mind off, and so he wrote: everything he knew about Grodescu's Paris operations, every lead he might try, contingencies and fallbacks, decision trees based on responses to the telegrams he'd sent in Barcelona. On the train, he had no new information, but at least he had five years of experience—mostly behind a desk, but it counted for something—and the few connections he still trusted. He had medical aid in the form of his brother. He was far from helpless, and he wasn't alone. Comforting himself with these thoughts, his eyes finally closed.

He woke when the train lurched to a stop at the first station outside Paris. They were only forty minutes out now. He turned to find Cheuk-Kwan watching him.

"What are we walking into?" Cheuk-Kwan asked, low and intent. It was time; Tinseng knew it was time. Still, it was awful betraying Jinzhao's trust. On the other hand, Jinzhao had run off and left Tinseng in misery, so maybe he deserved a little turnabout.

"Well, first of all, his name isn't Shan Dao. It's Mei Jinzhao. *That* Mei Jinzhao."

"Wh—" Cheuk-Kwan cut himself off to shift to a whisper no less intense: "What the *fuck?*"

"When everything with his family happened, Jinzhao told me everything. He knew I could help."

"First of all, when did you ... how long have you—and why would he think that? You're just a ..."

Tinseng stared until his brother said, resignedly, "You're not a translator, are you?"

"I am, actually. But not *just*."

Cheuk-Kwan rolled his eyes. "Fine. Okay. The Mei who came in from the cold, is that it?"

"With a different ending, hopefully," Tinseng said with as much false cheer as he could muster. "I've just been trying to help him survive."

"Ha. Where'd you go wrong?"

"Hey."

"Am I wrong?"

He wasn't. Cheuk-Kwan was due a little bitterness. Tinseng had never wanted his brother to know just how much he'd been lying to him.

"Well, after everything happened, we needed to get him out of Europe. And I'd been wanting to ... I'd missed Yukying's cooking. The plan was to get him to Hong Kong so he could lay low for a while. He hadn't decided what to do from there. But then we'd heard there'd been information stolen from his parents. The kind someone would kill over. The Americans, the Chinese, the Russians. This man, Lucas Grodescu, has the only copy of that information, and he's got them in a bidding war. And now he's figured he'll get a bigger payday if he sells Jinzhao along with them."

"And Mei Jinzhao went with him?"

Tinseng shrugged, unwilling to share that Jinzhao did it for him. If he thought about it, he wouldn't be able to function.

"Okay . . ." Cheuk-Kwan scratched his ear. "And what are you planning to do?"

"Get him back."

"So let me get this straight. Sh—Mei Jinzhao goes with this guy of his own free will, presumably. To maybe make a move of his own, or to protect all of us from the blowback, or something else you don't even know because he didn't tell you. But you're ignoring that and going after him anyway."

"If it were me," Tinseng said, "Wouldn't you?"

"Depends what you did," Cheuk-Kwan replied without missing a beat.

"Well then, good thing for Jianzhao it's me going after him. You're just along for the ride, right?" Tinseng brushed off the rest of the conversation, their motives and loyalties, with a final word: "It's the right thing to do, Cheuk-Kwan. He needs help."

Cheuk-Kwan shook his head. "You haven't changed at all, have you?"

"I tried to tell you. It's your fault you didn't listen."

Brothers would always be the same. It wasn't funny, but you had to laugh. Tinseng had no choice but to accept that his brother still betrayed that Tinseng wasn't the shining hero who'd saved his family. He'd only been thirteen, but already he had been a scholar, an orphan, a beggar, a thief, a drain on society, an adopted son, a bad influence, and a burden. He had worn many masks, which could also be called lives. He had no idea which one was most him.

Cheuk-Kwan sat back against the chair and crossed his arms.

"Who do you think Grodescu is trying to sell him to?"

"Doesn't really matter; the result will be the same. But my gut says Soviets."

"Is that who you work for?"

"Ugh! I'm insulted!"

"Well, how would I know?"

"You should know me better than that! Besides, don't think that way; I'm retired now. Officially. A brief but shining career."

"*Hmmph.* Anything else I need to know? Any little details that might've slipped your mind? *Your* name's still Tinseng, right?"

Tinseng snorted. "You think I've been lying since we met? We were six."

"Don't act like that isn't something you would've done back then."

The loudspeaker announced their final stop in Paris. Tinseng considered reiterating how serious this was; they were joking now, and he didn't know if Cheuk-Kwan really understood the severity of the situation. When he caught Cheuk-Kwan's gaze, he let his expression speak for him. Let the dark thoughts creep into his periphery; felt the weight of the gun strapped to his side. There would be death today. That was inevitable. It was his mission to ensure it was no one he loved. He let that thought fully surface and Cheuk-Kwan stared for a long moment, taking in the change. Then he nodded.

"Okay," his brother said. "Where to first?"

※

A spy who said they'd retired was a liar.

Even though Tinseng had signed his resignation papers, even though he'd told Jinzhao he was out, even though he was taking the job in Hong Kong, even though he'd just told Cheuk-Kwan he'd hung up his spook hat, those had only ever been half-truths. You could never really let go once they'd burrowed the paranoia under the skin.

When he'd left Paris a little over a week ago, he'd never intended to return. He'd said his goodbyes, absolutely confident he'd never see any of those people again. Julian—there was someone he thought he'd gladly left behind. Then why hadn't he thrown away the man's number? He knew why. Of the few replies he'd received in answer to the telegrams he'd sent in Barcelona, it had been Julian he'd most hoped would reply. He was the most useful connection Tinseng still had, and the one he had been most reluctant to contact. Tinseng had finished the goddamned chapter, the sordid page turned. Now here he was in this unwilling epilogue, a scene that had no purpose—except to bleed.

Just outside the train station, they queued for much-needed coffee. Tinseng also bought a box of pastries, ignoring a confused Cheuk-Kwan insisting he wasn't hungry. Box in hand, Tinseng hailed a taxi to take them across town. The streets narrowed and trash accumulated as they drove away from tourists and into the neighborhoods Tinseng used to frequent.

"What a charming place," Cheuk-Kwan drawled as the taxi dropped them in front of a tenement. Tinseng continued ignoring him as they walked up four flights of stairs.

"Don't react to anything," was the only warning he gave before he pounded on the door. After a few moments he knocked again, insistent, with the fist of the law. They heard a yell from the apartment and then the door flew open. A disheveled Frenchman stood on the other side, last night's hangover evident on his collar. A scar bisected his hairline, which Tinseng knew the man loved for the toughness of it, but no number of scars could hide the provincial air that still clung to him. The sun had permanently stained and wrinkled his skin, his wiry frame left over from a boy who'd grown up hungry, his hunched back from a childhood combing through garbage on the beach when the tide was low. The man scowled until he saw who stood in the hall. When his gaze fell on Tinseng, a light came to his eyes—nothing good promised.

"Wow. I thought your telegram was a joke," the man said in French as Tinseng shouldered past him. "Thought you said I'd never see you again. And who's this? New toy? Are we gonna break him? Can I play with h—"

"Touch him and lose another finger," Tinseng said without turning around. "I mean it, Jules. Did you follow my instructions?" he asked in English for Cheuk-Kwan's sake.

"The telegram messenger was so annoying," Julian drawled, ignoring the English and keeping to French. "I'm thinking of loosening his bike spokes. He's afraid of me, though, so that's something."

Tinseng ignored the prattle. "Did you get what I wanted?"

"What do I get if I did?" Julian asked.

*Your life*, Tinseng nearly snarled, but that wasn't how their game was played. Instead, he pulled a piece of paper from his pocket, torn from his notebook, and offered it between two fingers. Julian snatched at it, betraying his eagerness; when he read it, his smile widened.

"Naughty, Mr. Wu, very naughty. What would your superiors think of you giving me this information?"

"They're not my superiors anymore, are they?" Tinseng placed the bakery box on the grimy table. Julian grinned.

"*And* you're feeding me? Oh, you *are* desperate. It looks good on you, darling."

"Don't."

Julian shrugged and sat on the floor, folding his legs under the table and tucking into the pastries offered.

"What the fuck is happening?" Cheuk-Kwan intoned next to Tinseng as they stood above the other man.

"I needed a lead, fast. He doesn't sleep. I knew the telegram would reach him."

"Who is he?"

"No one you want to remember."

"I'm hurt," Julian placed a hand over his heart. He'd followed their conversation with shifting eyes, two marbles rolling in their sunken bowls. Already most of a croissant had disappeared past yellow teeth. "Didn't he tell you who I was? Who *he* was? He's a legend. I learned so much from him. But who *wouldn't* learn from—"

"Jules, do you *want* to die?" Tinseng asked in saccharine French.

"At your hand? You know I do." The other man leaned back against the couch, the long line of his body a twisted knife. He had a sharp, satisfied look, as though his glee had cut its way out of his mouth. It was pathetic.

Tinseng's exhaustion hit him then, inexorable as the horizon swallowing the sun.

"We're staying here. I'm sleeping. Cheuk-Kwan, watch this one. Read the file."

"What file?"

"Julian, where's the file?"

"In the icebox," the man on the floor sang. Cheuk-Kwan threw Tinseng such a look of long-suffering he had to laugh.

"You heard him: it's in the icebox. We want addresses. Places they might keep an asset. Associates who do his wet work and where they might have safehouses. That should be written up, Paris Station has been following Grodescu for a long time. Give Julian a list, and he'll go fetch more files. Won't you?"

Tinseng raised an eyebrow at his one-time associate, one-time lover. Julian met the look with no expression of his own. The little weasel patted his shirt pocket, no doubt where he was keeping the slip of paper Tinseng had given to him as greeting, his side of the bargain. It was a short list, two columns: next to each last name Tinseng had written a single word, maybe a short phrase. Everyone had their vices, even Paris Station's front desk men, supposedly chosen to be incorruptible. Perhaps Tinseng should feel guilty setting Julian loose on them, but after all, Whitehall had decided to recruit Julian in the first place after the DGSE would have nothing to do with him. Had, even after he kept having "accidents" in the field, kept him as a free agent in their stable for certain unpleasantness no real agent would ever touch. They had made their bed. Tinseng was simply ensuring they slept in it.

Besides, Julian had never been patient, or subtle. A smarter man would milk this blackmail for years. Jules would burn through it in two months and be right back where he started.

After a beat, Julian realized he wouldn't get the reaction he hoped for. He let his hand drop from his pocket and reached into the pastry box instead.

"Whatever you say, boss," he said, then stuffed half an egg tart in his mouth.

"Good." Tinseng looked away. "Great. Have fun. Wake me in an hour."

It was 4:00 p.m. when they left the tenement. Assuming Grodescu left around 3:00 a.m., he'd been in the city since 1:00 p.m. But even if Grodescu expected Tinseng to follow—and he must have—he wouldn't unload Jinzhao on the first willing buyer. There were sides to play and a price to inflate. A meeting to arrange, as well, one that suited everyone's paranoia and security and didn't tip off the French. Although Tinseng had been wrong at almost every turn, he still believed he knew Lucas Grodescu's character. Grodescu wasn't the type to waste an advantage. While he wove his web and pulled in his prey, he'd stash Jinzhao away somewhere safe for the long-term. Tinseng was counting on that; property would be easier to find than a person, and a slowly unfolding plan would even out Tinseng's time disadvantage.

With the names Cheuk-Kwan and Jules pulled from the file, Tinseng was fairly certain he knew where to look. But he only had one chance at this, so he flattened his hair with water from the sink, shoved a tartine into his mouth, then pushed Cheuk-Kwan out the door to take him to a place he shouldn't know about, to see a man who didn't technically exist.

A lot of bridges would be burned walking in and talking to one of the best informants in the city. It would almost certainly get back to MI6. It might even lose him the position waiting for him in Hong Kong.

"You'd get me a job if I need one, right?" he asked Cheuk-Kwan as they walked down the alley.

"Shouldn't you be asking *Laurence*? His father would love to finally have you under his thumb."

Tinseng made a sound of betrayal and shoved him. Cheuk-Kwan shoved back. Then they stood at the end of the alley in front of a door painted white. They looked at each other, a moment of silent synchronicity.

"Let me do the talking," Tinseng warned. "If you mess this up, Jinzhao dies."

Cheuk-Kwan didn't argue. There was flint in his eyes Tinseng hadn't seen since Cheuk-Kwan's mother had died. He'd hoped to never see it again.

"Okay," he breathed, then knocked on the door.

Inside, the smoke was so thick they could barely see the band on the raised platform at the other end of the room. It was better not to look too closely. In a place like this, in the middle of the day, the actors changed, but the roles were always the same: the barflies, the blackjack players, the strung-out girls, and the boys looking for someone to take them home—the addicted and the desperate, the low kind of humanity Tinseng always found alluring and strangely comforting. As if he were meant to be one of them and his soul knew it; perhaps like truly was always drawn to like.

The cigarette girls here weren't pretty, but they smiled all the same. One young woman with green eyes flicked a lighter with a tall flame as soon as they approached. Tinseng took out a cigarette and cupped the girl's hand, looking at her through his lashes.

"Merci," he murmured, dropping a handful of new franc coins on her tray. Continuing in French, he asked, "Say, you haven't seen Etienne, have you?"

"Not today," she said with an exaggerated pout, "but I can keep you company if you like."

Cigarette girls were the lowest rung in a club's pecking order, and each girl was always angling for a seat at a booth to prove her hostess potential to the boss. Usually, Tinseng would have helped out and invited her to his table. She looked like a nice girl. But Jinzhao didn't have time for him to be anything but ruthless.

"Well, I am a little lonely," he pulled at the string of her desperation, "but I have to work before I can play, honey. You don't want me getting in trouble, do you?"

"Never," she drawled, playing along.

"Good girl." He gave her a wink. "If Etienne isn't here, is there someone else?" He made a show of thinking before dropping the bait. "Casimir isn't around, is he?"

"Oh, yes, he just came in," the girl said, eager to show off her knowledge. "He's over there, in that far booth. But go ask Sammy at the bar if you can see him first."

"Of course—we have to follow the rules, don't we?" He winked again, and her giggle was good. Almost believable. "I'll try to be back later," he lied. He plucked up one of her matchbooks and slid it into his pocket as he walked away.

Cheuk-Kwan's incredulous gaze burned the side of his face, but he ignored it, turning the matchbook over and over in his pocket, a fidget of anxiety where no one could see. He would give the matchbook to Jinzhao later, he told himself, a little souvenir from his misadventure.

"I heard names," Cheuk-Kwan said after they'd bribed the bartender into letting them approach the booth. "Casimir? Etienne?"

"Local fixers. Both names listed as associates, but the file confirmed Casimir's the one supplying Grodescu his muscle. I know Etienne, but not this other guy."

Usually Tinseng had the luxury of time to get to know someone—how they worked, what motivated them. Instant rapport was not his strength; he was not good at fostering connections the way he could effortlessly see holes in a statement's logic or ask just the right question to break open an interrogation. He could only hope his instincts would serve him well today.

"Hope he's as easy to persuade as Etienne always is," he added.

"We'll make it worth his while," Cheuk-Kwan said grimly, eyes focused ahead on the booth barely visible in the haze. Cheuk-Kwan looked ready for a brawl. A surge of gratitude made him bump his brother's shoulder a little.

At the booth, Casimir and two cronies sat surrounded by fawning women. Tinseng didn't waste time he didn't have. He approached and laid down a stack of new franc bills, still wrapped in their bank ribbon.

"I'd like to buy five minutes of your time," he said in his best French, pushing the money in front of the man in the cheap wrinkled suit.

"So desperate, then?" The man asked with a lisp. Tinseng noticed a scar splitting open his lip and part of his nose. The scar spoke of enemies made and choices survived. "Kicking your feet roughly, you don't care what you disturb. Or is this supposed to impress me?"

"Neither. I'm simply an impatient man." Tinseng showed his teeth. "Why waste good whiskey and girls on me, when that's not what I'm here for?"

The man stroked his beard. "This is not the way things are done here, boy. You disrespect my hospitality."

Tinseng spread his hands. "Why accept an apple when you know the core is rotten?"

"It's a wonder you're still alive, with this attitude."

"Does Alonzo still hold court at the Savoy?" He angled the question at Cheuk-Kwan as he reached to take back the money. "Maybe *he'll* want to make a quick score."

The man moved fast for someone so clearly drunk, setting his hand on top of the stack before Tinseng could pull it away. "I didn't say I wasn't interested."

Tinseng placed his hands on the table and leaned forward. "So earn it."

"Tell me what all the fuss is about, then."

"Something hot. A lot of men needed quickly. A telegram early this morning, perhaps from Barcelona."

"I see." Casimir laughed and leaned back against the creaking leather. "You're a poodle picking a fight with a panther. I do not make a habit of getting on the bad side of panthers."

Agitation hummed under his skin. He shoved it down. *Patience*, Tinseng reminded himself. "All I need is an address. A neighborhood, even. If I'm caught, who knows how I got that information? It could have been a hundred ways." He set down another stack of money. "If I succeed, you won't have to worry about that particular panther anymore. His absence might leave some interesting opportunities for growth."

"Hmm." The man took a sip of his drink, taking his time. Tinseng dug his nails into his palm and kept his face placid. "I may have heard something this afternoon." His eyes flickered to the money. Tinseng sighed and added a third stack. Casimir reached into his jacket pocket and produced a small notebook and pencil. He scribbled down an address and set it on the table, a finger pinning it down. Tinseng lifted his hand off the cash and picked up the torn paper.

"Now, if you don't mind," Casimir said, "You're ruining my aperitif and you're blocking my view of the band. You can find your way to the door."

Tinseng turned to leave, his hand on Cheuk-Kwan's shoulder.

"Hey." For the first time Cheuk-Kwan spoke. He had to use English, not able to follow the French. "Your piano needs tuning," he told Casimir, clearly needing to get in a parting shot. "And your trumpet player's shit."

"Eh? *Qu'a t'il dit?*" Casimir asked the crony next to him.

A laugh tripped out of Tinseng, as startled as anyone else by his brother's recklessness but delighted in it. "He really is," he agreed, still laughing, hurrying them away before they were thrown out.

# CHAPTER THIRTEEN

*Two Days Ago. June 23, 1963. Paris, France.*

Telling his brother the truth about Jinzhao had been a risk, but he was glad now he'd done it. Partially, he was pleasantly surprised at how well Cheuk-Kwan adapted to the situation. Straightforward action seemed to suit him, to bring out a side of him Tinseng hadn't seen since they'd been back in Yichang. They hadn't felt this close in years. Mostly, though, he was glad because he had no idea how he would have explained this next part.

    The address led them down, in the way every city had an up and a down; not in geography but in atmosphere, the compass of acceptable and criminal, acknowledged and invisible, contributor and burden. Down they drove until they were deposited into an industrial stretch dotted with evidence of becoming a new immigrant neighborhood. A few restaurants, snatches of language as they scouted the area, the occasional flag hung in a window—it all spoke of something new emerging from old soil. Of writing to neighbors and cousins telling them to make the journey, there was something here for them: a job or a bed or a nice single boy with a grocer's salary. The threadbare hope of leaving home and praying what awaited you would be better. Tinseng thought of fleeing China for Hong Kong, leaving Hong Kong for Paris. They would have to fight, the quiet residents of this new community. He wished them more luck than he'd had. But they'd have help tonight. Rotten things should be excised. He was only too happy to cut it clean.

So then it was only a matter of staking out the place. The building itself was a standalone three-story on the corner. There were flats on the second and third floors; they watched an elderly couple enter, and a woman in her thirties leave. The first floor was their target. In the window hung a sign marking it as the satellite location of a construction company. A man left from the front door to smoke a cigarette. Tinseng watched, cataloging everything he could; he had been trained in this a little, though it was never his area of expertise. Thankfully, these men were hardly government-trained. They were hired muscle barely able to think past their noses. Tinseng hadn't been able to help scoffing as they'd scouted around the building earlier; even Cheuk-Kwan had said under his breath, "Not very careful, are they?" when they'd noticed the blinds half-drawn on a window. Watching the man now, he saw no sign of intelligence; he looked like one of his punches could knock Tinseng out cold, but they probably wouldn't be discussing Nietzsche. The man threw his cigarette on the ground, scrubbed his hand over his shaved head, and walked back inside.

Around the back, there were concrete stairs in the back leading down to a cellar. In all, they would have to cover the first floor and basement, two exits, four windows. From the half-drawn blinds they caught sight of their smoker and another man in gray slacks and a vest. Two on the first floor, possibly more. An unknown number in the basement. So many unknowns. No one would call this an ideal situation. In one of those, he would have a team watch this spot for days to learn their patterns, ready to intercept if they tried to move the asset. Tinseng didn't have a team, or time. This would have to be a smash and grab.

"You cover the back," Tinseng murmured from their spot across the street. "I'm going in the front."

"No fucking way," Cheuk-Kwan protested. "I'm coming with you."

"And if they hustle Jinzhao out of the cellar door we saw?"

"So we both go in the front, I rush the basement, and you sweep the first floor."

Tinseng tried not to lose his patience. "We don't have time to argue. I wouldn't tell you how to diagnose a patient. You have to listen to me on this. I know what I'm doing." He didn't, not really, but Cheuk-Kwan didn't need to know that.

They glared at each other until Cheuk-Kwan ground out, "I hate your plan."

"Got a better one?"

Cheuk-Kwan's mulish silence answered for him. Tinseng handed him a Walther PPK from the canvas bag Julian had supplied them with.

"Don't use this unless you absolutely have to; I don't know how clean it is." Jules would find it hilarious to use a dirty gun to connect two unrelated crimes; he liked playing those kinds of games with the police. But Jules was going to get caught one day—*wanted* to be caught some day—and Tinseng planned to stay a free man.

There were a few other details to cover: code words, when to flee, rendezvous points, how to reach Yukying if they were blown. Then Tinseng ran out of ways to ensure Cheuk-Kwan came out of this alive, and all he had left was to stand and watch as his brother walked away with his precious heart beating in his chest. He hated his plan too. But it had to be done.

Gripping the duffel tightly, Tinseng put his brother out of his mind. He counted to 200 slowly as they'd agreed—three minutes for Cheuk-Kwan to walk around back and situate himself. Then Tinseng started in on the door. Amateurs, he scoffed to himself as he examined the lock: He could kick it down if he really wanted, but he preferred the element of surprise and so set to work with the lockpicks Julian had packed. This must be a temporary spot, not usually used to keep assets. Grodescu probably didn't trade in human assets often; it was far messier than paper or film. They'd gotten lucky catching the man so unprepared. He thanked gods he didn't believe in that Grodescu had to rush this job, then thanked himself for being the reason Grodescu was worried. After a minute's tense labor, the lock clicked.

Tinseng put away the tools and pulled out his knife. He checked the street one last time then slowly turned the handle and moved inside like slow-rolling smoke.

He'd be like fire tonight—the kind that sparked while the family slept. He'd spread from room to room, silent and unforgiving, and then he'd kill them all in their beds.

A flash of a knife in the dark made quick work of the man on guard at the front, dead before he could stand from his stool. Tinseng caught the body and guided it to the floor. From his crouch, he took in the rest of the layout. There was a doorway with a hanging curtain separating the storefront from the back room; music from the radio drifted out from the other side.

Tinseng slipped off his shoes and tiptoed to the curtain. In the sliver between the fabric, Tinseng saw a man at the table, head down, more interested in his dinner than his job or his life. Tinseng used came up silently from behind to cover the man's mouth and slit his throat deep enough to turn his scream into a gurgle.

Tinseng watched the body long enough to ensure he wouldn't catch a nasty ambush later. Distantly, he hoped Cheuk-Kwan never saw this. But standing here, at a table with a dread feast and no witnesses to watch him gorge, he wondered if this wasn't who he was always supposed to be. It was what they'd wanted him to become, certainly. Their bright future for him: a war for the soul of the world, with men in faraway rooms telling nobodies like him to pull the trigger. "For queen and country," they had liked to say, but Tinseng was reminded of another mantra: "the most farsighted, the most self-sacrificing, the most resolute."

A raised voice from the street brought him back. There was no reason to think of either side anymore. He was on his own side with Jinzhao, whose voice whispered in his mind: *He who attains to sincerity chooses the good and firmly holds it fast.*

He walked over to the basement door and took a deep breath. He thought about getting Cheuk-Kwan, then thought about Cheuk-Kwan walking past two dead bodies. Just him, then, but that was okay. Whatever lurked down there, he would handle it. He slid his gun from its holster and hoped Jinzhao could forgive him for not choosing the good.

He opened the door to darkness. Only the dimmest light illuminated the depth of the basement. There was a light switch at the top of the stairs. *Perfect*, he thought, and flipped on the lights to blind the men sitting in the dark. With his knife and gun held one over the other, he surged down the stairs.

"*Que t'a-t-on dit sur le fait d'éteindre la lumière?*" A man snapped, expecting one of his companions. Then he saw Tinseng. "Ey, who—"

Tinseng threw the knife first, catching the man reaching for the gun on the table. A second man, the speaker, scrambled for the gun in his holster, but Tinseng shot him. The bullet caught the arm. Tinseng shot again and got him through the chest. The man swayed, then fell.

The first man had recovered from the knife in his shoulder and shot at Tinseng. Tinseng dodged as air stirred next to his head. He ran forward, shooting as he charged. The man flinched, not expecting his attacker to run at him. The hesitation cost his life: Tinseng shot twice in a row and hit once. One was enough.

As he stared at the man to ensure he wasn't breathing, he called, "Jinzhao, talk to me—can you hear me?"

Jinzhao grunted from a corner. They'd tied Jinzhao to a wooden chair. His shirt was ripped, his chest mottled. He struggled to lift his head, eyes on Tinseng. Tinseng felt the weight of them, Jinzhao's anger and relief under his bruised ego.

"He knew," Jinzhao told him, as if Tinseng cared about Grodescu right now. "Knew the buyer in Villefranche was false. He never had her papers on him and planned to kill whoever arrived at the meeting. When we approached him, he put it together. He strung us along to get me closer."

"That's all very interesting, Jinzhao, but how can you think of this right now? You know, I have a few things to say to you."

Part of him wanted to mention what Jinzhao told Yukying about his parents, but why invite ghosts? This moment was for them alone. Satisfied the room was empty, he walked over to the chair and crouched down in front of Jinzhao.

"The first thing is you can't ever do that to me again. I don't want to know who I am without you. Maybe you're strong enough to survive without me; maybe that's why you thought I could too. But I can't. I'm telling you right now. Or I won't. It's the same thing. Do you hear me?"

Tinseng whispered, a hand under Jinzhao's jaw to help him hold up his head. "You can't deny me this. I demand it, Jinzhao—promise me."

Slowly, Jinzhao wet his lips. His breath wheezed through him. "Promise."

"Okay. Okay." He kissed Jinzhao then, hard and demanding. The kiss seared life back into Tinseng's fear-cold heart and gave him the courage to pull back and say, "The second thing is I love you. I'm composed of Eros and dust and show an affirming flame. Every mote of me is yours. Do you believe me?"

"Every mote," Jinzhao repeated, still stunned. "Yes. Yes, I—"

"Live with me," Tinseng continued instead of letting him say it back. "Come live with me. Will you?"

Instead of answering, Jinzhao surged forward to kiss him again, chair rocking underneath him. For long moments the basement held still in deference to the two bodies hidden in the dark.

"I haven't even untied you," Tinseng said with a laugh when he finally pulled away. "You should have said."

"When?" Jinzhao asked archly. Tinseng cackled.

"Shouldn't you be unafraid to interrupt my speeches? Be resolute, fear no sacrifice, and surmount every difficulty to win victory, isn't that how it goes? Hmm," he looked at the ropes around Jinzhao's wrists and reconsidered undoing them himself. "Hold on, Cheuk-Kwan is here too. I want him to do this. Sit pretty, okay?"

He crossed the room to the cellar door and opened it to find Cheuk-Kwan pointing the gun unsteadily down the stairwell.

"Very intimidating," Tinseng commented as his brother followed him down.

"Shut up. How is he?"

"You shouldn't have come," Jinzhao had the audacity to say as Cheuk-Kwan crouched to check how they'd tied him to the chair.

"Don't be an idiot," Cheuk-Kwan said as Tinseng added, "What did you *think* we would do? Sail on to Villefranche and drink mai tais with fucking Laurence, wishing you the best on your journey?"

Cheuk-Kwan snorted. "Hand me that knife, A-Seng." He pointed to the knife sticking out of the man on the floor. Tinseng wiped the knife on the dead man's shirt then handed it to Cheuk-Kwan, who cut Jinzhao free. The rope pulled skin and hair as it untied; the wounds had started to clot around the fiber. Tinseng sucked in his breath as Cheuk-Kwan carefully peeled away the ropes to reveal raw, bloody wrists.

"Burns from pulling," Cheuk-Kwan diagnosed. "You kept trying to escape, didn't you? Stubborn bastard," he muttered, grudgingly respectful as he helped Tinseng pull Jinzhao out of the chair.

"Yep, stubborn bastard, that's him," Tinseng said, his outlook much better now that he could feel Jinzhao's living, breathing body against his. Jinzhao was alive, he wanted to live with him, he'd heard Tinseng's confession. They were both here! Alive! Tinseng almost laughed, and his shaking made Jinzhao look over, as though he could just sense anytime Tinseng wanted to indulge an inappropriate reaction. Instead of the glare he'd expected, Jinzhao's gaze was soft as the summer breeze.

*Oh no*, Tinseng thought, *but there is Heaven—it knows me!*

His joviality died as they stopped at the threshold of the cellar door. Had the neighbors called the police by now? Surely they had, after the sound of gunshots. The stairs up were dark and led into an unknown night. Grodescu was still out there, as were the people he'd promised the list to. Tinseng shifted Jinzhao's weight to keep a steady hand on his gun. Sensing the shift, Cheuk-Kwan pulled Jinzhao over to lean fully against him. Tinseng looked over to find his brother giving him a narrow-eyed look.

"Let me take him," Cheuk-Kwan said.

"I didn't want you to see that."

"You think I haven't seen worse?"

"It's different. This is different from your doctor's office."

"What do you think I've been doing for three years? There are riots in Hong Kong too, Wu Tinseng, and the only reason I'm not at the front is *because* I'm a doctor. They take the worst cases to me. I knew what I was getting into here. I know how to carry an injured comrade. You go ahead. Make sure it's clear."

"But—"

"You might be James Bond now, but you're still shit at strategy. Stop being emotional and go. I've got him."

"He's right," Jinzhao rasped. "Go."

"Jinzhao." Tinseng cradled his face in his hands as gently as he knew. Jinzhao's pupils were two different sizes. Blood pooled in one of his eyes and his nose bent unnaturally. They'd have to reset it. Dried blood matted a spot above his ear, near the divot where Tinseng's thumb could perfectly fit. They'd pulled out a chunk of hair; nothing professional in that, just hate. Jinzhao had seen the worst of it down here. Here in this basement and dozens like it where Tinseng had lived and had never wanted anyone to go; he had lost so much of himself in places like this, and he'd gotten it wrong, so wrong. Every move he'd tried to make had been anticipated. Grodescu had been ahead of them the whole time. *What if he was waiting above? What if—*

"Tinseng."

He resurfaced at the sound of his name.

"Yeah." It sounded tired. He was tired.

"Tinseng." His name again, more forceful. He raised his eyes and there he was—Jinzhao, *his* Jinzhao, who underneath it all seemed unchanged and met his gaze with steel.

"Get us home," Jinzhao said.

"Yeah?"

"Yes."

Tinseng cleared the gratitude and fury out of his throat. With a nod—first to the love of his life, then to his first and best friend—he stalked up the stairs with revenge in his heart, ready to do anything to carry out Jinzhao's order.

✤

They arrived at Hôtel Le Bristol to find Chiboon waiting for them on the sidewalk. His hand held a suite key, and his eyes widened at the sight of Jinzhao. They'd tried to clean him up but had few ways to hide all the blooming injuries; suspicion followed them through the sparkling lobby and stayed fixed as they made themselves as small as possible waiting for the elevator.

"Remember what I said about adventures?" Chiboon asked Cheuk-Kwan, who snorted.

"Yeah. And you're right: they're *exhausting*. Yingtung really had to stay at the fanciest fucking place, didn't he?"

"I told Yukying we needed to be inconspicuous," Tinseng agreed, adjusting his collar. "Did she have you use a fake name, at least?"

"She did," Chiboon said.

"And they didn't ask for anything else? Nothing special?"

"No, Laurence's flawless French accent was enough for them, apparently. Just like the hotels back home: no ID, no deposit, just filling out the registration form."

"Good, good." Tinseng tried to take heart; this part of the plan, at least, had gone off flawlessly.

"But why does any of this matter?" Chiboon insisted. "Yukying wouldn't say why."

"Because they'll forward our information to the DGSE."

"The who?"

"The D—the French equivalent of MI6?"

Chiboon shrugged.

Tinseng rolled his eyes. "Hotels forward on the information of any suspicious guests," he explained. "It's common practice. They'll give it to the police and the DGSE, who'll forward it to any foreign agency with connections to the suspects."

"We're *suspects* now?"

"Chiboon. We're a large group of Chinese people walking through the door."

The entire elevator stood in silence a moment, acknowledging the point. Chiboon clicked his tongue.

"Tinseng, you're so devious. But it's not like we haven't been hassled at every port, and we used our real names then. Why all this? And what's going on with you, anyway? Why is Shan Dao beat up?"

"Save it," Cheuk-Kwan snapped. Against all odds, Tinseng had to press his lips together to stop a smile. He glanced over at Chiboon to find him hiding his mouth behind his hand. It was a goddamned parody, he thought; Tinseng didn't know whether to laugh or cry. He focused on holding up Jinzhao until they made it to the suite; once Jinzhao was situated on the bed, Cheuk-Kwan left to fetch Yukying, pulling Chiboon out with him.

And then they were alone. Was it only last night he'd kissed Jinzhao's cheek and told him not to wait up? How arrogant he'd been. The price lay in front of him now, black eye and broken rib to match all the broken pieces inside Tinseng that made no proper human, only whatever people could cobble together from reaching in and pulling out. Jinzhao stared at him from the bed, and saw what? A savior? A curse? *I love you*, he'd said earlier, and Jinzhao had kissed him like . . . but wouldn't anyone be happy to be rescued?

The staring was getting to him. With a nervous chuckle, Tinseng fled to the bathroom.

He avoided his face in the mirror. *Get us home*, Jinzhao had said, as if they held the same definition. In the quiet of starched sheets and plush carpet, would reality sink back in? On the counter heavy glasses were set upside down to protect them from dust. He turned one over and filled it with water, wet a washcloth, then brought the whole ordeal out to the bed.

Neither spoke. Tinseng sat on the bed and began wiping Jinzhao's face. Most of the blood was quite dry by this point. His hair would have to be washed later. Easier to focus on the nose, though it made Jinzhao wince. Through it all, Jinzhao stared relentlessly. Tinseng looked anywhere but at the gaze he knew would undo him. Where was Cheuk-Kwan anyway? Wasn't he supposed to be fetching Yukying? If he knew Cheuk-Kwan at all, Tinseng would guess this long break was his brother's way of saying, in the most roundabout way possible: *Get on with it, you dumb bastard.* He hated having such a considerate family.

The water was getting too bloody to be useful. He tried to buy himself a reprieve by standing to get a fresh glass.

A hand around his wrist stopped him. There it was.

"Jinzhao. You're not looking so bad underneath it all. A little rest and you'll be back to your perfect self, shaming the rest of us with your mere presence."

"Tinseng." A note of hurt? Or was he imagining it? He couldn't confirm; he still couldn't look. It would be better, he decided, to wait Jinzhao out. This strategy had never worked before, not even once, but there was always a first time.

When he couldn't stand it anymore, he cracked and whispered, "Why? You didn't need to do that. *Why?*"

And now, of all times, he decided to raise his head. There were those burning eyes, the black always overlaying the brown. Only when the sun caught them did the embers glow. But there was no sunlight coming through the closed curtains, and Jinzhao's gaze would not have lightened even if it was.

"I did what you would have done," he said.

Tinseng couldn't refute it—Jinzhao did *exactly* what he would have done. What could he say now? That he wanted Jinzhao to admit he was right but never act on it? That he hadn't ever considered how he'd feel if the people he loved acted like him? Anything he thought to say made him sound like a fool or a hypocrite or both. He frowned and rubbed the dried blood above Jinzhao's ear rougher than he had to.

"They are *my* family's injustices," Jinzhao continued. "I have stood to the side while you sacrificed for me. But it is not right."

"You really are a righteous person, Jinzhao. It's very annoying sometimes."

"No more than you."

"Eh? Are you calling me annoying?"

"Righteous."

The heart couldn't take declarations like that. Not after what the hands still felt from their violence.

Jinzhao added into the silence, "You are wrong."

"About what?"

"My righteousness. I cannot be righteous until my actions reflect it. 'By nature men are nearly alike; by practice, they get to be wide apart.'"

"轻生重义.[11] What do your actions reflect if not that? Did you not despise life in order to value justice?" Flint tried to spark in Jinzhao's eyes but before it could light, Tinseng said, "What do you think of your father's actions, then? Has that changed?"

As he asked, he realized: For once, he was asking neutrally. The argument about that was over. Jinzhao seemed to feel the same. Instead of the knee-jerk defensiveness of the past, he answered softly, "I meant what I told your sister. At that moment, I understood not only what he did, but what you have been arguing."

"And don't think I don't regret it!" Tinseng cried, "I wish I'd argued that the most romantic thing you could do was wait for backup!"

Jinzhao's lips twitched. "I'm glad you didn't. I'm glad for your honesty. Your clarity. If you had not been so insistent, I would have stayed ignorant and . . . alone."

"Alone? You think it's so easy to get rid of me?"

Annoyance shadowed Jinzhao's features.

"Sorry, sorry. I'll stop interrupting. You were saying?"

Jinzhao chewed his words. Tinseng distracted himself trying to clean and bandage each of the injured wrists. Only after the second wrist was cleaned did Jinzhao say, "'To know a certain thing directly, you must personally participate in the practical struggle to change reality, to change that thing.'"

Tinseng hummed thoughtfully, then completed, "'Only through personal participation in the practical struggle to change reality can you uncover the essence of that thing and comprehend it.'"

"Love is participatory," Jinzhao said, "as is justice. Only understood through the struggle. I set myself apart and had neither."

"Jinzhao . . ."

"They chose to participate. How can I fault them for that?"

Tinseng sighed and smiled a soft, adoring smile. He really had no chance, did he? He should have known Jinzhao was going to play dirty,

---

[11] "To value justice above life."

with his ideals and his conviction like towering pillars in an ancient temple. He was his most beautiful like this: If Jinzhao ascended to heaven right now, he would question the very gods themselves about their choices. And he'd be right. He'd never see his own goodness and would insist on seeing goodness in people like Tinseng. It was insufferable, really.

"So you finally admit I'm right?" Tinseng said instead of anything he was thinking. "No, no, no, no need to acknowledge it. Ah, one thing though: Are you saying I should expect more of these heroics in the future?"

Jinzhao blinked, then asked with no expression, "Is there *another* list you know of?"

Tinseng laughed so hard that neither had the chance to say anything more before the others finally arrived.

---

Yukying started crying the moment she saw them and kept crying as she took the washcloth from Tinseng and kindly elbowed him out of the way. He considered pouting about it but, without a task to busy his hands, exhaustion hit him. Suddenly nothing sounded better than slumping down into a chair and never moving again. He floated into something like sleep as everyone swirled around him.

When he came back to himself, his siblings were talking quietly over Jinzhao. Yukying dabbed iodine to Jinzhao's face while Cheuk-Kwan rewrapped the bandages Tinseng had tied, probably muttering about poor technique if Tinseng cared to listen. When Cheuk-Kwan held out his hand, Yukying handed over the iodine; when Yukying needed a new washcloth, Cheuk-Kwan had already barked at Chiboon to fetch her one. This wasn't the first time they'd tended a patient together. Hadn't Yukying said her volunteering had included some nurse training? That sounded vaguely familiar; Tinseng probably should have paid more attention, or asked follow-up questions. He'd been so distracted. So neglectful of them both. Hopefully that would end soon.

To his left, Yingtung sat at the desk reading from a piece of paper into the phone—the room service menu, and *oh*, Tinseng was hungry. When was the last time he ate? The tartine at Julian's? He spared a moment's gratitude toward his sister's husband, who might be useless, but was at least the kind of useless who always remembered mealtime.

Chiboon, for his part, was upending an entire suitcase on the second bed and setting out their necessities. With any luck, they wouldn't be here more than a night, but to an itinerant like Chiboon, that didn't matter; he swore by the habit of unpacking everything to settle into a space. In the midst of upheaval, Chiboon wrote at the beginning of all his guides, the oldest routines bring the greatest relief. Clothes in the drawers, all in their neat stacks. Pajama sets laid out at the end of the bed for easy changing. Toiletry bag in the bathroom. There would be a toothbrush and paste for Tinseng when he wanted it, right there next to the sink, easy as home. Some strange pressure built up in Tinseng's throat at the thought. If he could just change his clothes and brush his teeth, he'd feel able to think again. Maybe there was something to Chiboon's routines after all.

Yingtung hung up the phone, then picked it up again, for who knew what; probably to complain to the concierge about the towels. Cheuk-Kwan finished on Jinzhao's injuries. The room's tide ebbed—his sister leaving, his brother going to the bathroom and closing the door. Chiboon followed Yukying out, and Tinseng couldn't pretend like he was asleep anymore: he had been watching Jinzhao's eyes droop and wanted a moment, just one more, before letting him sleep.

"I won't bug you for long," he said as he sat on the bed and took Jinzhao's hand, "but we never agreed what we should tell them."

"Tell them everything."

"Please."

"*Everything*. Why else are we here?" Jinzhao's eyes flickered around the room. Yingtung murmuring into the phone, the supplies Yukying and Cheuk-Kwan left scattered on the bedside table, the pajamas sloping off the bed, back to Tinseng looking at him adoringly. All the evidence of love. Why else were they struggling, his gaze seemed to ask. "Change reality, Tinseng."

And what was one supposed to say to that? What was there to do, except concede?

"For you?" Tinseng squeezed his hand. "Anything."

"For all of us."

"But you first," Tinseng lobbied.

He had no reason to expect Jinzhao to answer: "I love you."

"*Jinzhao!*" he hissed. Tinseng had needed grave peril to say it. How could Jinzhao just *say* something like that? How could he be this way? But of course, that was why Tinseng loved him. Once the floodgates were opened, it'd be like this forever from Jinzhao.

"I love you," Jinzhao said, in case it hadn't been devastating enough the first time, then said, "and it's for all of us, which you know."

Christ. Tinseng wanted to swoon, or dance; something absurd and spontaneous. It wasn't the moment. They'd have others. Right now, he could content himself to squeeze the hand he was holding and promise absolute hell with the twinkle in his eyes. "If you insist on the truth, I'll do my best. Leave it all to me, okay?"

---

Jinzhao fell asleep with his hand tightly clutching Tinseng's. Tinseng was reluctant to let go, even when the food arrived and Yingtung walked over to them with a covered plate for Jinzhao, eyes dropping to their clasped hands. Tinseng and his brother-in-law stared at each other for a moment, all the distrust of decades-long animosity flashing between them. Yingtung proved the bigger man, saying nothing when Tinseng almost certainly would have dug a knife in. All Yingtung suggested was that they all moved to his room, so they wouldn't wake Jinzhao with their talking. They left the plate and a note for the sleeping man, then piled into the other suite. Yukying and Yingtung sat close together on the couch, while Chiboon and Cheuk-Kwan took the chairs. Tinseng sprawled on the floor, pouring himself a large glass of wine from one of the bottles Yingtung had ordered.

"So, how was your day?" he asked, smirking at their reactions.

"A-Seng," Yukying admonished.

"Okay, okay, okay. So, two years ago, in '61, I met Shan Dao at a poetry reading in Paris. Only, he wasn't introduced as Shan Dao. He was introduced as the son of Mei Hankong, a Chinese cultural attaché assigned to the embassy in Bern. But of course, I'd recognized him right away. It was Mei Jinzhao."

Out of the corner of his eye he watched that ripple around the room. Cheuk-Kwan made a harsh sound to quiet the others, and Tinseng smiled down at his wine, thankful for his didi.

"We fell back into our close acquaintance right away," Tinseng continued. "Jinzhao knew they'd hired me to translate Mandarin and Cantonese into French, part of their bilateral intelligence agreement with France. But, well, by the time Jinzhao met me, I'd realized I might have miscalculated the nature of the assignment. I was unhappy, and Jinzhao helped me see that."

*The lie will be good for all of us*, he thought. They didn't need to know everything, and besides, Jinzhao was asleep. If he'd wanted to keep Tinseng totally honest, he would have made more of an effort to stay up.

"Anyway, I quit, so it doesn't matter anymore, but it's important because of what happened next. Around two years ago, his mother sent him a strange telegram. He was immediately concerned. He took the first train he could without sending a telegram back, and he didn't tell anyone he was coming. He thought if he had to get her out, it was better to have the element of surprise." Tinseng laughed once, a hateful thing. "He surprised them all right. He heard them leaving out the back."

"Oh," Yukying breathed, her hand over her mouth.

"He didn't even have a knife," Tinseng said, feeling very far away from himself. "They could have killed him. But they fled. Probably heard the front door. He found her in the bedroom. His father was in his study."

Yukying made a noise. In his periphery, he saw Yingtung put an arm around her, and she hid her face in his shoulder.

"He called the police and waited for them to arrive. But someone from the embassy arrived first. Strange, since he hadn't called the embassy yet. They kept him at the house for hours. Every time he tried to leave they stopped him. He started to wonder why. When he asked too many questions, they took him away to question him."

"They didn't think *he*—" Chiboon started.

"He's the son of two Chinese nationals. He's automatically suspicious to the Swiss."

"Bastards," Cheuk-Kwan spat.

"They keep files on their own children just for asking to see a Little Red Book for school reports," Tinseng said tiredly. "It's not exactly surprising. What *was* surprising was how the CID was acting. They did nothing to shield Jinzhao. Usually no one over here would act against a Chinese agent. If any of the CCP officials in Bern had so much as sneezed, the Swiss would have backed away from Jinzhao immediately. So why weren't they putting the full force of their diplomatic corps between Jinzhao and the Swiss?"

"Because they already knew Li Xifeng had flipped," Yingtung said.

"Right."

"And they were willing to lump Mei Jinzhao in with them?"

"A safe bet," Tinseng said with a shrug, "at least from their point of view. He's their son."

"What about the other one?"

"The other son? He'd been in China since he was fourteen and is now working in the Ministry of Foreign Affairs in Beijing. Jinzhao hasn't seen him in more than ten years. He actually comes into the story right now. Eventually, they released Jinzhao and he went straight to the embassy. That's when he *knew* something was wrong. They wouldn't let him past the lobby. So Jinzhao tried to get through to his brother. It was nearly impossible, probably because he was dodging the calls, but Jinzhao finally managed—only his brother said he had nothing to do with it and told him not to contact him about it again."

"Sensible," Yingtung murmured. Tinseng's imagination supplied a vivid depiction of throttling him.

"Was it? Both parents murdered, but not an ounce of curiosity why? *Sensible*. That's an interesting word for it, Yingtung; your insights are always so—"

"Tinseng." Cheuk-Kwan's hand put weight on his shoulder.

"Right." Tinseng tried for a smile. "Sorry. We must differ in opinion on how someone should react to the murder of their parents. Anyway, Jinzhao was crushed by this response. He stayed in town to take care of all the arrangements, but at every turn he was ignored. It was almost as if no one wanted to admit two people were murdered at all. And eventually they wrote in the papers that it was a robbery. The house had been cleaned out, but no one would tell Jinzhao anything. So he came back to Paris and asked me for help. We hadn't gotten anywhere when someone leaked the whole thing to the press. And we know what happened then. The Mei Affair. That at least made sense of why Jinzhao's parents had been killed, and why the CID acted the way it had. So that part was wrapped up, if you could call it that."

Tinseng took a long drink, nearly finishing his glass. No one else said anything.

"Anyway, as we were investigating the murder, we discovered something else. Just a rumor, at first, until the story broke. You see, there are lists of potential recruits maintained by every power. Too many lists to mention; MI6 probably has dozens. And in Switzerland, there was one in particular called 明单.[12] As far as we could tell, it was a very short list until a few years ago. Then someone took it over, and it became very successful: a list of Chinese-natives, in both Switzerland and China, who were sympathetic to the Soviets after the Sino-Soviet split. You can imagine how dangerous a list like that was."

Tinseng wished they had stayed in the other room after all; retelling the story would be easier if he could see Jinzhao.

"The person who maintained the list didn't care that they could ruin the lives of everyone they named. If the list was ever discovered, the reputation of those students would be tarnished forever. The journalists they named would never be able to live in China again. Any officials would have to fear for their lives. But that risk was worth it to the owner of this list." Tinseng finished his wine. "I think you know where this is going,

---

[12] "Bright list."

huh? A copy of the list got out. Grodescu has it, and he wants to sell it to the highest bidder. And I'd probably be trying to get it back regardless of the names on it, but the person who identified possible recruits so well was Jinzhao's mother. And she put Jinzhao's name on it."

※

A burst of pandemonium followed. Tinseng took the opportunity to eat a few bites of chicken and open another bottle of wine. Surprisingly, it was Yingtung who refilled his glass.

"But how'd you find this all out?" Chiboon asked when they'd all resettled.

"It doesn't really matter. Just research and connections. Knowing how to ask the right questions."

"You did all this in a year? While you were still working?"

Tinseng shrugged. "I was thinking of getting out anyway. Once Jinzhao showed up at my door, the decision was made for me. I told them I was out, that I'd gotten an offer at the new university they were setting up in Hong Kong. We lived off our savings."

That was a generous interpretation of events. Mei Hankong's will had given everything of value back to the state; the idea of inheritance ran counter to the basic tenets of communism, and he didn't want his sons to perpetuate societal inequality. Jinzhao had less than Tinseng, and Tinseng hadn't exactly had savings so much as scraps from his last few paychecks.

"Savings?" Cheuk-Kwan asked, too used to Tinseng's bullshit to buy it.

"We made it work," Tinseng said defensively. "Anyway, it was only for a few months. They let me go without too much fuss."

"On what condition?" Cheuk-Kwan asked, already picking up on the rules of the game. They exchanged a look, and Tinseng thought, *They chose the wrong brother.*

"If I happened to see any bright young things in my classes, they'd appreciate if I dropped them a line. A little 明单 of Britain's own. But if I don't see anyone I think is a good fit, that's not my problem."

"And so, what about this man?" Chiboon asked. "Grodescu? The one who apparently kidnapped Mei Jinzhao?"

"All you need to know is that he has a copy of the list. He doesn't know how to read it, but he doesn't have to; he just has to sell it. Our plans to get his copy haven't exactly worked out so far." Tinseng glared at his brother. "What, Cheuk-Kwan, would you like to say something?"

"Was there a single part of your plan he didn't see coming?"

Tinseng threw up his hands. "It was just the two of us! I think I did pretty good! Next time *you* plan it!"

"I would've done better than *you*. Did you even think about what we'd think? Were you going to tell us he'd changed his name if you managed to clear this up? Oh, everyone, by the way, Shan Dao is going by Mei Jinzhao somehow?"

"No, that part I get," Yingtung said unexpectedly. "You could say you were protecting his identity until he was safe on our territory."

"How does it feel?" Tinseng asked Cheuk-Kwan. "Even Yingtung's making more sense than you."

"What I don't understand," Yingtung spoke over the ruckus of the brothers fighting, "Is why Mei Jinzhao didn't ask for asylum. You know Whitehall would have slavered over the information he has."

"Why would he agree to that? At least his father loved his country; he might've betrayed it, but he still loved it. To follow in his mother's footsteps and become a pawn for a country that hates him? And why would he trust them? Why would he trust anyone?" Tinseng reached into his pocket for his cigarettes, needing something to do with his hands. "His father was a spy. His mother was a spy *and* a traitor. The country they'd raised him to love wants him dead. The country his mother betrayed them for wants him as long as he's useful, and then they'll discard him as scraps for the wolves. The English are imperialists, and the Americans are worse. Besides, I know exactly what Whitehall does to assets. It might not be as bloody on the outside, but they bleed you dry nonetheless."

Tinseng fell back against the couch, out of words. They left him alone, talking around him as he smoked through two cigarettes in a row, drifting now that the adrenaline had worn off completely.

"-nseng?" Someone had been saying his name. He blinked his vision clear to find them all looking at him.

"Tinseng," Yukying said gently, "we want to let you sleep, but we need to know the plan."

"What?"

"What's the plan?" Cheuk-Kwan's tone rippled with tension. "You have to include us this time, because your last plan was shit."

"What?" he said again.

"We still need to get the list, right? Or did you forget that detail?"

Tinseng hadn't forgotten, but he was a little surprised to hear Cheuk-Kwan so adamant. Even more surprising was how Chiboon, Yukying, and even Yingtung nodded or looked resolute. Any other day before this one, he would have fought their help. Yukying had said to do his best, and he'd always thought his best was done alone. He looked around the room at all the people gathered around to help Jinzhao. Something shifted inside him, something tectonic: it wasn't that he didn't have to do this alone—he *shouldn't* do it alone. He wasn't the only piece on the board. Maybe he wasn't a piece at all. There had to be a hand moving the pieces, and all his life he'd let others pick him up and discard him at will. Maybe it was his turn to play.

"Okay," he said. "Here's what we should do."

# CHAPTER FOURTEEN

*One Day Ago. June 24, 1963. Paris, France.*

After their talk, Tinseng curled up next to Jinzhao in the bed and slept. For once, he didn't dream. At 11:00 p.m., the ringing of the phone woke him. He sat up to find Jinzhao still asleep next to him. He rubbed the sleep from his eyes as Yingtung (was he going to have to start thinking of him as Laurence after his support earlier?) told Yukying the call was for her.

"Mrs. Grodescu?" he heard Yukying say, and his exhaustion instantly dropped away. "Hold on a moment." He bolted out of bed as she waved him over. They pressed their heads together over the phone to listen. "Are you all right?" she asked.

"There is not much time," a woman's tinny voice floated up between them. "I will leave something for you at the front desk."

"Oh, but—"

"Give it to that man," Marissa talked over her. "The one with the long hair you always talk to. He will know what to do."

"What about you?" Yukying asked.

"Do not worry about me. I am stronger than I look. They forget, Mrs. Li."

"They? They forget what?"

"Men. All they care about is that women can bear life. They forget the opposite is also true." Their connection crackled as Marissa Grodescu said, "I hope we do not meet again," and the phone line clicked.

253

Tinseng and Yukying exchanged a glance, then rushed down to the lobby. The clerk behind the desk handed Yukying an envelope. They walked a few steps away before Yukying pried it open. Inside was a single sheet of paper. She read it, then handed it to Tinseng.

It was blank except for two short lines of writing: an address, a note, and a time. The address was not in Paris; the name of the town sounded vaguely familiar to Tinseng, clicking in place when he remembered seeing it in a file at Julian's. It was Grodescu's home in the country. Next to the address was written, "Two lions mark the entrance. Wait in the WC attached to the study on the third floor." The time was 8:00 p.m. the following evening.

"What happens tomorrow evening?" Chiboon asked when they brought the note upstairs.

Tinseng handed him the paper. "We'll find out, won't we?" he grinned, feeling no humor at all.

---

Tinseng left the others to rest. A few hours of uninterrupted rest had reset him. Re-energized, he returned to Julian's apartment in search of the quietest piece he could find. He chose a Browning 1910 pocket auto slide combined with a 1922 .32 barrel. It was about as untraceable as a gun could get; thousands of 1922 Brownings had been manufactured by the Belgians while under German occupation, and thousands of 1910 models still floated around the market. To the barrel he attached a Maxim Silencer, modified from a silencer made for small-caliber hunting rifles. With hunting rifles still legal in several European countries, parts like a silencer were easy to buy without raising suspicion; naturally, a hunter would want their gun to be quiet. If one knew what they were doing, modifying the silencer to fit a Browning was no work at all. This specific make of slide, barrel, and silencer was known to both Jules and Tinseng as the type preferred by Belgian assassins. Tinseng didn't ask why Julian had it. He just hoped it hadn't been used for too many murders. It might be a fool's errand, but he was trying to make it as hard for the police as possible.

They were so close now. Thanks to Marissa Grodescu's help, he wouldn't have to run around the city bribing information out of contacts or try to track down where Grodescu was staying. Yingtu—*Laurence* and Cheuk-Kwan wondered if it was a trap, of course, but Yukying seemed certain Marissa had no love for her husband, and Tinseng had heard the woman's voice; if she'd been lying, she was a better actress than Lin Dai. Besides, Tinseng had another theory after listening to Yukying's description of the woman: Perhaps she finally saw a way out. By setting Tinseng on a path leading directly to her husband, she ensured a confrontation. What better way to kill your husband than to let someone else do it for you?

He might be wrong. If he wasn't, he was quietly impressed. He couldn't even resent the manipulation, since it suited both their needs. Anyway, she wasn't the one who deserved any of his anger.

When he returned, everyone had rearranged: Jinzhao on the couch, Yukying and Laurence sleeping on the bed, Cheuk-Kwan asleep on the floor next to Yukying's side of the bed. There was at least one other suite in Laurence's name, but no one seemed interested in leaving one another's sight. Tinseng was grateful; the same fear had him triple-checking the lock. Chiboon was the only one still awake at this early hour. He sat on the floor next to the couch, legs stretched under the coffee table, sketching in his journal. Tinseng peered over his shoulder to find the page littered with quick impressions: Tinseng raising an eyebrow, Laurence in profile, an unknown pair of hands gesturing. Chiboon's pencil hovered above a half-finished sketch of Jinzhao sleeping.

"How is it you're so talented," Tinseng asked as he sat at the table next to his friend, pouring himself wine, "yet you ran out three—no, *four*—art tutors?"

"Ah, I'm unappreciated." Chiboon nudged his journal over to Tinseng. For a few minutes, Tinseng flipped through it and asked questions, and Chiboon answered, and they pretended to forget together. It ended when Tinseng flipped back to find a full page of Yukying laughing in their cabana on Tamariz Beach.

"You're good with eyes," he complimented, staring down at his sister's kindness sparkling through a gaze that stared off the page.

"It isn't easy," Chiboon bragged. "And Yukying's a tricky subject."

"She is?" That surprised him.

"Oh, yes. It's difficult to capture in a painting. Have you ever seen Fu Baoshi's *Goddess of the Xiang River?*" Tinseng shook his head. "There's this fan . . . well, it isn't important. Yukying is an interesting subject, that's all. She knew about Grodescu before the rest of us, right?" Chiboon asked, then ducked behind his journal. "Ah, I mean . . ."

"No, you're right," Tinseng admitted. "She didn't put the whole thing together, but she knew he had something to do with Jinzhao. She thought Jinzhao was stepping out on me at first—can you believe that? So I had to tell her *something*. But I fucked up; I told her he was after me."

"Ah, Tinseng." Chiboon shook his head. "You've been a little brother for *how* long?"

"I know, I know," Tinseng whined, "but I didn't think she'd stick up for me so much! I'm not *actually* a kid."

"Doesn't matter, does it? When it's our siblings, there's really nothing we wouldn't do."

"You're right as always," Tinseng said easily, enjoying the cadence of their conversation too much to disturb it with his darker thoughts. "But you seem to have taken it all in stride. Aren't you a little impressed with all my spy craft?" He waggled his eyebrows in search of the praise Chiboon had always lavished on him in their younger days. Now, Chiboon just laughed.

"Asking for compliments like that, you're really shameless, Tinseng. But I am impressed you're running into danger so brazenly. Aren't you scared?"

"Should I be?" Tinseng lingered on a full-page sketch of the ocean viewed from the round window of their suite. On the opposite page, Chiboon had made notes for an article on how to make the most of downtime on a cruise. Tinseng could barely remember any of the activities Chiboon had written down. "I suppose it's just a matter of perspective."

"You're like your namesake. Saving those in distress, playing clever tricks, overcoming whatever the world throws at you. You even have a pretty maiden pining for you." Chiboon's gaze sliced over to Jinzhao before sliding back.

"Yes, he is very pretty, isn't he?"

"I hope he'll pose for me when we're home. Help me convince him, won't you?"

"Oh, I'd love to help you in that goal, my friend." Tinseng grinned with mischief. "He'll *hate* it. It'll be great."

"I knew I could count on you."

Chiboon took the journal back. "Oh, and of course you have the nefarious villain to face," he said. "And a showdown to attend. Then, all the story needs is an ending."

"Hmm, you're right. What kind of end would you give me, Chiboon?"

"Oh, I don't know." Chiboon poured Tinseng more wine. "Anything could still happen, couldn't it?"

"Come *on*," Tinseng wheedled, pouring for Chiboon in turn. "You're a writer, you must have some idea."

"Well . . . if you're twisting my arm . . ." Chiboon brought the glass to his lips and smiled to himself. "I like when the villain gets what he deserves."

"On that," Tinseng said, raising his glass in a toast, "we agree."

※

"Yukying and Yingtung are out renting the car," Cheuk-Kwan said without preamble the next morning, waking Tinseng with a ruthlessness Tinseng remembered from their school days.

"Great," Tinseng said. After consulting a map the previous night, they found that the address Marissa Grodescu provided led to a town about an hour and a half outside Paris. The plan was for Tinseng to scout the location with a touring car this morning to learn any peculiarities about the drive and find a place to hide the car. Then, later that night, he'd take a different car provided by Jules, one locals would drive and that wouldn't be out of place if seen on the road late at night. If he'd had time, he would have gotten fake plates. As it was, he'd have to risk it by taking them off entirely and hoping they weren't pulled over.

While Tinseng worked through his contingencies, Cheuk-Kwan said, "Sha—fuck. Mei Jinzhao, I'm checking your wounds again. Let's go." He led Jinzhao to the bathroom, then turned to point at the trailing Tinseng. "Not you."

"Why!"

"You'll distract the patient."

"Are you sure I won't distract you?"

"I'm very sure of exactly who you'll distract, and how," Cheuk-Kwan muttered darkly. Tinseng let them go. Jinzhao would be fine. Cheuk-Kwan was even a half-decent doctor. There was no reason to be nervous. He looked around the room for distractions. Chiboon was asleep in a lump of blankets on the couch but Tinseng decided to be generous and let his friend sleep. He paced around the room a few times, then gave it up for a bad job and went to listen beside the bathroom door.

"The ribs are the most concerning. You really need a hospital. And if you don't rest your eye, there will be permanent damage. No straining it. That means no squinting at maps in the dark or reading files all day while Tinseng is gone. What, you don't think I can see what you're thinking? You're as predictable as him. I'm telling you: a full day of rest. Do you *want* to go blind?"

"At least I would be spared certain sights," Jinzhao replied. The way Cheuk-Kwan spluttered, Tinseng imagined Jinzhao was looking directly at Cheuk-Kwan's face when he said it. Tinseng nearly burst trying to contain his laughter, but his mirth curdled to acid as Cheuk-Kwan hissed, "You're really meant for him, you know. The both of you acting so superior. You think Tinseng isn't out there pacing holes in the carpet over you? You should have seen him yesterday. You think he wants you straining your eye just so you can feel useful? You think that'd be fun for him, watching you be so selfish?"

This wasn't funny anymore, Tinseng decided, and opened the door.

"How's the patient?" he asked.

"A stubborn bastard," Cheuk-Kwan said.

"Such a glowing review! Jinzhao, how are you feeling? How are your wrists? Are you going to have handsome scars?" He examined each one.

"They will heal well, thanks to your siblings," Jinzhao said. Cheuk-Kwan huffed as he put away his tools.

"Good, good," Tinseng said. "Up for our evening drive?"

"Mm."

"What?" Cheuk-Kwan looked between them. "You're not seriously bringing him?"

"Why not?" Tinseng asked blithely. "They're his secrets—don't you think he deserves to see this through? Besides, I want him there." To Tinseng, that was all that really mattered.

"What time?" Jinzhao asked.

"Five-thirty. I want to stake out the place."

"His ribs—"

"He'll stay in the car."

"Yeah, *right*. When you get there and he looks at you with those eyes of his, do you really think you'll refuse him?"

Tinseng affected a sigh. "His eyes are enchanting, aren't they? I'm so glad you noticed too, A-Kwan."

Cheuk-Kwan bristled in frustration. "You're going to get yourselves killed!"

"We'll try very, very hard not to, I promise."

"You've never cared about anyone but yourself, have you?"

"Aren't you a little slow to only be noticing now?"

Cheuk-Kwan looked between them, caught their identical looks, and threw up his hands.

"It's like playing the qin to a cow," he muttered, stalking away. Tinseng and Jinzhao glanced at each other, then Tinseng grinned wide and unrepentant.

"I think he likes us. But really, Jinzhao, are you sure you're okay? I can do this myself, it's really—"

"No trouble," Jinzhao finished for him, and answered for himself. "I will rest today and be prepared for this evening."

"All right." Tinseng had no real plans to talk Jinzhao out of it; he believed what he said, about Jinzhao deserving to be there at the end. Chiboon was right about this being a story, but he got the main character wrong. It was Jinzhao's ending to write; Tinseng was just the ink. Or maybe the paper. Something for Jinzhao to use, at any rate. "I hope Laurence gets us a good car. Can you believe in all our time here, we never went to the country?"

"Yes," Jinzhao deadpanned, and Tinseng doubled over laughing, imagining a sour-faced Jinzhao chasing after chickens and milking cows.

"No sitting in these empty woods, silent mind sounding the borders of idleness? Okay, okay, no agrarian idyll for us. The seaside, then. We should have gone to the seaside, at least. We could have shucked oysters right on the boat!"

"We can shuck oysters in Hong Kong," Jinzhao said, and Tinseng heard, *We will be together in Hong Kong*. He heard, *I promise to agree when you want to drag me places*, and *We'll be companions*, and *We'll have adventures together*. He heard *we, we, we* resounding in his head like monastery bells. He spent a moment blankly staring before he gathered himself.

"You're right. You're *so* right. We'll go to Lao Fau Shan and help lay out the oysters to dry and then I'll eat so many I can't move."

Tinseng's brain suddenly spun like a top. He wasn't the type to imagine the future; he was usually too busy with the present and all its joys and challenges, and he'd shied away from picturing them together back home, for many reasons. Who knew if they'd get the list and ensure Jinzhao's safety? Mostly, though, Tinseng had never been sure where he stood with Jinzhao. But now he *knew*. Anytime he wanted, he could remember the way Jinzhao's lips moved around the word love.

"Hey, Jinzhao, you know what?" Tinseng took a step forward with a sly grin growing. "We should—"

"Cut it out," Cheuk-Kwan interrupted from the adjoining room, "There are other people here."

"Sorry, what was that?" Tinseng tilted his head to yell back, "was it a ghost? Is this room haunted? We should call and inform the hotel."

"Shut *up*, I'm still getting my beauty sleep," Chiboon moaned from the couch.

"Then give it up; it's not working," Cheuk-Kwan said, to which Chiboon threw a pillow at him.

"Are you ready for this to be your life?" Tinseng murmured quietly at Jinzhao's side. "Are you ready to never have a moment's peace again?"

"I don't need peace," Jinzhao murmured back, putting an arm around Tinseng's waist. Tinseng experienced a single moment of pure bliss before Cheuk-Kwan started pretending to gag.

"Chiboon, wake the fuck up. I need you to help me pry open this window so I can fucking throw myself out of it."

Still smiling helplessly at Jinzhao, Tinseng threw back, "Wait, before you do, we can get Grodescu's fingerprints on you and frame him for murder, and you'll finally be useful."

"You—" Cheuk-Kwan started as Chiboon sat up and whined, "Would you both—" and that ended the calm morning. Tinseng delighted in it, and, adding his voice to the chaos, set himself the task of needling Cheuk-Kwan into ordering him breakfast.

※

By the time Yukying and Laurence returned, everyone was showered, dressed, and fed, and Tinseng was in desperate need of distraction. He stood eagerly to meet them, already halfway across the room before the door even shut.

"She says she wants to accompany you," Laurence said with a tone that implied he'd already lost the argument. Tinseng only just contained his laughter. It was a really wonderful morning after all: Tinseng had everything he wanted. There was just one more thing to make the day perfect. By the end of the night, he hoped he'd be able to get Chiboon that ending.

"Thanks, dear." Tinseng plucked the keys from Laurence's hand. "Make sure to have dinner on by the time we get back."

Laurence rolled his eyes but held back his comment as Yukying walked up, telling Tinseng they should get on the road right away because of traffic. The touring car Laurence rented was a gray Peugeot 404 coupé, and Tinseng's soul nearly flew to heaven on the spot when Yukying led him to it.

"He must really like you," Tinseng commented as he slid into the leather interior and guided them out onto the busy Parisian streets.

"As much as Mei Jinzhao seems to like you," she teased, and he realized with shock this was—

"A trap! This is a trap!" Yukying had trapped him in a three-hour roundtrip drive with no escape. "You're going to put the screws to me! You're going to break the Geneva Conventions!" It was barely an exaggeration, in his opinion; with a nosy older sister, who knew what could happen? "Wait . . . did Laurence know you'd planned this?"

"I always thought he could be an actor," Yukying demurred, and Tinseng cursed all the way out of the city.

"So, he's your Mei Jinzhao from all those years ago," she said once he'd finished his theatrics and the scenery had started to emerge around them, verdant and buzzing under the June sun. "你们琴瑟和鸣。"[13]

Tinseng couldn't deny it, so he groaned instead.

"I'm so happy for you, A-Seng."

"Ugh, jiejie, stop!"

"Laurence is happy for you too."

"Happy enough to have us both underfoot?"

"There's plenty of room," Yukying insisted. "Nothing would make me happier, A-Seng. You don't have to answer now but—oh! Turn here!"

They had to pay attention to the map for a while. Outside Paris, the roads became rural quickly, visible scars on the body of a country still recovering from two hellish wars. Signage was haphazard at best, reflecting the French mentality that if you didn't already know where you were going, you probably weren't wanted. They passed fields still unable to grow anything, other fields that had fared better, orchards that stretched

---

[13] In blissful harmony. Colloquially: a match made in heaven.

on and on, white barns with huge painted letters to lure tourists to stop, low walls of neat white stone, rolling hills stretching in every direction. Between Yukying peering at the map and Tinseng paying close attention to the kilometers traveled, they only missed one turn, but the test run had been a good idea; it would have been impossible to do this for the first time in the dark.

At Yukying's instruction, Tinseng turned off the main road onto a road that cut across wide fields of sunflowers on one side, grapes on the other. While the rest of the drive had been marked mostly by working farms, these fields were maintained for show. The land used to be proper countryside, but now it had been bought up by the rich. Every few miles, they passed huge gates or statues marking the entrance to an estate. They could occasionally see the homes themselves at the end of long, winding driveways, with glimpses of guest houses, stables, pools, and gardens.

"Have you seen the two lions yet?"

"We're getting close," Yukying said with her nose in the map. "Slow down; let me read the number on that sign."

When they found Grodescu's home, Tinseng let the car idle as they stared down the long drive. It narrowed to a point and disappeared into the trees before the house could be seen. Tinseng got the sense that if they drove down, they, too, would be swallowed.

"Should we go look?" Yukying asked. It wouldn't be peculiar at all for someone to add this place to their sightseeing; it was a common pastime to go look at the stately country houses and grounds—they sold hand-printed guides in the nearby villages—and on the road, they'd passed many families on similar trips. After a moment, he nodded.

"Let's do it. Count the doors and windows on the first floor; I'll take the second and third."

Even closed up for the season, the house was impressive. Its three stories and newer addition were large enough to imply wealth without being ostentatious. The old wing—eighteenth-century if Tinseng had to guess—crumbled elegantly. Ivy grew in controlled chaos, and every brick and shingle gleamed from constant care. The addition was probably added after the war. The immaculate green lawn in the middle of the driveway spoke of incredible amounts of time wasted on upkeep. To the west side of the house, an entrance to a formal garden had been constructed from hedges and rosebushes. It *was* a beautiful old place. And yet . . .

"It's so empty," Yukying murmured, voicing what was in his heart just like always.

"Too quiet," Tinseng agreed. He could almost count on one hand the nights he'd spent without the sounds of barking dogs, gates slamming, arguments, drunks happily singing as they walked home. Yichang, Hong Kong, Paris—three different cities, but the sound of children's shouting laughter, that was a constant, the same in every language. Here, what was there of humanity? A person could so easily lose themselves in all this silence.

"'The lowest and vilest alleys of London do not present a more dreadful record of sin than does the smiling and beautiful countryside,'" Tinseng murmured, staring down the emptiness. They remained a few moments longer. Then, with a sigh, he said, "Come on. Let's get out of here."

※

At 4:00 p.m., Tinseng and Jinzhao left Paris once again, this time in a Citroën 2CV, a *deux chevaux* as the locals called it, a car no one would think twice to see on the side of the road. Only a few miles outside the city, Jinzhao fell asleep against the window, leaving the driver to make his own company. It was probably good, even if it left Tinseng bored; the brain healing, or something like that.

He slowed the car to a crawl. When he reached the farm service road where he planned to hide the car, he steered it down into the ditch and over until the wheels on the passenger's side crunched the edge of the field's crop.

Jinzhao had woken when the car had tilted, and now he looked over to Tinseng, sleep-mussed hair in his eyes.

"Hey, Jinzhao, if I threw green plums at you from my toy horse and then left for years, would you wait for me?"

"Is that not what I already did?"

"Well! For more years, then."

"Yes. Forever."

"Forever is a long time."

Jinzhao smiled. "Not long enough."

Their mouths crashed together, and time folded together to create an unbroken moment between this kiss and the one in the basement the previous day—as if this were a continuation, as if everything between had been a dream.

But no dream lasted forever, and eventually the crick in Tinseng's neck insisted he pull away.

"Grodescu's is a half-mile walk to the south," he explained as they slid out of the car. The wheat was taller than both of them; no one would see the car unless they were practically on top of it. "Come on, this way."

They began their journey stalking through the grass on the side of the road. Only three cars passed on their walk, and the lane gave them plenty of warning; it was so quiet they could hear the engines long before headlights crested the hill. When the first drove by, they made sure to lie down flat in the grass. It was only about 6:30 p.m. and the sun was far from setting; they wanted to be seen by no one.

That first time, Tinseng had pulled Jinzhao down without thinking; as he lay far away on the scratching grass, he'd realized what an opportunity he'd just wasted. The next time they heard a car, he fell to the ground and pulled Jinzhao directly on top of him.

"Tins—"

"Be quiet," he hissed against the shell of Jinzhao's ear. "Do you want them to hear us?"

Then he plunged his hand into Jinzhao's hair and kissed him like he was drowning. He arched his hips up and pulled every devastating move at once, then broke the kiss roughly to turn his head—Jinzhao bit the long cord of his neck on instinct—to look out at the road. Dark again. They were clear.

Tinseng sprung up, leaving Jinzhao in the dust. He looked down at his shocked lover with an air of impatience.

"Well? We're on a schedule, Jinzhao. Now's not the time to dawdle."

*Oh.* Jinzhao looked like he wanted to *murder* him. Tinseng wrestled down a maniacal grin and continued south toward the house. It felt exactly like turning his back on a hungry predator: Every hindbrain instinct wanted to flee. He didn't, remaining slow and steady as giddy anticipation raced through him. He didn't turn around, not even once.

When they heard the third engine, Tinseng shivered. All his senses sharpened. Jinzhao had been silent behind him but for the slight crunch of dry grass. He wasn't quite sure how close the other man was, whether he was a few meters away or right behind him; whether he would feel breath on his neck; whether a voice would be in his ear as he's being taken down—

Before they could even see lights, a hand covered his mouth. Tinseng's triumph followed him into the dirt.

---

During the day, Grodescu's country home was a beautiful old manse in the style of a brick farmhouse. At night, the house loomed. Its white exterior caught dusk's shadows, shifting and elongating them up its barren walls like fingers leaving traces of crime. None of the chimneys smoked; all the shades had been pulled. The house was abandoned, as promised. Instead of feeling relief at the sight, Tinseng only felt dread.

They approached from the side with the most trees to keep cover. The lock on the kitchen door only took a minute. Tinseng and Jinzhao slipped through the kitchen into the rest of the house, easy as that. Their movement left shapes like ghosts in the silence.

Grodescu's rooms were on the third floor, tucked into the far left corner of the new wing. It started as a library for entertaining, with clusters of tables, chairs, and small couches strategically placed around the room, expensive trinkets used as bookends on the edges of the shelves. The shelves themselves showcased a collection Tinseng couldn't help but admire. The bastard was either cultured or very good at faking it. He walked slowly through the room, running his finger along the spines of books, plucking out one here, another there. He checked the title page of one, then slid it into his jacket; the rest he tucked under his arm. When he caught Jinzhao staring disapprovingly, he winked, then moved on to the next room.

Attached to the library was the room they wanted, a study if Tinseng had ever seen one. An imposing mahogany desk dominated the center of the room; two red leather chairs made a reading corner, and a massive sideboard sat under a window overlooking the back gardens. The bookshelves in this room held more precious volumes as well as older antiques, the kind of rarities usually kept in cases to protect from the elements. Grodescu was clearly no collector for collection's sake but instead a man who believed in using what he owned.

After a few minutes searching behind paintings and pulling at possible trick books, Tinseng found the safe. One look was all he needed; his heart fell.

"I'm sorry, I can't. I don't have the expertise for this."

Jinzhao shook his head, rejecting the apology. "She asked us to wait. We will wait."

Tinseng nodded. They would have to wait now. And when they met Grodescu again, the safe would open, one way or another.

It was only 7:30 p.m. by Tinseng's watch, which meant they had an hour, possibly more, to spend cramped in a narrow bathroom. Jinzhao sank to the floor, probably to do something frumpy and endearing like attempt to meditate during a stakeout. Tinseng held a book in front of his face instead.

"See, you doubted my genius, Jinzhao, but I *knew* we'd need entertainment. Here's one of your favorites, and at least one of these you haven't read before, I'm almost sure." Jinzhao looked up at him; the naked affection made Tinseng want to take a step back. "Why are you looking at me like that? They're just books, not . . . here," he pushed them all into Jinzhao's arms, then sat on the toilet's closed seat.

"And you?" Jinzhao asked.

"Oh, I have a little something for me too." From his jacket, Tinseng pulled *Journal meiner Reise im Jahr 1769*, a travelogue that had looked most likely to hold his attention.

With nothing else to do, they settled down to wait.

---

After Tinseng had picked up and abandoned each book at least twice, he began checking his watch. It was driving Jinzhao to distraction, he knew, but he couldn't help it. The agitation was building like the swell of spring floods in the river. He needed time to move faster than its current glacial pace, and he needed to hear Grodescu's voice or get any kind of confirmation that this wasn't a trap. He'd never been able to do this part.

He checked the time again: 8:47 p.m.

As he pulled his sleeve over his watch, a door opened downstairs. *Finally*, he thought, and they both stood, getting their noisy rearrangement out of the way. There wasn't room to stand side by side, and after a silent argument, Tinseng gave in and let Jinzhao stand in front of him. It felt wrong, all wrong. But this was Jinzhao's revenge to take if he wanted. So Tinseng handed him the gun and wondered if any of the bullets would be fired tonight, and by whom.

It took almost ten more minutes for the couple to make their way upstairs.

"I want a drink," they heard Marissa say. Tinseng tracked their movements by footfall, placing Marissa near the sideboard and Grodescu in front of his desk.

"Pour me one as well," Grodescu said, "And then perhaps you can tell me what was so important it could not wait."

"The woman, Yukying Li—I know where she is. And the man you want. I know where he is too."

Tinseng tensed, and in front of him he felt Jinzhao do the same, but neither moved, both willing to trust Marissa a little while longer.

"Then tell me."

"I want something in return."

"Oh, yes? What? Another car?"

"My sister's papers."

"Please. Don't be so tedious; I've had a long day."

"Surely this is worth that. The man sounds valuable."

"I can find him a hundred other ways. There is only one you. There must be something else that your little heart desires. If it's your sister, she could come visit again."

"No." A pause. "Pardon me. I need a moment. Too much coffee today."

"Come back in a better mood," Grodescu called as they heard Marissa walk toward their door. "*You're* the one who insisted we drive out here. You promised a pleasant evening for us."

Tinseng crowded Jinzhao into the furthest corner and crushed himself against the wall. Marissa's expression remained unchanged as she closed the door behind her and turned toward them. They couldn't dare risk talking, and every movement was a risk, but Tinseng had to show her the gun.

"Signal?" he mouthed in French.

Marissa shook her head, pointed to the gun, and held out her hand. Tinseng looked at Jinzhao. Jinzhao frowned and gazed at Marissa. She met his inspection with a flat, even look. Jinzhao turned back to Tinseng and nodded.

Well, if Jinzhao said it was all right, who was Tinseng to argue? He reached over and flushed the toilet so he could whisper in her ear.

"The safety is off. There are six shots."

Then he placed the gun in her hand.

She ran the water and tucked the gun in the pocket of her flowing skirt. The gun disappeared into the folds, its weight and outline swallowed by the fabric. Tinseng nodded approvingly. She kept one hand in her pocket as she left, shutting them in behind her. If they were quiet before, now Tinseng barely breathed.

"You know, Marissa, you've always had options." Grodescu had become even more relaxed during the interlude. "We could always . . ."

A rustle, then a derisive huff.

"You won't use that," Grodescu said confidently.

"Won't I? Open the safe."

"I don't think so."

A gunshot cracked through the room. The sound wasn't deafening like the Grodescus might have expected; that was the silencer doing its work.

"I won't miss again. Open the safe."

Even with his ear pressed against the door, Tinseng couldn't hear what happened next.

The next audible sound was Lucas Grodescu saying, "There. It's open. Your sister's file is here, you can get it yourself. Are you satisfied?"

"No. Where are the papers the men on the ship were after?"

"Why do you care about them? Did they put you up to this?"

Marissa's laugh splintered like lightning across a red sky. "Where are they, Lucas?"

"Why waste your time on them? You have what you want. If you go now, you might even get away."

"Get away? From what? There is no one for miles. The cook is home; Marie is with her mother. You came without protection. You suspect everyone, *everyone*, but never me. You still think of me as the girl I was when you took me. But I've watched you, learned from you. You have lived mercilessly, and I see no reason to show you any. *Where is their file?*"

"In the fucking safe—where else do you think it would be?"

"Good."

"Now—"

Grodescu's bargaining cut off with a crack. One muffled shot, then another. A burst of them; Tinseng counted up to five. Then the clip was empty, and the silence after confirmed no struggle.

Slowly, Tinseng opened the door. Grodescu lay on the floor with the kind of bloodstain that meant only one thing. Assured of their safety, Tinseng led them both out. He passed Marissa on his way to the safe, who still had the empty gun pointed at her husband. He considered saying something, but what was there to say? He moved around her and knelt down in front of the safe; finding the files was the only thing he could do to bring Marissa and Jinzhao comfort.

Out of the corner of his eye he saw Jinzhao check Grodescu's pulse. Jinzhao looked up at Marissa and confirmed, "Dead."

Marissa made a small, broken sound. Jinzhao went to her, gently wrapping his hand around the gun and pulling it away. Marissa let it go. They both looked down at the man who had threatened them. Their faces held a very similar expression. Tinseng recognized it from the mirror.

Tinseng turned his back on the scene. He focused on rooting through files, pulling at random, then throwing them on the floor when they weren't the ones he wanted. Halfway through, he paused, then tossed one across the desk.

"Jinzhao." The file slid over to Jinzhao on the smooth mahogany. He flicked the cover open to scan the contents, then held it out to Marissa.

"Is this your sister's file?" Jinzhao asked Marissa.

"Yes. *Yes.*" Her voice cracked open, and for the first time Tinseng heard something besides grim resolution. "Thank you."

"No. We owe you everything. We would not be here without you," Jinzhao said. He took a breath to say more, but Tinseng interrupted, "Jinzhao."

It was real this time. He stood up and handed Jinzhao a slim file with familiar papers inside—the originals, taken from Li Xifeng's desk in Bern. Jinzhao stared down at the folder a long moment, then looked up helplessly at Tinseng. Tinseng smiled, then grinned, then—fuck it—started to laugh. The relief was so total, such a riptide, that his knees wobbled and he stumbled into Jinzhao's arms. Jinzhao buried his head in Tinseng's shoulder and shook. No one heard his mourning; only the silent heaving gave him away, a small boat on an infinite maelstrom.

But the storm passed quickly and soon they pulled apart, finding each other's eyes in perfect synchronicity. *That's enough of that*, Jinzhao's look said; *time to work*.

Tinseng nodded, then clapped his hands together. "We'll take the rest of it," he declared as he looked around. "Take all the files in the safe and burn them off-site," he said to Marissa. "Once we leave, you'll call the police. You came home and found him dead, you have no idea who could have done this, and so on. Don't play coy about his business; they know, you know, they know you know. Putting them on that scent is your strongest move. It'll be easy to frame it as robbery—because that's what it was. Robbery, revenge. Both. Exactly what happened, only with someone else holding the gun."

The longer Tinseng wove the story, the more confident he felt. But Marissa was shaking her head.

"I cannot stay."

"Marissa." Tinseng frowned. "It'd be just a few weeks. Close up the estate, talk to the lawyers—"

"You do not understand. I . . . I will not be convincing. It took everything not to scream at every moment. To look at him, speak about him without disgust. Now that he is gone, I . . ."

She had started backing up as she spoke, and Tinseng knew he was losing her.

"Everyone knew what he was," he tried to tell her. "The police won't expect you to be weeping in mourning clothes. Hell, you can be cold as—"

"The police won't be on my side."

"Just a few days, then. Marissa," he said with the voice he had used on rabbity assets. This was starting to fall apart. "If you leave in the middle of the night, they'll suspect you."

"Maybe I never came home."

"Do you even have a place to go?"

Marissa shook her head. "I did not think I would get this far. Even with—I could not believe it."

Yes, she was spiraling, now. She would run, and they would catch her, and it would be Tinseng's fault for not stopping her here.

"You won't be able to go to your sister," he said. "Or your hometown, or anywhere you've lived before. They'll look for you. If you're not very careful, they'll find you."

"I never expected to see her again," Marissa said with so much resignation that Tinseng imagined, wildly, abandoning all his plans to help this woman. She saved him by adding, "I can live knowing she is safe.

That is more than I had before. I will go wherever you tell me to go. But I must go."

"Please, I'm—" To have gone through all this, only to lose her now—Tinseng couldn't stand it. He wouldn't lose her. "I'm good at this. You have to listen to me; it's better to stay here. We, listen, I'll stay, too, protect you, talk you through it . . ."

A hand pressed between his shoulder blades. "Tinseng," Jinzhao said.

Tinseng blew out a huge exhale. Screwed his eyes shut. "Fine. Okay." When he opened his eyes again, finality made his voice flat. "You'll want to get across the border tonight. I can give you the name of someone who can make you a passport. You'll need money. A lot of it."

"That is not a problem."

"Okay. If you ever need help, we're easily found in Hong Kong." Marissa nodded her thanks and listened as Tinseng told her exactly what she needed to do. "Now, you should go," he said after he'd written down the address of a reliable fixer. "Time isn't on your side."

Tinseng listened to her footsteps for a moment, then turned and scooped up all the papers onto the desk. He started pulling out drawers, spilling their contents to the floor.

"Come on, help me."

Jinzhao started pulling everything out of the safe. They worked in silence, moving from room to room. There was no need to rush. The last thing they could do for Marissa was give her time to pack. He was pulling books down from shelves when they heard a car engine turn over: Marissa, leaving. She would never make it to where she wanted to go—but then, Tinseng never thought he'd make it out, and here he was, one house fire away from freedom. He let the book in his hand drop to the floor.

"I'm going to the kitchen. If we're lucky, they have gas." He pulled out his lighter and tossed it to Jinzhao, who caught it one-handed out of the air. "Light anything that will catch. Meet you outside."

Tinseng pressed a hard kiss to Jinzhao's willing mouth, then ran downstairs. There was humming in his blood. He couldn't call it joy; its teeth were too bloody for that. Something similar, though. Something he could revel in.

He wished Marissa a fresh start wherever she ended up. He hoped she didn't start having nightmares like him. Then he thought of the phone call, how she'd hung up saying, "I hope we do not meet again." He smiled in the dark, a wry little smirk just for himself. He hoped they never met again either.

***

They stopped the car on top of a hill twenty minutes away. Smoke was already visible for kilometers. In a city, they might have heard sirens; in a city, there was always someone watching. In the country, all they heard was the night symphony of creatures, the buzzing of high summer. If sirens interrupted this quiet, it wouldn't be for a long time. By the time the fire brigade reached the house, it would be smoldering down to its foundations, the body inside burnt to bone.

"You know," Tinseng said conversationally as they watched the distant fire grow, "Overall? One of my better vacations. What do you say we do it again next summer?"

# CHAPTER FIFTEEN

*Now. June 25, 1963. Épernay, France.*

An hour ago, the detective in the wrinkled suit had led her to a room with no windows, pointed to a chair, and told her to wait. Afraid to contradict him, Yukying sat underneath the vent and shivered. She was beginning to worry this would all fall apart. Cheuk-Kwan had won the argument in the end: They wouldn't risk complications from plane travel until Mei Jinzhao had been checked by a hospital—what was the point of going through all this if they lost him in the air to a blood clot? So Tinseng took them to a hospital known to Paris Station; the staff was used to looking the other way. If the attendant had suspicions about the fake passport, she kept them to herself, and she hadn't asked questions about the mugging story. But they must have gotten something wrong: That same day, French police had come to Mei Jinzhao's hospital room and asked Yukying and Tinseng to come in for interviews.

Now, in the interrogation room, the clock ticked slowly. Yukying rubbed one hand with the other trying to encourage circulation. She wanted to move, but there was Mei Jinzhao, Marissa, and Tinseng to consider. With the weight of all those secrets on the scale, who knew what might tip fate against them? She wrapped Li Xifeng's shawl tighter around her shoulders and imagined that stronger woman just behind her. Her own fingers felt bony, fragile; she thought about small things in cages and tried not to shiver. A chill, or anger? Her mother's rage had burned hot, something Cheuk-Kwan had inherited. Whose anger was in *her* veins, then, cold as glacial melt?

"Ah, yes, sorry," the detective grimaced as he walked in, file in hand. "The building is old. Survived the wars, so now the city thinks it should be preserved. I'd rather get decent heating, but what can you do? Can we get you some tea? A warm cup to hold always helps me."

He'd done a convincing job pretending to be thoughtful, until now. As he'd walked her back, he had asked about Hong Kong, and his society manners had made conversation easy. The civility had been so nice that she'd almost forgotten her fear. That, she supposed, had probably been the point.

"No thank you," she said, and moved her hands to her lap to hide her clenched fists.

"Are you sure? We have a good selection."

"That's a kind offer, but I would rather get back to my husband."

"I understand," the detective said in the tone of unmarried men everywhere. "So, Mrs. Li. Do you want to tell me how you got involved in all this?"

She took a deep breath, reminded herself of Tinseng's advice, and said, "I was hoping, detective, that you might tell me what exactly *this* is."

"Did they not tell you?"

"I'm afraid not." Turn it back on them, Tinseng had said. "I've been waiting over an hour, and all they've said is that I might have known someone related to a crime in France. I don't see how that's possible."

"Perhaps they didn't want to upset you unnecessarily. We've had hysterics before. Let's start with the simple facts. Who are you traveling with?"

"My husband, my brothers, and our friends Lim Chiboon and Shan Dao."

"Yes. Shan Dao. He's in the hospital now—is that right?"

"Yes. He was mugged."

"And who were the witnesses to that?"

"Myself, and my brother Tinseng."

"But you didn't file a report."

"They were young. A gang. The gangs get away with so much in Hong Kong, so we thought, well, it just wouldn't do any good." We'll blame it on a group we know they hate, Tinseng had said; they'll believe anything of people they hate. "We just wanted to go home."

The detective nodded sympathetically as he wrote. "How long did you plan to travel in France?"

"Oh . . . it's a cruise; I think there was just one port in France? Then on to Italy. It's been a whirlwind."

"Yet you ended up in Paris."

"My brother Tinseng—he's very impulsive. He's lived in Paris the last three years and decided he could be a better tour guide than the cruise." They'd agreed to this story beforehand, too. It wasn't unusual for people to leave the cruise early. She only hoped she wasn't asked too many questions about it; Tinseng would probably embellish his version.

"So you decided to travel to Paris. What night was this?"

"Two nights ago. The 23rd. We have suites at Le Bristol."

"Did you know that another couple from your cruise also traveled to Paris that same night?"

"No." She swallowed. "I didn't know that."

The detective's mouth twitched. "Hmm. What can you tell me about a woman named Marissa Grodescu?"

They weren't tracking Mei Jinzhao, then. This was hardly better, but at least Mei Jinzhao was safe.

"She was a woman on the cruise. We sat in the same sewing circle for a few days. Why, did something happen to her? Is she all right?"

"Tell me about her."

"She was . . . Polish? That's the one next to Germany?" She tried to sound as insipid as possible.

"Mm. What else?"

"She smoked. No children, I believe; she only worked on dresses for herself."

The detective suppressed a sigh and asked, "Did she mention her husband at all?"

"Oh, naturally! A husband always comes up in conversation." *Play dumb*, she reminded herself. *Be the stupid housewife.* "What meals you can cook in under half an hour, which starch is best for collars—we have such different products in Hong Kong than you do here! Women's topics. *You* understand." She smiled. "And she seemed happy enough. Every couple has problems, of course, but we're meant to weather those troubles. In sickness and health."

Did he believe her? It was impossible to tell; he kept his head down.

"Another guest said you two seemed close," the detective said.

"I enjoyed her company. She was an outsider, coming from Poland, and we had that in common. Is she—" She made her voice wobble.

"She's missing," the detective said, "and we're very worried about her, Mrs. Li. Anything you may remember, no matter how small, may help us find her."

*Liar*, she thought.

"Let's see . . . she went to the beach in Lisbon. She visited Gibraltar with her husband, and we played bridge together. Things like that?"

The detective struggled with his impatience.

*Good*, she thought, *be impatient with me. Think I'm a fool; send me away.*

"We're more interested in her feelings. Moods. Did she ever seem upset? Did she ever talk about getting away from it all?"

"Don't we all?" She tried to laugh like Mrs. Duncan. If they really thought Marissa was missing, she wanted to give Marissa as much of a head start as possible. If they thought her a suspect, Yukying wanted to muddy the water. But which would help more? "She loved travel. That's why they booked the cruise. She spoke of all the places she wanted to visit and always wanting to get out of the city. Maybe she's gone to the countryside? I think she mentioned a house not far from here?"

"Hmm." The detective ignored her bait about the house. "Did she mention any places in particular?"

"Cairo," Yukying said randomly. "New York." Based on what Tinseng told them about the couple's last conversation, Marissa was likely traveling to wherever her sister lived. Hopefully it wasn't either of those places.

"We discussed Hong Kong, and she seemed interested..." Yukying added before panicking. *What if the police came to Hong Kong? What if they started watching them? What if I've just—*

As sweat began pooling in her armpits, the detective spent a few moments writing. Was he trying to break her? It was working. She could feel gambits rising up, desperate attempts that might ruin everything, but she felt outside herself. She heard herself ask, "You don't think it was her husband, do you?"

"Why would you say that?"

Yukying leaned in, as if they were friends discussing a bit of gossip. "Well, that's always who it is, isn't it? Not in mystery novels—those have to keep you guessing—so it can't be the husband every time. But in the papers, in real life, it's always the husband or the father or the boss, isn't it?"

The detective stared at her. "Did you ever meet Mr. Grodescu?"

"Yes, a... a few times. At Casino Estoril, in Portugal—that was our first port. My husband and I had a drink with them, and we... we danced. My husband is a horrible dancer, you see, and the Grodescus looked so regal on the dance floor, so... happy. So I asked for a few dances with him. It was a very nice night."

"And the other times?"

"Just here and there. He borrowed a cigarette from our group once. It's hard to avoid people on a ship."

"Avoid?"

"I just mean, I couldn't have avoided them even if I wanted to." A bead of sweat rolled down her side. "But other than the dance, I only really saw her."

The detective wrote in his notebook.

"Anything else, Mrs. Li?"

"I don't think so," she said, then gave a fluttery laugh. "Nothing that isn't sewing patterns and tips about the casinos. I'm sorry I can't be more help. She was such a nice girl."

The detective hummed. His notebook flipped shut. Was that a good thing? Was she going to be let go?

"All right, Mrs. Li. We'll have you wait outside while we question a few others, in case they mention anything you might be able to confirm."

"Of course," she said, her stomach sinking. This wasn't over yet.

---

The station was a small outpost on the outskirts of Paris, and so Tinseng and Yukying were told to wait on a bench instead of an office.

*Better than a cell*, Yukying thought, thankful for small blessings.

The bench sat against the far wall and faced the door—and so they're able to see the moment Laurence walked in.

"Pardon me," Laurence called loudly in his plumiest English, "that's my wife you're holding without a warrant."

Laurence had dressed the part, and Yukying couldn't help but admire her husband: the three-piece suit was an unusual shade of yellow, the deep shade of a ripe fall gourd. Among a sea of black and gray, the color demanded attention. His shirt was a creamy butter, and the matching handkerchief stuck out of his breast pocket in three small triangles. With all his creases perfectly ironed, he looked like he owned any room he entered.

"Excuse me, sir—" The clerk hadn't given either Tinseng or Yukying honorifics; it was the attitude, more than the man, that had earned this respect. But of course Laurence knew that. He'd been raised to play this game.

"You were holding them for questions, yes?" Laurence asked.

"Well, yes, but—"

"And have they been questioned?"

"I . . . yes, I believe s—"

"Then they should be free to go, shouldn't they? As she's a subject of the British Empire, *and* the wife of an undersecretary in the Hong Kong government, I've already taken the liberty of calling the embassy. Additionally, the man you're holding there," he gestured to Tinseng, "my brother-in-law, is also an employee of the British government. That *is* in your file, isn't it?"

"I, I don't thin—"

"No, you *didn't* think, did you? Why don't you call this number and discuss the matter with them?" Laurence slid a piece of paper across the counter. "It's the number of the embassy head. He's awaiting your call, to discuss the holding of two of the Empire's *important* subjects."

The clerk looked around the room, but there was no one to help him; the few lingering men at their desks kept their heads low.

"Do you really think . . . ?" she whispered to Tinseng.

"I don't know," Tinseng whispered back, "but your husband might earn his dinner tonight."

She bit back a smile and sat back on the bench. They watched the clerk's face closely as he called, listened, and hung up.

Ten minutes later, Laurence escorted them out of the station.

No one spoke as they walked down one block, then another. They all feared breaking the spell. Around the corner of the fourth block, the other three waited in a nervous huddle. Seeing them cracked Yukying open; everything she had tried not to feel in that cold room spilled out in helpless tears.

"Did they hurt you, jiejie?" Cheuk-Kwan growled as the rest hovered in concern, Tinseng talking loudly and Chiboon trying to fan her face—all too close and too much. Laurence pushed them away, only to hover himself. They were such fools, and she had never been so grateful for them. She stepped into her husband's arms and pressed her cheek against his jacket.

"I'm fine," she assured them, "just relieved. Please, ignore me."

"Are you sure you're okay? They didn't do anything?" Cheuk-Kwan asked.

"No, no. I'm just being silly." She borrowed Laurence's handkerchief to wipe her eyes. Laurence plucked the handkerchief from her hand to do the job for her, staring down at her with a wry smile.

"I know what you need," he said as he dried her tears. "Why don't we go home?"

*Home.* "That sounds wonderful," she said.

*Two Months Later. August 30, 1963. Hong Kong.*

On the flight home, Tinseng and Mei Jinzhao turned down the invitation to live with Yukying. Instead, they moved in with Cheuk-Kwan. Cheuk-Kwan lived with their father in an older, more traditional part of the city, and Tinseng could be himself there, or at least could pretend convincingly as he relearned how the disparate parts of himself might fit together under one skin. Tinseng had felt guilty for a while, constantly apologizing to Yukying, until, after a week with his domineering aunt, Chiboon had showed up at Yukying's door begging for sanctuary and took up residence in the spare room. Then it was fine: The room would be used, and Yukying wouldn't be so alone.

It would all be fine, and maybe this time Tinseng could believe it.

The rest of the summer, the city filled their lungs and added calluses to their feet. It seemed they walked it end to end with their ever-expanding itinerary of friends to visit, markets to explore, oysters to shuck, lives to unpack and expand into a new place. When they weren't out, they piled onto Cheuk-Kwan's rooftop after sunset with other families looking to escape the heat, filling their cups as kids ran around their chairs playing games. Most often they made themselves at home at Yukying's, coming and going uninvited as the walls absorbed laughter and arguments. Yukying wrote to Mrs. Lanzette for Rebecca's address to send back her copy of *The Feminine Mystique*, and suddenly she had not one but three new correspondents, for Rebecca had been putting up Miss Duncan in New York.

The peace Yukying felt was cool and sweet, a river at dawn. So it surprised her, one day, to lift her head from the letter she was writing to find their summer almost gone. She tried not to let the feeling encroach on her happiness, but the realization hit her again on a muggy Saturday, all of them gathered in Yukying's living room with no plans in mind, one of Tinseng's records playing from the corner. Soon Chiboon would return to Singapore to visit his family, then fly back to New York. The new term would start in a week or two, filling Tinseng and Mei Jinzhao's schedules. Cheuk-Kwan was already back at his practice, and Laurence had more late nights than not; time was slipping away.

She could feel sad, she supposed. But like the river, like the dawn, their peace was never meant to be stagnant.

She leaned across the couch to snoop over Chiboon's shoulder.

"Are you writing for your article?"

"I should be, shouldn't I?" Chiboon grimaced. "Haven't even started, I'm afraid."

"Then..." Yukying looked down at the full page.

"Oh, this is nothing. Just some thoughts about the trip."

She hesitated, then asked, "May I read it?"

"Oh ... would you like to?"

"Very much."

He dithered, then flipped a few pages back. She read:

> *Of the Europeans with whom I spoke, most described their map of the world in simple strokes. I heard none of them mention any country to the West but America, unless it was to speak of other beaches to visit. The East, meanwhile, is a monolith of fear; they have little interest in putting faces to those who live on the other side of the Curtain—and none would call it living. They believe what the poet Kipling wrote: "East is East, West is West, and never the twain shall meet."*
>
> *In the middle, the only part that matters: their homelands, the seat of whichever empire holds their loyalty. On the periphery, like dragons on the edge of their map, exist those imperial possessions—or former possessions, thanks to the efforts of visionaries and the workers' support of those visions. Today, instead of pride, the European erudite speak of those possessions with disappointment. To hear a Frenchman speak of Algeria, or a Belgian mourn the loss of "their" Congo, is to relive sitting at the dinner table while disappointed parents discuss what is to be done about roughhousing at school. The dreams of colonies breaking their masters' chains are nothing more than the thrashings of an unruly child who doesn't know its place, while the hard-won independence of former*

> *colonies are spoken of like the press speak of this modern generation of youth: lost to the degeneracy of the new, because they will not follow what has always been done. These same people always forget the next line of that Kipling poem: "But there is neither East nor West, Border, nor Breed, nor Birth." There are new maps being drawn . . .*

It trailed off there, half a sentence crossed out twice.

"Not exactly publishable." Chiboon laughed helplessly as she handed back the journal. "I'd be blacklisted for sure."

Yukying looked over at Mei Jinzhao and Cheuk-Kwan playing chess with her father's board. The silence between them was almost companionable, a tentative alliance growing by the day. At the desk, Laurence sat penning a letter to the editor of *Ming Pao* about the government's mismanagement of the water crisis; she watched him pause, considering his words, then return to writing. On the floor, Tinseng chewed his pencil and mumbled about conjunctions, his tutoring students' papers in a huge circle around him. Between them all, they agreed on almost nothing. But the record played on, and the sun streaming in warmed them equally.

"Maybe someday it will be publishable," Yukying said.

"You think?" Chiboon asked idly.

"I do," she said, then said again, "you know, Chiboon, I do. It's never foolish to hope."

# ACKNOWLEDGMENTS

This book would not be possible without so many people: Claudia, my editor, who opened doors; Shu Mei, without whom none of the main characters would have names; Phi, my beta editor, without whom this would be still a half-finished draft; Lauren, Mike, Kyle, Pink, and Liz, for all the study halls and writing sessions, and for holding my hand when I needed it; Patrick, my husband, who let me turn full goblin as I wrote the first version of this book back in 2021; Harlan, who inspired me to dream bigger; my mom and dad, who always encouraged my creativity and never told me being an author was a dumb thing to want to be (even though it absolutely is); and all the readers of the fanfic version of this book, who wrote such kind things in the comments and helped me believe in myself. Finally, I want to acknowledge all the scholars, historians, and real individuals whose works and stories I learned from to write this work; a full bibliography is available at mythoscopes.substack.com.

# ABOUT THE AUTHOR

Ren Brooke (they/them), a queer Chicagoland native now immersed in the Pacific Northwest, is an author on a mission: to craft bold, unforgettable genre tales that ignite change. Witnessing the power of inclusive storytelling online, Brooke decided to bridge the gap between fandom and mainstream literature. With over two decades of fandom engagement penning three novels and dozens of short stories, Brooke's stories invite readers on genre-mashing adventures of exploration and empathy. When not lost in storytelling, Brooke enjoys bad movie nights, writing at their local brewery, and filling their Tumblr queue. Connect at adrienbrooke.com.